Tommy Nightmare

By JL Bryan

Published 2011

www.jlbryanbooks.com

Tommy Nightmare

ISBN-13:
978-1461058489

ISBN-10:
1461058481

Cover design by Phatpuppy Art (phatpuppyart.com)

For my son

Also by JL Bryan:

Jenny Pox

Helix

The Haunted E-book

Dominion

Dark Tomorrows (short stories, with Amanda Hocking)

Chapter One

Tommy heard the clatter in the hall, then a loud thump, followed by the old man muttering. The old man typically blabbered streams of incoherent mush, which occasionally contained a fully-formed word or two along the way.

Tommy tried to ignore the gibbering voice outside the door. Nobody else stirred at the sound. The other foster boys—Luke, and Jeb, and Isaiah—continued sleeping in the double bed they shared next to his.

Tommy had a bed to himself, though the boys were supposed to share them two apiece. None of the other boys would sleep in the same bed as Tommy because it gave them nightmares. For the first couple of months Tommy had been here at the Tanners' house, the two older boys—Luke, who was fifteen, and Jeb, who was thirteen—forced eight-year-old Isaiah to sleep with Tommy.

Nearly every night, Isiah's screaming and crying woke them all. In fact, Isaiah screamed his head off any time Tommy touched him. Tommy sometimes had that effect on people, especially if they were already scaredy-cats.

Eventually, Luke and Jeb showed mercy and let Isaiah sleep with them, probably just so they could have peace at night. Tommy had slept alone for a couple of years now.

Luke called him "Tommy Nightmare." The younger boys had taken up the nickname, too.

In the hall, the old man's muttering grew louder, accompanied by the sound of fingernails scratching the wall. The old man was just lingering there, on the other side of the wall from Tommy, making his pathetic blabbering and whimpering noises.

The old man was Mr. Tanner's father, and he lived in a room down the hall, next to the master bedroom where Mr. and Mrs. Tanner slept. The Tanners had no children of their own—as they put it, "The Lord had a different plan." They only had the four boys currently entrusted to them by the State of Oklahoma.

Outside the door, the old man's scratching and gibbering grew more insistent. Tommy sighed and slipped out of bed. The night was freezing cold, and the Tanners only gave him worn old pajama pants to sleep in, because they said suffering was good for a child's soul. The hardwood floor was so cold it burned his bare feet.

He tiptoed around the other bed, where the three other boys looked very warm, and he felt a pang of jealousy.

He eased open the door, wincing at the creak. He didn't want the other boys to wake up and start yelling at him. And he really, really didn't want to wake up Mr. Tanner.

Tommy peeked out into the hall.

Mr. Tanner's father—whom Mr. Tanner insisted the foster boys call "Pap-pap"—lay sprawled on the warped old boards, one arm draped across his overturned walker. His shaking, liver-spotted hand grasped and released the walker frame, over and over again. Tommy thought of a fish freshly pulled out of a pond, how its mouth kept opening and closing as it died.

The old man faced the floor, blabbering nonsense and drooling. His other hand scratched uselessly at the wall. His bathrobe had hiked up, revealing his withered old legs, the color of dead snakeskin. His ankles kicked in the air as if he were pedaling a bicycle.

"Pap-pap?" Tommy whispered. "Do you need help?"

"Muuhwuhh," the old man said. His whole body shivered on the cold wooden boards.

Tommy looked up and down the hall. He didn't know what to do. If he woke up Luke, Luke might get mad and punch him in the nuts. He ought to wake up Mr. Tanner, but that idea terrified him. He'd rather get punched in the nuts than walk into Mr. Tanner's room.

"Okay," Tommy whispered. "I can help you up, Pap-pap. I'm twelve now. I'm pretty big."

"Gaaaah," Pap-pap said. He turned his head and looked at Tommy with one rheumy eye. He stopped scratching the wall, and instead starting grabbing the air. "Guuuh…Guuuuh…"

"It's okay, Pap-pap. Sh!" Tommy walked softly to the old man, avoiding the two squeaky spots in the hallway floor.

He took the old man's hand.

"Guuuuh! Guuuh!" The old man trembled harder now. His mouth opened wide. His gray tongue flapped against his black gums.

"Shhh!" Tommy turned the old man over and slid a hand under his side. Tommy could feel his ribs through the threadbare blue robe, and the man was shaking hard. "I just got to prop you against the wall," Tommy said. "Then we can get your walker. You hear me?"

"Gaaaah.." The old man made a choking sound. He quaked and stared at Tommy.

"Okay, here we go." Tommy heaved and strained. The old man was frail, but Tommy wasn't really very strong himself. He wrapped both his arms around the old man's torso. Tommy tried to imagine he was a superhero, like Batman, sneaking around in the night and helping people. But mostly he felt scared. Pap-pap frightened him. Especially when you knew Pap-pap was the father of Mr. Tanner, who was truly scary.

Tommy pulled the old man up. Fault lines of pain ripped open along Tommy's back and across his shoulders, but he didn't give up. He leaned the old man against the wall, but Pap-pap began sliding back toward the floor.

"Careful!" Tommy pressed his hands against Pap-pap's cold, bony chest. Pap-pap wasn't wearing anything under his robe but stained yellow jockey shorts.

"Nuuuuuh…Nuuuuuuh!" Pap-pap's lips quivered and he swung his head from side to side.

"You got to be quiet!" Tommy said. He looked at the overturned walker on the floor. If he let go of Pap-pap, the old man would fall down again. He should have stood the walker up first. Stupid.

Tommy reached out one foot toward the walker, while pressing Pap-pap against the wall with one hand. Tommy could feel the old man's heart whamming under the loose, dry skin of his chest.

Tommy hooked his toes under the lowest rung of the walker. He pulled it toward him, and it clattered against the uneven floorboards.

"Nuuuh nuuh nuuh!" Pap-pap began slapping Tommy's head with both hands. "Nuuuh nuuuh!"

"Quit it! I'm trying to help you!"

"Nuuuuh!" Pap-pap stared at him with bright eyes, thick drool hanging from his chin.

Pap-pap's sharp fingernails dug into Tommy's cheek, slashing towards Tommy's left eye.

"Hey!" Tommy turned his face away. He could feel Pap-pap's heart jutting against his fingertips with every beat.

"Nuuuuh…uuhhh…" Pap-pap stopped struggling. He stopped shaking, and his heart stopped thumping.

"Pap-pap?" Tommy looked back at the old man. Pap-pap sagged against the wall now, not moving at all. His eyes stared somewhere past Tommy's shoulder, and his mouth dropped all the way open. The old man peed, making a fresh wet stain on his underwear.

Tommy was pretty sure he was dead.

"Oh, God damn," Tommy said. "Oh, no."

At the end of the hall, the door to the master bedroom banged open. Mr. Tanner stormed out, all six foot five of him, wearing only his sweatpants. He carried his belt with him, the one with the giant brass buckle shaped like Oklahoma. Mr. Tanner was in his early fifties, and the copious hair on his head and chest was gray, but he was still as big and strong as one of the bulls over on Mr. Whitson's ranch.

"What are you kids doing out here?" Mr. Tanner yelled. He snapped the belt taut, a horrifying sound. But his angry expression turned to surprise when he saw Tommy pinning the old man against the wall, with the overturned walker right next to Tommy's feet. "Pap-pap?"

Tommy gaped at Mr. Tanner, too terrified of the man to say anything.

"You leave him alone!" Mr. Tanner shouted. He sprang forward and slapped Tommy's head, hard enough to send Tommy stumbling down the hall. A painful ringing sound echoed in Tommy's ear.

Pap-pap slid down the wall, and Mr. Tanner caught him. He looked into the old man's eyes, but the old man wasn't looking back. His eyes were as cold and glassy as marbles.

"Oh, Pap-pap," Mr. Tanner whispered. He eased his elderly father down to a sitting position on the floor, against the wall. "Oh, Pap-pap." Mr. Tanner looked like he would cry, and Tommy felt like crying, too.

"What on Earth is all this commotion?" Mrs. Tanner stepped out of the bedroom, her blond hair tangled around her narrow, sour face. She wore her frilly pink night dress that barely covered her hips. She was at least twenty years younger than Mr. Tanner, and much shorter. She gasped when she saw Pap-pap and the walker on the floor.

"He's dead!" Mr. Tanner wailed. He stood up and pointed at Tommy, who cowered against one wall. "Because of him."

"I didn't!" Tommy said.

"Didn't what?" Mr. Tanner advanced on him and snapped the belt again. "Didn't what, boy?"

"I didn't do anything!"

"Looks to me like you attacked him. Why'd you do that?" Mr. Tanner loomed over Tommy. "You tell me."

"No!" Tommy said.

"Why's your face all scratched up?"

"I don't know!" Tommy wailed.

Mr. Tanner cracked the belt against Tommy's stomach. Tommy and slid down the wall. He covered his stomach with his arms, so Mr. Tanner began whipping his shoulders.

"Oh, goodness," Mrs. Tanner whispered. That was all she did when her husband beat the foster kids. She stood there and whispered, "Oh, goodness."

Tommy curled up on the floor, and Mr. Tanner whipped his back and legs.

"I told you this one had the Devil in him!" Mr. Tanner shouted. "I told you!"

"Oh, goodness," Mrs. Tanner whispered.

Luke and Isaiah, the oldest and the youngest, appeared at the door to the boys' room. Isaiah opened his mouth like he was going to speak, but Luke covered Isaiah's mouth with his hand.

"He done brought the Devil into this house!" Mr. Tanner yelled. He was still whipping Tommy, but he was losing steam. After a few more smacks, he turned his attention back to his dead father. He knelt by the old man's corpse.

"You think we ought to call the ambulance?" Mrs. Tanner asked, in her quiet voice.

"Can't do him no good now," Mr. Tanner said.

"We ought to call somebody."

"Then you go and call somebody!" Mr. Tanner roared. "When did I tell you to get out of the bed, anyhow?"

"I'm sorry!" Mrs. Tanner turned and scurried away to the bedroom.

"Get in the bed!" Mr. Tanner called after her, and then he turned to stare at Tommy. Tommy cringed against the wall, hurting all over, his arms hugging his knees.

"This is the Devil's work," Mr. Tanner whispered. "And the Lord demands a special retribution for those who help the Devil do his work."

Tommy shivered and looked at the floor.

"I'm gonna pray on it," Mr. Tanner said. "You just stay right there, Thomas."

Mr. Tanner turned back toward his bedroom, and Luke and Isaiah ducked out of sight. Mr. Tanner slammed his bedroom door and began shouting at his wife.

Tommy stayed where he was, like he'd been told, staring at Pap-pap's dead body sitting against the wall. An expression of horror was carved into Pap-pap's face, his eyes stretched wide and his toothless mouth gaping open, as if the old man had died in the grip of an unspeakable nightmare.

Tommy couldn't stop crying.

Chapter Two

The ambulance came in the night. Tommy cowered in his room while the other three boys went out to watch the circus of emergency medical workers and police. He lay in bed, shivering, as red and blue lights pulsed in the window.

They would come for him, Tommy was sure of it. Mr. Tanner would tell the police it was all Tommy's fault, and then Tommy would go to jail for life. The end.

But it didn't happen. The police and emergency people eventually went away, and Mrs. Tanner brought the other boys back to the room. Tommy lay in his bed, eyes closed and head turned aside, and pretended to sleep.

"Does Tommy really have the Devil in him?" Isaiah asked.

"Only God can know," Mrs. Tanner said.

"Mr. Tanner thinks he does," Luke said. "He said so."

"Then you'll have to talk that over with Mr. Tanner," Mrs. Tanner said. "Now, into bed, all of you."

Tommy listened as the three boys got into bed.

"Back to sleep, children." Mrs. Tanner turned off the lights. "God watch over you."

"Hey, Mrs. Tanner?"

"Yes, Isaiah?"

"Do we gotta say our prayers again?" Isaiah asked.

"No, just go to sleep."

"Mrs. Tanner?" Isaiah asked. "How come you always call your husband 'Mr. Tanner?' Don't you know his first name?"

"I've always called him Mister Tanner," she said. "Ever since I was his foster daughter. There was a different Mrs. Tanner then, but she's gone now."

"What happened to her?" Isaiah asked.

"Stop trying to put off your bedtime, Isaiah."

"But I don't want to sleep in the same room with Tommy. He's scary."

"There are scarier things in the world than him." Mrs. Tanner closed the door.

The room was silent and dark for a minute.

"You know what I think happened?" Jeb whispered. "I think Tommy gave him nightmares. Until he died."

"But the doctor said heart attack," Isaiah whispered. "Right?"

"That's what a heart attack means, stupid," Luke said. "It's when something scares you so much you die."

"Yeah, stupid," Jeb echoed.

"Ohhhhh," Isaiah said. He was quiet for a second. "Do you think Tommy can do that to us?"

"Maybe," Luke said.

"Or maybe just you, Isaiah," Jeb said. "Cause you're a little kid and a scaredy-cat."

"Why would he kill me?" Isaiah squeaked.

"Because you won't shut up and go to sleep," Luke said.

"You wouldn't let him kill me, would you, Luke?" Isaiah whispered.

"I would," Luke said. "I'd watch him do it, and I'd laugh."

Jeb laughed.

"Shut up, Jeb," Luke said. "Everybody shut up."

Tommy couldn't sleep, so he crept out of the house long before dawn and got started on his chores. That way, he wouldn't have to face anybody at breakfast.

He started by stacking up the firewood that Luke and Mr. Tanner had chopped the day before. Mr. Tanner wanted it in a very precise hash pattern.

Later, he let the horses out and mucked the stables. He couldn't get too close to the horses themselves, because he spooked them. The horses hated him, but he had to shovel their manure anyway.

He managed to avoid people for most of the day, but he was starving by late afternoon. Mrs. Tanner wouldn't want him in the kitchen unless he'd washed up.

Tommy scraped his muddy shoes outside the back door, then took them off and carried them into the house. Mr. Tanner and the other boys were still out doing chores. Tommy heard banging sounds and Mrs. Tanner's voice, swearing up a storm.

Upstairs, he found Mrs. Tanner in Pap-pap's room, which smelled like stale sheets and Ben-Gay. It sort of looked like Mrs. Tanner was packing up his things, because she was taking clothes out of drawers, shaking them, and then flinging them into cardboard boxes. At the same time, it sort of looked like she was searching the room, because she was leaving the drawers hanging open, and she had pushed the mattress off the bed.

She sensed him watching her and turned to him, a deep frown on her face.

"What are you looking at?" she asked.

"I don't know," Tommy said. "Can I help?"

She looked at him for a second, catching her breath. Then she nodded.

"Okay, Tommy," she said. "Help me find Pap-pap's money."

"Money?"

"He's got a bunch of cash in here somewhere," Mrs. Tanner said. "Now we need it."

"Where do I look?"

"Anywhere. Start anywhere. Don't worry about making a mess."

"Okay." Tommy looked around the old man's room. Where might he hide money?

Tommy looked under the bed first. There was a tackle box and a tool box, and the implements inside each were old and rusty. He found a photo album and flipped through it, thinking that it might be a good idea to hide money behind the pictures. He didn't find any, just a bunch of faded photographs of Pap-pap when he was younger, with people Tommy didn't recognize.

Mrs. Tanner moved on to the closet, checking the pockets of Pap-pap's coats and shirts.

The rattling sound of Mr. Tanner's truck approached the house, and Mrs. Tanner straightened up. She raced back to the dresser and slammed each of the drawers.

"Get out of here!" she growled at Tommy. "Go on and get washed up."

Tommy ran down the hall to the bathroom. He didn't know what was coming, but for sure Mr. Tanner had a punishment in mind by now. He scrubbed his face, hands and arms. He looked at the splintery handmade cross over the sink, and he prayed for protection against Mr. Tanner.

"Where is that boy?" Mr. Tanner shouted from the front door. "I'm ready for him now. The Lord has spoken to me."

"He's up here," Mrs. Tanner called.

Tommy crept out of the bathroom. Mrs. Tanner was hastily folding the clothes she'd flung into the cardboard boxes. As Mr. Tanner clomped up the stairs, Mrs. Tanner heaved the mattress back onto Pap-pap's bed and slid it into place.

Mr. Tanner paused at the front of the upstairs hall, his boots and jeans spattered in mud, his cowboy hat tipped back to reveal his angry face. His boots thudded on the boards as he approached. He glared at Tommy, who cringed by the door to Pap-pap's room, and then at Mrs. Tanner kneeling on the bedroom floor, folding clothes.

"What are you doing alone with him, Courtney?" Mr. Tanner asked. "What were you two getting up to?"

"Nothing, Mr. Tanner," Mrs. Tanner said.

"Why are you in Pap-pap's room?"

"I was just neatening up. Getting things squared away."

"And who told you to do that?"

"You always want me to do things without you telling me," Mrs. Tanner.

"This ain't one of them," Mr. Tanner said. "Put it back just like it was."

"But— " Mrs. Tanner said.

"Like it was!" Mr. Tanner grabbed Tommy by the sleeve and pulled him down the hall towards the stairs. Tommy stumbled along and fought to keep his balance. "And you got to come to church with me. You got to pray."

Tommy didn't want to go to church, but he didn't say anything. He didn't want a whupping.

Mr. Tanner took him downstairs and out the back door of the house, past the stables, and out past the goat pen.

“They say it was just a heart attack,” Mr. Tanner said. “Well, the Devil covers his cloven tracks, don’t he? I said don’t he, boy?”

“I guess so.”

“What’s that?”

“I don’t know, sir,” Tommy said.

“I knew something was wrong with you,” Mr. Tanner said. “From the day you got here. Right from your baptism. I told my wife, that one’s been touched by Satan himself.”

Tommy didn’t say anything.

Mr. Tanner had left the local church after getting into a dispute with the pastor. In fact, he’d gotten into disputes with every pastor and preacher in the county, often by standing up in the middle of a Sunday sermon and shouting fiery criticism about the church, its leadership, and its interpretation of the Bible. Mr. Tanner had his own peculiar religious ideas, which nobody else seemed to care about, at least not when he was screaming them in the middle of their church.

Since he couldn’t find a church to his liking, he’d cleaned out the ancient gray barn near the back of the property. Beyond it were the corpses of even older buildings that had collapsed long ago, blown over by the prairie winds and left to rot, their wood gone dry and brittle like bones in the sun. The gray barn itself was too decrepit for any working use, but Mr. Tanner had nailed a cross on top of it and held service for his wife and foster children there each Sunday. Sometimes other days, too, as the mood struck him.

Mr. Tanner pulled open the creaky barn door and waited for Tommy to step inside.

The inside of the barn church was already lit by a few candles. The rough, handmade benches faced towards the front of the church, where a big cross of nailed-together willow limbs hung on the wall.

Under the cross was the wooden platform Mr. Tanner had built from two-by-fours. Beside that was another platform, which held the baptismal pool, which was really just a dirty old bathtub.

Like each of Mr. Tanner’s foster children, Tommy had to be baptized within a day or two after he arrived. This involved the whole family coming out to the church, and some prayers by Mr. Tanner. Then you had to take off all your clothes and get in that cold water while Mr. Tanner dunked you again and again, saying he was casting out your devils and putting God inside you.

Tonight, Luke, Jeb and Isaiah were already here, dirty from working in the pasture. Luke held a length of rope and smiled at

Tommy, while the two other boys glared. Tommy wondered if he had to be baptized over again. But Mrs. Tanner wasn't here, and she never missed anything at church.

"Luke, the rope," Mr. Tanner said.

Luke nodded. He threaded the rope through an iron eyehole mounted in the wall above the willow cross. Then he grimaced as he bound Tommy's hands together.

"What's going on?" Tommy whispered, but nobody answered him.

Luke pulled the rope taut, raising Tommy's hands in front of him.

"Jeb," Mr. Tanner said.

Jeb stepped up to Tommy and unbuckled his belt. He pushed Tommy's pants down, leaving Tommy shaking in his underwear in front of everybody, embarrassed and terrified.

"Kneel," Mr. Tanner said. "Kneel before God. And beg for His mercy."

Tommy knelt on the dirt floor of the church. It was hard because his bound hands were stretched in front of him. Luke pulled on the rope, raising Tommy's hands even higher above his head, and then he tied the rope to one of the wooden posts holding up the barn roof.

Behind him, he heard Mr. Tanner unbuckle his belt.

"Say you're sorry," Mr. Tanner said.

"I'm sorry," Tommy whispered. The leather belt cracked across his backside, and Tommy yelped in pain. "I'm sorry! I'm sorry!"

Mr. Tanner kept whipping him. Tommy cried and repeated how sorry he was.

"Now stay there and pray," Mr. Tanner said. "Pray for the Devil to get out of you. Or I'll have to exorcise him myself."

Mr. Tanner and the boys left.

Tommy knelt in the dirt and cried, his arms stretched taut above his head. They were already starting to ache.

They left Tommy alone in the church all night, shivering with cold and pain.

Chapter Three

Pap-pap's body came back the next day. Tommy, who had been untied so he could attempt to do his morning chores with his weak and aching arms, watched Mr. Tanner, Luke, and Jeb unload the cheap pine casket from the back of Mr. Tanner's truck. They carried it into the gray barn-church. Mr. Tanner was going to conduct the funeral the next day, and then they would bury Pap-pap in the yard next to the church.

Tommy went to bed before supper. He hadn't gotten much work done, either, but nobody harassed him about it. They all acted like Tommy didn't exist.

After going to bed so early, Tommy woke just after midnight, when he heard a floorboard squeak in the hall. Then another one. Someone was trying to sneak down the hall. Tommy could tell because he'd done it so many times, trying to go to the bathroom without waking anyone. Tommy enjoyed it when he was the only one awake. He loved the deep hours of the night.

He looked at the other bed. In the moonlight, he could see all three boys were there. And Mr. Tanner wouldn't be tiptoeing around, he'd be clomping and banging as always. So it had to be Mrs. Tanner. Or a burglar. Or a monster.

Tommy lay very still and listened. He heard the squeak on the third stair, then the seventh stair. It was someone leaving, not someone coming. It had to be Mrs. Tanner.

He slipped out of bed and walked to the room's one small window, which looked out on the weed-and-dirt front yard. He watched Mrs. Tanner step down off the front porch and pull on a pair of boots.

A station wagon trundled up the front drive. Mrs. Tanner raced toward it, waving her arms. She leaned in at the driver's side, and the driver immediately turned out the headlights.

Mrs. Tanner climbed into the back seat of the station wagon.

Tommy watched it drive along the rutted dirt track towards the stables and barns. It drove around the corner of the house and out of sight.

Tommy pulled on a shirt and picked up his shoes. He followed after Mrs. Tanner, avoiding the squeaky spots in the hall, and the third and seventh step. She'd left the front door slightly ajar, so he did, too.

Tommy walked in the direction they'd gone, keeping himself to the shadows of the farm buildings as much as he could. The moon was bright overhead, leaving too little darkness.

The station wagon was parked next to the stable, with nobody inside. A crucifix hung from the rearview mirror. Tommy tracked them up to the church, where the barn door stood half open. Tommy circled around the barn, picked one of the knotholes on the side, and looked through.

Mrs. Tanner stood next to the pine casket, which was elevated on a pair of sawhorses. There were two other people with her. One was a very heavyset Mexican-looking woman in a loud dress, with bright scarves nested around her throat. She was shaking her head while Mrs. Tanner talked in a low voice.

The other person was the most beautiful girl Tommy had ever seen. She had deep, rich brown eyes and braided black hair, with skin that reminded him of butterscotch. She was about a year or two older than Tommy, dressed in jeans and a black T-shirt with a glittering butterfly on the front. She was chewing a giant pink wad of bubble gum.

"You bring us here, all the way out here," the older lady was saying to Mrs. Tanner, "All this sneaking around, and you have only twenty dollars for pay?"

"There's more," Mrs. Tanner whispered. "A lot more. The old man told me. I just need to find out where. Then I can pay your fee."

"What if he don't really have the money?"

"He bragged about it. He said his son—my husband—had no idea. I need that money."

"You going to keep for yourself?" the lady asked. "No telling you husband?"

"That's between us," Mrs. Tanner said. "I wiped this old man's ass for the last four years. I want to get paid."

The hefty lady sighed and eased herself down onto one of Mr. Tanner's homemade pews. She spoke in Spanish to the younger girl. The girl blew a big pink bubble and shrugged.

"How much money?" the older Mexican lady asked.

"Lots," Mrs. Tanner said. "Ten, fifteen thousand."

"You pay one thousand," the lady said.

"That's too much!" Mrs. Tanner said.

"Maybe you find the dead man's money yourself. Come on, Esmeralda. This lady is crazy."

The girl shrugged and started for the open door.

"Wait!" Mrs. Tanner said. "Wait. Okay. If you can really do what they say, and you find the money, I'll pay you a…a thousand dollars." She almost choked on the words.

"Good." The hefty lady pushed herself to her feet and approached the casket. "Open," she said.

Mrs. Tanner took a deep breath. She lifted the lid of the cheap coffin and slid it to one side. The big lady looked inside the casket and curled her nose.

"How long?"

"About two days now," Mrs. Tanner said.

"Is ripe." She waved a hand in front of her face.

"Well, that happens," Mrs. Tanner said. "Mr. Tanner doesn't believe in embalming."

The hefty lady sighed. "Esmeralda."

The girl turned to face them, and she pouted. She said something in Spanish. Tommy couldn't follow it, but from her tone and expression, she was obviously complaining.

The older lady—her mother, Tommy was guessing—snapped at her. The girl sighed and trudged over to the casket. She pinched her nose with one hand. Then she reached her other hand into the casket.

The girl closed her eyes.

"Wait," Mrs. Tanner said. "*She* is the one who—?"

"Sh!" the lady snapped. *"Silencio."*

Mrs. Tanner looked increasingly uncomfortable as the quiet minutes dragged on. She looked back and forth between the woman and the girl. She started clearing her throat every few seconds.

"*Si, si,*" the girl whispered. "I can hear him now. Questions?"

"The money," Mrs. Tanner said. "Where did he hide the money?"

"The money…" The girl scrunched her eyes. She licked her lips. Tommy was already developing a serious crush on her.

"This isn't working—" Mrs. Tanner said, but the lady cut her off with a glare.

"Yes, he hid the money," the girl called Esmeralda said. "It's in his duffle bag. From the Army."

"And where is that?" Mrs. Tanner said.

"In the trunk of his car," Esmeralda said. "In the barn. Not this barn, the one over there." She pointed in the direction of the newer barns. "His car under a sheet. He used to fantasize about jumping in the car and driving away. With his money in the trunk. He dreamed he would escape."

Tommy eased back from the barn. When he felt he was far enough away, he turned and ran.

Pap-pap's old Buick was parked inside the same barn where Mr. Tanner kept the horse trailer. Tommy lifted the mildewy canvas sheet and pushed it back, revealing the Buick's trunk. The car was a rusted heap, at least forty years old. It had been years since the car had its last chance of ever running again.

It was locked, and Tommy couldn't find a way to open the trunk. He might be able to pry it open with a crow bar, but that would make a lot of noise.

"God damn," Tommy whispered. He would have to go back into the house, up to Pap-pap's room, find the car keys. All without making a sound, all before Mrs. Tanner and the others came from the church to check the car.

Tommy pulled the canvas back into place. He ran back towards the house, where he eased the front door open and then left it ajar.

In Pap-pap's room, he found the car keys next to the scum-filled denture jar. No one had bothered taking Pap-pap's dentures out of them in over a year.

Tommy went out the back door, figuring Mrs. Tanner would soon be returning through the front, in search of the Buick keys.

Tommy jogged back toward the barn, but he heard a voice from inside. He ducked low against the building and listened.

"—can't get this fucking thing open," Mrs. Tanner grunted. "Christ. The keys are up in the house."

Mrs. Tanner stepped out and Tommy hid himself around the corner. He held his breath. He forced himself to count to ten before peeking around. Mrs. Tanner had walked out of sight. The barn was silent.

Tommy ran into the barn. She'd left the canvas off the back half of the car. Tommy hurried to the locked trunk and began sorting through Pap-pap's thick key ring.

"What are you doing?" a soft voice asked, and Tommy jumped.

It was the girl, Esmeralda. Tommy looked around, panicked, but didn't see her mother or Mrs. Tanner.

"Nothing." Tommy found two keys with the Buick logo. He tried the first one.

"You have the keys," she whispered.

"Quiet." The first key wouldn't slide in, so he tried the other one. There was a rusty squeal that sounded as loud as thunder to Tommy's ears. Then he lifted the trunk lid.

A green U.S. Army duffle bag lay inside, among assorted junk.

"We have to go tell—" Esmeralda started for the barn door. Tommy caught her bare arm in his hand, and she gasped.

"Don't tell anyone!" he hissed.

"Okay!" She shivered. She was terrified of him. He was probably giving her nightmares, and he felt bad about that. "Don't hurt me, okay?" she whispered.

"Stay right there."

"Yes, yes, yes." She nodded. "Whatever you say."

Tommy frowned and let go of her arm. He watched her for a second, to make sure she didn't run or scream, but she just trembled and stared at him.

"Are you the devil?" she whispered.

"Yes," Tommy said. He unzipped the duffle bag.

It was full of bundles of cash, each secured with a rubber band, and each bundle had a scrap of paper with an amount scrawled on it. The amounts were all in the hundreds of dollars, and he saw one or two that were over a thousand. Loose change sat at the bottom of the bag—a big handful of silver coins, plus one gold coin featuring an Indian head and an eagle on the back. "2 ½ dollars" it said, but Tommy thought it looked a lot more expensive than that. Pap-pap's life savings.

"That is her money," Esmeralda whispered.

"My money." Tommy zipped the duffle bag and hoisted it over his arm. "I need it because I'm leaving."

"Oh, no," Esmeralda said. "My mother will kill me."

Tommy stared at the frightened girl. He didn't want to cause her problems.

"I don't have much time," he said. He closed the trunk as quietly as he could and propped the duffle bag against it. He unzipped it part of the way, then he reached inside.

"This is for you," he whispered. He gave her one of the thousand-dollar bundles.

She gaped at it.

"Put it in your purse!" he said. "Don't tell your mother until you're a long way from here. Don't give any money to the Tanners. Okay?"

"Oh…I don't…" She continued gaping at the money.

Tommy grabbed her arm and shook her. "Do what I say!"

"Yes!" She crammed the money into her beaded purse and zipped it shut. "Sorry. Don't hurt me please."

"I wouldn't hurt you," he said. He could feel her trembling, but he didn't want to let go of her arm. She was warm. She almost seemed to glow.

"What are you?" she whispered.

"What are you?" he asked. "You can speak with the dead?"

"Sometimes," she said. "Mostly I listen. But you are like a…a…."

"A nightmare," he whispered. Tommy needed to run, but he couldn't quite let her go yet. She was different, in the same way that he was different. He felt like if he touched her long enough, he would understand.

Then he thought of Mrs. Tanner, on her way back any second.

And he did something that he later wouldn't believe he had the courage to do. He kissed Esmeralda, the mysterious Latin girl with the supernatural power, right on the lips. Then slipped the gold Indian-head coin into her hand.

She stared at it.

"That's for you," he whispered. "I love you."

Then he ran out of the barn and away across the pasture, towards the distant, flat horizon. He planned to never see the Tanners, or any other foster family, ever again.

He looked back over his shoulder and saw the girl gaping after him. He waved at her, then lowered his head and ran faster.

Chapter Four

The television in Bent River sat behind a shield of durable plastic in case of riots. Located in a crook of the Mississippi River, just before the State of Louisiana turned into the State of Mississippi, Bent River housed a mix of medium and high security prisoners. Tommy lived in a cellblock in the East Yard, along with a few hundred other violent offenders like himself.

Tommy sat on the hard bench at rec time, watching the TV. Next to him sat Doyle Vinner, one count of arson and two of homicide. Vinner had robbed and murdered an elderly couple and burned their house to the ground. He'd taken a shine to Tommy soon after Tommy arrived. Though Vinner was in his forties, probably a quarter-century older than Tommy, he followed Tommy like a duckling in awe of its mother.

The TV flipped from a baseball game to a 24-hour news channel.

"Teen pregnancy!" a fat, balding man shouted on the screen. "A shocking story about how the libs are wrecking our morals. Again. I'm Chuck O'Flannery, and this is the O'Flannery Overview Hour. Tonight's top story of teen girls and sex will turn your stomach! Keep watching the Overview." The promo ended, and cut to a commercial for Axe body spray.

Boos sounded from all the black prisoners.

"Shut your booing," yelled a big redneck named Patrick Headon, better known as Possum. A swastika was tattooed on the side of his shaved head. He sat with his hefty white-power cohorts.

Over in the guard station, behind another clear wall, the two guards smirked.

On TV, the commercials ended, and the O'Flannery Overview Hour continued.

“Welcome back to The O’Flannery Overview Hour,” he said. “My special guest is Ashleigh Goodling of Fallen Oak, South Carolina, population nine thousand. Thanks for coming today, Ashleigh.”

“Thank you for having me, sir.”

A wider camera angle revealed a very pretty girl with blond hair and hypnotic gray eyes. Tommy sat up. Her eyes looked just like his, a rare trait. For a moment, Tommy wondered if they were related—he knew nothing about his birth parents.

“I don't wanna watch this,” Vinner grumbled.

“Then get back to your room,” Tommy said. Vinner stayed.

“We hope you enjoy your visit,” Chuck O’Flannery said to the girl. “Now, for the Overviewers at home, give us a little background on this teen abstinence story.”

“Gosh,” the girl said. “Well, teen pregnancy is such a major problem, even in little towns like mine. Our group decided to promote the only moral choice, abstinence, at our school...”

Tommy wasn't listening. He was reading one of the many flickering sidebars on the screen, which told him all about the girl:

ASHLEIGH GOODLING, it said. FALLEN OAK, SC. Her name and town stayed fixed, but the line underneath it changed every five seconds:

SENIOR CLASS PRESIDENT

PRESIDENT, CHRISTIANS ACT! SCHOOL CLUB

CAPTAIN, VARSITY CHEERLEADING SQUAD

“…I’m not perfect,” the girl said. “I get tempted all the time. Your body wants it. That’s why you have to rely on your mind, and on prayer. When adults set the example, and they say abstinence is bad, it just tells us to go ahead and give in to our urges.” She was squirming in her chair as if agitated, and her tongue flicked across her lips.

“Ashleigh Goodling,” Tommy whispered.

“Looks like a sweet slice of tail, don't she?” Vinner snickered. Tommy slapped the lascivious grin off Vinner's face. Vinner fell quiet, but he didn't complain. He seemed to like a little abuse now and then, a little dose of Tommy’s fear. Some people did.

“...Christians get persecuted, but God takes care of us. I don’t care if everyone hates me. I have my faith.” The girl named Ashleigh touched the cross pendant around her neck.

Fallen Oak, South Carolina, Tommy repeated inside his head. *Fallen Oak, South Carolina.*

He watched the girl talk, entranced. A lifetime of violence and small-time robbery had given him a stony outer crust, but he felt something move inside him. Something big. Like those big plates under the earth, the ones that made earthquakes and volcanoes.

He'd had plenty of women, in his way—it was easy enough when you had Tommy's special thing, the nightmare that lived inside him. His touch filled people with fear. He could make them hand over wallets, car keys, the contents of a cash register.

This was a different feeling, though. He didn't just want to rip this girl's panties off. There was something else, a hint of something he hadn't felt in a long time. Not since he was a kid, and that had only been a glimpse.

He knew better than to trust the feeling. He'd never seen Esmeralda again, after all. That sense of falling for somebody seemed to hint at forever, but it was an illusion. In real life, you couldn't surrender to those feelings, or they would just rip you to pieces.

Tommy knew all of this. He thought of all this. But it was on the back burner of his mind.

On the front burner, red hot and smoking, was the need to find the girl on the television. And then...do something. He could imagine a lot of things he might do to her—he'd been in prison almost a year—but those weren't the main things that interested him. There was a lot more going on here. A mystery. He could feel things about that girl.

He tried to shake off the feeling. Stupid. He was just caged up and horny, and that was all.

“Thanks for having me, Mr. O'Flannery,” Ashleigh said at the end of the show. Then she smiled, and then she was gone.

Over the next few weeks, Tommy tried to push down his thoughts about the girl from the TV. He couldn't win: he kept catching himself daydreaming about her while he worked in the prison's cannery. She filled up his dreams, and he awoke hot, sweaty, and more miserable than he’d ever felt.

Tommy put together his plan. He had to be careful—he'd learned that the hard way, after he robbed that convenience store and the cops had taken him down with Tasers. Fucking shocking you to the ground from ten feet away, out of reach—that wasn't fair, in his book.

Tommy had found that if he could just get his hand on a cop for a moment, he could usually intimidate the cop into letting him go. He'd used that trick more times than he could remember. But if they were going to stay out of reach and zap him into a vegetable with electric wires, his special fear-inducing touch didn't have much room to play.

He made his move after lunch, on the way out of the cafeteria. Vinner was walking alongside him, jabbering away about his meth-addicted pregnant sister. As they passed a pair of guards, Tommy turned and punched Vinner in the face. Then he punched him again, and a third time. Vinner went down, bleeding from his nose and lip.

The two guards grabbed Tommy and hit him a few times, and Tommy went slack and fell on the floor, pretending to be semiconscious and groaning in pain.

"Good night, you crazy bastard," one of the guards crowed.

"Let's put this prick in the Hole," the other said.

They each took one of Tommy's wrists and dragged him away from the cafeteria. He could feel them shivering a little, as his touch began to work its magic.

When they dragged him into a side corridor, Tommy seized their wrists.

He didn't take any chances. Tommy's touch always made people afraid, whether he wanted to or not, but sometimes he could focus and make it really powerful, terrifying people out of their minds. He imagined pushing it out through his hands, pumping the guards full of fear.

The guards' arm hairs stood on end, and one of them gasped. They released Tommy and he fell to the floor. Tommy jumped to his feet and seized their hands again, not wanting to lose his moment. He pushed the fear as hard as he could.

"I'm leaving," Tommy hissed. "And you two are helping me."

"Okay, okay!" One of the guards was nodding as fast as a bobble-headed doll. "Whatever you want."

"Don't hurt me," the other guard pleaded. They both wore expressions like terrified little boys, and Tommy tried not to smile.

"You do what I say from here on," Tommy said. "Understand?"

They understood.

Tommy left the prison in the trunk of a guard's car. As Tommy instructed, the guard took him all the way to Baton Rouge. The guard also visited an ATM, emptied his checking account, and gave the cash to Tommy.

Tommy shook the guard's hand before the guard got back in his car. He squeezed tight, and stared the shuddering man in the eyes.

"You won't remember anything," Tommy said. "You won't tell anyone where you brought me. You're going to forget all about our adventure."

"Yeah, of course, of course," the guard said. He looked on the verge of tears. His voice came out small and squeaky. "Whatever you want me to do."

"Go home and forget about me."

Tommy stood on the side of the boulevard and watched the prison guard drive away. Part of him couldn't believe he'd pulled it off. Another part of him was beginning to feel like a real idiot for sitting in prison this long.

South Carolina lay several hundred miles to the east. Tommy started walking.

Chapter Five

Dr. Heather Reynard raced down the country highway at ninety miles an hour, while juggling her cell phone and a box of Zaxby's chicken nuggets. After two months of living on canned beans and U.S. Army MRE's, she thought the deep-fried chicken lumps tasted better than caviar.

"So, wait," her husband, Liam, said on the phone. "You're back home?"

"No," Heather said. "I mean yes, I left Haiti. No, I'm not on my way home."

"Then where are you?"

"In America."

"That narrows it down."

"I'm not supposed to say where I'm going, Liam." Heather hesitated. "It's somewhere in South Carolina, though."

"That's not far. Thank God you're finally back. You'll never guess what Tricia did to the dining room wall—"

"I am *not* back, Liam. Officially I'm still doing cholera in Haiti."

"And what are you unofficially doing?"

"I don't know!" Heather swerved around a slowpoke farm truck loaded with hay. "I'm guessing it's urgent, because I just flew from Port-au-Prince to Augusta on a U.S. Postal Service airplane, and this is my first chance to call."

"When did all this happen?"

"This morning. Early. Dr. Schwartzman sent for me. I don't know why. Nobody's telling me anything."

"I'm guessing it's not another salmonella outbreak, then."

"Why did you have to say that? I'm eating chicken nuggets here."

"You're probably safe. Like I was saying, your daughter is a real artist now."

"That doesn't sound good," Heather said.

"She painted a mural in the dining room. In the medium of ketchup and mustard."

"Ugh. That'll be a mess to clean up."

"Who's cleaning?" Liam asked. "I'll just slap a frame around it and tell people it's a Jackson Pollock."

"You're so unbelievably hilarious," Heather said. Following the directions she'd scrawled on her notepad, she turned off the main highway onto someplace called Esther Bridge Road, saw the National Guard roadblock, and hit the brakes. "Wow, this looks big. I have to go."

"I love—" she heard Liam say as she clicked the phone.

A Guardsman, about nineteen years old, walked towards her Heather's rental car, shaking his head. Heather lowered her window.

"Road's closed, ma'am," he said.

"I'm Dr. Reynard." Heather showed her ID badge. "CDC. I'm supposed to be here."

The Guardsman inspected her ID card closely, as if he were an expert in distinguishing between real and fake Centers for Disease Control badges.

"One sec. Wait here." He walked away and consulted with an older Guardsman, who consulted with someone else via walkie-talkie, and then nodded.

Soldiers moved aside the orange cones that blocked the road, opening a lane for her between two big National Guard trucks. They'd blocked off the left lane completely with their trucks, as if more concerned about people getting out than people getting in. Interesting.

Heather continued along Esther Bridge Road, which wound sharply through dense woods. She crossed a bridge over a creek, and then saw an old wooden sign:

WELCOME TO FALLEN OAK, it said. "*THE LORD HAS BROUGHT FORTH A BOUNTIFUL HARVEST*."

The little patch of downtown was surrounded by government workers—more National Guard, black Homeland Security vehicles, mobile CDC units. South Carolina Highway Patrol seemed to be lingering around the fringes, too.

Heather parked on the side of the road and checked in at the next National Guard blockade. As she walked into the scene, she dialed Schwartzman on her cell phone.

"I'm here," she said.

"Suit up and come meet me. I'm on my way there now."

"Where?"

"You'll find it." He hung up.

Heather found the CDC truck with the hazmat equipment. A young technician sitting inside the open rear door of the truck jumped to his feet.

"Dr. Reynard?" he asked. He grabbed one of the yellow hazmat suits from a hanging rack.

"That's me."

"You need to suit up," the technician said. "Schwartzman's waiting."

"What's going on here?" Heather asked. "I just flew hundreds of miles and I have no clue why."

"I'm not supposed to say. I'm just supposed to help you suit up." He held open the bulky yellow suit for her to step inside it. The suit would cover her from head to toe, keeping her protected from…whatever was going on in Fallen Oak.

"You must have seen something," Heather said. "Or heard something?"

"I haven't seen anything. I can't get close enough. Because I'm not wearing a suit." He gave the suit a shake and raised his eyebrows.

"But what are people saying?"

"Dr. Schwartzman is saying for you to hurry. But you can't do that until you put on this—"

"Okay, okay, give me the suit."

Heather let the young man help her into the heavy yellow suit. She fixed the radio speaker into her ear, and then he pulled the hood over her head. She smiled at him through the face shield. "How do I look?"

"Like an alien." He sealed the hood.

Heather followed the bustle of official activity toward the town square. She rounded an eighteen-wheeler truck, and then she saw the town green.

It seemed like a once-charming little town that had fallen on hard times, like thousands of little towns around the country. A nineteenth-century brick courthouse dominated the scene, with fat white columns and a sculpted frieze on the pediment. It depicted the goddess Justice, blindfolded and wielding scales and a sword.

There was a little white building with a sign identifying it as Fallen Oak Baptist Church, and there was a Merchants and Farmers Bank of Fallen Oak. The rest of the downtown was mostly empty brick buildings, the vacant shop windows whitewashed.

Immediately, Heather saw why Schwartzman had flown her up from Haiti in a rush.

The town green was covered in bodies. CDC workers in yellow suits like hers were sealing them in airtight plastic cadaver pouches and loading them onto two refrigerated box trucks. There were still at least a hundred bodies left scattered in front of the courthouse, the front doors of which were marked with a big splash of dried red. Heather guessed it wasn't ketchup.

She found Schwartzman supervising the collecting and sealing of bodies.

"What the hell happened here?" she asked him.

"Heather. Finally." His voice crackled over the radio, heavy with static, though he only stood a few feet away. She could hear other conversations fading in and out of the channel, from the other CDC workers.

"Yes, me, finally." Heather looked around at the carnage. Many of the bodies were badly contorted, rife with huge blisters, open sores, broken pustules, and dark tumors. She couldn't think of any known pathogen that would cause such a broad range of symptoms. Whatever biological agent had caused this was extremely nasty and needed to be killed immediately.

"Bioterrorism?" Heather asked.

"Possibly. But this town is about as far from a valuable national target as you can get."

"What are the local authorities saying?"

"We haven't found any," Schwartzman said. He nodded at the courthouse. "Mayor's office is empty. The little police department's empty. If I had to guess…" He gestured at all the dead bodies.

Heather shook her head. "My God."

"Don't say that," Schwartzman snapped. "The locals are already talking Biblical plague. Don't encourage."

"Maybe they're right." Heather knelt by one of the bodies. He was a heavyset man—obese by any measure—in a white dress shirt polka-dotted with his own blood. His face had peeled away into wide, curling strips. The muscles underneath were knotted with tumors. "I've never seen anything like this. It looks like leprosy, bubonic plague and cancer all wrapped together. How many cases?"

"We're still counting, but it looks like about two hundred. All of them right here. No suspected cases so far—just all these confirmed ones. Nobody alive to talk. Old lady found them early this morning." He nodded toward a shop with a big, hand-painted sign: *Miss Gertie's Five and Dime*. "She had no symptoms, but we took blood samples to send to Atlanta for analysis."

"So what happened?" Heather asked. "All these people came down to the courthouse, and they died all at once?"

"We don't know what happened," Schwartzman said. "We don't know what kind of pathogen we're facing. But answers are on the way."

"They are?"

"Yes," Schwartzman said. "Because I just pulled my best epidemiologist out of Haiti to find them."

Heather sighed and shook her head.

Chapter Six

Jenny awoke gradually, with a pounding headache. She was sore and hurting all over, inside and out. Her lungs still felt raw from drowning to death in Ashleigh's pond.

She'd thrown herself into the water because her body was already dying from her wounds and her massive-scale use of her curse, the Jenny pox. When that memory hit her, Jenny's eyes flew open.

It was twilight—she wasn't even sure what day. She was in her room at home, sprawled on her bed. Seth lay beside her, sleeping like a corpse. They still wore the tattered remnants of their Easter clothes.

A swirl of images flashed across her brain. How she'd run into the crowd, spreading the pox everywhere, watching people she'd known all her life die horribly, as spasms twisted their bodies and sores ruptured open all over them. Chasing them down, even when they'd given up trying to lynch her and started running for their lives.

She ran to the bathroom and puked. She and Seth had eaten everything in her house when they got home—frozen pizza, canned peas—and now whatever her body hadn't absorbed came burbling up.

Jenny sat on the worn tile floor and leaned her head against the cabinet door under the sink.

There was one rule, one absolute law that her father had taught her since she was little: *never touch people*. Because when she touched people, they got sick. And it didn't take long for them to die.

Seth was lucky. He was the opposite—when he touched people, he healed them. He'd even brought Jenny back from the dead. He didn't have to avoid people like she did, or obsess over how much of his skin was exposed where other people could touch it. He couldn't just flip out and slaughter a whole crowd of people.

All those people, Jenny thought. She could see their faces, from Mayor Winder and Coach Humbee and even people like Shannon McNare, who weren't really so bad, just caught in Ashleigh's spell.

Jenny stood on shaking legs. The weight of what she'd done pressed down on her like a million tons of darkness. There was no fixing this, no going back and undoing the damage.

She went back to her room and sat on the edge of the bed.

"What's happening?" Seth asked through a yawn. "Where are we?"

"My room."

"Oh." Seth sat up. "Don't let your dad catch me here."

"Who cares?"

"He might."

"Seth!" Jenny said. "I think we have bigger problems."

"Like what?"

"Like I'm a mass murderer! All those people."

"So? They tried to kill us first. They *did* kill us." Seth sat up and stretched. "What's for breakfast?"

"Are you kidding?" Jenny put her face in her hands. "I can't believe I...I..." She started crying. Seth hugged her, but she stiffened against him. "You don't know what it feels like."

"No, you're right," he said. "But remember what we saw when we were dead? This isn't anything compared to the past—"

"Oh, right. I was a mass murderer in hundreds of other lives, too. Thanks for reminding me." Jenny had a few broken memories of the time between when she'd been dead, before Seth brought her back with his healing power. She'd seen herself spreading plagues in ancient times, in medieval times, usually in the service of some king or emperor. "We're evil, Seth. I am, anyway."

"You're not evil. You were defending yourself."

"Maybe at first," Jenny said. "But then something came over me. All the evil inside came out. I wouldn't let anyone escape. It's like I was a different person. But that's who I really am, isn't it? A demon."

"That's a pretty strong word—"

"I should die for what I did," Jenny said. "I wish I could infect myself with Jenny pox."

"Don't do that." He kissed her cheek. "I love you, Jenny. We're not what we used to be. We're more human. We're learning, lifetime by lifetime—"

Jenny pulled away from him. "It's so easy for you. You can do so many good things with the power you have. I can only hurt people. And kill them. Lots and lots of them."

Seth didn't have anything to say to that. After a while, he asked, "Is your dad home?"

"He must still be at June's house." Jenny covered her eyes. "He's going to hate me. He spent his whole life teaching me not to hurt anyone, and what good did that do? He should have killed me when I was born." Jenny looked at the picture of her mother on the wall—young, cheerful, with Jenny's blue eyes. She had died at Jenny's birth, the first victim of the Jenny pox. This lifetime, anyway.

"We'll explain what happened," Seth said. "He'll understand."

"I'm not sure about that." Jenny took a deep breath. "Now what the hell do I do? Turn myself in to the police?"

"You killed the police."

Jenny slapped her palm against her face and groaned. Seth sang a verse of "I Shot the Sheriff," until she punched him.

"You can't turn yourself in. Nobody will believe you, anyway," he said.

"But I can show them." Jenny opened her left hand. With a thought, she summoned boils and blisters to the surface of her palm.

"Then they'll lock you up," Seth said. "Or kill you."

"Which is exactly what I deserve."

"No, Jenny!" He touched her hand, and all the boils and blisters healed. "You can't."

"Give me one reason."

"Because I don't want to live without you."

Jenny leaned her head against his shoulder. "I don't want to live without you either, Seth. But what am I supposed to do? Just keep going like it never happened?"

Seth scratched his head. His strawberry blond hair jutted out everywhere, in stiff clumps. "Well," he said. "When was the last time you fed Rocky?"

"Rocky!" Jenny jumped up. Seth followed her to the kitchen and lifted the big bag of dry kibble.

Outside, Rocky was knocking his empty clay bowl around the yard. The shaggy bluetick mix raised his head and wagged his tail when Jenny stepped out the door. He let out a throaty bay and kicked his bowl again for emphasis.

Seth carried the bowl back into the shed, placed it next to Rocky's dog house, and filled it with food. Rocky watched him from several feet away. He looked from Seth to the food, and then took a few cautious steps to the bowl.

Seth reached down to pet his head, and Rocky scurried back.

Seth squatted in the dirt.

"Come on, boy," he said. "Come on."

Rocky took a few more cautious steps toward Seth and the food. Seth rubbed the back of his head, and Rocky wagged his tail and began eating.

"Maybe you shouldn't get him too used to that," Jenny said. "I can only keep him because he's afraid to be touched by people."

"He likes me okay."

"I mean, what if he starts expecting me to do that? He'll get Jenny pox if he comes too close."

"So should he go the rest of his life without anybody touching him?"

"No." Jenny shook her head. "I know what that's like. Sucks."

Back inside, Jenny saw the red light flickering urgently on the answering machine in the living room. Lots of messages. She pushed PLAY, and the cassette inside whirred as it rewound.

"Jenny," her dad's voice said. "Are you all right? I tried to come home, but soldiers was blocking the road. Call me back at June's right now." *(beep)*

Jenny and Seth looked at each other. Soldiers?

"Jenny, you home or what? I done tried Seth's house and ain't nobody answering. I'm worried about you." (*beep*)

"Jenny, pick up the damn phone!" (*beep*)

"Jenny, are you there? We got to get you one of them cell phones. Call me back at June's soon as you get this." (*beep*)

"Jenny, just let me know you're okay. I'm over at June's still, and I guess I'm stuck here. The National Guard's got Fallen Oak all blocked, and don't nobody know what's happening. They're saying some kinda toxic waste or—"(*beep*)

"I got cut off. Just let me know what's happening. I'm at June's." (*beep*)

"Holy shit," Jenny said.

"The National Guard?" Seth ran to the front window and looked out, as if expecting to see uniformed men in Jenny's front yard. "You think they're still out there?"

"I have to call him back." Jenny picked up the old rotary phone next to the answering machine. No dial tone. She depressed the jack several times, but the phone was dead. "This ain't working!"

"Calm down," Seth said. He gave her his cell phone.

Jenny tried it. "It says 'no signal.'"

"What?" Seth looked at the phone. "I always get reception here. What's going on?"

"They're coming after me." Jenny sank onto the couch. "I ought to turn myself in."

"Come on, Jenny." Seth sat beside her and took her hand. "Even if somebody tells them, they'll never believe it. There's nobody left to talk about it, anyway."

"And that's supposed to make me feel better?" Jenny snapped. "Besides, you're wrong. All those girls saw what I did to Ashleigh." Jenny thought about it. "Or, I guess she was hanging out the window while they were all inside. But they had to see her body after, out in front of her house."

"I'm not going to let anyone hurt you."

"Yeah," Jenny said. "You'll unleash the healing touch on them. Clear up their colds and headaches. That'll show 'em."

"Very funny," Seth said. "I meant my family has some good lawyers."

"Lawyers…" Jenny shook her head. She tried the rotary phone again. "And this stupid thing is not working!"

Seth picked up his car keys. "I'll go check things out."

"Wait." Jenny stood up. "I'll go with you. I can explain what happened."

"No, Jenny! They'll think you're crazy."

"So what?" Jenny ran back to her room to put on some new clothes, replacing the shreds of Seth's Easter coat.

"And if they believe you, they'll lock you away from everyone." Seth followed her to her room.

"I ought to be away from everyone."

"Even me?" Seth asked.

Jenny didn't want to think about that. But she had to do the right thing.

"Just stay here," Seth said.

"No. I'm going with you."

They pulled out of Jenny's dusty driveway in Seth's blue Audi, with the top down. The Cure played from Seth's iPod, over his car stereo. It was April, the day after Easter, and honeysuckle and wildflowers bloomed alongside the road.

The beautiful afternoon seemed wrong to Jenny. She felt dark, cold and monstrous on the inside.

Seth drove toward downtown. Jenny gripped her armrest tight. She'd been there only last night, and she wasn't sure she was ready to see the carnage left behind. She steeled herself.

They quickly discovered they wouldn't be going into town, anyway. Armed men in green uniforms had constructed a roadblock, using trucks and plastic orange cones, cutting them off.

Seth slowed to a stop as two of the National Guard approached his car. One had a clipboard. The other, a heavy plastic shield and a Taser.

"Name?" the one with the clipboard asked.

"Um, Seth," Seth said.

"Last name?"

"Barrett."

"Address?"

"What's this for?" Seth asked.

"We keep a record of all attempted entries and exits," the Guardsman said.

"Attempted?" Seth asked.

"Address?"

Jenny noticed a police car parked by the side of the road. It didn't look like Chief Lintner's car, and anyway she'd left Lintner writhing with Jenny pox on the town green, after he'd supported Dr. Goodling's effort to lynch Jenny, like the legendary slave-sorcerer the town had lynched in the 1700s.

This police car was black and white, and had "Federal Protective Service POLICE" on the side. After that, it said "Homeland Security."

A uniformed officer inside the car snapped pictures of Seth and Jenny. Jenny tilted her head forward, so that her long black hair obscured her face.

The Guardsman studied Seth's driver's license, then nodded and gave it back to him. "No one in or out of the quarantine zone for now," the Guardsman said. "You'll have to turn back."

"What quarantine zone?" Seth asked. "What's going on?"

"I can't say," the Guardsman told him. "You are advised to stay calm, return to your home, and wait for instructions."

"Instructions from who?" Jenny asked.

"You know," the Guardsman said. "The authorities."

"I have to talk to someone in charge," Jenny said.

"I am in charge," the Guardsman said. "And I'm telling you to stay calm, return to your home—"

"This is important," Jenny said.

The other Guardsman, the one with the Taser, approached her side of the car. He raised the weapon toward her. She felt very exposed in the convertible.

"Okay, never mind," Jenny said. "We'll go home. Right, Seth?"

"Yep," Seth said. "We're staying calm, returning home and waiting for instructions."

The two Guardsman backed away from his car. Seth reversed, turned around, and drove back.

In the sideview mirror, Jenny watched the Homeland Security officer snap a picture of Seth's license plate.

Chapter Seven

The Devil came to Adelia's house after sunset, when she had just cooked up her small supper of collards and fatback. A sweet potato pie cooled on the window sill, destined for the mouth of her ten-year-old grandson Malik. He would visit tomorrow, along with his mother Renna. Renna was Adelia's youngest and wildest daughter, but Malik was as sweet as saltwater taffy, with none of his mother's attitude or stubbornness.

And Malik loved sweet potato pie more than just about anything.

Adelia dipped out collard greens into a chipped bowl with a faded floral design. She sat down at the kitchen table, where she could watch the television in the living room. She liked to watch the game show channel, where they reran all the good old shows from the 70s, like *Joker's Wild* and the original *Family Feud* with Richard Dawson.

She added one drop of hot sauce to her greens and stirred it in. As she folded her hands to say the blessing, she heard the squeak of the screen door on her front porch. She had the front and back doors and all the windows open to catch the evening breeze, since her aging little house had no air conditioning.

The screen door squeak meant someone was coming inside, and they hadn't bothered knocking or announcing themselves.

Footsteps approached her through the dark dining room. Adelia couldn't see anything through the folded wooden dressing screen that served as divider between kitchen and dining room.

"Who's there?" she called.

The wooden screen clattered as it folded up. The intruder set it aside, and he smiled as he stepped into Adelia's kitchen. He was a young white man, with black hair and strange gray eyes the color of rainclouds. He had a couple days' stubble on his face. She didn't recognize him, so he wasn't from around town. He wore a wide grin that unsettled her.

"Get out of my house!" Adelia pushed herself to her feet.

"I will," he said. "But I'm hungry." He crossed to the kitchen window, sniffing. "That's sweet potato pie, isn't it?" He leaned over the orange pie and took a deep sniff, closing his eyes. "It's got cinnamon, doesn't it? And brown sugar. I can smell it. They didn't serve nothing like this in Bent River."

Adelia eased over to the fridge and picked up her broom. It was old but solid, cut from hickory. If she could crack him across the back of the head, he'd be out. Or, at least, he'd be slowed down enough that she could hit him a few more times.

She stepped toward him and raised the broom handle above her head.

He opened his eyes.

"Oh, no," he said. He jumped toward her. She swung the broom, but he caught it easily in his hand and snatched it away. He hurled it like a spear into the dining room. Adelia backed away, but he grabbed both her hands.

That was when Adelia saw he was the Devil.

When she was a little girl in Grand Coteau, long before she moved down to this little village in East Baton Rouge parish, her idea of the Devil came from two places. One was the fiery Sunday sermons of Reverend Desmarais, since her parents took her to Opelousas every week for church. The other was Mr. Grosvenor, an old white man who lived across town. She wasn't too sure what he did for a living, but he had a big house behind a tall, spiked iron fence, and behind that fence lived a huge albino canine with pink eyes and long teeth that it bared at everyone who passed. It was rumored to have a particular taste for children.

Sometimes you could see Mr. Grosvenor walking the dog, Loki, around town, or driving his big black Cadillac with the dog growling at pedestrians from the back seat. Mr. Grosvenor usually wore a white hat and white suit, with sunglasses, and sometimes carried a gold-handled cane. Everyone was afraid of him. Eventually, Adelia understood people feared him because he was the biggest landlord in town, and most people were behind on their rents. When she was little, though—three or four years old—she thought Mr. Grosvenor really was the Devil.

When this young man grabbed her hands, Adelia immediately saw his true nature. He was like Mr. Grosvenor, the boogeyman of her childhood. In her mind, she could sense the big white dog circling her house, waiting to leap in her window. She could almost hear its heavy footsteps and its snarls through the thin walls.

"I need a couple of things," the Devil said.

"You can't have my soul," Adelia said. "That belongs to Jesus Almighty, Praise His Name."

"I want the keys to that Chrysler out front," the Devil said. "And I want that sweet potato pie. I don't give a damn about your soul. People don't have souls."

"The Devil is deceptive," Adelia said. "He knows his time upon this Earth is short, that the powers vested in him are temporary, and the New Coming of Almighty Jesus will cleanse us of the Devil's foul works—"

"Shut up!" the Devil yelled. For a moment, Adelia could almost see the great craggy horns sprout from his forehead and the scaly red skin of his true face. "Don't you talk Bible to me, or I'll leave you dead instead of just robbed. You hear me?"

Adelia closed her mouth and nodded her head. The fear was taking over, filling her veins like cold water. She had always been a bold, outspoken woman, but now she was as quiet as a mouse in a tiger cage.

His face appeared normal now, no horns or scales waiting to burst out, but Adelia understood his diabolical nature.

He opened her kitchen drawers until he found a fork. Then he began shoveling the sweet potato pie into his mouth, not even bothering to cut it into slices. "This is really good," he said through a mushy orange mouthful. "Really amazing."

Adelia said nothing. Flattery was one of the Devil's tools, she knew. She couldn't stop shaking, and she felt like she might wet herself. In her mind, she prayed to Almighty Jesus to surround her with a protective ring of angel fire. She kept her eyes on her shoes, occasionally glancing up at him as he wolfed down the pie.

When he'd eaten nearly the entire thing, he dropped it on the floor, along with the fork.

"The car keys," he said.

She pointed to her purse, sitting in one of the kitchen table chairs. The Devil picked it up and dug through it. He took out her car keys and cash.

"You only have twelve dollars?" he asked.

She nodded.

"That's pathetic." He threw the money down on the table. "Keep it."

"Thank you," Adelia said, then immediately chastised herself inside her mind. She should never show gratitude to Satan. The Lord wouldn't care for that.

He walked out her front door. She heard the old brown Chrysler chug to life and wheeze its way of her gravel driveway, and then it drove off into the night.

Adelia sat down at the kitchen table, folded her hands, and began praying out loud to the Almighty.

Chapter Eight

The Lowcountry Inn in Hampton, South Carolina became the unofficial operations center for the Fallen Oak investigation, since the Department of Homeland security leased the entire one-story, two-strip building, and provided some of the rooms to CDC investigators.

In her room, Heather dropped her suitcase on the floor and sprawled out on the double bed, soaking up the air conditioning. Heaven. She'd been sweating all night in tents down in Haiti.

She closed her eyes and dozed off, but the shrill telephone on her end table awoke her an hour later. It was a few minutes past midnight, she noticed on the room's alarm clock.

"Huh?" Heather whispered.

"Dr. Reynard." It was Schwartzman. "Room 117. Immediately."

"What's happening?" Heather yawned.

"Meeting. Urgent." He hung up.

Heather sat on the edge of her bed and stretched. She was groggy as hell, and her sandy hair was tousled from lying on the pillow. At least she was still dressed. She badly wanted to load up the room's coffee maker, but it didn't sound like there was time.

She'd meant to call home before falling asleep. Too late now—she would send a text to Liam's cell phone after the meeting.

Room 117 turned out to be a "corner suite," which was just two rooms with a connecting door propped open. Nobody seemed to be sleeping here—young men and women in suits, each wearing some form of federal ID card around their necks, sat at desks, end tables and dressers, punching furiously at laptops.

Schwartzman was at a table with two other men, and he rose to meet her.

"Dr. Reynard," he said. "This is Keaton Lansing, an assistant director of Homeland Security." A wiry man with glasses and a pinched-looking face nodded, and Heather shook his hand.

"And this," Schwartzman indicated the other man, who was silver-haired, with a dark Brooks Brothers suit and smooth manicured nails, "is Nelson Artleby, Special Advisor to the President."

Artleby smiled graciously as he took her hand. "It's nice to meet you, ma'am," Artleby said, and there was a hint of Texas twang somewhere at the back of his voice. After their handshake, he wiped his hand on the side of his pants.

Heather sat down with them.

"Here's our situation," Artleby began. "First, the White House has declared this whole sorry situation a matter of national security. We're keeping this thing more classified than the aliens at Roswell." Artleby chuckled, but nobody joined him. "On a serious note, nobody says anything to anybody about Fallen Oak. Not your friends, your family, and sure as hell not the media."

"We need to tell the public something," Heather said. "Lots of people are dead. They'll have families…" Heather trailed off. Schwartzman was cutting her a *shut the fuck up* look.

"Absolutely, little lady," Artleby said. "And we have a whole team of experts to sort out the best approach to that. So don't scramble up that sweet little face with any more worry lines."

Heather scowled.

"Pressing on, if we may…" Artleby raised his eyebrows at Heather, as if asking permission.

"Go ahead," Heather said.

Schwartzman removed his glasses, pinched his nose and squinted. That meant he was developing a migraine.

"Not one word about anything you see or do," Artleby said. "Official messages will be put out through official channels." Artleby looked at Heather expectantly, with an amused curl to his lip. She stared back at him, trying to look cold.

"Dr. Reynard will adhere to the *President's orders*," Dr. Schwartzman said. "Like the rest of us. Correct, Dr. Reynard?"

"Of course," Heather said. "Sorry, I was asleep. I'm just trying to catch up."

"Perfectly understandable," Artleby said. "Why, this must be a whole blizzard of information coming at you all at once. Would someone get the lady doctor a coffee?"

A twenty-something Homeland Security officer in a blue uniform hurried to fetch it.

"That's really not…" Heather began, though she was secretly relieved to have coffee on the way. Maybe she could fling it in Artleby's face, if she got bored.

"Mr. Lansing here has flown with me from Washington," Artleby said. "He's in charge of this situation. And he's my eyes and ears for the duration. You need anything, you hit any rough patches, you just come to him."

Lansing gave a small nod and waved his hand a little, as if everyone might have forgotten that the word "Lansing" referred to him.

"Now," Artleby said, "What is our first priority?"

"Identify the pathogen," Heather said. "I'll need to pull the medical claims histories of all the victims. And we're still looking for any hint of a source."

"No," Artleby said. "Lansing?"

"Contain the situation," Lansing said.

"Correct. You've collected all the bodies, is that right?" Artleby asked Dr. Schwartzman. "They're not laying around exposed to the public somewhere, are they?"

"They're in refrigerated transports," Schwartzman said. "Parked in an empty warehouse in Fallen Oak, until we find a facility. We've started our initial laboratory testing, but—"

"Good," Artleby said. "Now, priority two. Who else has the disease?"

"We haven't identified any suspected cases, yet," Schwartzman said.

"Test everyone in town," Artleby said.

"Test them for what?" Heather asked. Intuitively, she suspected a highly mutated, even genetically engineered, strain of bacteria, but there was no evidence for anything yet. "We don't even know what we're looking for."

"But we could perform a general screening," Schwartzman hurried to add. He cut Heather another sharp look. "The population is only a few thousand. We could survey for symptoms matching the known cases, or anything out of the ordinary."

"Could, should and will," Artleby said. "Make sure nobody gets overlooked. Get blood and hair samples from every yokel in that town. We won't break the quarantine until then."

Lansing nodded along, looking from Schwartzman to Heather.

"If you want to test every person in town, we'll have to set up a testing center in Fallen Oak," Heather said. "And communicate that to the public. And then door-to-door outreach to everyone who doesn't come voluntarily."

"And funding for that, and security for that," Schwartzman added, with a glance at Lansing. "I don't want my people getting shot as trespassers. You'll run across a few who don't really care for the 'feddle guvment' poking around."

Heather frowned. She hadn't thought of that.

"Sharp girl you got there, Schwartzman." Artleby winked at Heather. "Sounds like you've got everything thought out. Just let Lansing here know what you need. His decisions are final, and so is his approval for disbursement of emergency funds."

Lansing smiled a little at that.

"Not one word escapes this town," Artleby said. "And, while you're doing all this, can you please find one goddamn witness who can tell us what happened?"

"We'll do our best," Schwartzman said.

"Questions?" Artleby looked at Schwartzman, then at Heather. "Are you following all this, Miss Reynard?"

"Oh, I think I'm keeping up, thank you." Heather narrowed her eyes just slightly.

"Good." Artleby rapped his knuckles on the table, as if hammering a gavel to call the meeting closed. He stood up and shook hands all around. "I'm off to chat with the National Guard commander. Then look up who governs this ratty little state. Thank God for Wikipedia, am I right?"

Lansing and Schwartzman faked a little laughter.

Later, Heather tried to text her husband, but her cell phone got no reception.

She tried using her hotel room phone to call him. She couldn't get an outside line.

Chapter Nine

Jenny found the flyer stuffed in her mailbox the next day. The words were bright red, and the seal of the Department of Homeland Security was printed at the top.

> BY U.S. GOVERNMENT ORDER:
>
> All residents and visitors in Fallen Oak must report to the Fallen Oak High School gymnasium within the next 96 hours for emergency medical screening. Participation is mandatory. Screening facility will be open continuously for the next 96 hours.
>
> Due to the quarantine, emergency supplies of canned food, prepackaged meals and water will also be distributed at the school to Fallen Oak residents.

Jenny ran inside. Seth was eating a hot dog topped with baked beans and mustard, a ghoulish invention he called a "bean dog." They'd raided Seth's house for food while they were out. Since it was within the quarantine zone, nobody had stopped them, but Jenny was uncomfortable with how many National Guard and other official vehicles were out on the roads, and how few of anybody else. The bigger the situation grew, the smaller she felt.

"We have to do this." Jenny put the flyer in front of him.

"Are you kidding?"

"We'll go late at night," Jenny said. "When there aren't many people."

"Why, Jenny?" Seth said. "You know we don't have anything. We never get sick."

"I have something," Jenny said.

"Are you still talking about handing yourself over to them?" Seth asked. "That's a really, really bad idea. What do you think they'll find?"

"Maybe they'll find the Jenny pox," she said. "And a cure for it. Or an immunization. Or something. If somebody put some real science into understanding it, maybe I could figure out how to control it better."

"But that's not what will happen," Seth said. "I bet they try to make a weapon out of it."

Jenny had a flash of memory from the time when she was dead, tangled in weeds at the bottom of Ashleigh's duck pond. She'd glimpsed one of her past lives, riding in a galley, dressed in a black hooded cloak against the freezing sea air, on her way to cripple a foreign city with a plague. She was doing it for somebody else, some king or emperor. It was her job.

"Maybe," she whispered. "But they might help."

"And didn't all those pregnant girls see you drown in Ashleigh's pond?" Seth asked. "As far as anybody knows, you're dead."

"You, too," Jenny said. "Oh, wait. Everybody who saw you die is…gone now."

"But everyone will flip out when they see you," Seth said. "I'm sure the girls told everyone you're dead."

"While we've been holed up here for two days." Jenny looked out the window, to the hilly woods behind her house. "What will they think?"

"The same thing they've thought about us for months," Seth said. "Ever since I saved your dad in that tractor accident. Witchcraft, Satanism and that book from the *Evil Dead* movies."

"The *Necronomicon?*" Jenny said. "What does that have to do with anything?"

Seth shrugged. "Those are cool movies. We should have grabbed the DVDs at my house."

"Anyway, Ashleigh and Dr. Goodling aren't around to whip up that witchcraft bullshit anymore," Jenny said.

"But it's what people were saying," Seth said. "Those girls and their families all went to Fallen Oak Baptist. They've been hearing this stuff from Dr. Goodling."

"You think they'll tell the government that?" Jenny asked.

"Who knows? This is a batshit crazy town." Seth chewed his lip. "And that's something else I've been needing to talk to you about."

"That Fallen Oak is crazy? I figured it out a long time ago, thanks."

"I mean in the fall," Seth said. "My dad wants me to go to College of Charleston now, because he donated a bunch of money to some new international business school there. It's not so far from here, an hour or two. That's close enough to visit your dad. Or come have Christmas with my parents."

"Why are you even worrying about college right now?"

"Because I have to move to the city," Seth said. "And I want you to come with me."

"Seth, I can't even go out in public in my own town."

"But we can start over in Charleston," Seth said. "Nobody knows us there."

"That's not what I meant. It's a big city, Seth." Jenny pulled her arms tight around herself, as if walking through a crowded store, trying to avoid touching anyone. "All those people. There must be a million people."

"A *million*?" Seth rolled his eyes. "In Charleston? Are you kidding?"

"A lot, anyway."

"Come on, it'll be great. We can go pick out an apartment this summer. We'll get a place near the ocean. With a balcony. And your own room just for your pottery stuff. And we can—"

"Stop it," Jenny said. "I can't think about it right now. We have real problems, you know?"

"Think about it later." Seth pulled her close, and she looked up into his blue eyes. They were almost the same color as her own, she thought. "Think about it when you're thinking about turning yourself in. We could have a life together. We could have a future. And all you have to do is let everybody think you're dead, until this blows over."

Seth kissed her. Jenny was tense, but she relaxed after a moment, and kissed him back.

The school gym was transformed into a makeshift clinic, divided into little cubes by dark green curtain walls. Heather worked one of the cubes, taking mouth swabs along with hair and blood samples from those who responded to the flyers. She also carried out basic physicals to look for anything anomalous. She could have excused herself from this part of the work, but it was the easiest way to talk with locals about the event, and she was desperate for any kind of input at this point.

The first several people she tested were extremely tight-lipped, though, and offered no real information. Nobody seemed to know what had happened on the green, or wanted to admit knowing anything. Heather also had to structure her questions in a way that didn't give out information to people, which made things difficult.

Then a chubby teenage girl with mousey hair and thick glasses came into Heather's cube. She was very full around the middle, under her loose sundress.

"Hi," Heather said. "I'm Dr. Reynard. What's your name?"

"Darcy Metcalf," the girl said.

Heather looked her up on the laptop. Homeland Security had provided a database of all residents and their addresses. Heather and the other medical staff noted each person they examined on the shared database, along with any observations.

She found Darcy's listing. A nurse had pre-examined her, entering Darcy's height, weight, and age: eighteen. The file also noted that she had elevated blood pressure. And she was pregnant.

"Okay," Heather said. She took a tongue depressor from a jar. "Open up and say 'ah.'" She liked to start with this because it gave people the sense that it was a regular visit to the doctor's office.

The girl did as she was told, her eyes rolling nervously while Heather looked into her throat. No swelling, no pustules, no symptoms matching those of the outbreak. This girl was pale and sweating, clearly scared.

She asked if Darcy had experienced specific symptoms, and listed the symptoms associated with the bodies on the green, without mentioning the event itself. Darcy shook her head to all symptoms.

"Do you have any special medical conditions?" Heather asked.

"I'm pregnant."

"How far along?"

"Sixteen weeks."

"You know," Heather said, "You're the fourth pregnant girl I've met today, your age and younger. I see a lot of others in line out there. Doesn't it seem like a lot to you?"

Darcy shrugged. "I don't know. Yeah." She looked around, as if expecting somebody else to be watching them.

"Why do you think that is?"

"I…I'm not sure," Darcy said. "All I know is, I went on a date with Bret Daniels when I should have been studying for finals. And God punished me."

"Oh, no, sweetie," Heather said. "It's not a punishment. It's natural. It happens. Don't think of it like that."

"It shouldn't happen if you're not married."

"The important thing is to take care of yourself now," Heather said. "Are you seeing an Ob/Gyn?"

Darcy hesitated, then nodded. She kept looking back at the green curtain door.

"Are you all right?" Heather asked.

Darcy bit her lip.

"Is there something you want to tell me?"

"Well," Darcy whispered. "I don't know who else to tell. But listen…" Her voice dropped to an even lower whisper. "Jenny Mittens is *alive*. She is. I saw her riding in Seth's convertible."

"Who?"

"Jenny Mittens. Morton. Jenny Morton. Everyone saw her go into the pond at Ashleigh's house. People were there for like an hour after, and she never came back out. And people were watching, too, to see if her body floated up. But it never did."

"Jenny…Morton? How do you spell it?"

"Like the salt."

Heather looked it up. A Jenny Morton, and her father Darrell, were listed at a Fallen Oak address. Neither of them had come in for a screening, according to the database.

"She hasn't been in," Heather said, not sure why she was sharing that information.

"She won't be, I bet," Darcy said.

"Why not?"

Darcy frowned.

"You say she drowned in a pond?"

"At Ashleigh Goodling's house," Darcy nodded. She was actually shaking with fear now. "I should go."

"Wait!" Heather said. "Please. Just one minute." She searched for the surname Goodling, and found three people listed at a Fallen Oak address. Father, mother, one child. Ashleigh was the child. None of them had been in for testing, either.

"Are we done?" Darcy asked.

"I still have to take a few little things." Heather brought out a test tube. "I need to clip a hair sample."

Darcy sighed.

"Don't worry, I won't mess up your style." Heather clipped samples from the back of Darcy's head. Then she swabbed the inside of Darcy's cheek. She dabbed Darcy's fingertip with alcohol. "This will only hurt for a second," Heather said, and Darcy hissed as Heather pulled blood from her. Heather applied a small bandage to Darcy's finger.

"One more question," Heather said. "Why did you think it was so important to tell me about this Jenny girl?"

"Because she's at the middle of everything," Darcy said.

"At the middle of what, specifically?"

"All this!" Darcy pointed at the green curtains around them. "The terrible things happening around here."

"How is she at the middle of them?"

Darcy gave her a long, scrutinizing look. Then she spoke in a low whisper again: "Because she's into witchcraft."

"I can barely hear you. Did you say 'witchcraft'?"

"Yes!"

"What does that mean?"

"You know." Darcy made clawing motions in the air with her hands, and gave an exaggerated scowl. "Witchy. Witchy witchcraft. Her boyfriend Seth, too. They're both in league with Satan. People know. Ashleigh knew."

"Okay." Heather smiled a little. "And she casts spells, or what?"

"Oh, sure. Of course."

"What kind of spells?"

"I don't know," Darcy said. "Like all the girls getting pregnant. That was maybe one of Jenny's black magic spells."

"You said it was because you went on a date with a boy."

Darcy hung her head. "And I drank."

"This happens to a lot of people," Heather said. "It's very normal. The thing to do is focus on your future decisions. Nobody controls you with witchcraft, Darcy. You're in charge of your own life."

"Don't tell my dad I drank, okay? He'd get so P.O.'d."

"I won't. Everything you tell me is confidential, Darcy. In fact..." Heather gave Darcy one of her cards. She had plenty of them, in case she found chatty townsfolk who might actually help her investigation. "You give me a call if you think of anything else. Or just want to talk. I'll be in town for a while. I know the phones around here aren't working too well, but the Homeland Security guys say that should be fixed in a few days."

"Why aren't the phones working, anyway?" Darcy asked.

"I'm not sure," Heather said.

"Whoa," Darcy said, reading Heather's card. "'M.D.' 'Epidemiologist.' That's awesome. I thought about being a doctor, before I blew my GPA and got pregnant."

"I'm sorry," Heather said. "But it looks like you're in good health. I'm sure things will get better for you. Life does get easier as you get older."

Darcy slouched as she shuffled out through the curtain.

Heather watched the girl join her father, an obese man in a wheelchair, who looked like he was missing a foot. Maybe it was an injury, but from his inflated size, Heather wouldn't be surprised if he'd lost it to diabetes.

"Hurry up!" Darcy's father barked, while Darcy pushed his wheelchair. "Jog that big ass of yours!"

On the database, Heather added an extra notation to Darcy's listing: "Possible psych. issues related to religion, parents."

Heather sterilized the area, changed out her disposable rubber gloves for new ones, and greeted the next subject.

Her name was Brenda Purcell, seventeen years old, five months pregnant.

Chapter Ten

Tommy roared along the highway. He had ditched the old lady's piece-of-crap Chrysler in Alabama, walked three miles to a biker bar, and picked out a machine he liked. He wanted something fast, but he couldn't keep his eyes off one particular Harley-Davidson with a stylized, devilish red gargoyle painted on the side.

He didn't know how to hotwire a motorcycle, so he'd waited in the shadows of the abandoned gas station next door. Eventually, the machine's owner came out, staggering and drunk, a balding man with a long mullet and a long goatee. He was short but very stout. In Tommy's experience, you had to watch out for the short guys—they were the most eager to fight, as if they had something to prove.

The man sat on the bike and tried a few times to insert the key into the ignition, but he kept missing. Once he got it in, he seemed to have forgotten how to turn the key.

"Howdy," Tommy said as he approached the man. Then he pulled out a wad of cash. He still had most of the prison guard's bank account.

The drunken biker eyed Tommy's cash wad with great interest. Tommy tucked it back into the pocket of his own jeans, which he'd bought at Kmart. The biker's eyes followed the money.

Tommy stuck out his hand. "Name's Freddy," he said. "And I'd like to make you an offer."

"How's it going, Freddy?" The biker shook Tommy's hand.

Tommy squeezed the man's hand and pushed fear into him.

The biker's eyes swelled, and his hand trembled in Tommy's grasp.

"Why don't you step off that bike?" Tommy suggested.

The biker reached for the keys.

"Leave those there," Tommy said. He didn't let go of the man's hand, so they ended up holding hands over the Harley-Davidson.

"Aw, look, Beater's got a girlfriend," another biker hollered. Two of them had just stumbled out of the bar. The shouter wore a Confederate flag do-rag, and his friend wore a very faded T-shirt featuring the band Poison.

"Hell, prettier than his last one!" the guy in the Poison T-shirt yelled, and the two of them laughed. Both men were big, disheveled, and clearly favored denim.

"I've just purchased your friend's bike," Tommy said, though he hadn't given the man any money. He shook Beater's hand again. "Right, Beater?"

"Yeah," Beater said. "Yeah, man. You got it."

Beater's friends stopped laughing when Tommy got on the man's bike and started it up.

"Hey, that's not cool," Rebel Flag Guy said. "You can't take that."

"He sold it to me," Tommy said. "Isn't that right? The bike's mine now, right?"

"Yeah, man." Beater took several steps back. "Whatever the guy says."

Rebel Flag and Poison T-shirt stepped up to Tommy.

"I don't think you made a fair trade," the rebel-flag guy said, and he poked Tommy in the chest. "I think my buddy's drunk, you come over and run your mouth, try to steal his bike. That's what I think."

"You don't want to touch me," Tommy warned them. He tried not to let them see how bad he was shaking. Rebel Flag Guy put a calloused hand around his neck, and Tommy felt the fear move into him. Maybe Tommy could use that.

"Look out!" Tommy shouted. He seized Rebel Flag's wrist and pushed the fear as hard as he could. Tommy had always imagined the fear as a kind of low-grade current of black electricity, something that flowed out from him when he touched other people. Now he imagined turning up the voltage. He wanted to make the guy panic, lose his mind. People were much more open to suggestion when they were frightened.

"That guy in the Poison shirt, he's trying to kill you, man!" Tommy shouted at Rebel Flag. Tommy pointed at his friend in the Poison shirt, who was walking up behind him "Protect yourself! Fight back!"

"What?" Rebel Flag turned on his friend and punched him in the nose. "You ain't gonna kill me! You ain't gonna touch me!"

"I didn't do nothing!" the Poison T-shirt guy yelled, but Rebel Flag kept punching him, so he started fighting back.

While the two of them struggled, Tommy noticed Beater, proprietor of the red-gargoyle Harley, easing back toward the front door of the bar.

"Wait," Tommy said to him, and Beater froze. "Stay right there. Stay."

"Okay." Beater held up both hands. "I'm not doing nothing to you, okay?"

"Right. So just wait there a while. And forget about me. Forget what I look like. Just remember you sold some guy your bike and blew the money."

Beater broke into a goofy smile. "Hell, yeah, man. I'm happy to do that."

Then Tommy took the man's bike and rode across Georgia, and into South Carolina.

Now Tommy approached the town of Fallen Oak. He missed the turn-off onto Esther Bridge Road, but it was a good thing. He saw some kind of roadblock down that way. Not just police, either. It looked like the Army or something.

Tommy kept going. He couldn't risk being identified as an escaped convict, especially when he was so close to her.

He couldn't give up his obsession with Ashleigh Goodling, either. His dreams about her grew more powerful, even addictive, so he couldn't wait to sleep and dream about her. She would know things about him, he thought. She would have the answer to the insane riddle of his life. His intense dreams had convinced him of that.

There was only a small voice, somewhere in the back of his head, suggesting that he might be crazy for letting his dreams control his waking life. He ignored that voice.

He drove on. Nobody was going to stop him. They might block off the roads, but they couldn't block off every field, pasture and deer path in a place this rural. He had a flashlight and a stack of Google maps in the bike's saddlebag. He could find his way to Ashleigh Goodling's house, even if he had to ditch the bike and do it on foot.

Chapter Eleven

Heather sat crossed-legged on her bed at the Carolina Inn, facing two laptop screens, her scribble-filled notepad, and an increasingly uneasy sense of dealing with the unknown.

After three days, laboratory studies had yielded nothing. They couldn't find anything like a common cause, even though most of the cases had symptoms of extremely damaging infection throughout the skin, muscle tissue, internal organs, and even skeletal structure.

The voluntary phase of the screening had brought no suspected cases, either. They might find more when they pushed out into the community. For now, everyone who exhibited signs of the disease had already died in that singular incident. No source had been identified.

Heather was beginning to suspect a bioweapon. Any wild virus or bacterium with such a powerful effect would have been teeming all over the deceased bodies. Humans, on the other hand, had an incentive to engineer deadly bacteria with a programmed cell suicide clock. Something that could quickly sweep through a population, and then break itself down so that it left no trace, would be a powerful weapon.

That was only speculation, though. The pathogen would have to be programmed, not just to die, but to decay into undetectable components. And that sounded like science fiction. She couldn't begin to suspect a motive, either. But something had swept through those people and left them in that condition.

Neither Heather nor the other investigators had turned up any clear explanation of what all those people might have been doing there, on the town green, on a Sunday night. It didn't seem like any planned event, such as an Easter evening church service, had been happening. Nobody, not even the immediate relatives of the deceased, seemed to want to offer any reason why two hundred people had suddenly converged in the middle of town a few nights ago.

Based on their medical records, the two hundred and seventeen deceased had a statistically normal distribution of minor and major illnesses, their ages ranging from teens to the elderly. Only one African-American case had been identified, a teenager named Neesha Bailey. The town itself was forty-five percent African-American. Heather wondered at the discrepancy. Maybe it indicated some geographical division.

The other big anomaly was the teen pregnancy rate, which was far above the statistical norm. With a few exceptions like Darcy, there was a cluster of expected due dates near the end of July, indicating a cluster of conceptions in late October. Heather wondered if there was a single event involved there.

Researching on the internet, she found that the town's pregnancy epidemic was quite documented. Ashleigh Goodling, the preacher's daughter, had made an amazing number of press appearances talking about the surge in pregnancies. Heather even found a YouTube video of Ashleigh on Chuck O'Flannery's blowhard TV show.

She watched Ashleigh talk with the most obnoxious man in show business:

"So of course the left has unleashed the crazy hounds," O'Flannery said. The man was even fatter and uglier than Heather remembered. "I've seen awful things about you on the web, Ashleigh. Just hateful bile. Cartoons and Photoshop pictures that aren't suitable for this program. Even The Onion has attacked you. All this attention must be hard on a kid your age."

"I think it's sad the left has to resort to attacking little girls," Ashleigh said. "But you know what? My daddy's a preacher, and he always tells me no matter what I suffer, it's nothing compared to what Jesus and the Disciples suffered. Christians get persecuted, but God takes care of us. I don't care if everyone hates me. I have my faith." Ashleigh rubbed the cross pendant at her chest, and just happened to skip her fingers over her breast as she brought her hand down.

"I think you must have incredible strength to cope with all this vitriol," O'Flannery said.

"All I ever said was teens shouldn't have sex," Ashleigh said. "How is that controversial?"

"Never underestimate the sheer hatred of the left," O'Flannery said. "The truth makes them howl. In fact, I think it's time to call out the Liberal Moondogs."

A sound effect of several barking dogs played, and four cartoon dogs paraded across the screen.

"Now let's look at the victims of this radical atheist principal," he said. There was a slideshow of black-and-white photos, pregnant girls looking depressed and ashamed, accompanied by slow, sad music. Heather had seen a few of those same girls in the gymnasium over the last couple of days.

Heather paused the video. This Ashleigh person seemed strange to her. Unnaturally self-possessed and in command, she thought, for a high-school girl from a flyspeck town.

On her other laptop, Heather looked up the Goodling family. None of them had checked in for medical screening. None of them were identified among the deceased, either. She might have to put the Goodling household at the top of her community outreach efforts.

Then Heather looked up the other girl again, the one Darcy had accused of witchcraft. When Heather asked the other pregnant girls, a couple of them had reluctantly admitted to seeing Jenny Morton fall into a pond and never return to the surface. They had described Jenny as covered with blisters and sores at the time.

So Jenny Morton was Heather's first suspected case. But it might mean dredging the pond at the Goodling house to see if it held an infected body, whether the body was Jenny Morton or somebody else. Of course, that sort of thing was what all the Homeland Security money was for.

Unless Jenny had slipped unnoticed out of the pond and was still alive, as Darcy had said. A visit to the Morton house would also be high on her priority list.

She had so little to go on, she might as well investigate these anomalies.

The bodies were slowly being identified and their listings marked DECEASED in the database. When that process was complete, she might have more useful information.

For now, all she had was Darcy Metcalf and her odd talk of witchcraft.

Late in the afternoon, Darcy brought some fresh-cut daisies and pansies from her mother's garden to lay them on the walkway in front of Ashleigh's house. Her flowers from two days ago had withered, of course, but her note was still there.

She frowned as she stepped closer. The little envelope had been torn open. Darcy lay the bouquet down and picked up the envelope.

The hand-written note, where she'd poured out to Ashleigh how much she missed her, was gone.

Darcy frowned.

"Hi there," a voice said, and she jumped

The boy who approached looked her own age, or a little older. He had scruffy patches of early beard growth, midnight black hair, and cloud-gray eyes that immediately reminded her of Ashleigh. And he was incredibly cute.

"Oh!" Darcy said. "Hi."

"You're the one who's been leaving flowers for Ashleigh," he said.

"Um. Yeah. I'm Darcy Metcalf." She held out her hand, tentatively, but he didn't shake it.

"I'm Tommy." He folded his arms.

"Are you Ashleigh's…cousin, or something?"

"Yeah," he said. "Yep. Her cousin. Tommy Goodling."

"Wow. I didn't know…I mean, I…"

"They don't talk about us much. They probably wouldn't want anybody to know I'm in town. We're sort of the bad branch of the Goodlings." Tommy winked.

Darcy giggled.

"So, I've been waiting here for hours," Tommy said. "Where is everybody? Where's Ashleigh?"

"Oh." Darcy felt sad for him. "You don't know."

"Don't know what?"

"Um, maybe Dr. Goodling or Mrs. Goodling will be home soon." Darcy didn't know how to tell him the bad news. It should probably come from family, she thought. Dr. Goodling would know just what to do. "I mean, they're kind of missing. A lot of people are missing right now. The authorities are straightening everything out, though."

"I don't understand," Tommy said.

"Um…oh!" Darcy pulled her key ring from her purse. "I have a spare key to the Goodlings' house. I feed Maybelle when they're out of town."

"Maybelle?"

"She's de-barked, so she's creepy." Darcy led him to the front door and unlocked it. "I was going to feed her and take her out. Want to help?"

Darcy led him into the house. A Welsh Corgi jogged up to them, then opened its mouth and rasped at Tommy.

"She's really sweet, actually." Darcy rubbed the dog's head. Maybelle gave a few more soundless barks at Tommy, then followed Darcy deeper into the house. In the laundry room, Darcy filled Maybelle's bowl with food.

The Goodlings made pretty good money, Tommy thought. Their house was spacious and full of sunlight. Some of the rooms were two stories high.

He wandered into the living room and looked at the photographs on the wall. There was the object of his obsession, the girl whose face filled his dreams. Golden hair, enchanting eyes, mysterious smile. In the pictures, she was every age, selling Girl Scout cookies, playing the Virgin Mary in a children's play, kneeling in her cheerleading uniform with her fist tucked under her chin.

While Darcy filled the dog's water bowl, Tommy went upstairs.

He found Ashleigh's room right away. It was large and frilly, with a private bathroom and walk-in closet, and everything here smelled sweet.

Tommy sprawled on her bed and buried his face in her down-stuffed pillows. He sniffed deep. This was the right place, the right girl.

"Um, hey, Tommy?"

He lifted his face from the pillow. Darcy stood in the doorway, watching him.

"What?" he asked.

"So I guess I should go," Darcy said. "You can wait around here."

"Wait!" Tommy stood up. "Where is Ashleigh? I have to know."

"Um…"

"Tell me!' Tommy shouted. He seized the girl and shook her. "Where is Ashleigh?"

"She's dead!" Darcy wailed, and then she broke down crying. She sank to the carpet. "She's dead! Jenny Mittens killed her!"

Tommy squatted down and looked her in the eyes. He squeezed her arm tight, pushing fear into her.

"Explain," he said.

Darcy led him into the back yard, past the duck pond and the shaded outdoor swing to a magnolia tree with sprawling arms and royal purple blossoms.

"It's called a Purple Queen magnolia," Darcy said. "It was Ashleigh's favorite. That's why I buried her here."

Darcy pointed to the giant gnarled roots of the tree, which might have been hundreds of years old. A section of the otherwise immaculate lawn had been churned up between the roots, leaving a muddy mess.

"Ashleigh is…buried here?" Tommy asked. He felt dizzy. This wasn't how it was supposed to go.

"Well, Jenny turned her all to bones and little pieces," Darcy was blubbering, with a little drizzle of snot running from her nose. "It was so bad. And Dr. Goodling never came home. And I couldn't just leave her there. She was my best friend," Darcy sobbed.

Tommy felt kind of bad for the girl. He wanted to reach out and comfort her, but he could never do that. His touch never comforted anyone.

"I wish she could come back," Darcy said. "I wish it was me instead of her. I'm the one who sinned. I'm the one God should have taken."

Tommy stared at the churned earth. Fury swelled inside him. The girl had been alive only a few weeks ago. Alive and ready to give him answers, bring him understanding. But something had happened, and he'd missed her completely.

If he'd been faster, and if he'd been here for her, she would still be alive.

Tommy screamed and punched the solid trunk of the magnolia. "Fuck!" he said.

Darcy cringed. Tommy seized her by the shoulders again, and he snarled into her face.

"Who did this?" he shouted. "Where are they?"

Darcy told him.

Chapter Twelve

When Jenny heard the engine in her driveway, she thought it would be one of the government vehicles. Or maybe her dad, if they were finally letting people back into town.

She stood up, walked to the front door, and grabbed a pair of light cotton gloves from the basket by the door. Seth sat on the couch in front of the TV.

"Where are you going?"

"Out to see who it is."

"Wait," Seth said. "Maybe they're just turning around or something."

"You can come with me if you want." Jenny pushed open the screen door and stepped onto the front porch.

It wasn't a Homeland Security or National Guard vehicle in her driveway, though. It was a Harley-Davidson, painted with a fire-red gargoyle. The man who stepped off it wasn't in a uniform, either, but a denim jacket and black jeans.

"Hey!" Seth opened the screen door and stepped in front of Jenny. "Who are you?"

The biker was a young man with black hair, maybe a year or two older than them. He didn't wear a helmet. He took off his sunglasses as he approached.

"Are you Jenny?" he demanded.

"I asked you first," Seth said.

"Did you?" He glared at Seth. His eyes were a rainy shade of gray, and Jenny had only seen one other person with eyes like that.

"What do you want?" Seth asked.

"I want to find the person who killed Ashleigh Goodling." He pointed at Jenny. "Was it you?"

"You still haven't told us who you are."

The young man kept walking toward the porch, so Seth descended the steps to meet him.

"Seth," Jenny whispered, but he ignored her.

"You better get out of here right now," Seth said.

"I'm leaving soon," the young man said. "After I take care of this."

He threw the first punch, and Seth dodged out of the way. Seth landed a fist in the young man's stomach, and he doubled over and backed away.

"Go," Seth said.

The man sprang up and clapped his hands to either side of Seth's head. He bared his teeth.

Seth shuddered in his grasp, as if being electrocuted, and then he screamed. The man punched Seth in the face twice, one quick jab with each fist. Then he used one foot to sweep Seth's ankles out from under him, and Seth crashed to the ground.

The man spun around and stalked up the steps toward Jenny.

Jenny backed up. She took off her gloves and let them fall to the porch floorboards.

"You don't want to touch me," Jenny said.

The young man hesitated a moment, as if her comment had thrown him off guard. Then he ascended the final step.

"I'm serious," Jenny said. The cold shadow was taking over inside her, the ancient and evil thing that had killed so many over the millenia. It seemed particularly strong when Seth was hurt or in danger.

"You killed Ashleigh Goodling?" the gray-eyed young man glared at her.

"You're right. I killed her." Jenny folded her arms and glared back. "You want to be next?"

He seized both her hands and squeezed. Jenny pushed the pox into him, willing her infection to burn in deep.

Something lashed out at her from his touch, like a lightning flash of dark, twisted energy.

And then she was terrified. She'd had a recurring dream, the last few nights, of all the diseased people from the town green, all surrounding her, closing in on her, accusing her of murder, and then tearing and slashing at her.

Now she had the sense that they were coming for her. Any moment they would pour out the windows and door onto her porch, or smash up through the floorboards, grabbing and biting at her. They would come boiling out of the woods, screaming her name.

And the attack would be led by the young man squeezing her hands now. Already, he looked like one of her victims, open sores and bloody rashes spreading up his arms, boils and blisters opening on his face—

He screamed and let go of her hands. He stumbled down her porch stairs, lost his balance and fell into the dirt.

Jenny trembled where she stood, still terrified of him.

He pushed up to his feet.

"What the fuck are you?" he screamed. His face was covered in pus and black swellings.

"What the fuck are you?" Jenny whispered.

He ran to his bike, turned a wide circle in Jenny's front yard, and then roared away.

Jenny stumbled down to Seth, on her shaking legs, and helped him up. He still wore a shocked look on his face.

"Was it my great-grandfather?" Seth whispered. "Was he here?"

"Let's get inside, Seth," Jenny whispered. "I want to lock up."

They went into the house and bolted all the doors and latched all the windows. Without discussing it, they pulled all the window curtains tight, then turned off all the lights so no one could peer in at them.

They huddled together under her blankets, shivering, gripped with their individual fears. Shapeless monsters seemed to threaten them from the dark all night.

Jenny didn't want to admit it, but she was even feeling a little scared of Seth, too.

Just before sunrise, Tommy rode out of Ashleigh's driveway. He was covered in mud. He'd left the clay-smeared shovel on the floor of the workshop, which was built onto the garage, and closed the door. Maybe nobody would notice it for a while.

Tommy had found Ashleigh's remains, wrapped in a Sunday dress, just as Darcy had told him. Along with the skull and broken bones, Darcy had thrown in a gold cross necklace and some kind of silver ring.

Tommy then stuffed Ashleigh's remains into a backpack he found in Ashleigh's house—Ashleigh's, he assumed, from the colorful, girly patches added to it, lots of flowers and animals and hearts.

He'd crammed the backpack into one of the motorcycle's saddlebags. And now he was leaving town.

He passed a convoy of vehicles going the other way, towards Ashleigh's neighborhood. There were a couple of the Homeland Security cars, a yellow Caterpillar excavating machine, and some kind of truck full of pipes and hoses.

Tommy kept his head low as he drove past them.

He didn't fully understand what had happened the night before. He'd put the scare in both those kids, for sure, but they'd given him a little parting gift, hadn't they? The infection was all over his arms, his torso, his neck and face.

You don't want to touch me, she'd said. The same thing Tommy had said himself, countless times. It was sometimes a threat, sometimes a warning. Sometimes just a matter-of-fact observation.

And she'd been right. She had a thing inside her as bad as Tommy's. Worse, even. Tommy didn't know if he would heal—his sores had run bloody all night as he worked the shovel. But he was pretty sure that if he'd held on to that Jenny girl for another minute, he would have died.

Chapter Thirteen

The day was uncomfortably warm for a biohazard suit. Heather was sweating as she watched men in similar suits handle the pumping of the pond.

They'd dropped a pair of long, fat hoses into the duck pond. Pump machinery on their truck slurped up the black water. The water shot out of another hose, turning the far end of the Goodlings' back yard into a swamp.

Nobody had answered the door when they arrived that morning. Attempts at interviewing neighbors hadn't gotten far, but nobody had seen the Goodlings in days. Heather felt like there was something the town just didn't want to tell outsiders like her.

Draining the pond was a sluggish process, so Heather went in to explore the house. They had broken in the back door to confirm nobody was there before they brought the pumping equipment into the yard.

The house was airy and bright, with huge picture windows and open modernist-style staircases. Everything was cheerful. Every room, she noticed, included a shrine to Ashleigh—her ribbons and awards and trophies and pictures. It was clear Ashleigh's parents adored her, maybe even to an unhealthy extent. Like they all but worshiped their only child.

She identified Ashleigh's room, a frilly princess-style theme with a canopy bed, and lots of pictures of Ashleigh and her friends on the wall. Prominently featured were two girls, one a freckled girl with red hair, one a pretty black girl. Heather recognized her. Neesha Bailey, the sole African-American caught in the outbreak. Another piece of the puzzle.

In some of the picture frames, half the picture had been cut out, leaving Ashleigh posing by herself.

In an end table drawer, Heather found the missing halves of those pictures. They each featured a handsome boy with blue eyes and strawberry blond hair. The pictures seemed to be taken over a period of years. They'd been together a long time, for a couple of teenagers.

Heather wasn't sure how any of this could be relevant to the investigation. But data was thin. No hint of a pathogen had been identified, despite the laboratory trucks running night and day inside the old warehouse that Homeland Security had assigned for the testing of the bodies. The two refrigerated trucks were parked in there, too, and the whole interior of the warehouse sealed with white plastic sheeting. Nothing was to be moved out of the town yet, per Homeland Security.

The broad public screening hadn't yielded much, either, as far as anyone could tell. Nobody had any unusual illnesses, or any symptoms similar to those of the confirmed cases. It was as if the disease had snuck into town one night, killed two hundred people, and then vanished without a trace.

That didn't sound possible to Heather. It sounded supernatural. And she did not believe in the supernatural.

She found signs of a struggle in Ashleigh's room. The window over the bed was smashed out, the curtains puffing in the breeze. Heather leaned out and looked down at the paved white walkway that curved from the Goodlings' driveway to their front door.

If there had been any wreckage below, shattered glass or broken window frame, someone had cleaned it up. The only thing on the walkway beneath her was a bouquet of assorted flowers. They looked fresh and bright from here, as if someone had just set them out last night.

Heather would have to jot her observations on her small personal notepad, as soon as she was out of this bulky suit.

She returned downstairs and walked back outside.

The back slope of the Goodlings' lawn was flooded. Much of the water had collected in a deep puddle between the roots of a large magnolia tree.

Heather tromped toward the pond.

It was mostly empty. The hoses sucked mud at the bottom.

She didn't see a body down there, infected or otherwise.

Schwartzman would probably grouse about the money, but Heather knew emergency funds were coming from Homeland Security. Besides, if there had been another case, it would have been important to get the body quarantined.

Or maybe not. Nothing contagious had been found. There was no disease, only symptoms. Heather couldn't imagine what that might mean.

And Heather had checked off two items on her list, visit the Goodling home and drain the pond. She'd discovered nothing conclusive. She didn't hold out much hope for her next stop, either, but sometimes epidemiology required the baleen whale approach—suck in all the information you could get, and hope you picked up something you needed.

Heather left the drainage crew to take their equipment apart and go home. She tossed her hazmat suit into the trunk of the federal police car driven by Officer Boele, her assigned security detail. Though Heather had a rental car at the hotel, Schwartzman ordered her to ride everywhere with Boele, a taciturn young man in a blue uniform.

"We're going to Jenny Morton's house," she said. She gave him the address, and he plugged it into his dashboard computer.

Jenny and Seth found their panic subsiding as the sun rose. They took turns peeking out the window to see if the frightening young man had returned.

"This is crazy," Jenny finally said. "We're acting like kids who saw our first scary movie."

Seth nodded. "Why are we so afraid of him, anyway? You hit him pretty hard with Jenny pox. Why would he come back, knowing you could kill him?"

"Yeah." Jenny looked down at her hand and wiggled her fingers. Her lethal touch. It had almost made her life not worth living, until she met Seth.

Jenny went to him and slid her arms around his waist. She laid her head against his chest and listened to his heart.

"He looked like her, didn't he?" Seth asked after a minute.

"The eyes," Jenny said. "He had her eyes."

"You think he's a relative or something?" Seth asked. "He seemed pretty hell-bent on revenge."

"No," Jenny said. "That's not what I think."

"You have some ideas, feel free to share."

"Look at my eyes, Seth."

Seth pulled back from her so he could look down into her face. He smiled and cupped the back of her head, and his touch sent warm ripples through her, chasing away the black cobwebs of fear. "Beautiful," he said.

"No, I'm not," Jenny said. "And I wasn't fishing for compliments, either. Come here."

Jenny took his hand and led him to the bathroom. They stood next to each other, surrounded by fading floral wallpaper.

"What am I looking for?" he asked.

Jenny stood on her tiptoes and laid her cheek against his. Two pairs of deep blue eyes stared back at them.

"They're the same color, aren't they?" Seth said.

"Because we're a pair," Jenny said. "Opposites. That's what keeps drawing us together, through all these lifetimes."

"We've been enemies, too," Seth said, and she gave him a puzzled look. "I'm just saying. I saw that in my memories. We killed each other, a bunch of times."

"Long ago," Jenny said. "The last few times, we've really worked on becoming human. Learning to love." She looked at him.

"Becoming human." Seth shook his head. "That's a weird way to put it."

"It's true."

Seth turned away and left the bathroom, as if he didn't want to look at himself anymore. She followed him into the kitchen, where he was pouring a Dr. Pepper. "Your dad have anything stronger I can put in this?" he asked. "Whiskey?"

"No, he threw it all out."

"I need something." Seth sat at the table and looked out through the window into the deep woods that shadowed Jenny's house.

Jenny leaned against the wall and folded her arms. "You get what I'm saying, though?"

"Yes," Seth said. "We're evil. We're not normal human souls. We don't belong here."

"I mean about us being opposites. Ashleigh must have one somewhere, too. Someone whose touch doesn't spread love, but the opposite."

"What's that?" Seth asked. "Hate?"

"Or what we felt last night," Jenny said. "Fear."

"His touch spreads fear." Seth drummed his fingers on the table and shifted around, looking agitated. "Jesus. Think of what he could do with that."

"I bet he can control people," Jenny said. "Like Ashleigh. Just in a different way. They fear him instead of love him, but still."

"I wonder where he came from," Seth said. "Why's he here now? Because Ashleigh's dead?"

"You've never seen him before?" Jenny asked.

"Why ask me?"

"She was your girlfriend for three years? You were up her ass all the time? She made you her slave—"

"Okay, I get your point! No, I've never seen him, or heard Ashleigh talk about anyone like that. But she never admitted having a power in the first place. He wasn't a part of her life, unless she kept it totally secret."

"Which she was good at," Jenny said.

"You really think he's like us?" Seth asked.

"He did something to us," Jenny said. "Don't you wish there was some kind of expert on this stuff we could ask? It's hard figuring it all out by ourselves."

"There's not even a name for what we are," Seth said. "If we were, I don't know, vampires or werewolves or something, maybe we'd have some clues."

"Vampires." Jenny laughed a little, without any pleasure. "I'm worse than that."

"If that guy comes back, I'll deal with him," Seth said.

"I'm pretty sure that'll be my job." Jenny looked out the window again. "And if there's another one of *us* to deal with—another one like Ashleigh—then this isn't a good time for me to turn myself in."

"I totally agree." Seth grabbed her hand. "But we really should move over to my house. You'll be safer. There's a thousand places you can hide."

"A thousand scary places," Jenny said.

"They're not all scary." Seth stood up and embraced her from behind as she looked out at the woods. He pulled her close to him, and he kissed her neck. "You like the navigator room. The bed hung with old sails…"

She closed her eyes as he turned her and kissed her mouth. His hand slid under the hem of her shirt, to cup her left breast. She tried to catch her breath. He was putting her off guard…but they needed to…

"We need to go!" Jenny pulled away from him. "If I'm hiding and playing dead, we can't stay here."

"But I was thinking—"

"I know what you were thinking." She kissed him, then went to her room and stuffed clothes and a few other things into her school backpack. "Go make sure Rocky has food. You'll have to come check on him every day until this is over."

When the dog was fed and Jenny was all packed up, she made a last circuit of the house, checking that the windows and back door were locked tight. They'd done a very careful job of securing the house last night, though, when they'd been scared out of their brains.

They stepped out onto the porch. As Jenny locked the front door, a black-and-white police car pulled into the driveway.

"Shit," Jenny whispered. "Too late."

The car parked, blocking them in. It was one of the federal cop cars, Homeland Security.

"What do we do?" Jenny whispered.

"Just smile and nod until they leave," Seth whispered back.

A guy in a blue uniform stepped out of the driver's side. The woman who emerged from the passenger side had a short, professional haircut and wore a dark suit. She carried a black doctor's bag. Some kind of ID badge was clipped to her lapel.

"Hi," the woman said. "Are you Jenny?"

"Um," Jenny said.

The woman walked all the way to the porch. Jenny felt pinned. She looked at Seth, but he wouldn't know what to do, either.

"I'm Dr. Reynard," the woman said. "Centers for Disease Control. I'm looking for Jenny Morton. It's urgent."

Jenny thought those were among the scariest words she'd ever heard. *I'm from the Centers for Disease Control and I'm looking for Jenny Morton.*

"You must be her," the lady continued. "You look just like the picture."

"Okay," Jenny said. "What's going on?"

"Did you get a flyer like this?" Dr. Reynard held up the flyer ordering medical screening for everyone.

"Maybe," Jenny said. "I don't know."

"Things have been crazy," Seth said. "Nobody knows what's going on."

"Unfortunately," Dr. Reynard said. "We can't leave town and let things get back to normal until we've screened everyone. That's not my choice. I just have to do my job."

"Where do we need to go?" Seth asked. "When?"

"Actually…" Dr. Reynard thumped the black medical bag in her hand. "We can do it right here. It's very simple."

Jenny stared at the bag. She was scared to think what they might discover about her. And kind of curious, too. She hadn't been examined by a doctor since she was born, and that had led to tragedy.

"Wait," Seth said. "You can't just show up at Jenny's house and force her to do this."

"Yes, we can." The Homeland Security officer reached for his belt, either for a Taser or a gun.

"I can handle this," Dr. Reynard told him.

"We have lawyers," Seth said. "We'll fight you."

The Homeland Security officer looked at Jenny's crumbling old house and smirked.

"This is considered a state of national emergency," the Homeland Security officer said. "You will follow orders."

"Look, I'll do it," Jenny said. "Don't worry about it, Seth. It's fine with me."

Jenny and Seth went inside, and the Homeland Security officer followed. He let the screen door bang shut behind him, so the doctor had to switch her medical bag to the other hand and open it herself. "Thanks," she muttered.

The uniformed officer stood just inside the door, hands at his belt, spine straight.

"What do we need to do?" Jenny asked the two strangers in her living room.

"We're actually in a pinch," Dr. Reynard said. "I'm supposed to be getting some mobile lab units in tomorrow, so we can test people at their homes. But we don't have them yet."

"So why not wait until tomorrow?" Seth asked.

"Seth," Jenny said.

"Because we want to get out of this town as much you want us gone," Dr. Reynard said. "Is there a table where we can sit?"

Jenny led her into the kitchen. "I'm sorry it's messy," Jenny said. "We weren't expecting doctors."

Dr. Reynard laid the medical bag on the table and sat down across from Jenny. Jenny let out a small sigh of relief when the doctor strapped on a pair of rubber gloves. No skin on skin contact.

"Let's start with a quick blood pressure check." Dr. Reynard strapped a cuff over Jenny's arm.

Jenny kept herself frozen in place. She didn't want to accidentally bump against the doctor when she was leaning so close.

"Just relax your arm," Dr. Reynard said. She squeezed a bulb to pump up the cuff with air. "Have you had any unusual medical conditions recently, Jenny?"

"Like what?" Jenny asked. The question made her very nervous.

"Oh, anything," Dr. Reynard said. "Like sores, blisters…any strange growths or rashes…anything like that?"

"No." Jenny's voice was too small to hear, so she made herself say it again. "No."

"Blood pressure looks fine." Dr. Reynard clicked a button, and all the air hissed out of the inflatable cuff.

Jenny stiffened again when the doctor pulled out a penlight to inspect Jenny's eyes, ears, and throat. Though the lady wore gloves, it still made Jenny nervous to have her fingers so close.

"Any special medical conditions?" Dr. Reynard asked.

"No," Jenny said.

"You aren't taking any prescription medicine? Or pregnant?"

"No."

Jenny kept her hands folded in her lap. She wore light blue cotton gloves today. She never left the house with her hands bare.

"This is weird," Seth said. "You're just going to do this in somebody's kitchen? That doesn't seem very, what do they call it, sanitary."

"You got a problem?" the Homeland Security officer said.

"I've worked in worse conditions," Dr. Reynard said. "I've been in places where they've never seen running water." The doctor removed a Q-tip from a case in her bag. "Now just a couple of quick samples, and we'll be done. Can you open your mouth for me, Jenny?"

Jenny felt her heartbeat pick up as the doctor swabbed the inside of her cheek.

"This town hasn't been easy, though," Dr. Reynard said. "Seems like nobody wants to tell me why two hundred people got together at the town square on Sunday night."

Jenny's hands grasped each other tighter.

"I just need a quick hair sample." The doctor clipped a few of Jenny's hairs and dropped them into a test tube. "I tell you what, it's like nobody wants us to figure anything out. Any idea why that is?" Dr. Reynard looked intently into Jenny's eyes.

"It's a strange town," Seth said. Jenny nodded.

"Do you two know anything?"

Jenny and Seth stayed quiet.

"Hm. Well, I'm going to need a blood sample, and I'll let you go." Dr. Reynard looked at Jenny's folded hands. "Isn't it a little warm for gloves?"

"I just like them," Jenny said. She hated how small and pathetic her voice sounded.

Jenny peeled off a glove and watched the doctor swab her fingertip with alcohol and prick it with a little sharp-tipped tube, which slowly filled with Jenny's dark red blood. *That's it,* Jenny thought as Dr. Reynard sealed the sample inside another test tube. *All my secrets are yours.*

"The only thing anybody will talk about is witchcraft," Dr. Reynard said. "Why are people so interested in that around here?" She looked closely at Jenny.

"I don't know," Jenny said. "I don't really go to church."

"No thoughts?" Dr. Reynard asked. "Do *you* have any idea what happened on the town green?"

Jenny shook her head. "Are we done?"

Dr. Reynard changed out her disposable gloves for a fresh pair. She'd even brought a small container where she could stuff the used ones. She winked at Seth. "Your turn."

While she'd taken a lot of time with Jenny, her testing and sampling of Seth was quick and efficient. She didn't seem very interested in him at all, Jenny thought. Which meant she was very interested in Jenny. That worried her.

Dr. Reynard thanked them and packed up her bag.

"Do you have any questions?" the doctor asked, smiling at Jenny again.

"When do we get our results?" Jenny asked.

"Results?"

"From the tests," Jenny said.

"Oh." Dr. Reynard looked puzzled. "We aren't really getting back to individuals unless we find something unusual. So, no news is good news. Is there something you're concerned about?"

Jenny shook her head.

"Anything you want to ask me? Or tell me?"

Jenny looked down at her own shoelaces.

"If you change your mind, call me." Dr. Reynard gave Jenny a business card. She offered one to Seth, too, but he turned it down, so Dr. Reynard laid it on the coffee table. "I'm in charge of the investigation."

"Okay," Jenny said.

Dr. Reynard turned toward the front door, and the Homeland Security officer pivoted to accompany her out.

"Oh, one more thing." Dr. Reynard turned to face Jenny. "It's a little bit of a strange thing. Several people told me they saw you drown in a pond on Sunday night. Over at the Goodling residence. Any idea why people are telling me that?"

Jenny didn't know what to say.

"They must be confused," Seth said, but Jenny didn't think his comment helped anything.

"Were you at the Goodling house Sunday night?" Dr. Reynard asked. "Or at the town square?"

Jenny wasn't sure what to say. The woman seemed trustworthy, but a lot of people seemed that way. And the Homeland Security guy didn't seem like he would be very sympathetic.

"No," Jenny said. "We were home."

Dr. Reynard studied her, then gave a quick nod.

"Okay," Dr. Reynard said. "Thanks so much for your cooperation today. Jenny, get in touch any time."

Jenny watched the doctor and the uniformed man leave her house. She closed and locked the front door as they pulled away.

"I am so screwed," Jenny said, leaning against Seth.

"You said you wanted someone to study you."

"But this could be really bad. I don't know what to do. What should I even expect?"

Seth held her tight. He didn't have any answers, but at least he was warm.

Chapter Fourteen

Tommy loved the open road, with the Harley roaring beneath him and infinite blue space before him. Oklahoma was very flat, which made for dull scenery, but it really let you open up the throttle.

Using the fear inside him, he'd mugged somebody in Evans, just outside of Augusta—a man in a suit who was able to withdraw six hundred dollars at the ATM. He'd bought a black motorcycle helmet to avoid getting pulled over. Considering he was an escaped prisoner riding a semi-stolen bike, it would be stupid to get busted on a minor helmet law. He could usually deal with a lone police officer just fine, but it was always risky, and he didn't want the hassle.

He was in a hurry. Daylight was starting to break in the east. He'd been driving for eighteen hours, with only a brief stop for a nap in the Ozark National Forest.

The sores on his hands, arms and face were healing, but slowly. He didn't know what that bitch had done to him, but he couldn't focus on her until the immediate business was handled.

He sped through the dreary countryside, past collapsing farmhouses and rusty barbed wire, towards the miniscule town of Sulphur. There was a bright grin on his face. He was going to sort some things out today, and sort them good.

In his childhood memories, the Tanner house and the outbuildings made up a massive compound, almost like a town. When he pulled up the dusty gravel driveway, he almost thought he had the wrong place. The main house looked tiny and gray, many of its exterior boards crumbling to dust. The outbuildings seemed much smaller than he remembered, too.

Tommy parked in front of the house, next to a big rusty pick-up truck, and he looked up to the tiny window on the second floor. Then he knew he had the right place. That window had been his eye on the world for nearly three years.

The lights in the house were already on. Mr. Tanner liked everyone to be up by sunrise, to get started on chores around the farm.

Tommy stepped off his bike, hung his helmet on it, and walked past the chickens scraping and pecking in the yard. The front door opened as he approached it—someone must have heard his engine.

Mrs. Tanner stood behind the screen door, a few years fatter and grayer. A boy of about ten stood beside her, his eyes bulging with fear.

"Howdy," Tommy said with a wide smile. He wondered how he looked to them, with the oozing infections leaking down his face.

"Who are you?" Mrs. Tanner asked. "What do you mean making all this noise so early in the morning?"

"Don't you remember me?" Tommy took off his sunglasses and stared at her with his gray eyes.

"Thomas?" she whispered.

"Fuck yeah." Tommy pulled open the screen door and stepped inside, forcing Mrs. Tanner to take a step back. The little boy stared up at him. "What's your name?" Tommy asked.

"Paul," the boy whispered.

"Did Mr. Tanner baptize you when you got here, Paul?" Tommy asked.

"Yes," Paul whispered. "He baptizes me all the time."

Tommy scowled and looked past the boy and Mrs. Tanner. Two more kids ate breakfast at the kitchen table, staring at Tommy over spoonfuls of shredded wheat (not the frosted kind, as the Tanners believed that would spoil children). The boy looked about fourteen or fifteen, while the girl looked twelve or thirteen.

"Oh, look." Tommy nodded at the girl. "It's the future Mrs. Tanner."

"That is disgusting!" Mrs. Tanner snarled.

"You're getting a little ripe, aren't you?" Tommy poked Mrs. Tanner's doughy arm. His touch made her gasp and back away. "A little old for Mr. Tanner."

"He was right," Mrs. Tanner whispered. "You do have the devil in you."

"True." Tommy picked up a bowl of unsweetened shredded wheat from the table and ate a spoonful. "This stuff is nasty. You kids like this?"

The two kids at the table shook their heads.

"What in the Lord's name is happening down here?" Mr. Tanner tromped down the staircase, dressed in overalls and boots. He glared at Tommy. "Who are you?"

"You forgot me already, Mr. Tanner?" Tommy asked.

"This is Thomas," Mrs. Tanner whispered. "He ran away. Remember?"

"I don't care who he is," Mr. Tanner said. He jabbed a finger into Tommy's chest. "You gonna get out this house right now, less you want me to grab my shotgun and plow a trench through your skull."

Tommy seized Mr. Tanner's hand.

"Get the shotgun if you want, old man," Tommy said. "It'll end with your brains splattered on the ceiling. I promise."

He squeezed tight, giving Mr. Tanner a good dose of fear, then released the man's hand. Mr. Tanner just gaped at him.

"Mrs. Tanner," Tommy said. She jumped at her name, but he had her attention. "When the old man died, you brought a couple of witches here to talk to his corpse. To find some missing money."

"You did what?" Mr. Tanner stalked toward his wife. "Witches? I'm gonna whup you so bad. Get upstairs and take them britches off."

Tommy grabbed Mr. Tanner's throat and slammed him back against the kitchen wall. The pots and pans hung overhead crashed to the scuffed linoleum floor. The little girl at the table started crying.

"You stay put there," Tommy hissed to Mr. Tanner. "Or I'll kill you like I killed your daddy."

Mr. Tanner's face looked fishlike, big cold eyes and lips gulping at the air, reminding Tommy of Pap-pap on his way into death. Tommy could feel the darkness flowing out in a river now, washing away any doubts Mr. Tanner might have had about Tommy's devilish nature.

Tommy turned back to Mrs. Tanner.

"I'm looking for them witches," Tommy said. As always, his deep-country accent grew thicker when he was angry, or scared, or just excited. He was a little of each right now. "You tell me how to find 'em."

"I don't know," Mrs. Tanner whispered. "It's been years—"

"Tell me!" Tommy snapped, and she cringed.

"I have the phone number upstairs," Mrs. Tanner whispered. "I'll go get it."

"Don't try to pull any tricks on me," Tommy said. He was still pinning Mr. Tanner against the wall. "I can kill him. All I got to do is think about it."

"Do what he says," Mr. Tanner whispered. "Do anything he says."

Mrs. Tanner whimpered and scurried from the room.

The ten-year-old, Paul, was crying louder than the girl now. He knelt on the kitchen floor, weeping.

Tommy pulled Mr. Tanner off the wall and turned him so his back faced the doorway where Mrs. Tanner had gone. If Mrs. Tanner tried to pull anything—if she came back with that shotgun, for instance—she would have to go through her husband first.

Fortunately, Mrs. Tanner was timid. How could she be otherwise, Tommy thought, after a lifetime with Mr. Tanner? When she returned to the kitchen, she was holding nothing but a scrap of yellowed paper in her shaking hand.

"What's that?" Tommy asked.

"Her phone number," Mrs. Tanner whispered. "It's all I have. I'm sorry."

"Bring it." Tommy tightened his grasp on Mr. Tanner's throat. He reached out his other hand to Mrs. Tanner.

She approached Tommy with small, trembling footsteps. When she was close enough, Tommy snatched the paper from her hand, and she gasped and darted away.

The scrap of paper was a grocery store receipt.

"On back," Mrs. Tanner whispered.

Tommy turned it over. GUADALUPE RIOS was hand-written on the back, along with a phone number.

"What area code is this?" Tommy asked.

"Texas," Mrs. Tanner said. Her voice was almost too quiet to hear. "Fort Worth."

"Okay. Perfect." Tommy folded the paper and stuffed it into his jacket pocket.

"It won't do you any good," Mrs. Tanner added. "They're scam artists. They never did come up with any money."

Tommy smiled. He looked at Mr. Tanner, who was downright terrified from being in Tommy's grasp so long. He could let the man go now. Then Tommy looked at the three frightened children. He remembered his own childhood, how often Mr. Tanner's twisted, insane ideas about religion seemed to involve stripping and beating the children.

"You were right," Tommy said to Mr. Tanner. "I do have the Devil in me. And today, the Devil wants you."

Tommy let the black lightning rip out of him, filling Mr. Tanner. Mr. Tanner's shuddered hard in Tommy's hand, and a trickle of blood leaked from Mr. Tanner's nose. Then the man slouched, and Tommy let him fall to the floor.

Tommy kicked him, but Mr. Tanner didn't respond. His eyes stared into empty space. Heart attack, stroke or seizure—one way or another, Mr. Tanner had died of fright.

Mrs. Tanner screamed and dropped to the floor to embrace her husband's corpse. "Oh, Jesus!" she cried. "Oh, Jesus. Oh, Jesus…"

Tommy ignored her. He grabbed a box of long kitchen matches and walked outside.

In the biggest barn, where the horse trailer and the ancient canvas-sheathed Buick were parked, there were also large plastic jugs of gasoline for the tractor. Tommy picked up two of them.

The three children trickled out of the farmhouse to look at him. They trailed him, at a great distance, as he walked to the old barn Mr. Tanner had converted into a church for his weird little personal cult.

Tommy pulled open the barn door. He splashed gasoline on the handmade pews, the wooden dais, the willow cross. He splattered more along each of the four walls.

The children stood outside, several feet from the open door, and watched him with open mouths.

When he'd emptied both containers, he walked to the door, and the children ran back ten or twenty feet. Then they turned to watch him again.

Tommy gave them a grin as he struck a kitchen match. Then he flicked it into the barn. The burning matchstick tumbled end over end, until it landed in a gasoline puddle in the middle of the dirt floor. For a moment, he thought the match had simply gone out.

Then a gout of fire belched up, and rivulets of flame rushed out to the four walls of the barn. The cross and the whole altar area went up in a bright red whoosh.

Tommy walked along the dirt-rut road. The children cleared off of it and ran up the slope to the stable, to watch him from a safe distance as he passed.

"Do yourselves a favor," Tommy said to the three of them. "Run off. There's nothing good here. You got to sort out your own life for yourself, sooner or later."

Tommy walked past the gaping children, and on past the farmhouse, where he could hear Mrs. Tanner wailing over her dead husband.

Then he got on his bike and headed for Texas.

Chapter Fifteen

Almost three weeks after she'd been called to Fallen Oak, Heather sat on the edge of the bed in her room at the Carolina Inn, and she watched the local TV news with an open mouth.

South Carolina Governor Calhoun Henderson stood at the microphone, looking a bit solemn for his press conference.

"We've held off any public announcements until the situation was clear," he said. "We did not want to feed into any speculation or false rumors—and there have been plenty of those. Let's put 'em to rest now, folks.

"Some of you have been asking my office for an explanation of the National Guard presence around the little town of Fallen Oak," he continued. "As usual, the rumors are far wilder than the reality. There was a small dye factory in Fallen Oak, back when cotton was king, but it's been closed since the nineteen-fifties. Apparently certain industrial chemicals were left behind and never properly disposed. The chemicals had a volatile reaction, in connection with a storm—lightning may have been involved. A deadly gas was generated, resulting in injuries and fatalities. Specific details on those harmed are being kept confidential for the sake of the families."

"What the hell are you talking about?" Heather yelled at the television. She was on her feet now.

"I want to commend the South Carolina Highway Patrol and other first responders, as well as the South Carolina National Guard, the Department of Homeland Security, the CDC and other federal agencies, for their rapid response and quick containment of the situation. Our state and federal officials acted with speed and professionalism in protecting the people of this great state. Homeland Security assures me that the situation has been cleaned up, and no further hazards exist.

"Thank you for your time." The governor visibly grimaced as he left the podium, ignoring the shouted questions from the press. His press secretary moved into place, a clear sign that there would be no further information of significance.

Heather raced outside, down along the walkway under the flickering fluorescent light bars, and pounded on the door to Schwartzman's room.

He opened the door looking tired and rumpled, as if he hadn't slept much the night before. The TV news was jangling in his room, too.

"What was that?" Heather asked. "A chemical spill? That doesn't even make sense—"

"Keep your voice down! You want to talk, do it indoors." Schwartzman stepped back to let her in the room.

Heather glanced at his bed. His suitcase was open, and most of his clothes were already packed. A few more items, including his shaving kit, sat beside it.

"You're leaving?" Heather asked.

"The White House pulled the emergency funding," he said. "The quarantine's over." He rolled a pair of black socks and tossed them in the suitcase.

"That doesn't make sense," Heather said. "It's only been a couple of weeks. We don't even know what happened."

"We don't know why so many ships disappear in the Bermuda Triangle, either."

"What are you talking about?"

"Look, our resources are limited," Schwartzman said. "We're up against budget cuts." He put his toiletry kit into the suitcase and zipped it.

"Two hundred people are dead, and you're worried about budget cuts!"

"It's not me," Schwartzman said. "I'd like to keep looking until we find answers, even if it takes ten years. But then there's reality. There have been no additional cases, not even suspected. There's nowhere for the investigation to go. The labs have been running night and day, and there is no pathogen in those bodies. None, Heather."

"But there must be something. It's just very elusive—"

"We're transferring them to frozen storage, for further study. But we can't do more. We have to keep things calm." Schwartzman double-checked each drawer in the hotel room's dresser. They were empty. "Maybe after the election…"

"The election?"

"Forget it." Schwartzman turned off the TV.

"Oh, my God. That Nelson Artleby guy from the White House. He did this."

"The White House did this."

"But we have to fight it," Heather said. "This could be really important."

Schwartzman sighed and sagged to the edge of his bed. "The President's party is facing a very difficult midterm. They might get swept out of Congress. One big negative event like this—"

"But this doesn't have anything to do with politics."

"Everything has to do with politics."

"So, the Governor's announcement…"

"Calhoun Henderson's running for the Senate," Schwartzman said. "He's desperate for the President's endorsement."

"So Artleby cut a deal to bury this story."

Schwartzman nodded.

"And screw any actual concern for public health and safety. Am I right?" Heather sank down in the room's easy chair. "This is crazy."

"The National Guard's leaving," Schwartzman said. "Everybody's leaving. We'll continue to study what we've collected here. But the field investigation has been squashed. It's time for you to pack your things, Heather."

"What was the point of me coming here at all?" Heather could hear the bitterness in her own voice.

"No one expected it to go this way," Schwartzman said. "You should take some time off. It's been a while since you've seen your husband, hasn't it? And your daughter? She's, what, three years old now?"

"Four," Heather said. "And when I leave, who takes over the investigation?"

Schwartzman just looked at her.

"Nobody?" she asked.

Schwartzman laid his hotel keycard on the table by the bed, along with a few dollars to tip the housekeeping staff. "You'll need to check out today. Give my best to your family."

He left the room, and the door closed behind him.

Heather stayed where she was for a few minutes, feeling like she'd been hit by a giant truck. A refrigerated truck, full of mysterious dead bodies, with no explanation for their demise.

Chapter Sixteen

Jenny suffered recurring nightmares after the events of Easter night—usually just a replay of what had happened, Ashleigh whipping up the mob, and then blasting away Seth's chest with a shotgun. The mob closing in on Jenny, and Jenny killing all of them with her horrific pox.

A couple of weeks after Easter, she had a new nightmare, even more vivid.

Jenny wore some kind of rough cloth tunic that felt scratchy on her skin. Her long black hair was pulled into a simple braid. She walked across a battlefield littered with bodies, spears, plumed bronze helmets and circular shields. A horrific slaughter had occurred, and the iron tang of blood hung in the air like smoke.

She was accompanied by soldiers carrying tall, iron-tipped spears that extended high above their heads. Their round shields were slung over their left shoulders, and their helmets had bronze cheekplates to protect their faces. They wore stiff linen tunics with bits of bronze sewn into them. An old man on horseback accompanied the group, dressed not in armor but in robes dyed red, with golden rings on his fingers. Jenny knew he was some kind of priest.

The band of men surrounded Jenny, but they kept their distance from her. They were terrified of touching her.

They led her into an encampment with a few large fires and numerous tents, the largest of which was guarded by a pair of soldiers with spears. This largest tent was their destination.

As they approached, one of the guards leaned into the tent and spoke. Jenny didn't know the language, yet in her dream she understood the meaning of his words. He was telling someone inside the tent they had arrived. The guard leaned back out and looked at them.

"The priest and the girl may enter," he said, in his strange language.

The soldiers helped the old priest dismount, and one of the guards held open a tent flap for him to enter.

"Follow me," the priest said to Jenny.

Inside the tent, two men sat on hard wooden folding stools with squarish seats and legs in an "X" shape. The bottoms of the stool legs were carved to resemble lion's feet, pointed inward. They ate bread and roasted meat from a low, simple square table.

One of the men, the one who sat off to the side, wore a white linen tunic, trimmed with geometric green patterns. The other man was tall, with a thick beard, and wore a tunic of purple with intricate gold designs sewn into it. He had bracelets of gold in the same style.

The man in white and green stood to formally greet the priest. The man in purple remained seated. He glanced at the priest with little interest, but he studied Jenny intently. She felt uncomfortable in his gaze. He was a king, and she was a slave.

"This is the girl?" the king asked the priest.

"We have studied her," the old priest said. "I have seen with my own eyes. She has a gift from Aphrodite Areia. The power lies in her touch."

"Is this true?" the king asked Jenny.

"Great king, the war goddess has blessed me," Jenny heard herself say.

"Give us a demonstration," said the man in white and green. He offered his chair to the priest, who sat.

Jenny held up her hand and splayed her fingers. Her hand turned a feverish red, and then pustules and ulcers broke out across her palm and along the insides of her fingers.

The man in the green-edged tunic, who was the king's advisor, turned pale and gaped. The old priest, having seen far more than this, was interested only in the king's reaction.

The king leaned forward to the edge of his stool. "Come closer."

Jenny took two steps toward him. The advisor stepped back, as far away from her as he could manage.

"Great Archidamus," the old priest said to the king. "The touch of the goddess slays all. No man can touch her and long survive."

"That is a great shame." The king favored Jenny with a smile. "Come closer," he said, and Jenny stepped toward him.

"Careful," the advisor said. "She is a helot."

"You would not wish to slay your rightful sovereign?" the king asked Jenny.

"I would not," Jenny said. "But I am a slave to the goddess, as I am a slave to Sparta. She chooses whom to slay. I do not. I am merely her vessel."

"I have sacrificed many fine rams and ewes at the temple of Aphrodite Areia," the king said. "The goddess loves me. She bears me no wrath." The king reached for her hand.

"Do not touch her!" the priest shouted.

The king scowled at the old priest. "Do not command your king!"

"Neither beast nor man are spared," the old priest said. "The goddess destroys all that the girl touches."

"If the goddess harms me," the king said, "then the rites of your priesthood are false."

The old priest said nothing.

The king took Jenny by the wrist and brought her hand closer to inspect the signs of disease.

Jenny shivered in fright. She waited for the touch of Aphrodite Areia to flow into him, for sores and ulcers to break out on his hand and spread up his arm, across his body. Then the king would scream, the old priest would shout, and perhaps the advisor would draw the short sword at his waist and attack Jenny.

But this did not happen. The king studied her fevered, ulcerated hand. The plague did not spread into him, and she marveled. And she trembled, for now she knew the king was no ordinary man. The gods must have favored him.

"It looks strong," the king said. He looked up at her. The irises of his eyes were a deep, rich amber color. "And you may inflict a deadly suffering upon men, if you wish?"

"If the goddess wishes," Jenny whispered. In all of her fifteen years, she had never touched another without causing disease.

The king released her.

"You spoke falsely," the king said to the priest. "The goddess loves me, yet you said she would do me harm."

"I have never seen otherwise," the old priest said. He was pale now, frightened at having displeased the king. "I only sought to protect the king."

The king eased back on his stool, which was cushioned by woolen fleeces. He studied Jenny.

"You must know of the recent evils of Athens," the king said to Jenny. "The Athenians formed the Delian League under pretense of constructing a shield between Persia and Greece. Yet Athens has reduced her allies to mere subjects, and thinks only of expanding her influence, not of protecting Greece. She will not cease until the world lies prostrate under the sword of the Athenian tyrant. Do you know of these things, helot?"

"I have heard such talk," Jenny said. "But it is not my place."

The king smiled at her, and she trembled at the powerful energy in his gaze.

"The Athenians hide now behind their walls," the king said. "The walls reach all the way to the sea. We have ravaged the Attica countryside, yet Athens remains free to command the seas. No army may enter the city."

He paused, looking at her. Jenny did not know what she might say to this, so she remained silent.

"We cannot assault her from without," the king said. "But my priests advise me that you may assault her from within."

"We should not put any trust in a helot," the advisor said, but the king ignored him.

"The priests tell me they have prepared you for this," the king said.

"Yes, my king," the old priest said. "Years of exercises at the temple have uncovered the reach of her divine touch—"

"I wish the girl to speak," the king said.

"I can do as you wish." Jenny's voice was soft and low.

"A woman cannot win a war," the advisor said. "Curses will rain down on us if we follow this course."

"If I wanted to hear of curses, I would ask a priest or a magician!" the king bellowed.

"Magic and sorcery will lead us to suffering," the advisor said. "Wars must be fought by men, with bronze and iron, on a properly blessed field—"

"What do you think of this?" the king asked the priest. "My advisor's prattling?"

"It is clear the goddess favors my king," the priest said. "Her blessings will be upon you."

The advisor sneered.

“Before we proceed,” the king said. “I must satisfy myself with a demonstration of your abilities.”

“I will do as the king wishes,” Jenny said.

“Let us find a beast,” the priest said. “Great or small, as the king wishes.”

“I do not wish to send a plague among the beasts of Athens,” the king said. “But among the men.” He looked to his advisor, and a cruel smile appeared on his face. “Perhaps she might demonstrate upon a worthless general, who can himself offer no means of breaching the Athenian walls.”

“My king!” The advisor shuddered, looking sick. “You cannot mean this.”

“Lay your hands upon him, lovely girl,” the king said. “And see what the judgment of the goddess shall be.”

Jenny approached the advisor. He tried to back away from her, but he had already reached the wall of the tent.

“Surely you have made your offerings to Aphrodite Areia, and do not fear her judgment,” the king said.

Jenny reached for the advisor’s hands.

The man screamed and ran along the wall of the tent.

“Coward!” the king bellowed.

Jenny, wishing to make the king happy, ran after the advisor and leaped onto his back. She wrapped one hand around his throat, and slapped the other across his face.

The advisor squealed and fell to the ground. He writhed on the dirt while Jenny clamped her hands tighter on his head and neck. His skin turned feverish, the fever spreading to his fingers and down his legs, and then dark, bloody sores burst open all over him.

When he lay still, Jenny stood.

“Is he dead?” the king asked.

“Yes, my king, as you instructed,” Jenny said.

“Can my men touch him?” the king said. “Or will they grow diseased?”

“There is no contagion in the dead,” the priest said. “Unless she wills it.”

The king called a guard from outside the tent and instructed the young man to turn the plague-ridden corpse of the advisor face up, so that the king might look upon him. The guard looked at the body, and showed great hesitation at the order to touch it.

"You need not fear the goddess," the priest said. "You will not grow sick."

The young hoplite soldier hesitated a moment more, then laid his hands on the dead man's green-edged tunic, taking care not to touch his skin. He turned the body, and the king smiled at the bleeding tumors that had arisen on his advisor's face.

The jarring sound of a telephone woke Jenny from her sleep. She lay on her bed alone. It was daylight, and for a moment she wasn't sure what century it was, or who she was.

The phone rang again. It hadn't worked in two weeks.

Jenny pushed herself to her feet and stumbled groggily to the living room. She picked up the phone and mumbled a hello.

"Jenny?" asked the voice on the other end.

"Oh! Daddy! Hey!" Jenny said.

"Are you okay?"

"Yeah, I'm fine," Jenny said. "It's just the phone's been out. All the phones."

"I've been worried sick," he said. "Couldn't even get the answering machine after that first day."

"Guess it's working now," Jenny said. "Where are you?"

"I'm driving home now," he said. "The National Guard cleared out, left all the roads wide open."

"Oh, good, they're leaving!" Jenny said.

"I'd say they're about gone. Haven't seen one."

"So it's over," Jenny said.

"I guess," her dad said. "But nobody's too sure what it was all about. What happened, Jenny? Did you see anything?"

"Um," Jenny said. The last thing she wanted to do was tell him what she'd done. "It's just been crazy."

"Well, you can tell me about it when I get home."

"I'll be here," Jenny said.

After the phone call, Jenny chewed her fingernails. She didn't know how to explain to her dad what had happened. She hurried to throw on jeans, a long-sleeved blouse, and a pair of light gloves. She added a stocking hat, though it was very warm outside, bordering on hot.

She found Seth outside, pacing in the back yard, between rows of her dad's partially finished projects—motors, furniture, and appliances in need of repair, or else waiting to have the useful pieces stripped out of them. The stuff used to be all over the yard, but Seth had helped Jenny and her dad build a fence, from the house to the shed, to hide her dad's mini-junkyard. The front yard actually looked half-decent now.

Seth turned and walked along the fence toward her. He was talking on his cell phone, looking annoyed.

"What is it?" Jenny asked when he was done.

"They're saying it was a chemical leak at the old Lawson dye factory," Seth told him. "Which our bank owns. But that's crazy, because the factory was just a little concrete shell. It's been totally empty forever. My dad's worried about the liability now, with the insurance company or something, and he wants me to go out to the factory with Mr. Burris. Talk with the Homeland Security guys. Or listen while Mr. Burris talks, anyway."

"When do you have to go?"

"Right now," Seth said. "Before they leave town."

"Wait—who came up with that story?" Jenny asked.

Seth shrugged. "Let's just be glad there's a story, and it doesn't involve you. Want to come with me? Should be long and dull."

"Not really," Jenny said. "And I can't, anyway. My dad will be home any minute."

"Wish I could stay, but I have to do this. My dad's so worried, he's flying up from Florida to try and get control of the situation."

"What happens when he figures out there wasn't a chemical leak?"

"I don't know," Seth said. "I just hope he doesn't start prying too deep."

Jenny slouched. "I wish your parents didn't hate me."

"They don't hate you."

"Right."

"I don't hate you." Seth took her hands and looked into her eyes. "Not at all."

He kissed her, and Jenny felt herself relax. She always felt as if she were feeding on him somehow, as if his touch made her stronger.

Sometimes it made her too strong, maybe. Strong enough to wipe out a town square full of people.

Her dad's Dodge Ram rumbled into the driveway.

"I have to go," Seth said.

"Great," Jenny said. She'd been dreading telling her dad what had happened, but she'd imagined Seth would be there with her. Now she would have to face it alone. "Seth, how much do you remember from when you were dead? On Easter?"

"Not much now," he said. "Right after I came back, I could have told you all kinds of things. But it's like my brain couldn't hold all that stuff. Past lives. Crazy stuff."

"I don't remember very well, either." She heard her dad get out of the truck and walk up the front porch steps. "Do you ever have dreams about your past lives, since that?"

"Maybe," Seth said. "I don't remember my dreams for long. Except this one where I was a giant rubber duck, being chased by soap bubbles. That was weird. You think it means anything?"

"Jenny?" her dad said. He walked out the back door to join them in yard.

"Daddy!" Jenny ran to him and hugged him tight, careful to keep her exposed face against his shirt. He arranged his hands cautiously on her back, avoiding the skin of her head and neck, and hugged her back.

"It's so good to see you, Jenny," he whispered. He sounded like he was about to cry.

"I missed you, Daddy."

"I missed you, too."

Seth watched them for a minute, then he said, "It's good to see you, Mr. Morton. I actually have to run into town."

"Take care, Seth," Jenny's dad said, not deeply interested. To Jenny, he said, "I got some groceries in the kitchen. Figured you might have been running low on things, with the town cut off."

"That's great!" Jenny said. "I'm tired of baked beans."

"How could you get tired of those?" Seth asked.

They went inside, and Seth hugged Jenny and continued on out the front door.

Jenny helped unload the groceries. Her dad had picked up a sizable brick of hamburger meat.

"Thought Seth would be eating with us," he said. "That boy can put it away."

"I bet I could eat two hamburgers right now," Jenny told him. She opened the Piggy Wiggly bag on the counter. "Oh, and fresh lettuce, fresh tomatoes…this is great!"

Her dad made patties and took them out to grill. Jenny took cabbage and carrots and put together a slaw, and then she grabbed a pitcher and squeezed juice from the plump lemons he'd brought.

She carried two glasses of lemonade outside, gave one to her dad at the grill, then relaxed on a lawn chair, soaking up the sun.

"You feeling okay, Jenny?" he asked.

"I guess."

"Sure you don't have any idea what happened?"

"Well…" Jenny said. "I didn't want to say on the phone."

"I figured."

"Did I ever tell you Ashleigh Goodling had a power like ours?" Jenny asked. "Like me and Seth?"

"The preacher's daughter? No, I think I'd remember if you said that."

"Well…she was like us. Only a lot worse."

"What kinda sickness did she spread? Or could she heal people?"

"Neither one," Jenny said. "Her touch made people feel love. That's why everyone in town loved her and did whatever she said."

"Hell, I can believe that," he said. "I always thought there was something off about them Goodlings. Dr. Goodling puts me in mind of them people that travel with the carnival."

"So, here's the thing," Jenny said. "Ashleigh turned the whole town against me and Seth. Or maybe not the whole town, but a lot of people. And she had them all together at the courthouse, ready to hang us for being witches. Honestly."

"Like Gabriel Joe?" her dad asked. That was the name of the slave that had supposedly been hung from the giant gnarled oak in front of the courthouse in the 1700s, on the charge of practicing sorcery. There hadn't been a courthouse then, just the giant oak.

It was a story usually told at night, by a campfire, somewhere around Halloween.

"I'm not kidding," Jenny said. "I think that old story helped get everybody together. Kind of made it easy for Ashleigh to tell everybody what to do. And then she killed Seth with a shotgun." Jenny pointed to her chest, to show where Seth had been shot.

"What?"

"He got better," Jenny said, thinking of Monty Python. "And then everybody tried to hang me from the tree. And then...don't you need to flip them?"

Her dad was staring at her, the metal spatula in his hand forgotten halfway to the grill.

"What happened, Jenny?"

"Then I lashed out."

"Did people get hurt?" he asked.

Jenny didn't say anything.

"Did people die, Jenny? They said on the news..." His mouth dropped open. He understood now. "How many people, Jenny?"

"A lot."

"What's a lot?"

"I don't really know. A hundred? Maybe more?"

"*A hundred people?*"

"Yeah, I'd say...at least a hundred people. The Goodlings, and Mayor Winder, the police department, a bunch of kids from school, Coach Humbee and some other teachers, some deacons from the church, that realtor guy with his face on the benches all over town—"

"You killed Dick Baker?" her dad asked. "He still owes me a check." His voice was detached, as if he were mentally drifting away. "That's a lot of people, Jenny."

"I know!" Jenny said, and then she broke down and began to sob. She rested her elbows on her knees and buried her face in her gloves.

A fatty lump of the neglected beef fell through the grill and ignited in a gout of greasy flame. Her dad set the metal spatula down on the little platform attached to the grill, and he turned to walk inside.

"I got to think this over," he muttered, walking toward the house.

"What about the hamburgers?" Jenny asked.

"You can finish them if you want them," he said. "I tried to teach you better than this, Jenny."

"I know, Daddy! I should never touch people. I know."

He walked into the house, looking tired and old.

Chapter Seventeen

A few days after the quarantine ended, Jenny took some new clay pots down to the Five and Dime, to see if Ms. Sutland wanted to put them out for sale.

She arrived to find the door propped open and half the store's inventory packed into boxes. A couple of men were moving furniture out on hand trucks.

"Ms. Sutland?" Jenny asked, though the bell had tinkled loudly when she entered.

Ms. Sutland emerged from the back office, dabbing at her eyes.

"What's happening?" Jenny asked.

"Oh, it's the Morton girl." Ms. Sutland brightened a little. "How's your mom and dad?"

"They're fine, ma'am," Jenny said. Jenny's mother had died at birth, but Ms. Sutland was foggy about anything outside her store. "What's going on?"

Ms. Sutland looked around, puzzled. "What do you mean, Jenny?"

"Why is the store all packed up?"

"Oh, let's have a nice cup of tea," Ms. Sutland said. "I've only just brewed it. Have you ever been to a ladies' tea party, Jenny?"

"I don't think so. But why is the store all packed—"

"You just sit right here." Ms. Sutland pulled out a chair at one of the remaining antique tables. Last time Jenny had been here, the furniture was crammed together so tight you couldn't begin to think about actually using any of it. Now the maze of furniture had thinned out considerably.

Jenny sat, and Ms. Sutland brought out tea cups, along with sugar cubes and tongs. She returned with the tea pot, poured some for Jenny and herself, then set the pot on a quilted square of cloth.

“There.” Ms. Sutland sat across from her. She lifted the tea while the men came back with the hand truck and began loading a grandfather clock. “Isn’t this pleasant?”

“Yes, ma’am,” Jenny said. “But why—”

“Your mother used to come here,” Ms. Sutland said. “Pretty girl with the blue eyes. I remember.”

“You do?” Jenny asked. “What was she like?”

“Oh, she was just the nicest little thing,” Ms. Sutland said. “Always bought something, too. Even if it was just a refrigerator magnet, salt shaker, something small.”

“Did you talk with her much?” Jenny asked.

“Some. She always had friends around her, though. Always laughing. Didn’t stay and talk like you do.”

Jenny sipped her tea, not sure what to say.

“She always said she wanted a daughter,” Ms. Sutland said. “She did say that a time or two. Looking at the cribs and children’s furniture.” Ms. Sutland nodded toward an empty corner.

“Where is everything going, Ms. Sutland?” Jenny asked.

“Oh, all of this?” Ms. Sutland waved her hand around. “Well, it’s just shameful to say how far behind I am on the rent. The Barretts are so nice about it, such lovely people, the Barretts. Don’t you think?”

“I like one or two of them,” Jenny said.

“Mrs. Barrett even shops here. The young Mrs. Barrett. Haven’t seen the old Mrs. Barrett in ten, twenty years.”

“You mean Seth’s grandmother?”

Ms. Sutland’s forehead wrinkled, and she toyed absently with her tea spoon.

“Are you…moving the store?” Jenny asked. “Where are those men taking your stuff?”

“Listen, Jenny,” Ms. Sutland said. “Have you ever used a computer?”

“Yes, ma’am.”

“Well, on the computer, there is a thing called eBay,” Ms. Sutland said. “You just take a photo of whatever you’re selling, and then all kinds of people offer to buy it. Can you believe a thing like that?”

“I’ve heard of it,” Jenny said.

“So my nephew insisted on putting up some pictures of things, on the eBay computer,” Ms. Sutland said. “Some of them things I’ve had forever. And do you know that I found buyers for just about everything? Not always at a price I'd like. But then, for a few items, some people offered too much, in my opinion, but I suppose you have to take the highest bid."

"That's good, Ms. Sutland! So you're not closing up the store, right? You're sticking around?"

"Goodness, no," Ms. Sutland said. Her voice dropped to a whisper. "Some terrible things happened here." She nodded out toward the green. "Not everyone understands it. But I saw it the day after Easter. I came to open the store, and there were such horrors…" Ms. Sutland shuddered. "I shouldn't even speak of what I saw that morning. Before sunrise, even."

"I'm so sorry," Jenny said.

"I called the police chief, but nobody answered, so then I called the governor's office."

"The state governor?"

"You would not believe how difficult it is to get the governor on the telephone," Ms. Sutland said. "I told them I'm a citizen with an emergency, but they still made me leave a message. Can you believe that?"

"I sure can't, Ms. Sutland."

"Now how can I keep coming back here, every day, after seeing a thing like that? I've been thinking about pulling up and leaving out, anyway. None of my friends are left in this town, except the ones in the cemetery."

"I'm your friend," Jenny said.

"Thank you, Jenny. But I want to live by the ocean. And I want to move somewhere the people are nicer."

Jenny laughed, but Ms. Sutland just gave her a puzzled look, as if it hadn't been a joke at all.

"I didn't sell any of your things on the computer." Ms. Sutland pointed to the shelves near the front of the store, where Jenny's pottery was displayed.

"That's okay."

"I mean, I didn't put it for sale on the computer. Because, I thought, Jenny ought to put them for sale on the computer herself."

"Okay," Jenny said. "So I need to take everything home with me today?"

"That would probably be best," Ms. Sutland said. "I'll have to lock up the store when I leave."

Jenny felt like crying. Ms. Sutland had always been nice to Jenny, when nobody else was. Probably because she was too eccentric to notice how weird Jenny was.

"You can't go, Ms. Sutland," Jenny said. "This town won't be the same if you leave."

"The town already isn't the same," Ms. Sutland said. "It's a different place now."

Jenny drank her tea and looked out the dusty window at the town green.

Chapter Eighteen

Esmeralda studied the face of the dead man on the table. Fernando Aguilar Ortiz had lived seventy-one years, and his face was leathery from a lifetime of hot sunlight. Thick calluses covered his hands. According to the pictures provided by his family, he had a cheerful smile but a dark, serious look in his eyes.

Her job was to bring him back to life for a day.

Esmeralda glanced at the embalming room door to make sure no one was coming. Then she touched her right hand to his cold, stiff face.

Immediately, she was in the village of Rio Pequeño in Mexico, caught in a swirl of bright costumes, the sound of maracas and guitarron and vihuela, clapping hands, rhythmic voices. It was a saint's day festival, though she wasn't sure which one. She looked up as she held tight to the hand of an older man with a gray beard.

This was Fernando Aguilar Ortiz's first memory.

His life unfolded around her. It had not been a very easy one. When he was a little boy, a deadly fever had swept through the village, taking several cousins, an older sister and a younger brother, and his mother.

Fernando had attended a little bit of school at the Catholic church in town, but mainly he worked for his father, who raised goats. When he was sixteen, he fell in love with a neighbor girl, Lucia, and they were married, but Lucia had not survived her first childbirth. Neither had the child.

Soon after, Fernando made his way illegally into America. He worked first on a farm, and then got a better-paying job with a landscaping company. He met another girl and married her, and they had five children. In time, he created his own landscaping company with one of his good friends and two of his sons. He had seventeen grandchildren, who gave him delight without measure.

He'd been diagnosed with cancer when he was sixty-nine. His two devoted sons and his eldest daughter came to see him over the following two years, as did five of his grandchildren. The others lived too far away or were too busy, and this brought him sadness, but in his heart he forgave them.

He had died nine hours ago at the UCLA hospital, with one son at his side.

That was Fernando Aguilar Ortiz's last memory.

Esmeralda had embalmed the body and dressed it in the coat and tie provided by his family. Now the real challenge began, using cosmetics to bring the semblance of life back to his face. The art of the mortuary cosmetics included using color to make the body appear to have a living circulatory system. Small, careful traces of red mixed in at just the right spots could bring a healthy and vital appearance to the deceased's face.

Once she had seen someone's life, Esmeralda's understanding of the person helped guide her in making up their face and styling their hair. Maybe it was just small touches—a little shading here and there—but she did her best to subtly bring out the personality and emotional richness the deceased had possessed. The final viewing created a lasting memory image for the person's loved ones, and Esmeralda felt it was important that the families have a positive experience.

And it was much better than working with the living.

Esmeralda became absorbed in her work. On her headphones, she listened to Vivaldi. Esmeralda had not always listened to music while she worked, but in the last few weeks, she'd had a few nightmares about work. In these dreams, the embalming room stretched on forever, with mortuary tables as far as she could see, each with a body waiting for her attention. She couldn't work fast enough—the bodies were rapidly decaying and crumbling, putting her into a panic to preserve them.

Then a young man would slowly approach her, tall and handsome, with dark, shaggy hair, and deep brown eyes that were identical to her own. He had a dazzling smile. He would touch each corpse as he passed it. At his touch, the corpse would sit up on the mortuary table and turn to look at Esmeralda.

Esmeralda cranked up the volume on her headphones and tried not to think about those dreams.

By six o'clock, Esmeralda had Mr. Ortiz looking as if he were in perfect health, just taking a siesta on a warm summer afternoon, instead of the gaunt and pale look with which he'd arrived. She hoped the family would be pleased.

Esmeralda stripped off her gloves. Mr. Ortiz was now dressed and styled for his family, and Jorge and Luis would move him into his casket for the viewing.

She straightened up the embalming room, washed her hands and rubbed them with sanitizer. She removed her smock, said goodnight to the elder of the two Mr. Garcias, and stepped outside.

Garcia y Garcia Funeral Home had operated in eastern Los Angeles for more than twenty years. Esmeralda had graduated high school two years earlier, and now she was two classes away from her Associate of Applied Science in Funeral Service degree. Technically, she was an intern at Garcia y Garcia, but since neither of the Garcia brothers really cared to do much embalming anymore, and both were impressed with how well Esmeralda prepared the bodies, she often found herself working alone.

As she walked into the parking lot, she noticed a man in dark sunglasses watching her. He sat on a motorcycle with a huge engine and some kind of gargoyle design on the side. She didn’t recognize him. He was Caucasian instead of Latino, which made him stick out in this neighborhood, where none of the signs were written in English. Strange scars dotted his face, and his hands were sheathed in black leather gloves.

He smiled at her, which made her uncomfortable. She turned her head away from him to watch the road. She would have liked to turn her back on him entirely, but that seemed a little dangerous. Esmeralda stared at the passing traffic and watched him from the corner of her eye while she waited.

She thought about going back inside, but she didn’t want to get stuck explaining how she was scared of a man in the parking lot, who was probably just an early arrival for the Ortiz viewing.

Hurry up, Esmeralda thought, watching the cars pass.

“Hi,” the man spoke behind her. She ignored him, as if she believed he was speaking to someone else. “Esmeralda,” he said.

She tensed. She turned back to give him her best “crawl away and die” look.

"I don't know you," she said.

"Are you sure?" The man slid off his bike. As he walked toward her, he removed his sunglasses.

When she saw his gray eyes, she heard herself draw in a sharp breath, and then she completely turned her back on him. She didn't know what her face looked like right now, but it would be full of emotions she didn't want him to see.

"You are Esmeralda, aren't you?" He was walking towards her. "You have to be. You're as beautiful as I remember."

Esmeralda wanted to roll her eyes at him, but she would have to turn and face him to do that. And then he might see how she really felt, or how her knees had gone loose and wobbly.

"Don't you recognize me?" he asked. He was standing just behind her now.

"Yes," she said. She got her face under control—cool, distant—and finally turned to look at him. She flicked her eyes up and down him, trying to appear indifferent, but her heart was skipping. She didn't even mind the weird dotting of scars on his face. "You are the devil."

He laughed, and she liked his smile.

"Your mother said I was a fraud," Esmeralda said.

"Foster mother," he said. "And who cares what she thinks?"

"She was very insulting. And my mother was angry."

"I bet your mother didn't care once you gave her the money," he said.

"I did not give her the money," Esmeralda said.

He gave her a surprised look, then laughed again. "You are sneaky. That's how I've always imagined you. Clever and sneaky."

"I didn't do it so I could keep the money."

"Sure. You gave it all to starving orphan puppies."

"That's not what I mean," Esmeralda said. "You wouldn't understand."

His gray eyes looked into hers. He was only inches from her now. Her heart gave a flutter.

"I've thought about you," he said. "Over the years."

"Have you?" Esmeralda asked. Of course, she'd thought about him, too. He was the first boy who had kissed her, and there had been something in his kiss, electric and powerful, that she had never again felt. Mentally, she scolded herself for feeling anything at all about him—it had only been one moment, very long ago.

He reached out a leather-gloved hand and lay it next to hers, then he wrapped his fingers around her hand. Esmeralda caught her breath. She didn't want him to think he could just grab her up after all these years…but she didn't exactly want him to let go of her, either. His touch made him feel more real, and less like a dream.

Then Pedro's Acura pulled into the parking lot.

"Shit!" Esmeralda pulled her hand away and took a few steps back from him.

"What is it?" the gray-eyed boy asked. He looked at the Acura pulling into the parking place beside them, and at Pedro in the driver's seat. "Is he a friend of yours?"

"My boyfriend," Esmeralda said.

The gray-eyed boy didn't bother hiding his scowl.

Pedro got out of the car and stepped between the two of them.

"Esmeralda," Pedro said. "Let's go."

Esmeralda hesitated, and Pedro noticed. He looked again at the gray-eyed boy. Esmeralda knew the boy was her own age, or younger, so Pedro had to be five or six years older than him. Pedro was shorter, but much bulkier.

"Who are you?" Pedro took a step toward him.

"I'm Tommy," the boy said.

"Tommy. That's cute, man. Maybe when you grow up, they'll call you Tom. Or Thomas, no?"

"I hate Thomas," Tommy said.

"Okay, Tommy," Pedro said. "*My* name is Pedro Ortega Hernandez. And I want to know why the hell you're talking to my girlfriend."

"Pedro," Esmeralda said. "It was nothing. Let's go."

"I was not talking to you, Esmeralda. You get in the car." Pedro glared up at Tommy. "You. Why are you talking to her at her job? Why you trying to grab her hand?"

"I wanted to," Tommy said. He didn't look very scared by Pedro, but he had never seen Pedro angry.

"Well, I don't want you to." Pedro thumped Tommy in the chest. "I see you near her again, you'll have to hire old Mr. Garcia to bury you. You understand?"

"Okay." Tommy held up his hands defensively, but he was smirking. "Take her on home."

"I'll take her where the fuck I want to take her."

"It's been nice meeting you, Pedro," Tommy said.

Pedro glared up at him a moment longer, then stalked back to his car. "Get in," he said to Esmeralda.

Esmeralda looked at Tommy again, and he just folded his arms and winked at her.

"Get in the fucking car!" Pedro yelled.

Tommy didn't say anything, so Esmeralda got in the fucking car.

Pedro drove in silence for a couple of miles.

As they passed the grocery store near her neighborhood, Esmeralda said, "I need to stop by *la tienda* for a couple things—"

"Who was he?" Pedro snapped.

"He was nobody."

"It's so good to know," he said, "While I'm building houses for my uncle, and studying law at night, and fixing your mother's plumbing because her landlord is lazy—it's so good to know you're out there making new friends."

"He's just someone I knew when I was a kid."

"First he's nobody, then he's an old friend?"

"It's not like that—"

"Then tell me what it's like."

"You missed the grocery store."

"You can walk." Pedro lit a Camel as he turned into Esmeralda's apartment complex. "Or use your mother's car."

"I wish you wouldn't smoke so much."

"Good. Because I was hoping to take a little more shit from you today." Pedro stopped in front of her apartment, but he left the engine running and didn't park. "Maybe tomorrow your friend with the motorcycle can take you home from work."

"Pedro, stop it!" She kicked open the car door.

He took her arm and pulled her close.

"Let me go!" she said.

"I just don't like to see you with some other guy," he said. "I love you, Esmeralda."

"And I love you. Don't be so jealous."

"Look in my eyes and tell me he is nothing to you."

Esmeralda looked Pedro in the eyes. "He is nothing," she said, but her eyes blinked involuntarily when she said "nothing."

He frowned at her. "I have to get to class. I'll call you later."

Esmeralda stepped into the two-room apartment she shared with her mother. Immediately the sound of a Telemundo soap opera, weeping confessions backed by sappy music, jangled her ears. Her mother sat on the couch, watching the TV.

"*Hola, Mamà,*" Esmeralda said.

"You should not upset Pedro like that," her mother said in Spanish.

"Like what?"

"I was watching you through the window, and he did not look happy. What did you do?"

"You spy on me and you take his side," Esmeralda said.

"What were you fighting about?"

"It was nothing. He is jealous of everything."

"You should keep him happy," Esmeralda's mother said. "That boy is going to be very successful one day."

"A very successful asshole," Esmeralda muttered in English as she walked into her room.

"What did you say?"

"Nothing!" Esmeralda closed her door. Then she locked it, which she rarely did. She even made sure the blinds were down, as if Pedro would be outside her room, staring at her. Sometimes she felt like he was. She'd had enough of her mother always taking Pedro's side, too. Her mother wasn't exactly a master in the art of picking good men, anyway.

Esmeralda opened her closet door, stood on her tiptoes, and felt around on the top shelf. She brought down a Reebok shoe box, which she had long ago decorated with glue, glitter, butterfly stickers, and markers. Much of the glitter had fallen off over the years, and the butterflies were curling off the cardboard.

She sat down on her bed and took off the box lid.

The shoe box held a few pictures from her childhood, a letter from her grandmother in Matehuala, one of Esmeralda's baby teeth, some Valentines she had received in middle school. Esmeralda dug through these to the bottom of the box.

She took out the gold coin. It was engraved with an Indian chief's head, and the word "Liberty," on the front, and a bald eagle on the back. The coin was dated 1908. She had never taken it to a coin shop to check its value, for fear her mother would somehow find out and ask questions.

Esmeralda had also never turned over the thousand dollars to her mother.

When Tommy suggested she hide the money, it was the first inkling Esmeralda had that she could hide anything from her mother, even for a minute. The farmer woman who had called them to the middle of nowhere, in Oklahoma, had been livid when she opened the dead man's trunk and found nothing. Esmeralda's mother had screamed at her, but Esmeralda had kept the secret.

As they drove home, Esmeralda wasn't sure how to tell her mother what happened. The longer they drove, the more possible it seemed that Esmeralda could keep the secret forever.

The real secret, though, wasn't about the stolen money.

"What is wrong with you?" her mother had screamed as they drove back to Texas. "Why did you lie?"

"I can't do it anymore," Esmeralda had whispered.

"Can't do it? Can't do what?"

"I can't talk to the dead anymore," Esmeralda had said. "I don't remember how."

"Remember? What is to remember? You have always done this."

"Yes," Esmeralda said. "But maybe I am too old now." At the age of thirteen, Esmeralda was sick of her mother dragging her around like a freakshow attraction, charging people money to hear from their dead relatives. The dead didn't bother Esmeralda, but the living did—people greedy to find money, jealous wives wanting to know whether their husbands had cheated on them or not, and too often, there were children crying and upset as they learned the pain of losing someone close.

Esmeralda didn't like it. And if she could get away with lying about money, maybe she could get away with more.

And she had. Her mother hadn't dragged her out to read the dead again. Instead, her mother had finally gone back to her housekeeping job at the hotel and stopped living off her daughter's strange gift.

As far as Esmeralda's mother knew, Esmeralda hadn't had the special touch in nine years.

Esmeralda rubbed the gold coin. The paper dollars had trickled away over the years, on movies and candy and shoes, but she kept this because it reminded her of him. His unreal gray eyes, the power in his hands and lips. He had frightened her deeply…but she had liked it, and relished the memory again and again.

Until today, she had almost forgotten he was a real person, and not a dream or a fantasy.

He had found her, after all these years. Esmeralda didn't know what it meant, but she felt scared and exhilarated. She needed to see him again.

She closed her hand around the gold coin and held it tight.

Chapter Nineteen

When Fallen Oak High School re-opened at the beginning of May, Jenny drove herself there for the first time ever. She'd always ridden the bus, until the past few months when Seth had started picking her up. The school issued a limited number of the jealously guarded student parking passes, and those were earmarked for certain juniors and seniors—student council, varsity football players, people like that.

Jenny had killed a lot of those people, though, so there was probably room for parking.

She drove to school, listening to Willie Nelson and Merle Haggard sing "Pancho and Lefty" on the country-gold radio station. Her dad had been distant for days now, ever since her confession. Jenny knew he didn't see her the same. It was hard to adjust to your only child being a mass murderer, she thought. And it looked like she was going to get away with it, which, in a weird way, only made things worse.

Not that Jenny really believed she would get away with murder. People were investigating. They'd taken the bodies, and they'd taken all kinds of medical samples from Jenny. Someone was going to put it together.

She now understood the meaning of the phrase "living on borrowed time."

School was strange and quiet. Several teachers were dead, and the state had brought in some befuddled substitutes. People trudged through the hallways, saying very little to each other.

They did whisper, though, when Jenny walked in the front door of the school. They whispered a lot, about how she was supposed to be dead, everyone had seen her drown.

As usual, nobody talked to her directly. She sensed something different, though. Where there had once been cold dismissal, if not outright loathing, the feeling she got from people now was one of fear. Ashleigh, and even Dr. Goodling, had accused her of witchcraft, and now a bunch of people were dead with no explanation. Including all of Jenny's enemies.

Notes and photographs were taped all over Ashleigh Goodling's locker, and there was a heap of flowers and a couple of little teddy bears in front of it. People had even left packs of Twix and unopened cans of Cherry Coke—Ashleigh's favorite morning vending-machine treats—at the foot of her locker, like an offering to a pagan god.

In Jenny's homeroom, there were a lot of empty desks. Several of the girls were pregnant, and they gave Jenny the strongest looks of fear or revulsion. Alison Newton, Brenda Purcell, and Ronella Jones, all former cheerleaders now quite visibly pregnant, whispered to each other in the front row, looking back over their shoulders at Jenny.

Jenny sat in the back corner of the back row.

Darcy Metcalf arrived, and her pregnancy was really starting to show. She sat in the back row, too, at the opposite end from Jenny, away from everybody. Abject misery radiated from Darcy's face and slumped posture. Jenny knew the feeling.

Assistant Principal Varney—now acting principal, since Ashleigh had gotten Principal Harris suspended—gave the morning announcements over the intercom.

"First," her deep bass voice crackled over the boxy intercom, "Let us have a moment of silence for the teachers and students lost in the tragic accident."

Jenny's substitute homeroom teacher, an elderly man with a bulky hearing aid, closed his wrinkled eyes solemnly.

The pregnant girls, and a few other kids, stared at Jenny. Jenny lowered her head, and her eyes, but she didn't close her eyes all the way. She had a feeling that people might pounce on her if she gave them a chance.

"All students are invited to visit with our guidance counselor, Mrs. Gerbler, for grief counseling." Assistant Principal Varney said over the intercom. "She will be available in the main office all week, along with Mr. Ellerton, a grief specialist sent by the State Department of Education. Now, despite the tragedy, we must finish out the school year. Contrary to rumor, final exams will be held." This brought groans from all over the school. "Other announcements will follow as plans become finalized."

Jenny wondered what that meant.

"Please be respectful of the new substitute teachers around the school," Mrs. Varney continued. "They're here to help us through these difficult times. Major extracurricular activities are suspended until further notice. Lunch today will be Salisbury steak, tater tots and okra medley. Now rise for the Pledge of Allegiance."

Jenny rose with everyone else and quietly pledged allegiance to the rectangle of cloth hanging over the chalkboard, and to the republic for which it stood.

The school remained quiet as a funeral parlor all morning. At lunch, Jenny sat with Seth in their usual lunch place on dry days, under the shade of one of the big, gnarled old oak trees that were everywhere in town. This was one of three big oaks on the narrow lawn between the school and the student parking lot. The roots were wide enough to use as benches and tables, if you didn't mind sitting close to the ground.

Jenny had brought a peanut butter and jelly, plus an empty butter container full of carrots. She eyeballed Seth's lunch with a little disgust. He'd not only bought the mystery brown rectangle of Salisbury steak, he'd actually paid extra for a double order.

"Well, all my friends are gone," Seth said. "But they did all gang up and murder me. True friends don't really do that."

"They couldn't help it," Jenny said. "They were under Ashleigh's spell."

"Could she really keep that many people under control at once?" Seth said. "She got them going, but it's not like they tried real hard to stop themselves. I mean, they kept coming at you, right?"

"At first," Jenny said.

Seth wolfed down a Salisbury slice. Jenny barely had any appetite.

"What's it like having your parents in town again?" Jenny asked.

"Back to the old family sitcom. Mom's medicated and talking on the phone with her old sorority friends. Dad's drunk and talking to my great-grandfather's ghost. Or fighting with Mr. Burris about the stupid bank. They try to parent me around like they didn't just leave me by myself since Christmas."

"Do they know we're still together?" Jenny said.

"That's kind of hard to do," Seth said. "Last time my mom saw you, she was busting you with cocaine at our Christmas party."

"It wasn't mine!" Jenny said. "It was Ashleigh's. And not even hers, but some of your stupid preppy rich-kid friends."

"Not my friends," Seth said. "My parents and their parents are friends. And not even real friends, most of them, it's just business."

"Whatever," Jenny said.

"I told them what really happened," Seth said. "But they don't believe me."

"Because Ashleigh was such a perfect angel."

"And you're a wicked devil, trying to suck out my soul." Seth grabbed Jenny, bit at her head and made sounds like a starving zombie.

"Stop it!" Jenny slapped him, but not very hard, and she let her fingers linger on his face for a second. She was wearing gloves for school, as always. "I'm eating."

"Actually, you're not."

"I was thinking about it."

"I also heard prom might be canceled," Seth said.

"Could be," Jenny said. "I killed the whole prom planning committee."

"Jenny!" Seth looked around. "You can't just say that out in public."

"There's nobody close by. Nobody would sit near us if we asked them to." Jenny looked around at the scattered little groups of people. There was no big central crowd at the picnic tables now, orbiting Ashleigh like she was the sun. Everybody had broken off into tiny clumps here and there. The entire social order of the school had been destroyed.

A lot of people, like Darcy Metcalf, sat all alone—Darcy's main purpose in life had been to suck up to Ashleigh Goodling. Isolated people like Darcy seemed to have no friends left in the world, which was just the way Jenny had been most of her life. She felt sick.

"Everyone's talking about how many people are missing," Seth said. "The news made it sound like it was only a few deaths, and with the phones out, people didn't realize just how many people—"

"Okay, Seth!" Jenny said. "I get it. It was a lot of people. I think I'm going to puke now."

"Sorry." He rubbed a hand along her back. "I think a lot of people are skipping, too, though. I mean, who really wanted to come back?"

"It's so weird now," Jenny said. "I just feel sick all the time, thinking about what I did. It's going to be like this forever, too. What can I even do?"

"I don't know."

"I wish somebody knew," Jenny said. "I wish somebody could tell me."

And then the bell rang.

In her dream, Jenny rode in the back of a cart towards the center of Athens, awed by the city. Sparta had been little more than a rough and sprawling village, despite its military might and its position as chief power of the Peloponnesian League of cities.

Athens, in contrast, had fed well on its Delian League cities as its empire grew, and put up massive monuments and temples to the entire pantheon. Everywhere she looked, she gaped at marble steps, marble columns, imposing statues of heroes and gods, all of them masterfully cut and brightly painted.

No wonder Sparta feared this city, she thought. It looked like an imperial capital. According to King Archidamus, that was exactly what Athens had become, a provoker of wars so that it might conquer, a threat to civilization itself.

It was her job to destroy this city, and thereby save all of Greece from tyranny.

She rode in a two-wheeled cart drawn by a horse, and two other girls rode with her. The three of them had arrived by galley in Piraeus, the port of Athens. She and the other girls were heavily made up, lots of black around their eyes and dark red on their lips. They were allegedly slave girls from a distant island near Persia. The man driving the cart would sell them to a certain wealthy Athenian citizen who stocked his household with exotic women.

Jenny reflected on how she had come to be here.

The old priest, whose name was Kyrillos, had taken an interest in her soon after she was born. (In this life, she now understood, she was called Euanthe.) Euanthe had been discovered as an infant, wailing and kicking in the low, filthy shed where her helot family lived. The rest of her family had died of some horrific disease, but Euanthe had survived, though cranky and hungry.

This apparent immunity to disease brought the attention of the priest Kyrillos, who had taken her for healthy slave-breeding stock. Soon he recognized her true nature. He entrusted her care with the priestesses of Aphrodite Areia, who served the warlike side of the love goddess, the sometimes consort of the war god Ares, and the most beloved goddess in Sparta.

The priest himself provided much of her education. His main interest was in testing her abilities, helping her to control them and discover what they could do. They tried her magical infection on animals, and later he procured criminals and undesirables whom Sparta had sentenced to death. By experimenting, they learned a great deal, though the experiments themselves were nightmarish events.

He taught her that she had been cursed by the goddess, that Euanthe or her family must have done something to displease the goddess, and consequently she needed to spend her life in service to the goddess (and, by extension, the priest Kyrillos himself) until she regained the goddess's favor and the curse was lifted.

And, she now understood, he had also been preparing her for this, intending to use her as a weapon on behalf of Sparta.

According to the story that the slave merchant had told the wealthy Athenian, the girls spoke no Greek at all. This freed Euanthe and the other girls from any need to craft and maintain careful lies.

The magnificent house was high upon a hill, much of it built from marble, painted bright blues and greens. The slave merchant led them on foot into the grand courtyard, and she gaped up at the second-floor galleries, on their thick marble columns.

Euanthe trembled. She did not know the other two girls, though she understood they might have been prostitutes. They seemed to know each other, and they wanted nothing to do with Euanthe. They stayed close together, even holding hands, and spoke only by whispering in each others' ears.

The slave merchant presented them to the withered old slave who administered the wealthy household. He looked the three girls over and paid the merchant a few silver coins.

Euanthe and the other girls were sent into a side gallery, in which women were crammed together, weaving. The three new girls were put to work.

Soon, the lady of the house entered. She was a few years older than Euanthe, her golden hair coiled into fine braids and set atop her head with jeweled pins and clips.

A pretty servant girl trailed behind her like a dog.

"These are the new ones?" The lady of the house looked over the three girls with her disturbing gray eyes, and then she addressed the eldest of the slave women. "Do they work hard?"

"They need training," the woman said. "Lots of training. And they only speak their barbarian tongue."

The lady touched the shoulder of one of the girls who had accompanied Euanthe. The girl's face lit up with a smile, as if she suddenly adored the gray-eyed Athenian lady.

"We shall break them in," the lady said. "My husband, at least, will have great enjoyment of them." She looked at Jenny/Euanthe, then leaned in for a closer look, her eyes narrowing. "What is your name?"

Euanthe said nothing, pretending not to understand.

"I don't like the look of this one," the lady said.

"Shall we dispose of her?" the lady's servant asked.

"No, no, she's already paid for." The gray-eyed lady turned to leave, with her servant again at her heels. "At least they aren't ugly. Ugly slaves are unacceptable in a fine household."

"Yes, my lady," her servant agreed.

Euanthe set her fingers to the hard work of weaving. The elder slave women slapped her each time she made an error.

Chapter Twenty

Tommy waited in the parking lot of Esmeralda's apartment complex and watched her door as the sun rose behind him. He sat on his stolen bike, wearing gloves and a long-sleeve shirt though the weather was very warm, almost hot. He didn't want to risk touching her and making her afraid of him.

Her apartment complex was ugly, built of concrete and cinderblocks, with wrecked car husks occupying a few of the parking spots. The outer walls, the dumpster, and the stop signs were all sprayed with gang tags.

Never mind the blue sky and the palm trees from the movies, Tommy thought, this city was crap. It was like Panama City Beach or some low-rent tourist trap like that, only stretched out for mile after mile and then slathered in smog.

When she stepped out of her apartment, Tommy cranked the engine of his motorcycle. The sound drew her attention, and she smiled immediately when she saw him. Then she seemed to remember herself, and the smile disappeared.

She turned away from him and walked toward the bus stop at the front of the complex.

Tommy swooped out until he was alongside her, then slowed down and walked his bike along with her, the engine grumbling beneath him.

"Hi, Esmeralda," he said.

"You know my name." She kept walking, kept trying to hide her smile.

"I couldn't search the whole country for you without learning your name," he said. "Esmeralda Rios."

"The whole country? Where did you start?"

"Forth Worth."

"Wow." She laughed. "That was years ago. Did you stop in Albuquerque, too?"

"Yep."

"Arizona?"

"Flagstaff."

"I am impressed." She gave him a sidelong look. "And a little creeped out."

"But you remember me," he said.

"A little. I don't even remember your name."

"I never told you."

When she reached the graffiti-coated Plexiglas bus shelter, she finally turned to look him full on in the face. Tommy felt something move in his heart—but he pushed the feeling down quickly. He needed to handle his business, not stare all droopy-eyed at this gorgeous girl.

"Want a ride?" he asked.

"I like the bus."

"My bike's a lot nicer," he said. "Cleaner, too."

She eyed his stolen Harley. "I doubt that."

"More fun."

The bus approached down Sepulveda, pausing only one intersection away to load and unload passengers.

"I don't ride with strangers," Esmeralda said.

"My name is Tommy."

She raised an eyebrow.

"You have beautiful eyes," he said.

Her eyes responded to the compliment by rolling upward. "You are so original," she said, but she was smiling again.

The bus trundled towards them.

"Do you want the ride?" Tommy asked. He could take off his glove, grab her arm and make her do anything he said. But he didn't want to do that. He wanted her to choose to come.

"I still don't know your last name."

"It's Krueger," he said. It was a surname he often used. His favorite, actually.

"That doesn't sound very Spanish to me." The bus arrived, and the door folded open. Esmeralda looked at the steps inside. "My mother won't approve of it."

"We can change it. I just made it up, anyway."

She laughed. “You chose to be named after a movie monster?”

“I always kind of identified with him.”

“You are crazy.” The bus door folded, and the bus lurched away. “Look, you made me miss my bus. Now you must take me to work.”

“Hop on.”

Esmeralda slid into the seat behind him. She wrapped her arms around his waist. He felt her fingers on his abdominal muscles, pressing him tight through his shirt, and now it was his turn to smile.

“You don't have an extra helmet,” she said.

“I'll have to fix that.” He took off his helmet and passed it back to her. “Just pull the chin strap under—”

“I know. You're not the first boy on a bike I've dated.”

“Are we dating now?”

“I didn't mean to say that. Okay, I'm ready.”

Tommy gunned the bike and they shot out into the road. He curved steeply, almost tipping over on one side, and she squealed and clamped her arms tight around him.

He straightened up the bike and drove.

The funeral home was only about ten minutes away, but when they reached it, Tommy didn't pull into the parking lot. He kept going, not stopping until the next red light.

“You missed it,” Esmeralda said.

“Take the day off,” he said. “We’ll have fun instead.”

“But I told Mr. Gonzales I would come in for a few hours.”

“Let the dead bury the dead,” Tommy said. “Isn't that what they say?”

“It’s a bad plan,” Esmeralda said. “The dead don’t work very hard.”

The light turned green, and Tommy opened up the throttle.

She never asked him to turn back.

When Jenny dreamed of being Euanthe again, she was bringing food to the grand dining hall along with a few other slave girls. One girl carried a platter of roast lamb, another a skin of wine, another a loaf of bread. Euanthe herself carried a wooden platter with an assortment of olives.

The gray-eyed lady and her husband reclined on couches near the fire. Her husband had the same gray eyes that she did, as if husband and wife were somehow related.

Euanthe and the other slave girls stood near them, ready to serve food and drink on demand.

"Your plans are too bold," the man said to his wife. "Pericles remains popular, despite all the talk we've spread of corruption and impiety. We have removed a few of his supporters, but the man himself remains in power. The moderates in the assembly will not turn against the leader in a time of war."

"Pericles is weaker than he seems, Cleon," the gray-eyed young woman said. She held out a cup for a slave girl to fill it. "People will blame him for the Spartans ransacking our countryside. This is the opportunity we've sought for years. We have undermined his support in the assembly, we have gathered embarrassing information on his most powerful friends, and soon we will topple him. Athens is nearly ours, whether you see it or not."

"Athens may soon belong to King Archidamus and his barbaric Spartans," the man called Cleon said. "And then the internal politics of Athens, whether Pericles rules or I rule, will no longer matter." He bit into a meaty leg of lamb.

"Cleon, that is why you should lead Athens," his wife said. "This will be our argument. Pericles is too weak, too old, too much a lover of peace. Athens needs a man with fire in his blood. A man who can make the Spartans quake in fear." She took his hand and smiled.

Euanthe tried to wear a bored look while listening carefully to the conversation. The politician against whom these two were plotting, the man named Pericles, had been leader of democratic Athens for decades. He was Euanthe's target, too. Her instructions were to keep herself quiet and invisible until she had an opportunity to infect him.

She knew how to make her plague contagious—the old priest Kyrillos had helped her discover this, using both sheep and convicted criminals. Pericles would die, and then Athens would follow.

The gray-eyed lady gestured to Euanthe and opened her mouth. Euanthe approached and fed her an olive, careful not to touch her lips.

The lady stared up at her, holding the olive between her teeth. Euanthe tilted her head forward, so that her hair covered her eyes, and she looked down at the floor. She knew the lady didn't like her, and she didn't want to draw more of the lady's wrath.

"These olives are of poor quality." The lady spat the olive on the floor, having never bitten into it. "Go and feed them to the swine."

Euanthe pretended not to understood her words, so one of the Athenian slaves snapped her fingers in front of Euanthe's face, and Euanthe followed her out of the room.

As she departed, she heard the lady say to her husband, "I do not want that slave girl touching our food again. She has an evil look about her."

Chapter Twenty-One

Jenny and Seth hiked through the woods, towards a place they liked to go, while Rocky bounded on and off the trail around them.

"Have you had any weird dreams lately?" Jenny asked.

"Um...there was one where I was standing at the counter at Hardee's, and I had to order something, but I couldn't remember what. And I couldn't read the menu. And then I realized I was naked and everybody was pointing at me. And then I ordered a cheeseburger."

"That's sort of not what I meant," Jenny said. "Anything flashing back to past lives? Like we saw when we were dead?"

"Not that I can remember. I don't usually remember my dreams for long after I wake up, though."

"I've had some strange ones," Jenny said. "Weird ancient history stuff. I actually looked it up at the library—"

"—because you're the last person on Earth who doesn't have Internet at home—"

"—anyway, some of it checks out. Especially the name 'Pericles.' There's a lot of stuff about him."

They rounded a bend in the trail and arrived at a high, sprawling rock formation, nestled in a valley of the hilly, stony Morton land. Jenny climbed up the biggest rock, using the rock beside it for leverage. When she reached the top, she looked down at Seth, who was just standing and staring off into the trees.

"Come on, don't be a turtle," Jenny said.

"Sorry." He shook his head and began to climb after her.

"What are you thinking about?"

"Just my dad. He's really being a dick."

"Because of me?" Jenny asked.

"No..." Seth reached the top of the boulder and brushed dirt from his hands. "They don't really know I'm still seeing you."

"That's probably best." Jenny sat down on the rock.

"He says I have to major in international business, economics, something like that."

"I thought you wanted to do physical therapy, so you could heal people."

"Not good enough for him. Also, he says I have to learn to speak Mandarin. Or Hindi. My choice." Seth gave a thin smile. "I barely made it through Spanish." He sat down and put an arm around her, drawing her close to him.

Jenny leaned against his strong, warm body and listened to his heart. She didn't want to think about him moving out of town, or about the future at all. She was having enough trouble figuring out the past. "So, Pericles," she said.

"Yeah, sorry," Seth said. "What's up with Pericles?"

"He was like the ruler of Athens for years and years," Jenny said. "In ancient Greece. I looked him up, and they say he built up the city, the Parthenon, all kinds of stuff. And Athens kind of ruled the ancient world while he was in charge.

"But then Athens got into a war with another powerful city, Sparta. And there were all these rumors and accusations about Pericles and his friends, religious crimes and embezzling gold. And then the Athenians weren't happy with how the war was going. Another politician named Cleon accused Pericles of some crimes, which knocked Pericles out of power. And then Pericles died of the plague. And then Cleon took over Athens, and he controlled the city for years, until he died."

"That's totally interesting." Seth kissed her. His hand drifted down to the hem of her shirt, then began to pull it up. "I know you didn't sneak out in the woods with me to talk about ancient Greece, though."

"Yeah, actually, I did." She laid back on the rock, out of his reach, and tucked her hands behind her head. "In my dream, there was this gray-eyed woman who was Cleon's wife. It seemed like she was behind a lot of the rumors and accusations, and basically destroyed Pericles' reputation behind the scenes. And then I read today that Cleon, her husband, ends up as the most powerful man in the city."

"Sounds like Ashleigh," Seth said.

"Exactly like Ashleigh. I think it *was* Ashleigh. You see what I mean?"

"Okay," Seth said. "Ashleigh was a manipulative bitch in all her lives. Gotcha. And who were you, in ancient Athens?"

Jenny didn't want to say it. "I helped destroy Athens."

"You should put that on your college application." He lay down beside her and kissed her. Jenny wanted to just give in and let him do what he liked to her, but this was too important. She fought down her feelings and nudged him back from her.

"You're the one going to college, not me. Anyway, I was working for the king of Sparta. His name was Arky…Archidamus. He sent me to Athens to spread a plague there, and to kill Pericles. And I looked it up, and Athens really was hit by a huge plague during that war, and Pericles died from it, too. And Cleon and his people took over Athens, and they were vicious. And eventually Athens lost the war against Sparta. It was called the Peloponnesian War. After that war, Athens stopped being a powerful, important kind of city."

"Okay," Seth said. "But I don't see how it matters now. That was like hundreds of years ago."

"Um, thousands," Jenny said. "And it matters because of this guy Cleon. You know that guy who had Ashleigh's eyes?"

"Old spooky-touch?" Seth said. "I don't think I'll forget him."

"That was him, I think. I've got it worked out here." Jenny leaned up on her elbow. She took a folded sheet of notebook paper from her pocket and spread it out on the boulder between them. "This is what I've figured out so far."

The page had two columns of names:

Euanthe = Me

Cleon's wife = Ashleigh

Cleon (politician, takes over Athens) = that scary guy (Ashleigh's opposite)

Archidamus (king of Sparta) = Seth (???)

"Hey, how did I get on the list?" Seth asked.

"The king of Sparta," Jenny said. "When he touched me, the Jenny pox didn't infect him. He was immune. So it had to be you. Right?"

"I don't know. It's your dream."

"I don't know, either," Jenny said.

"So who was Pericles?" Seth asked.

"I don't know if he was one of us or just a regular person," Jenny said. "Anyway, who else is there for me to recognize, besides you and me, and Ashleigh and her guy?"

"So…what does any of this mean, Jenny?"

"I just wanted to tell you. That guy and Ashleigh have a long history together. And he knows I killed her. So I think he'll be back."

"After that nasty infection you gave him? I bet he'll stay away."

"What if he brings a gun and shoots me?"

"Then I'll heal you," Seth said. "After I kill him."

"I'm serious, Seth."

"Me, too." Seth folded up the paper and tucked it in his pocket. "I'll study this stuff later, when I'm stuck at home. Right now, I'd rather talk about you."

Seth kissed her again.

This time, Jenny didn't resist him.

Chapter Twenty-Two

Tommy drove them out of the city, into the vast lonely universe of the Mojave desert, where the air was clear and the sky was a bottomless blue overhead. She gripped him tight with her arms and thighs.

He followed a narrow unpainted spur road up the top of a bluff, and then he stopped at the edge of the cliff, looking down over a sea of sand and rock.

"That was a long ride," Esmeralda said.

"You loved it."

"Maybe."

She got off the bike and stretched her arms. He dropped the kickstand and killed the engine, then stood beside her, looking over the cliff.

"Why did you come looking for me?" she asked. "Why now?"

"I should have come years ago," he said. "I keep thinking about you."

"Thinking what about me?"

"Take off your helmet."

Esmeralda took it off and shook her long black hair. She smiled at him.

"I have a magic touch like yours," he said. He took off one glove.

"What do you mean?"

"You can talk to the dead when you touch them," he said.

"Maybe when I was a kid. It kind of faded away as I got older."

"I don't believe you."

"You shouldn't. I'm lying. But I can't really talk to the dead."

"Then how did you find out about the old man's money?"

"What I do is more like listening," Esmeralda said. "It's like all their memories are left behind in their bodies. And I can find them. But it's not like talking to dead spirits or anything. Their souls are gone."

"Gone where?"

"Wherever souls go." Esmeralda shrugged. "What do you do?"

"I can make people feel fear."

"I'm not afraid of you."

"Everyone is. Let me see your hand."

"Don't do anything creepy." She held out her hand to him.

"Everything I do is creepy." He took her hand and watched the inevitable chill bumps spread up her arms. She trembled and pulled away.

"You see?" he asked.

She touched her fingers to her lips, staring at him.

"I did warn you," Tommy said.

"No…it's okay," she said. "It's like a shock. I remember from when I was a kid. When you…" She blushed. "Let me try again."

She took his hand in both of hers. She shuddered, but she kept looking him in the eye. Tommy felt his own heart move faster at her touch. She was going to drive him crazy.

"How scared are you?" Tommy asked.

"It's kind of a rush," she said. "It makes you feel alive." She stepped closer and looked up at him. "I want to scream. But I like it. I want you to touch me more."

She reached up and laid a cold, sweaty palm against his neck.

"I need you to do something for me," he said.

She pushed closer against him. "What do you want?"

"I have the body of a third person. Like us. I need you to read it, or whatever you do."

She took a breath and stepped back, releasing his hand. "Is that why you came?"

"I'm trying to understand more about what we are. Don't you want to understand?"

"It can't be understood," Esmeralda said. "We are as God created us."

"I'm not sure God did," Tommy said. "We aren't like normal people."

"So who is this person?"

"A girl," Tommy said.

"Oh. And what do you want to learn from her?"

"I saw her on television," he said. "She seemed very together, very in control. And I can't stop thinking about her."

Esmeralda looked over the cliff and said nothing.

"I think she's like us," Tommy said. "Whatever we are. Only she knew what she was doing."

"And you could see all this on the television?" Esmeralda asked, still not looking at him.

"I just felt it. I keep dreaming about her. I keep seeing her face and hearing her voice, all the time."

"So you did not come out here for me," Esmeralda said. "You came for her."

"It's all the same thing," Tommy said. "It's all about figuring out what we are, and what we can do—"

"It is not the same thing! You either came here for me, or for her."

Tommy looked at her, not sure what to say. He hadn't really thought very deeply about any of this.

Esmeralda sighed. "Take me to the body. I'll do it. But then take me home."

"If that's what you want." Tommy opened the saddlebag on the side of the bag, and he brought out the backpack with flowers and hearts sewn into it.

"What's that?" Esmeralda asked.

"The body." He unzipped the backpack and brought out the muddy wad of the dress. He unrolled it across the rocky sand, revealing a third of Ashleigh's skull and a pile of bone fragments, with black crust flaking off them.

"Gross!" Esmeralda said. "That's been right there the whole time?"

"This is all that's left of her."

"It won't work," she said. "It's too old and broken up. Usually I do it soon after they're dead."

"It's not actually old," Tommy said. "Just wrecked."

Esmeralda sighed. "I can try it, but I don't promise anything."

"Go ahead."

She knelt on the sand next to the desiccated bones. She took a breath, then picked up the broken hunk of Ashleigh's skull.

She closed her eyes.

Tommy watched her, feeling very nervous. If this didn't work, he didn't know what else he could do.

Esmeralda began to hum—not a song, but a drawn-out, tuneless noise.

Her eyes flew open, and she was staring right at Tommy.

"Finally!" she shouted. "Why did you wait so long?"

"What?" Tommy asked.

"I've been screaming at you day and night. 'Get out of that prison and come get me!' It took you forever!"

"What are you talking about?"

"God damn it, I hate being between incarnations," she said. "Nobody sees you, nobody hears you, your powers are worthless…I missed the flesh." She looked down at herself. She squeezed her own breast with her hand. "This isn't a bad body, either! Not as pretty as my last one, but I'll take it. Too bad she's Mexican, though. And no money. Yuck."

Tommy just stared at her until she looked back. Her eyes seemed a little different—as if their deep, rich brown color had turned a very dark shade of gray.

"Oh, guess you want a reward," she said. With the hand that wasn't holding Ashleigh's skull, Esmeralda began unbuttoning her white blouse. She wore a flimsy, lacy bra underneath, and he could see the dark circles of her nipples. "Do you want to screw her body?"

"What?"

"Come on." She stepped close to Tommy. Everything was different—her posture was taller and straighter, and she had a commanding tone to her voice. She hooked her fingers into Tommy's belt. "It's been a long time. I wanted to keep up the whole unattainable virgin thing in my last life, and there wasn't a boy in Fallen Oak who wouldn't have bragged about fucking me. So I went that whole lifetime without doing it."

"Are you…Ashleigh Goodling?" Tommy asked.

"How are you this dumb again? You get dumber every time you're born. It takes forever to train you."

"I still have no idea what you're talking about."

She sighed. "Okay. I am Ashleigh Goodling, or that was my name in my most recent life. But I didn't remember my past lives then. I didn't remember what I really was. And if I wanted to come back, I had to go through the whole process of being born and being a baby and forgetting everything again. And I can't let Jenny and Seth win like that."

"Okay," Tommy said. "Past lives?"

Ashleigh rolled her eyes. "Do we have to do this now?"

"What do you want to do?"

"I want to get your pants off." Ashleigh tugged at his belt buckle but couldn't pry it open with one hand. She used two fingers of her other hand, the one holding the broken piece of skull. The skull slipped out and fell to the ground.

"Fuck that!" she screamed. She let go of his belt and scrambled back from Tommy. "What are you doing?" She looked down, saw her shirt hanging open, and hurried to cover herself. "What are you doing to me?"

"I didn't do anything," Tommy said. "You started taking off your clothes."

"It wasn't me. It was *her.*" Esmeralda shuddered. "That's not how it's supposed to work. The soul is supposed to be gone. It's like she was still there, just waiting to…" She scowled at Tommy. "You planned this, didn't you?"

"I didn't know that would happen."

"But *she* knew," Esmeralda said. "She was waiting. She jumped right into me. I didn't even know that could happen."

"Is it because she's like us?"

"How would I know?"

"She talked about past lives. Like reincarnation," Tommy said.

"I don't believe in that." Esmeralda's dark amber eyes smoldered with anger. "I did what you wanted. Now take me home."

"You have to let me talk to her again."

"No." Esmeralda's voice grew quiet. "She scares me."

"I thought you liked being scared."

She glared at him. "I'm not letting her take control of me again."

"I have to talk with her." Tommy reached for Esmeralda's arm.

She walked backwards towards the road, keeping her distance from him, watching his reaching hand warily.

"Esmeralda, wait—" Tommy said.

"I said no!" Esmeralda turned to run, tripped over a stone, and sprawled in the road.

"Let me help you." Tommy shed his other glove and reached for her with both hands.

"No! Don't touch me! Don't…"

He seized her arms and pushed fear into her, the way he had with the prison guards. She shook hard in his grasp.

"You will do as I say," Tommy told her. "Pick up the skull."

"No," she whispered, though she was shaking in fright. "Find someone else."

"There is no one else."

Mentally, he pushed harder, and she cried out.

"Then find someone else…who will be possessed by her," Esmeralda whispered. "I'll put her in someone else. But I would rather die than let her inside me again."

Tommy was impressed by her ability to resist him. Maybe it was because she had a power of her own, he thought. Or maybe she was just incredibly stubborn.

"Okay," Tommy said. "But then you have to come with me."

"Yes," she whispered, close to tears now. "Whatever you want."

"That's right," Tommy said. "Whatever I want."

Chapter Twenty-Three

When Alexander stepped up into the rear of the box truck, the two men with machine guns stopped talking with each other and watched him warily, their hands tight on their weapons.

In this part of Mexico, people knew Alexander as *El Brujo*, the sorcerer. His hair and eyes were dark, his skin a deep bronze from life in the sun. He wore a black Egyptian cotton t-shirt and dark, mirrored sunglasses. From a distance, it would be hard to guess that he was a gringo from Brentwood, a recent Stanford drop-out pursuing an interesting opportunity south of the border.

Inside the truck, three dead bodies lay in a puddle on the floor, flies already crawling on them as they rotted in the heat. The fourth *bandito*, the one that was still alive, knelt with his hands roped behind him. One eye was swollen shut, and he bled from both nostrils, but he kept his spine upright like a well-trained soldier.

The survivor was tough and wouldn't speak, and this was why Papa Calderòn had sent in *El Brujo*.

"Hello, Carlos." Alexander spoke to him in Spanish. Alexander had known both English and Spanish from the moment he was born, along with hundreds of other languages, most of them dead. "My friends tell me you aren't cooperating. They say you refuse to speak. This is very rude of you, Carlos."

Carlos glared defiantly at Alexander and said nothing.

"Who sent you, Carlos?" Alexander asked. "If you don't tell us, we will unleash the greatest horror you have ever seen. The remainder of your life will be a long waking nightmare, if you do not speak now."

Carlos did not speak.

"I don't want to be here, Carlos," Alexander said. "I should be on a plane right now. I have important business in the north. Don't slow me down, Carlos. I don't have time to play."

Carlos didn't answer.

"You killed our driver," Alexander said. "And his bodyguard. You stole our shipment. Now the situation is simple, no? You tell us where to find our missing product—you tell us who has it now—and you live. If not…" He gestured to the three bullet-riddled bodies on the floor. "Who sent you? Was it Toscano?"

"Nobody sent us," Carlos said. "We are independent."

"Independent?" Alexander laughed. "You want to say you moved against Papa Calderòn, in this state, with the blessing of no one? I am to believe you are that stupid?"

Carlos just stared at him.

"We do not believe you are that stupid." Alexander knelt in the pool of three dead men's blood, paying no mind to the damage done to his Armani jeans. He grabbed the hair of a dead man lying face down in the congealed blood.

"Leave him alone," Carlos said.

Alexander lifted the dead man's face from the blood. The man had a bristly moustache and thick jowls. His mouth hung open. "This guy, your friend," Alexander said. "I believe *he* is that stupid. He has a stupid face." Alexander slammed the dead man's face into the floor of the truck, and Carlos jumped.

"Or this guy." Alexander touched the second corpse, and then the third. "Or him. They all look like stupid little men."

Carlos snarled, just a little. Alexander was getting to him.

Alexander smiled as he stood. He gave one of the bodies a hard kick for good measure. "Your friends, stupid. But you do not look stupid." Alexander approached Carlos. "You look disciplined. Smart. Maybe ex-military, no? Or a former *federale*?"

Carlos gave a hard stare, his eyes full of anger.

"Anyway," Alexander said, "You are a man who follows orders. We only want to know whose." He paused to give Carlos an opportunity to speak, which Carlos didn't take.

Alexander walked in a slow circle around Carlos.

"We know that Toscano and his friends do not like what Papa Calderòn is doing," Alexander said. "But Papa Calderòn has ended his past relationship with Toscano. That won't change. We are…what did you call yourself? We are independent of Toscano's organization now.

And if Toscano doesn't want to do business on our terms, this is fine. But he must leave our men and our shipments alone. Do you understand?"

Alexander knelt beside Carlos and spoke directly into the man's bloody, bullet-nipped ear.

"I will tell you a secret thing," Alexander said in a lower voice. "We do not need your confession. Papa Calderòn knows who sent you. He simply wants you to deliver a message back to your boss. Can you do this?"

Carlos looked back at him, but didn't answer.

Alexander held out a hand toward the three dead men.

They began to rock side to side in their own blood.

Carlos watched them with wide eyes.

"You know what name they call me, don't you?"

"El Brujo," Carlos whispered. "Papa Calderòn's witch."

"They call me this for a reason." Alexander lifted his hand a few inches, and the dead men rose to their knees. "It is because I am a high priest of the devil. A necromancer, and a wielder of black magic." Alexander lifted his hand higher, and the three dead men stood, swaying like palms in the wind, unsteady on their feet. Alexander backed away from Carlos.

The three corpses shuffled around, bumping into each other as if drunk, until they all managed to turn and face Carlos.

Alexander crooked his fingers, and the bullet-riddled corpses advanced on Carlos, one sluggish dragging step at a time, heads lolling and limp, eyes blank, mouths open and drooling.

Carlos began to whisper a prayer to the Virgin Mary, and the two machine-gun men, Papa Calderòn's foot soldiers, crossed themselves.

"And so, Carlos, here is the message," Alexander said. "If the raids against Papa Calderòn do not stop, I will unleash horrors on Toscano and all his friends. I will send an army of demons to their homes to eat their families."

The reanimated corpses closed in around Carlos, grabbing and clawing him, biting at his face. Carlos screamed.

"Tell your boss that God has been banished from this land, and the Devil walks among us," Alexander said.

Carlos cried out as the corpses of his friends bit and tore at his flesh.

"You tell him I am here, and I will come for him." Alexander snapped his fingers. The three corpses fell to the ground like rag dolls.

Carlos remained on the blood-spattered truck floor, curled in a fetal position, weeping softly, bleeding from bite marks all over his body.

"Release him," Alexander said to the men with machine guns. "Let him go back to his boss, and don't cut his tongue out. We want him free to talk."

Alexander stepped down from the truck. Outside, a scorching wind blew through the arid Mexican countryside. The box truck was parked inside a weathered old barn that was missing much of its roof.

Alexander walked to his own car, a black Mercedes convertible, parked in the huge empty doorway of the barn.

He was running late. There was a girl up north he needed to find, if he was going to do what Papa Calderòn wanted him to do. Alexander had been waiting his entire life to meet her.

The rural highway took him through vast open pastures with sparse grass and skinny cattle. The hot, dry pastoral landscape was broken only by an occasional farmhouse or old church, with a graveyard full of huge pastel sculptures.

His name in this lifetime was Alexander, but he'd had a thousand names, and if he had to, he could list them all. He was twenty years old, but his memories spanned all the way back into the deep primeval world, long before the dawn of civilization.

In all of those lifetimes, ever since his kind had first found their way here and learned to incarnate among the humankind, his touch had possessed the power to command the dead.

By himself, he couldn't make the reanimated dead do much—just a few repetitive tasks, or continuous marching. The dead were stupid. But if he charged up his power, he could make them wield swords, and maybe guns.

From his past lives, he knew how best to amplify his power. He hadn't met her in this lifetime, not yet, but he was on his way to reconnect with her. And he planned to bring her back with him, whether she liked that idea or not.

He drove north.

Chapter Twenty-Four

Darcy Metcalf lived in a ranch-style house with windowboxes full of dandelions and other weeds. Tommy parked his motorcycle in her driveway, behind a pick-up truck with Chuck O'Flannery bumper stickers, featuring the sweaty talk show host with dialogue balloons: "No Healthcare for Hippies!" and "Save A Bullet, Stab a Leftie!"

Tommy smiled, taking it as a good omen. The O'Flannery Overview Hour was where he'd first seen Ashleigh.

He and Esmeralda stepped off the bike. A beady-eyed woman peered out a window, probably drawn by the sound of his motorcycle.

Tommy led the way up the steps to Darcy's front door. Esmeralda trailed behind him. He felt bad about having to keep Esmeralda in fear, but he needed her.

He knocked on the door.

The jowly, beady-eyed woman opened the door. She was in her late forties or early fifties, and she didn't look friendly.

"We ain't buying nothing," she said through the screen door.

"We're just here to visit Darcy," Tommy said.

"Who are you?"

"We're friends."

"Darcy don't have no friends. They all died in the witchcraft."

"Mom!" Darcy ran towards the door. She was wearing a long-faded Fallen Oak Baptist Kids' Kamp T-shirt, which didn't cover her swollen pregnant belly. She also wore yellow rubber gloves and smelled like Clorox. "That's Tommy Goodling!" Darcy beamed through the screen door at Tommy, but her smile fell when she saw Esmeralda.

"Who's the Mexican?" Darcy's mom asked. "Bet she's illegal!"

Esmeralda gave her an angry glare.

"Mommm!" Darcy said. She pushed opened the screen door. "Come on in, Tommy."

"You didn't tell me you was having friends over." Darcy's mom eyeballed Tommy and Esmeralda with disgust as they walked into her foyer.

"I didn't know they were coming!" Darcy said.

"Did you clean both bathrooms?" her mom asked.

"Just about," Darcy said.

"Did you scrub the commodes?"

"Mom, do you have to *say* that?" Darcy turned bright red, looking at Tommy.

"Well, did you?" her mom asked. "You can't go nowhere until you scrub the commodes."

"Okay, okay!" Darcy said.

Darcy's dad wheeled into the room. The man was obese, with a thick moustache and an angry look on his face. He was missing one foot. Tommy could hear *Wheel of Fortune* in the living room from which he'd emerged.

"Who in Christ is this?" her dad demanded, staring at Tommy.

"Language, Morris," Darcy's mom said softly.

"Is this the boy who knocked you up?" Darcy's dad growled. His hands balled into fists on his wheelchair arms.

"No, Dad!" Darcy's face was deep red now, and she covered her eyes with one yellow glove. "I told you a million times, it was Bret Daniels. He disappeared like everybody else."

"Pretty convenient for him!" he barked. "Now I got to pay for a baby with nothing but disability and the shit money your momma makes at the fabric store! When you gonna get a got-damn job?"

"Language, Morris," Darcy's mom said.

"I *told* you, I applied at the Hardee's and the Wal-Mart already," Darcy said. "Nobody's hiring! So why can't I just hang out with people for once?"

"You can't go nowhere until you give me my insulin," her dad said.

"And scrub the commodes," her mother reminded her.

"Okay! I'm doing it!" Darcy marched down the hall. "I'm scrubbing the dumb commodes!" To Tommy, she said, "You guys want to hang out in my room and wait for me? I've got a radio you can turn on, if you keep the volume below 3."

Tommy and Esmeralda followed her down the hall.

"No boys in your bedroom!" her father yelled.

Darcy turned around to face him, and cupped her swollen belly in both hands. "Oh, gee whiz, Dad, what's gonna happen? I mean, get real."

"Don't you tell me to get real!" her dad yelled, his face turning bright crimson. "I ain't got no foot! That's as real as it gets!"

Darcy gave an exaggerated sigh and pointed to a bedroom door with a poster of Kermit and Miss Piggy thumbtacked to it. "That's my room. I'll be there in two shakes."

Tommy and Esmeralda stepped into Darcy's bedroom, and Tommy closed the door behind them. A few stuffed animals sat on the bed, and there was a cartoonish plastic piggy bank on the end table. Tommy looked at the collage of pictures on the wall. Some of them were Darcy's family, but more of them were pictures of Darcy with Ashleigh Goodling, or just pictures of Ashleigh. Darcy also had a few posters of Jesus and seemed to prefer pictures where Jesus was muscular, cut and bronzed like a movie star, his loincloth barely clothing his loins.

Tommy sat in a small armchair by a window, next to a bookshelf crammed with C.S. Lewis and L. Frank Baum paperbacks.

"So, that's the girl." Esmeralda kept her voice low.

"She worships Ashleigh," Tommy said. "It's perfect."

"Let's just get it over with."

Tommy felt a little hurt. He'd been so happy to find Esmeralda again, but he had to keep dosing her with fear, since she didn't really want to help him.

They'd driven straight across the country, eighteen hours a day, stopping once to spend the night in a cheap motel. He'd worried that she might find the courage to leave in the middle of the night—but Tommy was a light sleeper. In Bent River, you never wanted to sleep too deep.

Esmeralda hadn't even tried to leave, though.

Now Darcy returned, sans rubber gloves, and hurried to close the door behind her.

"Sorry, guys," Darcy said. "My dad's such a lame-o."

"It's fine," Tommy said.

"He's handicapped, you know. Type II diabetes got him." Darcy looked at Esmeralda and forced a smile. "Hi. I'm Darcy."

"I am Esmeralda."

"Nice to meet you. So, I guess you're Tommy's girlfriend or…?"

Esmeralda looked at Tommy, waiting for some instruction.

"Oh, gosh, sorry if that's an awkward question!" Darcy said. "I'm such a dodo about things like that." She sank to the bed, leaving plenty of space between herself and Esmeralda, and she farted. "Whoopsie! Sorry. Being pregnant sucks. Anywho, what's going on? Has anybody heard from Dr. or Mrs. Goodling?"

"Darcy, I have to tell you something." Tommy moved over to the bed and sat next to Darcy, so that Darcy was stuck between Tommy and Esmeralda. He smiled. Time to make use of Mr. Tanner's craziness.

He took Darcy's hand, and he pushed fear into her. He tried not to do too much—he didn't want her a panicked, gibbering idiot, but he needed her awestruck.

"I am an angel of God," Tommy said. "Can you see it now?"

Darcy's eyes widened, and her lips trembled. "Yeah. Yes. Yes, sir."

Tommy squeezed her hand.

"Ashleigh's work on Earth isn't quite done," Tommy said. "So God is sending her back from heaven on a special errand. But she can't use her old body, since it's ruined."

"Yes, sir," Darcy breathed. "It's way ruined."

"So Ashleigh needs to borrow yours," Tommy said. "Just for a little while. This angel here can put her soul into your body." He nodded at Esmeralda.

"Okay," Darcy said. "If that's what God wants."

Behind Darcy's back, Esmeralda frowned and scowled at Tommy.

"But wait, sir," Darcy said. "I'm pregnant."

Tommy didn't know where she was going with that, so he just watched her quietly.

"So," Darcy said, "If you put Ashleigh's soul in me…does that mean my baby will have Ashleigh's soul? Ashleigh will be my little girl?"

"Is that what you want?" Tommy asked. The gleam in the girl's eyes when she talked about Ashleigh was unsettling.

"Oh, holy cow, yes," Darcy said. "I mean, if I can, sir. If it's okay with God."

"Then that's what will happen," Tommy said.

"Oh, wow," Darcy said. "And is it okay to say 'holy cow' or is that swearing? Cause I've never been sure and I figured you would know, sir."

Tommy reached into his jacket pocket and took out a wad of tissue. He unwrapped one of Ashleigh's finger bones and handed it to Esmeralda. Esmeralda grimaced, but she curled her fingers tight around it.

"What's that?" Darcy asked.

"Are you ready, Darcy?" Tommy asked. "Are you ready to do this for God?"

"Yes, sir!"

Tommy released Darcy's hand. "Then let her do it."

Darcy turned toward Esmeralda. "You're an angel, too, ma'am? Wow, two angels!"

"Quiet," Esmeralda said. She took Darcy's hand in her own, and then closed her eyes.

Darcy closed her eyes and bowed her head, as if praying. Tommy could feel something shifting in the room, like a huge build-up of static electricity thickening the air, waiting to discharge.

Darcy shuddered. Esmeralda hissed and jerked her hand away from Darcy.

Darcy's eyes opened, and she scowled at Tommy.

"Darcy Metcalf?" Darcy's mouth asked. "Are you serious?"

"Ashleigh?" Tommy asked.

"Oh, God, look at this body." Ashleigh looked down at herself, then around at the room. "Ugh. She smells so bad. But this is actually a good place to get to work against Jenny."

"Jenny?" Tommy asked. "The girl who killed you?"

"Who the fuck else would I be talking about?" Ashleigh tried to jump to her feet, but Darcy's body was too heavy for the move. She landed clumsily and took a few steps to regain her balance, and then she farted long and loud. "And what the hell has Darcy been eating? Smells like Hamburger Helper."

"I brought you here to answer some questions," Tommy said. "Last time, you said something about past lives—"

"Yeah, whatever, we'll get to it," Ashleigh said. She turned to Esmeralda, who looked frightened. Ashleigh's voice turned sweet. "Oh, thank you so much. I'm sure Tommy's explained the whole situation to you, right?"

"Not really," Esmeralda said.

"That figures." Ashleigh took one of Esmeralda's hands, the one that wasn't holding the bone fragment. For the first time in two days, Esmeralda visibly relaxed. There was even the ghost of a smile on her lips. "You see, there's a girl in town. Jenny. And she's a murderer. She has an evil power in her touch."

"Like us?" Esmeralda asked.

"Just like us." Ashleigh brushed stray hairs back from Esmeralda's face and cupped her chin. "She killed hundreds of people, and she's going to get away with it. She'll probably kill thousands more, if we don't stop her."

"Oh," Esmeralda said. "I didn't realize it was like that."

"Yeah," Ashleigh said. "So you're being a big help. And look, I've seen you do this before, in past lives. What you need to do is keep holding onto that little piece of bone. Never let it go."

"Never?" Esmeralda looked at Ashleigh's finger bone in the palm of her hand.

"You can hang it on a necklace, under your shirt," Ashleigh said. "That helps me to stay connected to this world. You'll keep helping us, won't you?"

"I don't know…I should—"

Ashleigh squeezed her hand hard, and pressed her palm and fingers against Esmeralda's face, pushing Esmeralda's head against the wall.

"Please keep helping us!" Ashleigh's eyes were big and tearful.

"Of course! Yes!" Esmeralda said. "I don't want to hurt your feelings."

"Good." Ashleigh released her. "Now, first thing, let's get out of this dump. We're going to my house."

Ashleigh led the way to Darcy's front door.

"Whoa, whoa." Darcy's dad wheeled into the room. "Where do you think you're off to?"

"I have to help weed the flower beds at church," Ashleigh said. "Nobody else is doing it, and we can't let it look all grody."

"Who's gonna give me my insulin?" Darcy's dad demanded.

"Jeepers, I don't know," Ashleigh said. "Do it yourself." She opened the door, and Tommy and Esmeralda followed her out.

"What? What did you say to me?" Darcy'd dad wheeled after them, but Ashleigh slammed the door before he reached it.

They walked out to the driveway.

"Wow, this stupid baby is heavy." Ashleigh slapped her stomach. She looked at Tommy's bike. "Okay, genius," she said. "Three of us, one motorcycle. What were you thinking?"

"I like the bike," Tommy said.

Ashleigh rolled her eyes. "I'll go get the keys to Darcy's mom's car."

Chapter Twenty-Five

At school, Jenny and Seth sat again under the old oak by the parking lot. Seth ate a square of school pizza.

"Did you get a chance to research that stuff I told you about?" Jenny asked.

"Huh?"

"The Peloponnesian War?"

"Oh," Seth said. "Um."

"Hi," a small voice said. Jenny and Seth looked up to see Darcy Metcalf standing over them, holding her own square pizza on a Styrofoam plate. "Could I...like…sit with you guys?"

Jenny felt a little bit stunned. Nobody had ever asked her that in years, if ever.

"Sure, Darcy," Seth said. "Are you feeling okay?"

Darcy sat on a fat tree root next to Seth. "Thanks so much!" she gushed. "I hope it's okay I'm here. I didn't want to bother anybody."

"It's fine," Seth said. "Right, Jenny?"

Jenny looked at Darcy. On one hand, Darcy had always sucked up to Ashleigh and tried to be part of her group—but so had most of the kids in school, because Ashleigh had a magic touch that made people feel love. Darcy had been a committed Cool Crusader and part of all Ashleigh's groups, and Ashleigh had treated her like a servant.

On the other hand, Ashleigh was dead. Nobody was under her spell anymore.

In a lot of ways, Darcy was like Jenny. Darcy was awkward and regarded as an oddball by the other kids. Plus, Darcy didn't have any real friends, and even her fake friends weren't around anymore.

"It's okay," Jenny said. "How are you taking all this?"

“Gosh, the whole place is just bonkers now, isn't it?” Darcy took a big bite of pizza, and talked with her mouth full. “I mean, where did everybody go? Do you really think they're all dead?”

“The news said only a few people died,” Seth said.

“But so many people are missing!” Darcy said. “And I don't know what to think about Ashleigh anymore, even. Since she's gone, I feel so different. I don’t know why I tried so hard to make her like me. You know what I mean?'

“Definitely,” Seth said. Jenny nodded.

“But maybe that's good,” Darcy said. “Because I have to grow up and be a mom now.” Darcy patted her big belly. “Babies are miracles right from Jesus, aren't they?”

Jenny thought of her own mother, dying of Jenny pox as Jenny was born, and she doubted it.

“Anywho,” Darcy said, “Jenny, I've been praying a lot. And I know it's been kinda rough in school for you, with all us popular kids kinda picking on you.”

Jenny wanted to smirk at the idea that Darcy considered herself “popular.” But she just nodded instead.

“I mean, I don't know why you wear gloves.” Darcy nodded at the pink gloves on Jenny's hands. “But we're all goofballs somehow. I just want to make amends before graduation. Like, maybe we could hang out?”

Jenny automatically distrusted Darcy. Darcy had been the last person Jenny spoke to before she died. Darcy had seen her drown, like all the other pregnant girls. But she was acting like that had never happened. Which was perfectly fine with Jenny.

Though Darcy had gotten sucked into Ashleigh’s spell, Darcy herself had always seemed like a nice, earnest person on the inside, trying to do the right things, but also desperate to be accepted. She was probably just lonely.

“Okay,” Jenny said.

“Cool beans!” Darcy said. “So do you want to hang out after school today?”

“I don't know,” Jenny said. “I've got some chores at home.”

“I'll help!” Darcy said.

“You don't have to.”

“Come on, Jenny. I really want to make things up with you. I really think it's what God wants me to do.”

“Well...” Jenny thought it over. She'd never really had a friend, until she met Seth. She would have to be careful to avoid any skin-on-skin contact with Darcy, but she had a lifetime of practice avoiding contact with people. “I mean, if you really want to...it's cool with me.”

“Yay!” Darcy pounded her sneakers up and down in the dirt, as if she couldn't contain her excitement. “This is gonna be so rad!”

Jenny looked at Seth. He gave a slightly amused smile, but he didn't look worried.

Jenny tried not to worry, either.

At Jenny's house, Darcy really dived into the chores with enthusiasm, gabbing away while she helped Jenny straighten up, do the dishes, sweep and mop the floors. Her main topic was memories from church camp, but she avoided mentioning Ashleigh, as if aware that this might annoy or upset Jenny.

Jenny tried to make her stop working—she hadn’t really intended to have Darcy do housework. Jenny hadn’t even really planned on doing any, it had just been an excuse to try and avoid being social.

Darcy insisted on cleaning Jenny’s house for her, though. “That’s what friends do,” Darcy had explained.

Jenny carried a bag of dog food out back to feed Rocky. Darcy trailed behind her, talking about the time she'd come to pick the tuba over the trombone when she joined the school band.

Rocky stepped out of the shed, tail wagging. The moment he saw Darcy, he began to bark.

“Rocky!” Jenny said. “Relax.”

But the dog grew more agitated, jumping and barking.

“Is he gonna chomp me?” Darcy said.

“No, he's okay,” Jenny said. “He just don't like strangers. Rocky! Quit barking!”

As they approached, Rocky darted off into the woods. He let out a long, low bay, as if he were frightened or hurt. Or had trapped a raccoon in a tree.

“I don't think he likes me,” Darcy said.

"He's just shy." Jenny poured the food and filled his water dish from the garden hose. "I guess that's all my chores. Thanks for helping."

"No prob." Darcy winked.

"What should we do now?"

"I dunno. What do you usually do for fun?"

"I kind of do this pottery thing." Jenny led her inside, to the dining room, where Jenny's old potting wheel was waiting. She showed Darcy the assortment of flowerpots she'd made, plus her attempts at sculpture, like a statue that was supposed to be Rocky but looked more like a mutant cow.

"Coolsville!" Darcy said. "I didn't know you did stuff like this."

"It's just a hobby," Jenny told her. "Ms. Sutland used to sell them at the Five and Dime, but that's closed now."

"Oh, the Five and Dime closed?" Darcy said. "I didn't know that. What a bummerino, huh?"

"It feels like the town's falling apart."

"Good thing we're outta here, right?"

"What do you mean?" Jenny asked.

"You know, college. Aren't you going?"

"No," Jenny said. "Seth is, though."

"Where?"

"College of Charleston."

Darcy snickered.

"What?" Jenny asked.

"Oh...nothing," Darcy said. "It's just, well...um, that's where I'm going!"

"Really? Charleston?"

"I wanted to go to Duke, but I blew my GPA." She tapped her big stomach. "Hooked up with Bret instead. And now he's not even around anymore. God's punishing me for everything I did." Darcy looked like she was about to cry.

Jenny reached out with a gloved hand and gave her an awkward pat on the arm. Darcy gasped and pulled away from her.

"Are you okay?" Jenny asked.

"Oh..." Darcy looked down at the place where Jenny had touched her arm. "Yes. I guess I'm fine. I guess I wasn't expecting that."

"You just seemed upset." Jenny felt weird for trying to touch her.

"Yeah, I know. Sorry."

“Who wants cheese sandwiches?” Jenny's dad asked as he walked in the front door, carrying two Piggy Wiggly bags. He paused when he saw Darcy. “Oh, I didn't know you had company, Jenny.”

“This is Darcy Metcalf, Dad,” Jenny said.

“It's very nice to meet you, Mr. Morton.” Darcy shook his hand, and Jenny's dad smiled.

“You too, Darcy,” he said. “Want a cheese sandwich? I got some good hoop cheddar at the Piggly Wiggly. On sale, too.”

“Oh. Actually, I need to get going,” Darcy said. “My mom'll have an orangutan if I'm not home by sunset. Thanks, anyway!”

“I'll give you a ride.” Jenny picked up her car keys and Darcy headed out the door.

“Y'all gonna miss some good cheese sandwiches.” Jenny’s dad laid the bags on the counter and began unpacking them. “Got Miracle Whip, too.”

“I'll have one later, Dad.”

He watched through the front window as Darcy got into the car. “That Darcy seems like a real nice girl.”

“She does seem nice.”

“It's good to see you having friends, Jenny.”

Jenny's eyes stung a little at his comment. Jenny rubbed them with the back of her glove before she went outside to take Darcy home.

Chapter Twenty-Six

That night, Ashleigh searched Darcy's room. She knew Darcy kept a diary, and Ashleigh wanted to read it. She needed to piece together what had been happening in Fallen Oak since she died.

While she was dead, Ashleigh had quickly found her way to her opposite, Tommy, and devoted all her energy and attention to haunting him and trying to get him to do what she wanted. That had probably only worked because he was so deeply connected to her.

When she wasn't incarnated, Ashleigh had all her memories of all her lifetimes, but no power to be seen or heard or influence the world. When she was incarnated, she was usually focused on that single lifetime, usually with no clue about her past lives or what she really was.

Now, possessing Darcy's body, she had a weird mix of both. Her power seemed intact, if her effect on Esmeralda and Jenny's dad were any indication. At the same time, she had a huge store of past-life memories—jumbled together, not linear or organized at all, but they were there. The past-life memories gave her insight into her past relationships, and into her own power, and into the powers wielded by Esmeralda and Tommy.

And the horrific power wielded by Jenny.

Ashleigh found the diary under Darcy's bed, a pink journal decorated with kitten and puppy cartoons. It was full of Darcy's bulging handwriting.

She began to read. Darcy had seen Jenny stagger into the pond at Ashleigh's house. She'd been shocked to see Jenny alive and well at school.

From her past lives, Ashleigh knew what that was about. Seth, if he was really determined to come back, could sometimes heal his own dead body and return to life—if he was fast enough. And he'd healed Jenny's body, too, to restore her to life.

Opposites, when close to each other, had the effect of amplifying each other's power. That was why Seth had been able to come back, and why Jenny had been able to unleash hell on Fallen Oak.

There were other issues, too—something called "cross" powers, and "complementary" powers, a whole tangle of information that was jumbled inside Ashleigh's head. She would have to think long and deep to figure it out, if she needed to.

The main thing, though, was finding your opposite. Your opposite could be a powerful ally, or a dangerous enemy.

Ashleigh read on. Darcy described a conversation with a CDC doctor, to whom Darcy had tried to explain about Jenny.

The squeaky sound of Darcy's dad's wheelchair approached. After only a day of pretending to be Darcy, she had already learned to hate that sound.

Darcy's father arrived at the open door to the bedroom. She had to keep it open all the time, or Darcy's parents would knock and demand that she open it. The Metcalf household was a semi-fascist state.

"Darcy!" he shouted. It seemed easier for him to shout than to talk normally.

"Hi, Dad."

"Your cousin Heywood just got promoted to assistant manager," he said. "Over at the Taco Bell in Vernon Hill."

"That's...great." Ashleigh wasn't sure if she was supposed to be excited. Maybe this represented a huge step forward in life for Cousin Heywood.

"He says he can get you a job," Darcy's dad continued. "You got to start working nights at the drive-through, and then work your way up. I bet you could make assistant manager in a couple years."

"Um...can't it wait until after graduation?" Ashleigh asked.

"Jobs don't wait, Darcy!" he shouted.

"But I have finals coming up. I need to study."

"I don't see why. You ain't going to college no more. You got to earn some money and take care of that baby."

Ashleigh thought it over. She had no intention of working at Taco Bell, or anywhere else. That was Darcy's problem, not hers. Just like Darcy's pregnancy. Darcy's mother insisted she take prenatal vitamins, but Ashleigh secretly spat them out, because they made her feel sick.

"If I graduate with good grades," Ashleigh said, "Maybe I can go to college later, when the baby's older—"

"Yeah," Darcy's dad snorted. "And maybe Santa Claus gonna come down on a flying carpet and make you shit diamonds and gold."

"Okay." Ashleigh heard the wonderful sound of her beloved caramel Jeep rolling into the driveway. She dropped Darcy's diary into Darcy's big canvas purse to take with her. "Well, I gotta go."

"Where you goin'?" he shouted as Ashleigh squeezed past him.

"Out!" Ashleigh hurried to the front door.

Outside, she climbed into the passenger seat of her Jeep. Tommy was driving, and Ashleigh gave him her biggest smile. He was nearly immune to the enchantment of her touch, but he mostly did what she wanted, anyway. They'd been married several times, in other lifetimes. Ashleigh had murdered him several times, too, but happily, he didn't remember any of it.

He was cute in this lifetime. She especially liked his eyes.

"Hi!" Ashleigh said. "Let's get the fuck out of here. I've always hated Darcy's family."

"You got it." He stomped the accelerator and peeled out as he left the driveway, leaving smoking rubber tire tracks behind him.

Darcy's father glared at them through the screen door as they roared away.

"Where's our pet necromancer?" Ashleigh asked him.

"She's watching TV back at your house."

"Damn it, Tommy, you can't let her out of your sight like that. If she gets control of herself, she can knock me out of Darcy's body anytime she likes. And if she runs off—"

"She's not running off," Tommy said. "She likes me."

"Don't get cocky. I hope you dosed her up with fear before you left."

"I did!"

"Good," Ashleigh said. "We'll make her fear you and love me. Between those, she'll be way too confused to try anything."

"Sounds like a plan."

"It's not a plan, it's common sense."

"So," Tommy said. "While we're alone, I wanted to ask you about our past lives—"

"Not right now, Tommy," Ashleigh said. "I've got a headache, a backache, a footache...Darcy's body sucks."

"But I was wondering—"

"Just get me the fuck home."

At Ashleigh's house, Esmeralda was on the couch, watching a movie on the big plasma screen, and she jumped up when they arrived.

"There's nothing to eat here!" Esmeralda complained. "I'm so hungry."

"There's stuff in the fridge," Ashleigh said.

"It's all spoiled," Esmeralda replied.

"Whatever." Ashleigh opened the fridge.

The smell hit her like a mule kick to the gut. Mold was growing on everything, and the milk jug had expanded until it was almost ball-shaped.

Ashleigh covered her mouth, but she puked through her fingers. She ran to the kitchen sink and puked her guts out into it. There were strange, rotten smells from the sink, too, which just made her vomit more.

"God, that's horrible," Ashleigh said.

"I told you." Esmeralda had a little smirk on her face.

Ashleigh grabbed Esmeralda's arm with one barf-splattered hand. Esmeralda scowled and tried to pull away, but Ashleigh clamped tight, smearing vomit across the girl's bicep.

You'll like it, bitch, Ashleigh thought. She hit her with a golden wave of love.

Out loud, Ashleigh said, "Oh, this pregnancy is really hitting me hard."

Esmeralda's face softened. "I forgot you were pregnant."

"Yeah, it's so hard to do anything," Ashleigh said. "You don't mind cleaning all that puke up, do you? I'd do it myself, but it's so hard. With the pregnancy."

"Oh, sure!" Esmeralda said.

"In fact, you don't mind cleaning the whole kitchen, do you?" Ashleigh asked. "It would be such a help."

"Yeah, that's fine."

"And take out the trash when you're done, so it doesn't reek?"

"Whatever you need." Esmeralda smiled. "I helped my cousin Lucia when she was pregnant."

"Good! I could really use your experience and help." Ashleigh injected her with another dose of love and then released her. Esmeralda immediately dug out cleaning supplies from under the sink and went to work.

"Tommy." Ashleigh gave him her sweetest smile. "Can you go to the Piggly Wiggly for us? I'll make a list."

Tommy shrugged.

When she'd sent him on his way, Ashleigh went up to her own room. It was very spacious, with floor-to-ceiling windows, a walk-in closet, and a private bathroom. It was, in fact, the master bedroom of the house. Years ago, Ashleigh had persuaded Dr. and Mrs. Goodling that she should have it, while they moved into a smaller room.

Past-due notices had arrived for all the utility bills, so Ashleigh found one of Dr. Goodling's credit cards and went online to pay them, to keep the house running. Apparently the credit card company didn't yet know that Maurice Goodling was dead, with no living heirs, because the charges were accepted.

In her desk, Ashleigh had a PayPal debit card. This was linked to the account where people all over the country had made donations to "Ashleigh's Girls," after Ashleigh's appearance on Chuck O'Flannery and other national media. The account held over two hundred thousand dollars, last time she'd checked, and maybe more donations were still trickling in through the website. She wouldn't use that money unless she had to—better to clean out her father's bank account and max out his credit cards first.

Ashleigh sat on her bed and opened Darcy's diary, ready to learn more about how the town had been quarantined and investigated. A small white card fluttered out from the back of the journal. It must have been tucked between the last page and the back cover.

Ashleigh picked it up.

HEATHER REYNARD, M.D., it read. OFFICE OF SURVEILLANCE, EPIDEMIOLOGY, AND LABORATORY SERVICES. CENTERS FOR DISEASE CONTROL. ATLANTA, GA.

"Interesting," Ashleigh said. She continued reading the diary.

Chapter Twenty-Seven

Friday evening, Jenny waited at home, feeling anxious. She played an old Jean Shepard record to soothe her nerves, but she had to play it low because her dad had gone to bed early. The bank manager had hired him to fix up some foreclosed properties around Fallen Oak, and he came home exhausted every day.

When it reached seven o' clock, Jenny drove her old car across town to pick up Darcy. Darcy didn't live in one of Fallen Oak's nicer neighborhoods, but it was an actual neighborhood. Jenny's house was a little way out of town, basically in the woods, and Jenny didn't have any neighbors close by.

Darcy stood at the end of her driveway with a huge canvas purse slung over her shoulder. She opened Jenny's passenger door and jumped inside.

"Let's scoot fast," Darcy said. "My dad's being a total tool biscuit."

"Okay." Jenny pulled out of her driveway.

"Cool car!" Darcy said.

"Thanks."

"It's kinda old, isn't it?" Darcy asked. "But I mean in a good way."

"Yeah, I like it," Jenny said. "Seth bought it for me for Christmas. From Merle Sanderson."

"He bought you a fucking *car*?" Darcy scowled for a second, then quickly went back to her smile.

"I don't think it was very expensive," Jenny said. "It clunks a lot. Not really that great of a car."

"Yeah, I guess I'm just jealous because I don't have one," Darcy said. Her tone attempted to be pleasant, but Jenny thought she could detect something nasty underneath. "I mean, a car or a boyfriend. I've never even had a boyfriend. Just that one time with Bret Daniels, when we sinned really bad. I mean, he sinned my brains out. But he never acted like he cared about me after that."

"I'm sorry."

"That's how boys are, I guess. They act like they love you, but then they don't really care at all."

"They aren't all like that," Jenny said.

"But I think they are," Darcy said. "I bet even Seth might leave you. They really are jerks underneath."

"I don't think so," Jenny said. "We're pretty happy."

"I mean, I saw how he just dropped Ashleigh all of a sudden, and she cried so much after that."

Jenny found it hard to imagine Ashleigh Goodling in tears, unless it was to manipulate somebody into doing something for her. "Seth's been really nice to me," she said.

"Oh, I don't mean to say anything bad about him," Darcy said. "Just guys in general."

Jenny glanced at Darcy's pregnant belly and decided not to argue. Darcy had her own bad experience to cope with. A huge, life-changing bad experience.

"Anywho," Darcy said. "You like *Chronicles of Narnia*, right? 'Cause I brought the DVD's."

"Sure," Jenny said. She'd never seen it, nor had a strong desire to, but she was trying to make friends.

"I also brought the *Lord of the Rings* trilogy if you want to watch that." Darcy grinned. "We can do a movie marathon!"

"Okay," Jenny said.

They stopped by the Little Caesar's, located in a half-empty strip mall on the edge of town, and got a pair of pizzas for dinner, plus a two-liter of Coke. At Jenny's house, they set up camp on the living room couch.

They played the movie on the cheap DVD player Jenny had bought with her own money, since her dad thought there was no point moving on from VHS, even though DVD players were only like twenty bucks now. They had to keep the volume low because of Jenny's dad sleeping at the back of the house.

"We should have gone to Seth's house," Jenny whispered as *Chronicles of Narnia* began. "But his parents are in town."

"His parents don't like you?" Darcy asked.

"Pretty much. They think I'm a dope fiend who corrupts their perfect son. They don't even know we're together."

"Oh, that won't work," Darcy said. She bit into a pepperoni-topped square of pizza.

"Hopefully they'll get over it."

"I doubt it. People like that—rich people, you know?—they only like their own kind. They can tell we don't belong with them."

"They just never gave me a chance. But they *loved* Ashleigh."

Darcy smiled, then quickly pushed it to a frown. "That's what I mean. The Goodlings had more money. I mean how's it going to work when he goes to college, anyway?"

"I don't know," Jenny said. "I don't really want to move to Charleston. I just don't like big cities. The idea of leaving town scares me. And my dad needs my help around here." Jenny had the odd feeling that a weight was lifting from her shoulders, one she hadn't even noticed. She never got to talk about her relationship with Seth, or anything girls might talk about. Just sharing her fears made her feel better.

She was almost tempted to tell Darcy everything—about the Jenny pox, and why Jenny couldn't live anywhere with a lot of people—but she swallowed back that urge. As much as she needed to talk about it, it was much too dangerous to tell anyone.

"Did you tell Seth you don't want to move to Charleston?" Darcy asked.

"We've talked about it," Jenny said. "He just acts like I'll get over it and move there with him. But big cities make me panic."

"What does he say about that?" Darcy reached for the two-liter and refilled her own cup. "Want more Coke?"

"Sure, thanks," Jenny said. "The thing is that Seth used to want to go to Clemson, where his grandfather went. And that would be totally fine, because it's *tiny* and it's in the middle of nowhere. I could cope with that. But his parents are really the ones who want him to go to Charleston, because his dad donated a bunch of money there, I think. And they say he'll make more 'connections' in the city."

"Meaning other rich kids," Darcy said. "People his parents will like."

"I guess."

"But then that means…huh." Darcy chewed on her lip and turned toward the TV.

"What?" Jenny asked.

"I kinda don't want to say. Let's skip it."

"It's okay. What are you thinking?"

"Well, you know," Darcy said. "If he always ends up doing what his parents want, and his parents don't want you together…"

Jenny thought about it. Seth's dad did seem to have a lot of control over Seth's choices. Seth and Jenny had been together for almost five months now, and he'd kept it secret from them. He'd even changed his mind about colleges when his dad told him to.

"I don't think…" Jenny began, but she couldn't finish the thought. Darcy might actually have a point.

"Plus all those other girls he'll meet," Darcy said. "I mean, tons of pretty girls, from richer families that his parents will like. You know?"

"Yeah, but…" Jenny knew she was right. Seth wasn't just cute and nice, and even funny when you didn't expect it. He also had his healing touch, the one that made everyone feel better when he touched them, erasing anything from a cold to cancer.

"The girls will be all over him, too," Darcy said. "And I mean there's gonna be thousands of them. Not like here."

"But Seth can't leave me. He's the only one—" Jenny cut herself off. She had almost said, *he's the only one I can touch.* She began to feel panicky. There wouldn't be any other relationship options for her, but he could have any girl pretty easily. It hit her just how vulnerable and powerless she was in their relationship. He was really holding all the cards.

Her eyes stung, and she fought back tears. She didn't want to think about losing Seth.

"Oh, crapsies," Darcy said. "I'm such a dodo. I didn't mean to make you feel bad. I was just thinking about how guys are."

"No," Jenny said. "It's okay. You're right. I need to figure out what I'm going to do. I just wish he wasn't moving to such a big city."

"Here, let's do a toast." Darcy raised her glass, which featured Joanie from *Happy Days*. Jenny's mom had bought the whole set of commemorative *Happy Days* glasses at the flea market, not long before she died. "To guys. And how much they suck."

Jenny laughed and raised her matching Richie Cunningham glass. The two girls clinked their glasses together, and they drank.

Chapter Twenty-Eight

Tommy stood in the giant kitchen at Ashleigh's house, making preparations for a huge pot of chili. Esmeralda was shouting in Spanish over in the living room. She'd been on her cell phone for twenty minutes.

"My mother is giving me so much shit," Esmeralda told him when she returned to the kitchen. "I told her I needed a break and I went to Mexico. Are you actually cooking?" She looked at the pinto beans, the beef he was browning in the skillet.

"One of my specialties." He touched a small bowl holding chopped jalapeno and habanero peppers. "Think you can handle these?"

"Oh, please. You should try my mother's cooking." Esmeralda unscrewed the small glass jar of habanero peppers. She lifted one out by the stem.

"Careful," Tommy said. "Those can burn you. You don't want to get the juice in your eye."

"You think you are so tough." Esmeralda lifted out a second hot pepper and offered it to him. "I bet you won't eat this."

Tommy took it by the stem and looked at it. "That's a lot to eat all at once."

"Maybe for you." Esmeralda put the entire pepper in her mouth and bit it off at the stem. She gave him a closed-mouth smile as she chewed.

"Okay," Tommy said. He put the habanero in his mouth and chewed.

Fire spread across his tongue, up to his nose and down his throat. The pain filled his head, burning his nostrils, and he wanted to run to the sink and guzzle ten gallons of water. He didn't let her see any of this, though. He held it in and smiled back, though he was pretty sure his face was a scalding shade of crimson. If not purple.

"Very impressive," Esmeralda said. "I almost believe you aren't in agony right now."

"It's just a pepper."

She moved closer to him. "How long do we have to stay with Ashleigh?"

"She says we have to stop Jenny before she kills more people."

"And what happens after that? Can we leave?"

"You don't like Ashleigh?"

"She's actually not so bad," Esmeralda said. "I like her more as I spend time with her. But then, when I'm alone with you, I remember why I really came."

"And I'm glad you did." He slid an arm around her, avoiding the band of exposed brown skin between the hem of her short shirt and her low-slung jeans. She was dressing in Ashleigh's old clothes.

"I know you use your power against me sometimes," Esmeralda said. "But you don't have to."

"I can't turn it off," he said. "I don't have a choice."

"I want to be with you," she said. "I hate my life. My job is nice, but my mother…and Pedro…" She rolled her eyes. "I don't stay with you because you make me. I stay because I want to."

"You do?"

"Yes." She opened her beaded patchwork purse, which was hung over a kitchen chair. She rummaged inside it, then handed him a gold coin. "Do you remember this?"

Tommy looked at it. The head of an Indian chief, complete with headdress, was engraved on one side, an eagle on the other.

"I gave this to you," he said. "I'm surprised you haven't sold it."

"It makes me think of you," she said.

He looked at her. His heart skipped in his chest, the way it had when they were kids. She was looking up at him with beautiful brown eyes, her hand floating close to his waist.

"You really do remember me," he whispered.

"I never told about the money," Esmeralda said. "Even my mother. I told her I lost my power. It freed me from that horrible work."

"You are sneaky." He reached a hand toward her bare waist, but he didn't want to touch her and fill her up with fear. He felt extremely frustrated.

"It is okay." Esmeralda pressed his hand to the hot skin of her stomach. She shivered, and she sucked in a gasp of air through her teeth, but she kept his hand there.

"I fill people with fear," Tommy said. "Whenever I touch them. I've shattered people's minds, once or twice. And I didn't even mean to."

"I know," she said. "I can feel it. But I…kind of like it." She closed her eyes. "It makes me feel so *alive*."

Tommy leaned down and kissed her. She tensed, then pushed her face against his. She shuddered as their tongues touched each other. She tasted like the habanero pepper, and her kiss burned his lips and tongue.

Tommy pulled her close and held her tight against him, and she kissed him harder. She slid both her hands to the back of his head and curled his dark hair in her fingers.

He realized he was going to take her right here, in the kitchen, against the counter, and he'd never wanted anything more in his life.

A high-pitched scream pierced his eardrum. The smoke detector, bleating its warning.

Tommy opened his eyes. Lost in each other's lips and hands, they hadn't noticed the ground beef turn to a charred black pile in the skillet, or the kitchen fill up with smoke around them.

"Fuck!" Tommy pushed the skillet onto a cold burner, then ran to the wall, jumped up, and slapped the smoke detector, which was mounted on the wall near the high ceiling. It gave a short beep as a parting shot, and then it shut up.

Esmeralda looked at the thoroughly burned meat. She smiled at him through the smoky air.

"This is your specialty cooking?" she asked.

"I got a little distracted."

Esmeralda took another habanero from the jar. "Looks like it's vegetarian chili tonight."

Jenny woke to the sound of Darcy whispering.

"Huh?" Jenny said. She forced her heavy eyelids to open.

Darcy stood in the doorway of Jenny's bedroom in the early morning light. Her purse was slung over her shoulder.

"Jenny," Darcy whispered again. "I have to go home. My dad said I have to be home early or I'm in deep doo-doo."

"Christ," Jenny sighed. She looked at the clock. It was 6:34 a.m. on a Saturday.

"Don't take the Lord's name," Darcy whispered.

Jenny stretched her arms. Darcy had said she didn't like sleeping with other people, due to a certain cousin named Heywood who used to share her bed when he visited and always peed in his sleep. That was perfect for Jenny. She'd given Darcy blankets and pillows to use on the couch.

"Let me get my car keys." Jenny yawned.

"Oh, no, that's okay," Darcy said. "It's only a mile or so if you go through the woods. And I feel like hiking in the woods for a while."

"Okay." Jenny knew what Darcy meant—there was nothing better than the solitude of those woods, away from everybody. She sat up.

"It's cool, you don't have to get up," Darcy whispered. "I was just letting you know so you didn't think I was a disappearing spaz or something. I left you *The Return of the King*, cause you don't want to miss that one when you just saw the other two! No, seriously, don't even get out of bed. I insist."

"All right." Jenny rubbed her eyes, feeling disoriented. She'd been lost in a terrible dream, one where all the people she'd killed were back for revenge, chasing her through a dark tunnel somewhere. "Um, see ya, Darcy. Thanks for coming over."

"Thanks for inviting me," Darcy said, though it had really been her idea. "God bless!"

When Darcy left, Jenny dropped back into bed and pulled the covers over her face to block the daylight. It was way too early.

Ashleigh clomped through the woods, cursing Darcy's hefty body at every thudding step along the way. She felt like an elephant lumbering through the jungle. An elephant with an aching back.

She wasn't really going back to Darcy Metcalf's house—she intended to avoid that place as much as she could, without blowing her cover. So far, nobody seemed to have noticed the renewed activity at the Goodling house, which was tucked at the back of a cul-de-sac. The house to their left had never sold, and the one on their right had been foreclosed on and lay empty. The only other house on the cul-de-sac had belonged to Dick Baker, the realtor/lawyer whose face was all over town, and who had been put to a miserable death the night Jenny Mittens went psycho.

She arrived at her house red-faced and puffing for air, her socks squishy with sweat inside her tennis shoes. She trudged up the front steps, staggered inside, and locked the door behind her.

Exhausted, she crawled upstairs on her hands and knees. She felt the baby flip around inside her.

"Fuck you, baby," she whispered.

She glanced into the guest room, where Esmeralda was staying, and a snarl came to her lips.

Esmeralda sure hadn't run off. She lay in her bed, still deep asleep. Tommy lay beside her, one arm over her hips.

It looked like they'd done it. Tommy was wearing only his boxers, and Esmeralda wore Ashleigh's favorite flannel pajama bottoms, which were polka-dotted with the Superman logo. They were too small for Ashleigh, now that she was stuck in Darcy's fat, pregnant body.

Esmeralda wore a simple, thin gold chain they'd found in Ashleigh's mother's jewelry box. Tommy had taken one of the Ashleigh's finger bones to the garage and drilled a hole in it, and now it hung around Esmeralda's neck, on her chest between her bare tits.

Ashleigh looked up and down Esmeralda's gorgeous dark body, and she felt a sharp sting of jealousy. Tommy was falling for her. But Tommy was Ashleigh's opposite, her property.

And Esmeralda was Ashleigh's doorway to the physical world. She had the power to kick Ashleigh right out of Darcy's body at any moment, and then Ashleigh wouldn't be able to do anything except try to get born again as an infant somewhere. Ashleigh would forget everything again, like she did each time she was born, and Jenny would have a long, peaceful, and possibly happy life.

But Jenny had killed Ashleigh, and Ashleigh wasn't going to let her get away with that.

Besides, Jenny would be watching for Ashleigh now. She might track Ashleigh down when Ashleigh was still a small child and kill her all over again. Jenny had done that before, in India, maybe two thousand years ago.

Now, Ashleigh had to worry about Tommy and Esmeralda getting too close. A bond between them could lead, in time, to an alliance against Ashleigh. She needed their primary loyalties to her, not to each other. She would get to work on that, too.

Ashleigh went to the computer in her room and hopped on the Internet to gather up some information.

It was time to build a Jenny trap.

Chapter Twenty-Nine

The same Saturday, Seth sat in a leather armchair in the library at his house, studying for his chemistry final. This basically meant trying to memorize some formulas and getting a reasonably good idea of where to plug them in, once you puzzled out the word problems. Hopefully, the information would stick for at least the next forty-eight hours.

He heard his dad approach and he looked up. Seth thought his dad looked unusually old today, a little more stooped, a little more gray in his hair.

“Seth,” he said. He raised his whiskey glass, and the single large ice cube clinked against the side as he drank.

“What’s up, Dad? How’s it going with the dye factory thing?”

“Not bad, really. The government paid the bank a ridiculous compensation for use of the old factory. They said we didn’t have to worry about EPA or anybody. Our insurers wanted to investigate the dye factory themselves, and the government even paid them to shut up and go away.”

“Well, that’s great!” Seth said. It meant Jenny was in the clear, he thought, if the government was burying the incident.

His dad looked at him, maybe a bit surprised by the excitement in Seth’s voice.

“I mean, right?” Seth asked. “Isn’t that what you wanted?”

“Hell of a lot better than I expected,” he said. “Almost scary how well it’s going now. Although they’re full of horseshit. That dye factory’s been emptier than a politician’s heart as long as I can remember.”

“Well, if they want it to go away, and we want it go away…” Seth said.

“No, no, I’m satisfied. I could go for a walk. You want to go for a walk?”

“I have finals tomorrow.”

“Just take a minute.”

Seth didn’t like the sound of it. His dad was clearly in one of his melancholy, semi-drunken moods.

He followed his dad across the back lawn, through the blooming peach orchard where bees hummed their way from one sweet nectar snack to the next.

Seth’s dad kept walking, on and up the far slope. He was heading right for the family cemetery, up the staircase of big granite slabs, toward the wrought-iron gate in the old brick wall.

Seth trailed behind. The family cemetery was mostly the sign of his great-grandfather’s insanity, his master plan for his descendants. Like how the third floor of his house was a sign of Seth’s grandfather’s insanity. There was plenty of crazy to go around in this family.

Seth’s dad took out a key ring and unlocked the iron gate.

“Ted Burris at the bank says he’s seen you driving around town.” He pushed open the gate. “Says you have Jenny Morton in your car.”

Seth sighed.

“You still dating her?” Seth’s dad stepped inside the high brick walls of the cemetery. Inside, rows of identical monuments marked the burial sites of Barretts past and future. His dad walked past the blank monuments of generations to come, back to where his grave and Seth’s had already been carved—Jonathan Seth Barretts III and IV, their birthdays already inscribed, years of death to be added as needed.

“This isn’t going to be that conversation about Jenny again, is it?” Seth asked. “And how much you hate her?”

“I don’t hate her. And this is not that conversation. I only have one thing to say about her: Use protection. Get her pregnant and you’ll never really shake her loose.”

“Dad!”

“I’m not kidding. You have your fun with the town girls if you want, just be careful. You’ll grow out of her once you meet some decent girls at school.”

“Whatever,” Seth said. “I really care about her. I don’t want to meet anyone else.”

“You’re young,” his dad said, in a dismissive tone.

They walked all the way to the back of the cemetery, to the megalith commemorating the first Jonathan S. Barrett. Seth's great-grandfather had made the family extremely wealthy, but he'd been obsessed with death. He'd built this miniature necropolis and even disinterred his own ancestors to move their bodies here.

"I never told you the most important thing about your great-grandfather," Seth's dad said. "I never talked about it at all, even with my own father. He knew it, though, you can bet on that."

"Knew what?" Seth asked.

"There's a reason your grandfather believed that your great-grandfather's ghost would haunt the family."

"Didn't Great-Grandpa threaten to do that?"

"That's true. J.S. Barrett the First lived to be almost ninety, and he got meaner and crueler every year. He died before I was ten years old, but I can remember his screaming and his horrible laugh, and how he would threaten my father with every kind of thing. The monster on the third floor, that's how I thought of him. He was shriveled and half-senile by then, or at least he acted that way. He had the coldest, darkest eyes, and you could feel him studying you…." Seth's dad shuddered. "Those eyes were as dark as hell."

"I know," Seth said. "I kind of got he was terrible."

"He was more than that," Seth's dad said. "He was terrifying. When I was six years old, he insisted on taking me out to one of his farms, even though my father tried to stop him. We had a huge amount of land back then, I don't know how many hundreds of thousands of acres. But a lot of it was a good distance from town, a good distance from anybody.

"He took me out there in his big black Cadillac. He must have been more than eighty years old, but nobody would even think about saying he was too old to drive. Nobody forbid Grandfather anything he wanted. We were all scared of him. And I'm about to tell you why.

"He drove down one dirt road after another, far away from any town. And he drove out into a field, where there must have been thousands of rows of tobacco, and he told me, 'Look, boy. That's how you keep your margins high on a plantation.'"

Seth's dad eased down onto granite bench and finished his drink.

"What was he showing you?" Seth asked.

"The workers. I saw them out there, slowly harvesting the tobacco leaves into baskets." He shook his head. "It's the most goddamned horrible thing I've ever seen in my life."

"Were they slaves?" Seth asked.

His dad sighed. "No, Seth, we didn't have slaves in 1966."

"Oh, yeah. Sorry."

"They were…" He shook his head. "They were dead, Seth."

Seth looked at him, expecting more.

"They were *dead*," his dad repeated.

"Who was dead?"

"The workers in the fields. I mean they were corpses. Rotting. Missing skin. Some of them, you could see through to their skulls, bones, the daylight on the other side. Pieces of them were falling off while they picked that tobacco."

"How much have you had to drink, Dad?"

"I'm not making this up." He scowled at Seth. "He could animate dead bodies. Make them do simple, repetitive tasks. They were sluggish and they fell apart after a while, but they were free. And you can always find more dead people."

"Okay," Seth said. "It sounds like you're seriously telling me Great-Grandpa was a…what? A zombie master? Like *Evil Dead* zombies?"

"My father thought he sold his soul to the Devil, to get rich," Seth's dad said. "Because that's how he made his money first, farming all that land with free labor. Then he started investing in Charleston, and then New York…"

"The devil," Seth said.

"Look." His dad sighed again, looking down at the dirt. "This thing happened. It happened for decades, and they kept working right up until he died. Then they all fell over and stopped working. My father had to fill pits with lime to get rid of all the bodies."

Seth just looked at his dad. He had no idea what to say, or even what to think.

"So that's where the Barretts come from," his dad said. "Black magic and pacts with Satan. So when I say your great-grandfather told us his ghost would watch over and rule this family from the other side…"

"Kind of sounds more believable now," Seth said.

"I tried not to believe it," his dad said. "But I just can't forget how it looked, all those poor bastards out there working day and night until they fell to pieces. When the wind blew through them, they would make this sound…this awful groaning sound, like they were in agony, and just wanted to be dead again—"

"Okay! I get it."

"And then there was your brother." He nodded to the marker inscribed CARTER MAYFIELD BARRETT, 1986-2000. Seth's brother had died when Seth was ten, and Carter was fourteen. "Your great-grandfather insisted that the firstborn son in every generation continue his name. But he'd been dead for more than fifteen years. And your other grandfather, Carter Mayfield, we needed his influence right about then to pull some strings in Washington, protect a major overseas investment of ours."

"What do you mean?"

"Better you don't know. Old Carter was adamant that our boy be named after him. So I ignored what your great-grandfather said. And Carter paid for it."

"You don't really think Great-Grandpa's ghost killed Carter?"

"In his will, he threatened horrors against the living if he wasn't obeyed. You can read it yourself."

"That's crazy," Seth said. "But Carter…that could have been a regular accident. People die in car accidents every day."

"We were being punished."

"How can you believe that?"

"Seth, you've never seen a hundred and fifty corpses working a tobacco field. Death was nothing to him. He had powers over death."

Seth thought about how Ashleigh had blasted him through the heart with a shotgun. He'd managed to heal his own body, but he couldn't remember much about how. He could only remember a powerful determination to get back to Jenny.

"So do I," Seth muttered.

"What?" His dad looked up at him sharply.

"Nothing."

"So that's why your grandfather wasn't crazy when he turned the third floor into a maze to confuse your great-grandfather's ghost. Your great-grandfather really was supernatural. And that is why we must maintain things as he wishes. Because he's watching. And he's ruthless."

Seth looked at Jonathan Seth Barrett's granite monolith. "Wow. Thanks a lot, Great-Grandpa."

"Don't mock him."

"He doesn't have a sense of humor?"

"No."

Though it was a hot day, almost June, Seth felt very cold. He didn't want to believe anything his dad had said. But he couldn't deny there were supernatural things in the world. Seth was one of them. So was Jenny.

For a moment, he thought about telling his dad everything—about his own healing abilities, and Jenny's deadly touch. But he didn't know whether that would encourage his dad to approve of the relationship, or if his dad would solidly forbid him to ever see Jenny again.

So he kept his mouth shut.

"Can we go back now?" Seth asked.

"We can try."

Chapter Thirty

Ashleigh made a dozen scrambled eggs and six pieces of French toast, which she dusted generously with powdered sugar, then drizzled with some raw honey. She made coffee and filled a silver pitcher with cream. She poured tall cups of orange juice.

She played Jason Aldean on the stereo, and she gradually turned up the volume with short blasts of the remote while she set the kitchen table. She opened the big kitchen windows to let in the sunlight and the warm spring air. Then she turned up her stereo a bit louder.

Soon, Tommy wandered down the stairs, in his boxer shorts.

"Want some breakfast?" Ashleigh asked.

"Hell yeah!" Tommy sat down at one of the place settings and slurped up a mouthful of scrambled eggs. "Nice!"

"I know," Ashleigh said. "There's love in every bite."

He smiled and forked a whole piece of French toast into his mouth, then slurped down a glass of orange juice.

"Help yourself," Ashleigh said.

Esmeralda came down a few minutes later, but she'd gone to the trouble of getting dressed and applying a little makeup. She looked uneasy and a little scared when she first saw Ashleigh, but then she noticed the elaborate meal on the table and relaxed a little.

"Esmeralda!" Ashleigh squealed. She threw her arms around the girl and hugged her tight. She even kissed her on the cheek. Esmeralda melted like hot taffy in her arms.

"You look so happy," Esmeralda said.

"I am!" Ashleigh released her and stepped back. "Everything is just going perfectly, isn't it?"

"Hell yeah," Tommy said. "Are you gonna eat that piece of French toast?"

"No, go ahead," Ashleigh said.

“I’m so glad you’re safe,” Esmeralda said. She sat at the table and poured cream into her coffee. “You took a big risk going to Jenny’s house.”

“I really did,” Ashleigh said. “She could have killed me again. But you guys would have brought me back again, right?”

They both hurried to agree that they would.

“But anyway, I gathered some good intelligence, and I figured out how we’re going to destroy Jenny.”

“Why don’t we just shoot her?” Tommy asked. “Bury the body, done.”

“Duh, tons of reasons,” Ashleigh said. “First, Seth could bring her back.”

“Kill them both,” Tommy said. “Make it look like they ran off together.”

“That, Tommy, is actually not a bad idea,” Ashleigh said. “I actually respect you a lot more now that you came up with that.”

“Thanks!” Tommy said.

“Hold on,” Esmeralda said. “You two are kidding, right? We’re not actually going to kill these people.”

“The mass murderer girl, with the disease touch,” Tommy said. He raised his hands, which were pockmarked with little scars from his Jenny pox infection. “She has to die. She’s too dangerous to live. Especially if she might come after us.”

“Why would she come after us?” Esmeralda asked.

“Because she hates me,” Ashleigh said. “If she knows I’m back, she’ll come and kill me, and she’ll kill anyone who gets in her way. That’s exactly what happened last time.”

“That’s scary,” Esmeralda said.

“Very,” Ashleigh agreed.

“But this French toast, it’s amazing,” Esmeralda said.

“Thank you! So, Tommy, killing her is more complicated than it seems. Then her soul gets free, she gets incarnated again. Then she’s a newborn baby somewhere on the Earth, and I have no idea where.”

“So we do reincarnate,” Tommy said. “All of us. Right?”

“All of us,” Ashleigh said.

“I don’t believe in that,” Esmeralda said.

“Well, I wouldn’t either,” Ashleigh said. “Except I just recently died, and now I remember the past lives.”

“Do you remember me in any of them?” Tommy asked.

"Bunches!" Ashleigh said. "All three of us. We've been friends for thousands and thousands of years. We always help each other. But some of our kind are evil, like Jenny and Seth, and we end up fighting wars against them. That's why it's important we stop them now, while we're all young, before they can get too powerful and kill a whole lot of people. Like millions of people."

"What do you mean by 'our kind'?" Esmeralda asked.

"We're old," Ashleigh said. "Older than any human soul. But we were cast out from where we originated, and we found our way to Earth, and we learned to incarnate as human beings."

"Like fallen angels?" Esmeralda asked.

"I don't know," Ashleigh said. "It's hard to even remember things clearly. That's the bad thing about being human, we have to focus so hard to incarnate that we forget everything that came before. The good part of being human, of course, is we get to use our powers. Plus, all the other pleasures available in the flesh. But you two know all about that, don't you?" Ashleigh winked at Esmeralda, who blushed and looked down at her plate.

"So." Ashleigh slapped the table, as if calling a meeting to order. "It's time we get on with the old game. What I want to do is have Jenny Mittens kept alive, but in deep captivity. For the rest of what will hopefully be a very long, very boring life. We need her out of the way before we can hope to do anything else of significance."

"What do you want to do?" Tommy asked. "Keep her in the basement?"

"No," Ashleigh said. "And I have to say, my respect-o-meter did just drop a notch. I will not 'keep her in the basement' so that she can kill me in my sleep. I want her locked away, underground, maximum security, fed through a slit in a door. That is my dream for Jenny's future."

"Sounds expensive," Esmeralda said.

"I'm not going to *pay* for it," Ashleigh said. "I'm going to *arrange* it."

"How?" Tommy said.

"I need your special power for the first thing, Tommy. You'll have to drive down to Charleston, though. You can just take your bike."

"What am I doing there?" he asked.

“You can go down there tonight,” Ashleigh said. “Talk to somebody for me. Then grab a hotel room. I have a list of errands for you.”

“We’re going tonight?” he asked.

“No,” Ashleigh said. “*You’re* going tonight. Esmeralda and I are staying here.”

“She’s staying with you?” Tommy asked.

“It’s okay with me,” Esmeralda said. She gave Ashleigh a big smile. “I’m really starting to like it here.”

“I like having you!” Ashleigh said. She took Esmeralda’s hand and held onto it. “Anyway, I’ll keep on Jenny with the whole poor-Darcy-needs-a-friend act. And I need Esmeralda to help me with a few things.”

“You really have it all planned out,” Tommy said.

“Of course,” Ashleigh said. “That’s what I do. I’ve made you into powerful men before, Tommy. Kings. Emperors. Think of how much fun we’re going to have in this crazy modern world.”

Tommy grinned.

“I’m so glad we all found each other again!” Ashleigh said.

“Me, too,” Esmeralda sighed, beaming at Ashleigh and holding her hand.

Chapter Thirty-One

Seth was in the library again late Saturday night, trying very hard to focus on Beowulf for his English final. He was relieved when his cell phone rang, because he thought it would be Jenny. He needed a break.

It wasn't Jenny, though. His Blackberry identified it as WOOLY. That was Chris Woolerton, one of Seth's friends from Grayson Academy. They were friends on Facebook, but Seth hadn't actually spoken to him in person in a couple of years. Wooly's family lived in Charleston.

"Hey, Wooly," Seth said.

"Seth! What's up, man? What have you been doing?"

"Just hanging out."

"Yeah? That's great, man, that's great! Hey, I saw on Facebook you're coming to Charleston for school."

"Yeah. Where are you going to college, Wooly?"

"Right here, man. We're going to be freshmen together. Where you pledging?"

"Huh?"

"What fraternities?"

"Oh," Seth said. "I don't know if I'm doing all that."

"Come on, you don't want to miss out," Wooly said. "We're all Sig Alphs in my family. I can get you in, no problem. We got a phat, phat mansion, right off-campus so we can do what we want. The best parties. Puss, puss, pussy all over your face."

"Okay, thanks. I'm still not sure—"

"When are you coming down for orientation?"

"On the website, it says I can go any weekend in June, July, early August—"

“Yeah, you *can* come any weekend,” Wooly said, “But you *have* to come two weeks from today. The Southeastern Funk Fest. All weekend, in the streets. Blink 182’s gonna be there, *Incubus* is gonna be there, Willie fucking *Nelson* is gonna play—*everybody*. I’m taking four tabs of ex and a thermos of vodka. We’re gonna get crunked like skunks, chipmunk.”

“Sounds pretty good,” Seth said. Wooly had always gotten under his skin a little, but most people seemed to love him.

“Fuckin’ *A*,” Wooly said. “And you can meet my Sig Alph boys. I’m basically already a brother ‘cause I’m so legacy. I’ve been going to their parties all year and *damn*. Just *damn*.”

“Okay. I’ve got finals this week, but I’ll call you—”

“Come on, man. Two weeks from *today*. And check it out—maybe I can set it up so you can crash at the Sig Alph house. Like I said, pussy, pussy, pussy.”

“My girlfriend’s probably coming with me,” Seth said. “Probably just get a hotel room.”

“Yeah, if you want to make it lame, make it lame, bring your girlfriend,” Wooly said. “Oh! Okay, sorry! Um, I mean, don’t do that, man. We need to hang out and catch up. Bunch of Grayson guys will be around, too. This is a very bros-before-hos situation.”

“I’ll see, man,” Seth said. “But we can definitely hang out when I’m in town.”

“What’s this *I’ll see* shit?” Wooly asked. “You’re coming. You *are* coming. I’m telling people you’re coming.”

“Okay, I’ll come that weekend.”

“Fuck yeah,” Wooly said. “And you gotta let that high school pussy go, man. Repeat after me: I am *not* fucking married.”

“Nah, we’re pretty serious—”

“I am *not* fucking married. I’m not hanging up until you say it, bro. I am *not* fucking married. I am *not*—”

“Okay!” Seth said. “I am not fucking married.”

“Fuckin’ *A*. I will see you in two weeks. If you don’t come, you’re a fucking dead man.”

Seth laughed. “All right, Wooly. I’ll be there.”

Wooly hung up the phone. "Okay? Was that okay?" he asked.

The man standing over him gave an evil grin. "That was fine."

Wooly shuddered. The man's voice sounded like a razor cutting through ice.

The man had come in through Wooly's French doors, which led out to his balcony overlooking Charleston Harbor. Wooly had been sitting at his desk rolling a fattie of kush for a concert that night. Pink Floyd's "Learning to Fly" was thumping his subwoofers, and the room was lit only by his black-light posters.

The man had stepped in from the darkness, dressed all in black, with that crazy grin. His freakish gray eyes locked onto Wooly instantly. Wooly had started to stand up and yell for help—maybe his brother would hear him downstairs—but the man grabbed his forearm and squeezed it tight, making Wooly spill the bag of bright green, eight-hundred-dollar-an-ounce kush all over the carpet.

And that was when things got fucked up.

When Wooly was a little kid, there was one movie that scared him more than any other. *Pumpkinhead.* A witch summoned a demon to carry out revenge against some teenagers, and that demon, with his swollen wrinkled head, his evil sneer, and his blank eyes, had given Wooly nightmares and wet beds for months.

The guy's gray eyes reminded him of that demon's eyes. And this guy's face seemed to flicker a little, and Wooly could swear he kept glimpsing Pumpkinhead's sneering face underneath.

His grip on Wooly's arm was definitely as tight and strong as a demon's.

"Okay," Wooly whispered. "Okay. I called him. I did what you wanted. Right?"

"You will welcome him," the guy growled. "You will keep him with you."

"Okay."

"You won't say anything about me to anyone." The gray-eyed dude put a finger on Wooly's ear, and Wooly tensed, thinking he might tear it off. "No matter where I am, I can hear when someone is talking about me. Do you understand?"

"Yeah!" Wooly gasped. "Yeah, man, no way would I tell anyone."

"Good," the guy said. He finally let go of Wooly's arm, and Wooly cradled it in his other hand. "Do what I told you. I'll be watching." He stepped out onto the dark balcony, and he closed the French doors behind him.

Wooly didn't dare go and peer out through the glass onto the balcony, or turn the light on to see whether the demonic guy was gone. He felt like the guy was just standing out there, watching him, and might pounce on him and kill him any second. He was too scared to move.

Chapter Thirty-Two

Alexander had tracked the girl all the way to Fallen Oak, South Carolina, which made him smirk. He'd spent a previous lifetime here, infusing the place with his energy, really having fun with it. It only made sense that it would attract others of his kind. He should have checked up on this place. But he was into bigger things now, bigger experiments far south and west of here. Things he needed *her* to power.

He sat inside the empty, never-sold house in Ashleigh's cul-de-sac, watching out through the window curtains in the master bedroom. He could watch them through the side windows. He'd been occupying this house a couple of days, curious to watch the convocation underway.

There was the fear-giver and his opposite, the love-charmer.

And then the third person. Esmeralda, Alexander's opposite, the one who could listen to the dead, while Alexander could command them. He watched her closely.

She was infatuated with the fear-giver, it seemed. Alexander had watched them in the kitchen. When they'd finally gone upstairs together, he guessed they would be distracted for a while, especially with the stereo blasting downstairs.

So he'd crept into the house and planted a couple of tiny microphones here and there. Since then, he'd sat here in the empty house and listened to their conversations. Interesting stuff.

Tonight, the fear-giver had left town on an errand, but the two girls were here.

He tore open a yogurt-granola bar—he'd bought a case of them, and he'd been living mostly on those and some cheese crackers while he spied on the others. He stretched out on the bare hardwood floor, closed his eyes, and listened over his headphones.

"What's all that?" Esmeralda asked.

Ashleigh was coming down the stairs with a big wicker basket stuffed with lotions, gels and big, fluffy pink towels rolled up inside.

"Since he's off doing his thing, I thought we could really girl out tonight," Ashleigh said. "I've got stuff for your feet, face, and hair, and I've got every single Hugh Grant movie on Blu-Ray."

Esmeralda laughed. "Whatever you want to do."

"This is what I want to do." She dropped onto the couch next to Esmeralda and put a hand on her, and poured the love into her. "I want to thank you for bringing me back to life, and keeping me alive. I don't even know how to say how much I appreciate it, and how deeply grateful I am to you."

"It's okay," Esmeralda said. "I'm glad I brought you back. It's been a great time."

"You may not know this, but there are some real benefits to my touch, and I want to share them with you." Ashleigh said. She stood up and unrolled one of the fluffy pink towels across the couch. "Lie down on your stomach."

Esmeralda looked puzzled, but she was still smiling. She stretched out facedown on the pink towel. "What are you going to do?"

"You're going to get the best thing in the world." Ashleigh uncorked a bottle of expensive organic lotion. "An Ashleigh massage."

"You don't have to do that."

"I know. People used to beg me for these." Ashleigh lifted the back of Esmeralda's shirt and hiked it up to her shoulders.

"Hey!" Esmeralda said.

"I'm going to use my best lotion, too." Ashleigh unhooked Esmeralda's bra. "It's got royal bee jelly, and like twenty South American herbs." She spread the lotion on her fingers and began to rub Esmeralda's back. She poured her special energy into it, infusing Esmeralda's deep muscle tissue with love.

Esmeralda gave a deep sigh.

"I told you, I'm awesome at this," Ashleigh said.

"Yeah," Esmeralda said.

Ashleigh rubbed her way up Esmeralda's back, feeling the girl relax under her fingers.

"So, did you have fun with Tommy last night?" Ashleigh asked.

"Oh, yeah."

"What did you guys do?"

"We made chili." Esmeralda giggled. "Vegetarian chili."

"Yeah? Was it good?"

"Oh, yeah. It was hot."

Ashleigh moved her hands down to Esmeralda's lower back and started over, working her way up to Esmeralda's shoulder blades. "Then what did you do?"

"We danced. I showed him how to salsa." She giggled again. "He was funny."

"Yeah? Don't you get scared when he touches you?"

"Oh, yeah," she sighed. "So scared. But I like feeling scared."

"Oh?" Ashleigh said. "That's interesting."

"I like your touch, too. Keep touching me."

"Take your shirt off."

Esmeralda slowly tugged away her shirt and bra, moving at half-speed as if tranquilized. She dropped them on the floor and snuggled into her thick pink towel.

"Then what else did you guys do?" Ashleigh rubbed her shoulders and neck.

"We played around."

"Did you kiss?"

"Yes." Esmeralda giggled again, drunk on Ashleigh's energy.

"And he played with your tits?" Ashleigh rubbed her hands up along Esmeralda's sides.

"Yeah."

"And then you had sex?"

"No," Esmeralda held up a finger and wagged it. "No, no. But I sucked his dick."

"And then what?"

"He came in my face and fell asleep."

Ashleigh snickered. "Turn over, Esmeralda."

Esmeralda turned over. Ashleigh looked at her old finger bone, resting between Esmeralda's erect nipples. Esmeralda held too much power over Ashleigh to be trusted.

"You're so important to me," Ashleigh said. "I can give you a massage like this every day if you want."

"Oh, yeah?" Esmeralda looked at her with dilated pupils and languid eyes, and gave her a drugged smile. "That would be perfect."

"I know." Ashleigh tugged down Esmeralda's pajama pants, and the girl didn't even protest.

Ashleigh slid a finger into the damp between Esmeralda's legs and rubbed the girl's clit. Esmeralda gasped.

"Do you love me?" Ashleigh asked.

"Yes, I love you." Esmeralda's eyes closed.

Ashleigh rubbed her faster, and she turned her love-energy way up, pumping it into her. Esmeralda's body quivered, and her hips hitched up off the couch.

"Do you love me more than you love Tommy?"

"Yes, more!"

"A lot more?"

"So much more!" Esmeralda cried out.

"You belong to me, don't you?" Ashleigh asked.

"Yes."

"Say it."

"I belong to you…I belong to you…"

"That's right," Ashleigh said.

Chapter Thirty-Three

The day of Jenny's high school graduation was overcast, but the Weather Channel said it wouldn't rain, so graduation was outside on the football field as usual.

Jenny stood in her rented cap and gown on the temporary bleachers set up on the field. The graduating class was sparse and scattered on the bleachers, as were the groups of parents watching from the permanent concrete bleachers. With so many people dead or missing, it was a gloomy day in more ways than one.

Jenny found her father among the parents. He'd dressed in his best suit, which was a brown corduroy artifact of the 1970s. His girlfriend June sat beside him in a flowered church dress.

A few rows away from them, she spotted Seth's parents. Mr. and Mrs. Barrett were dressed quite a bit better than Jenny's dad, but they all looked equally miserable.

"Hey, Jenny!" Seth called to her as he climbed up the bleachers toward her. "Did I miss anything?"

"Just a lot of standing around." Jenny welcomed him with a hug and a quick kiss. She noticed his eyes glance warily towards his parents.

"Have you talked to your dad about Clemson?" Jenny asked.

"I wish I could go there, Jenny. But he's like iron on this one."

"But you know I can't live in Charleston."

"You can!" Seth said. "It's not even a big city like Atlanta."

"Charleston has too many people," Jenny said.

"My dad's insisting. I have to go there because they 'have the right focus on global market integration.'" Seth jabbed a fist in the air as he imitated his dad's voice.

“Ooh, are we talking about Charleston?” Darcy asked. She'd joined them on the bleachers, and now stood on the far side of Seth from Jenny. “I can't wait! Can you?”

Jenny shrugged.

“When are you guys going for orientation?” Darcy asked.

“I'm supposed to go in a couple of weeks,” Seth said. “Meet up with some of my friends from Grayson Academy.”

Jenny didn't like the sound of that. Before high school, Seth had attended an all-boys private school with a bunch of other rich kids. He’d only come back to Fallen Oak for high school because of his parents’ weird ideas about tradition. Jenny had met a couple of Grayson types at the Barrett Christmas party, and they were jerks.

“Ooh, nifty,” Darcy said. “Do you think I could hook a ride with you guys? My parents won't take me. They're still mad about the precious miracle in my belly. I'm giving it up for adoption, so it's not like it's gonna matter, but....” Darcy shrugged.

“You can ride with Seth,” Jenny said, and Seth gave her a sharp look. “Right, Seth?'

“Well, yeah...” Seth said. “It's just, there's the big music festival that weekend. Lots of drunk people, crowds...”

“Ooh, yeah,” Darcy said. “I want to go to a music festival.”

“Really?” Seth asked.

“Hell yeah. I never have any fun,” Darcy said.

“Darcy Metcalf,” Jenny asked, in a mock-scolding tone. “Did you just swear?”

“Fuck yeah I did!” Darcy said, and Jenny and Seth laughed. “I'm graduating. I can do what I want.”

“So you're taking her, Seth?” Jenny asked. She smiled. How much trouble could Seth get into with Darcy Metcalf up his ass?

“Uhhh...” Seth said.

Darcy beamed at him.

“Yeah, okay,” Seth sighed. “It'll be fun.”

“Bet your bumpers it will be!” Darcy said.

When the students were assembled, Assistant Principal Varney approached the loudspeaker podium on a little platform in front of the students. She addressed the parents and other audience members.

“Parents, students, and members of our Fallen Oak High community,” she said. “We all know this has been a difficult year for our town. But today is a happy day, when so many of our young people move forward to begin their lives in the world..." After a few platitudes, she introduced Reverend Bailey for the commencement address.

"Brothers and sisters in Christ," he began. The man looked a little stooped, and much grayer than Jenny remembered. His daughter Neesha was among the missing—and Jenny knew that all the "missing" were really dead. "In this time of need, let us remember and celebrate those we have lost. And let us also remember that, wherever they are, the Lord watches over them...Let us pray for understanding. Let us pray for hope. Let us pray." He bowed his head, and everyone else in the stadium did the same.

The Reverend's prayer referred to the Book of Job and trials and tribulations. When he mentioned Job's affliction of boils and disease, Jenny peeked open one eye to see if anyone was looking at her, but nobody was.

Then Mrs. Varney returned to introduce the class valedictorian, Raquisha Higgins, who said things like "now we move on into the springtime of our lives, like butterflies hatching from the high school cocoon..."

At least I saved us from one last speech by Ashleigh, Jenny thought.

Mrs. Varney called the students to receive their diplomas.

The whole experience was surreal. Jenny was the reason so many people were gone, but nobody knew except Seth and Jenny's dad. Seth was adamant that she shouldn't turn herself in—but if he was moving away from her, how much could he really care?

Out in the audience, half the people were crying. So were some of the students around her. The short list of graduates made it clear how many people they had lost.

She looked at her dad. He didn't look happy, either.

Then she looked at Seth. What kind of person was she, if she could kill so many people and still worry about her own happiness? So what if Seth moved away? She deserved far worse. She was a monster.

Seth took her hand and gave her a small smile, but Jenny wasn't feeling it at all.

Chapter Thirty-Four

Heather got to work early Monday morning, which was her new habit. The CDC had continued testing the bodies, and still failed to come up with anything that might explain their horrific demise. Heather couldn't leave it alone, so she kept checking the data for any developments.

Fallen Oak presented her with two big anomalies: the day of death and the teenage baby boom. Heather had crunched the numbers on that and determined that most of the conceptions must have happened in late October and early November, almost as if a single event were responsible for the whole thing. She wondered what had been happening in Fallen Oak on Halloween.

There was no more information on Ashleigh Goodling, or her parents. They hadn't been identified among the bodies. The whole family seemed to have vanished in a puff of smoke. She found that extremely suspicious, but it was getting her nowhere.

There was, of course, no explanation for the magical disappearing pathogen, either. Over two hundred people had simply developed extreme symptoms for no reason. That was good enough for the White House, so long as the event didn't recur. It wasn't good enough for Heather. She came in early and worked late to crunch the numbers collected by the lab techs. The government was keeping the bodies in frozen storage now, presumably in case some new information or investigative technique turned up, and fending off inquiries from the families. Most of the bodies currently in storage were officially “missing” instead of deceased, in order to downplay the scale of the event.

That didn't sit right with Heather, either, but it was beyond her control. The White House, no doubt, had no interest in her opinion. Not in an election year.

The phone rang, which surprised her. She wasn't officially here for another half hour. She thought about letting it go to voice mail, but then she noticed the area code: 803. That was South Carolina, maybe Fallen Oak.

"Dr. Reynard," she answered.

"Um, hi." The voice on the other end was young, female, and very nervous. "Is this, um, Dr. Reynard?"

"Yes."

"Um, hi," the voice repeated. "You were in Fallen Oak when all the stuff was happening?"

"Yes."

"Okay, I think I met you. My name is Darcy. Metcalf."

Dr. Reynard tried to put a face with the name, but couldn't. She had screened a lot of the girls in town. She wrote "Darcy Metcalf" on a Post-It pad.

"Yeah," the girl said. Her voice fell to a whisper. "I tried to tell you about Jenny. About the witchcraft, or whatever it is."

Dr. Reynard remembered a mousey-haired pregnant girl pushing her angry father's wheelchair.

"Oh, Darcy!" she said. "I remember you."

"Okay, good," Darcy said. "Now, I've thought about it a lot, and I think maybe it's not witchcraft."

"I'm sure it isn't, Darcy."

"No, there's gotta be some science involved. Like she carries the disease, but it doesn't hurt her, but she can infect other people. Is there a word for that? You know, like how mosquitos can infect you but they don't get sick themselves?"

"An immune carrier?"

"That sounds right! She could be an 'immune carrier.'"

"Who are we talking about?" Heather didn't know what to make of this phone call yet.

"Jenny Pox. I mean, Jenny Morton. Jenny Pox is just what people call her."

"Why do they call her that?"

"Because, like I said, she can infect people and make 'em sick. But she doesn't really get sick. She can suck it back in when she's done."

"Darcy, you're whispering too low. I can barely hear you."

"Okay, sorry. It's just, I don't want my dad to know I'm talking to you."

"Why not?"

"Cause he'd get mad. Cause he doesn't want me to get involved. Nobody wants to get involved. But I think you should know about it."

"Well, thanks for calling, Darcy. Is there anything else?"

"You don't understand," Darcy said. "I have pictures. I have to email them to you."

"What kind of pictures?"

"Of Jenny. Only she's all infected and gunk. Just like the people who died in the square."

"Did you see what happened in the square, Darcy?" Heather asked.

"No. But everybody kinda knows. It was Jenny, she flared up with her disease and infected people. They die fast once they get it. That's why everyone's scared to talk. Everyone's scared of her."

"Well, send me the pictures, Darcy—"

"I already did. Can you look at 'em now? Please?"

Heather sighed. She opened her Outlook and saw the email from Darcy. She opened the attachment.

A photo of Jenny Morton filled her screen. The girl leaned close to a blond-haired boy, who looked drowsy or asleep, and she had pried his mouth open with her fingers. Her chin and lips were full of leaking blisters and broken pustules. Her tongue was fully extended, reaching down towards his mouth, dripping pus, blood, and clear fluid onto the boy's lips and face.

Heather sat up in her chair. The girl had the symptoms of "Fallen Oak syndrome," the mystery killer that they couldn't identify. She was the first live suspected case.

"Darcy," Heather said. "When was this picture taken?"

"That's from, like, months ago," Darcy said. "Somebody took it during Christmas break, I think."

"This isn't recent?"

"No. Like I said, she brings it out, then she threatens people with it, then she sucks it back in. Or, you know. Kills people. She says she can get away with it because it's not murder, it's disease. And she laughs. She terrorizes people with it. The whole town's like in fear of her."

"Darcy, listen to me very carefully," Heather said. "Is what you're telling me true? All of it? Or is there any part you might be exaggerating, or not explaining clearly?"

"It's true," Darcy said. "And I prayed on it, and then I started thinking maybe it's not witchcraft, maybe it's science. Like that immune carrier thingy you were talking about."

"But you're saying she can express her symptoms at will?" Heather said.

"Yeah. Or maybe she can't really control it—like when I get hives on my butt after I eat cheese—it breaks out, and then she just acts mean when it breaks out. I dunno. I've been thinking about it too much."

"So you're saying she has occasional breakouts, but then they go away?" Heather asked.

"Right," Darcy said. "But you don't want to touch her because she's contagious. That's why she wears gloves all the time. Jenny Mittens, that's something else people call her. She's kind of a freako."

Heather remembered her visit to Jenny's house. The girl had been wearing a pair of blue cloth gloves—that stuck out because it had been a hot, sticky day, no reason for her to wear them. The gloves were too clean and lightweight for gardening. Also, Heather thought it was odd that the girl never took them off, even when Heather was examining her, until Heather asked to take her blood.

And Heather remembered one more thing—the girl had sighed in relief when Heather strapped on the disposable rubber gloves. She remembered that because *nobody* felt relief at the sight of a doctor strapping on gloves. Taking them off, maybe.

"Dr. Reynard?" Darcy asked.

"Yes. Hold on a moment." Heather's mind was racing. There were three possibilities. One, the photo was a fake of some kind. Two, the girl Jenny had previously been infected with the x-pathogen, but showed no signs when Heather examined her. Three, the picture was newer than Darcy said, and Jenny had become infected after Heather examined.

Options two and three each indicated a separate outbreak from the single incident they knew about. Either possibility required immediate action.

"Okay, Darcy?" Heather said.

"Yeah?"

"What else can you tell me about this?"

"Uh…that's about it, I guess."

"How certain are you about when this picture was taken?"

"Kids were passing it around school in January. That's all I really know."

"Okay. If you think of anything else, you call me. In fact, here's my cell number." Heather gave it to her. "Have you seen Jenny lately?"

"Just around town," Darcy said. "She's usually riding with Seth Barrett. He's the boy in the picture. He never gets sick, though."

"You've seen her since you saw this picture?"

"Oh, yeah. That picture's from a while ago. I kept it 'cause it was so weird."

"Does she look sick to you?"

"No, she looks fine," Darcy said. "Like I said, that disease thing comes and goes with her."

"Okay. Thank you so much, Darcy. I'll call you back if I have any questions."

"Um, better text my cell phone," Darcy said. "My dad's kind of a lame-o. He gets mad if the phone rings too much."

"Okay, I'll text you. Bye, Darcy."

Heather looked up Jenny Morton's lab results on the investigation database. If there was anything unusual, it was the girl's completely perfect health.

She wasn't satisfied. Never mind the lab reports—she wanted to go look at the specimens herself.

But first, she would stop by Schwartzman's office. He would know somebody discreet at Homeland Security, somebody who could get her every available piece of information on Jenny Morton. And on the Goodlings, while they were at it.

It looked like Jenny Morton might be carrying something deadly. Heather didn't want to think about what could happen if Jenny decided to leave her little house in the woods and carry the pathogen right into some unsuspecting city.

In her dream, Jenny was Euanthe again.

Cleon had taken her among his retinue of servants to a grand holiday banquet at the home of Pericles, an intimidating marble mansion surrounded by gardens. Cleon liked Euanthe because she never spoke and always hurried to do as he asked. Euanthe had pretended to learn a few Greek words, like “wine” and “bread,” so that he could communicate with her. In reality, of course, she understood everything that was said around her.

Cleon's wife had stayed home, as women were not invited.

The great hall of Pericles' house was filled with nobility, politicians and wealthy merchants, as well as their servants. They reclined on carved wooden couches thick with cushions, and they drank wine and ate fruit from bowls carried by servants. Cleon greeted some of his friends and political allies and took a couch among them.

Euanthe's job was to stand near Cleon's couch and fetch him things on demand. In reality, her main purpose—along with the other servants Cleon had brought with them—was simply to be there as a statement of Cleon's wealth and status. She wore a clean white tunic with a blue floral pattern, much nicer than anything she wore at Cleon's house, and her hair was braided and pinned up around the crown of her head.

After the guests had arrived, a tall man with a thick gray beard stood near the giant fireplace, holding up a golden bowl filled with wine. He had striking blue eyes, and Euanthe thought he was very handsome.

“Great men of Athens!” he said. “I welcome you to my home. May wise Athena continue to protect us from the Spartan scourge.”

Shouts of agreement went up from the crowd.

So this man was Pericles, Euanthe thought. The man she'd been sent to kill.

“War is always cause for sorrow,” Pericles said. “And it is a time for men to stand strong together, shoulders together as in the phalanx, each man's shield protecting the man to his side. If one man falters, the phalanx is broken. We have our quarrels, and we will always quarrel—that is the blessing and curse of democracy.”

Cleon muttered something to a friend, a wealthy merchant on the next couch, and the man smiled and nodded.

“While the Spartans ravage the countryside outside our walls, we cannot present a weak front line,” Pericles said. “Therefore, we must set aside our differences until the Spartans are defeated. Vicious lies have been whispered about us all—let us cease whispering. You know I am not a man given to banquets and other extravagances. But I have invited you, the leadership of every major party and faction in the Assembly, to offer the branch of an olive tree. While there is war without, there must be unity within. Let us all find a way to work together for the good of Athens."

Pericles looked directly at Cleon.

Cleon regarded Pericles with a stoic face, his gray eyes cold. All heads in the room gradually turned toward Cleon.

When he had the room's attention, Cleon raised his gold-embossed silver cup, and he nodded his head very slightly.

"Let there be peace," Cleon said.

The room erupted in cheers and stomping feet. Pericles and Cleon both drank wine, and all the other men did the same.

Then musicians played lyres and harps while the guests busied themselves with eating and drinking, gossip and debate. A poet standing by the fireplace recounted from memory the story of Odysseus and his long journey home from Troy.

Euanthe stood quietly, listening and pretending not to listen, until Cleon instructed her to fetch him a leg of roasted lamb, his favorite food.

She left the banquet hall and walked into a large kitchen, where slaves roasted lambs and pigs over huge fires. At a long wooden table, more slaves hacked the roasted beasts into smaller pieces and stacked them on serving platters.

Euanthe approached the long table, looking for the meatiest leg to bring her master.

"You there!" a drunken voice called. Euanthe turned to see two young men approaching her, both of them in tunics stitched with gold and silver. Nobles. "Yes, you, girl!"

Euanthe just looked at them, remembering that she allegedly did not know Greek, being an exotic foreigner.

"She is Cleon's slave," the second young noble said to the first.

"Cleon is a filthy dog," the first noble said. "Enemy of all that is Athens."

Euanthe remained silent.

"Nothing to say in his defense?" The first noble was almost upon her. "Nothing for Cleon? Do you deny he plots against Pericles?"

“She's only a slave,” the second noble said. “She is too stupid to know of politics.”

“She is *his* property. Let's defile her, as a message to him.” The first noble reached for Euanthe's arm, but she pulled back.

“You should not touch me,” she warned him.

“Insolent!” the second noble said. He reached for her, too, and she had to dodge in the opposite direction.

“Leave me to my work,” Euanthe said. She looked around the kitchen, but no slave would stand up for her against the noblemen.

“I do not take orders from slaves!” the first nobleman said. “Least of all, slaves of that lowborn cur Cleon.”

They had backed her against the long wooden table now, and both men reached for her.

Euanthe summoned the special pox, the contagious one she had prepared for the destruction of Pericles and Athens. She was meant to infect Pericles directly, but launching the plague in his household would have to be close enough. She was not going to let these drunken noblemen drag her off and have their way with her.

She lashed out, filling them both with the pox. Sores and tumors ruptured open along their arms and spread to their faces and legs.

The noblemen fell to the ground, howling in pain and surprise. Now the other slaves paid attention, closing in from all sides to see what was happening.

Euanthe breathed out a cloud of black spores, infecting them all. She felt bad for the other slaves as they writhed on the ground, but they were all doomed to die anyway. Archidamus, her king, had ordered it.

She pulled the contagious plague back into herself, as much as she could. As the slaves fell to the floor, Euanthe found the biggest, juiciest leg of lamb and grabbed it for Cleon.

Chapter Thirty-Five

Heather strapped on a cleansuit, sealing herself from head to toe in plastic, with a breathing mask connected to a bottle of oxygen at her hip. Since the pathogen's means of transmission remained as unknown as the pathogen itself, the Fallen Oak specimens were treated as maximally dangerous and maximally contagious. A high level of security clearance was necessary to enter the lab dedicated to the investigation.

The entire situation was still tightly stage-managed by the President's special adviser Nelson Artleby. The test samples had all been collected here in Atlanta. In a fairly bizarre move, the White House had ordered all the bodies stored in a guarded facility outside the city. The warehouse had been quickly configured for refrigeration in a special contract given to SyntaCorp, LLC, a giant defense firm where Nelson Artleby happened to sit on the Board of Directors.

Heather couldn't imagine how gruesome that place must be. She imagined shelf after shelf of dead bodies, each one wrapped and sealed in layers of plastic. She wondered how their families would react if they discovered what had happened to their missing loved ones.

Heather shook her head to try and clear away those thoughts. She was here to gather data.

It amazed her to find the lab deserted. It had run round the clock for weeks while the samples were analyzed, but it looked like nobody was even assigned here full-time anymore. Nothing had been discovered by all the testing, which was the scariest fact of all.

Heather located Jenny's blood sample in a refrigerator full of them. They were labeled with tracking codes—each person in Fallen Oak had been assigned one.

She extracted one red drop and dripped it onto a microscope slide, then laid a clear plastic slide cover on top of it.

She peered at Jenny's blood cells.

Jenny had the world's rarest blood type, she knew, AB negative. Jenny's little boyfriend Seth had the opposite, O positive, the universal giver. Heather had developed a related interest in Seth, because he was either immune to the pathogen or he was a handsome teenage boy who didn't mind having a girlfriend he couldn't touch. Heather wasn't sure which of those possibilities was more far-fetched.

Heather zoomed in closer. She couldn't see anything unusual here. Just normal, healthy blood cells, floating sluggishly because they'd been stored at freezing temperature. She knew there was nothing unusual about Jenny's white blood cells or platelet count.

"Okay," Heather whispered. "Tell me something new."

Since she couldn't find anything, and every standard test had already been run, she decided to try a slightly crazy experiment.

Heather brought out a clean sample of AB negative from a different person, a blood donor from somewhere around Chicago, someone who had almost certainly never been exposed to Jenny before. She added a couple of drops of the sample to the slide with Jenny's blood, then returned the slide to the microscope.

She watched the sample blood mingle with Jenny's blood. Nothing happened. She'd contaminated the diminishing specimen of Jenny's blood for nothing, she thought.

Then, some of the blood cells began to quiver, their outer membranes vibrating like guitar strings.

In front of Heather's eyes, some of the cells shriveled, others contorted into strange, spiky shapes, and others burst altogether. Other blood cells—Jenny's, she guessed—remained perfectly healthy as they floated among the destroyed ones.

"What the hell was that?" Heather stood up straight and looked around at the empty lab. "Somebody tell me what the hell I just saw."

Jenny floated on her back, gazing up at the billions of blue and white stars. The water around her was very warm, heated by the June sunlight all day. She knew if she swam down far enough, she would reach the deep place where the water held the winter cold year round.

"It's quiet out here," Seth whispered. He floated beside her. "Used to be so many people during the summer."

They were swimming at the small body of water a couple of miles outside town, which Seth called "the reservoir" and everybody else called "Barrett Pond." It was almost midnight.

"It's weird, isn't it?" Jenny said. "Never going back to school. It's like people tell you what to do your whole life, and then, all of a sudden, nobody's in charge."

"We're in charge," he said. "We can do whatever we want."

"You can. I still have the Jenny pox, and I don't know what to do with myself now."

"Come with me and Darcy this weekend," Seth said. "You'll like it. We're staying at a pretty cool hotel, an old mansion in the middle of downtown. Darcy said she stayed there with her family once and it's really nice."

"Cities scare me. All those people I could infect. I've done it to whole cities before, in other lives." Jenny had begun to think that Pericles, the man she'd been trying to kill in her dream, was a past-life incarnation of Seth. But he never seemed interested in her past-life dreams, so she didn't see any point bringing it up.

"Are you really worried about that?" Seth asked.

"I have to worry about it every second I'm alive, Seth. It's what my whole life is about"

"You don't think you might be hiding behind the Jenny pox a little bit?"

She turned her head in the water to look at him. "What do you mean?"

"Maybe you're scared of change," he said. "A little bit scared of the world beyond this town."

"That's not it!" she snapped. "You don't understand."

"I do, though. I'm kind of scared, too, and I'm used to being away. But that was boarding at Grayson. This is different. Nobody in charge anymore, like you said. But it won't be scary if you're with me, you know? It'll be fun."

"If I go," Jenny said, "Can you get a place outside the city, more in the country? Then you could drive into Charleston for school, but I won't have to be surrounded by people."

“I don't know. My parents might get suspicious about that.”

“Suspicious?” Jenny flipped down from her back float and started treading water. “You've been insisting I come and live with you, and your parents don't even know that's your plan?”

“Well...”

“You don't think they would figure it out?”

“They wouldn't allow it if I told them. I'm just trying to do what will work for us now.”

“And what about the future?”

“Why are you freaking out?”

“Because you act like you have it all settled for us, but you don't. What am I supposed to do, hide when your parents visit? Do I just live out of a suitcase the whole time? What’s your plan?”

“We'll deal with it.”

Jenny finally asked the question that had been eating at her, ever since her talks with Darcy Metcalf. “Do we have a future, Seth? If your parents are so against us being together?”

“I can handle my parents.” Seth took her hand and towed her close to him. He tried to kiss her, but she dodged it.

“Oh, yeah.” Jenny swam back from him. “Like you handled them when they told you what school to go to, and what to study, and every big decision you've ever made about anything.”

“Come on, Jenny. I love you. I'll take care of everything.”

“I don't think I believe you,” Jenny said. “I'll think you'll do what you're told, eventually. And where does that leave me? You want me to build the rest of my life around you...until it gets inconvenient for you. And you can move on to some girl your parents want you to marry.”

“That's not true!”

“Prove it,” Jenny said.

“I can't show you the future. We're together today. Tomorrow, next year, we'll keep finding ways to be together.”

“That's what you say.”

“What the hell do you want me to say, Jenny? What do you want me to do?”

“Nothing,” Jenny said. “You have fun with Darcy this weekend. And all your little pals from Grayson Academy.”

Jenny swam away from him, toward the rocky shore. The night was growing a little cold.

Chapter Thirty-Six

"Where are you going?" Darcy's mom asked.

Ashleigh was packing Darcy's suitcase. The clothes all seemed unreasonably big to her, especially the underwear. But that was the crappy body she inhabited.

"I'm just going on a little weekend trip," Ashleigh said.

"A trip? Where?"

"The beach."

"With who?"

"Just some friends." Ashleigh zipped up the suitcase.

"Morris!" Darcy's mom screamed toward the living room. "Morris!"

"What now?" Darcy's dad yelled back.

"Darcy says she's going to the beach for the weekend! With *friends*!" Her voice grew shrill.

"Like hell she is!" Darcy's dad wheeled from the living room to the hall. He glowered at the sight of Darcy's suitcase. "I didn't give you permission to go nowhere!"

"I'm eighteen years old. I'm a high school graduate. I can go on a trip if I want."

"Who the *hell* put that idea in your head?" Darcy's dad yelled.

"The United States Constitution," Ashleigh said. "Look, it's no big deal. I just need a vacation."

"All you *need* is a job!" Darcy's dad said. "How the *hell* you gonna pay for a vacation?"

"Yeah, how?" Darcy's mom asked.

"Seth's paying," Ashleigh said. "For everybody."

"Seth?" Darcy's dad asked. "You don't mean Seth Barrett?"

"That's the one," Ashleigh said.

"Who else is going?" Darcy's mom asked.

"Um..."

"Not those two you've been running around with, I hope," Darcy's mom asked. "I don't trust them."

"Mom, Tommy is Ashleigh Goodling's cousin. How bad can he be?"

"But he's always with that Mexican girl," Darcy's dad said. "I never thought I'd live to see the day, my little girl running around with Mexicans."

"Don't be racist, Dad." Ashleigh pushed by them, walking towards the front door. She had no intention of ever coming back.

"Don't you pull that politically correct horseshit on me!" Darcy's dad wheeled after her, and Darcy's mom trailed behind him. "I ain't no racist, but Mexicans are filthy, weird people! Chuck O'Flannery did a whole show about it! Diseased welfare-suckers, taking up our jobs and our schools."

"What job?" Ashleigh snapped. "You don't work. You live on welfare."

"You take that back!" Darcy's dad shouted. "I ain't on welfare, I'm on disability! I can't get no welding job when I ain't got no foot!" He jabbed one sausage-shaped finger at his missing foot, in case she just hadn't noticed yet.

Ashleigh watched out the window, gripping the suitcase tight.

"I know what this is about," Darcy's mom said. "You're going to the beach so you can have sex with those boys."

"Yeah, that's right," Ashleigh said. "Gang-banging the fat pregnant chick is every boy's fantasy."

"Don't use language like that under my roof!" Darcy's dad said.

Mercifully, Seth's blue Audi convertible pulled into the driveway.

"Seth's here," Darcy said. "I'll see y'all Monday."

"Don't you go sinning!" Darcy's mom said.

"But I am," Ashleigh said. "I'm gonna have sex with Seth, and I'm going to let him stick it in my ass, too. Because that's where I like it. Right in the butthole."

Darcy's mom gasped and covered her mouth.

Ashleigh flung open the front door, and Darcy's dad wheeled out after her. She ran down the front porch steps two at a time.

"Darcy Hortence Metcalf, you come back here now!" he screamed. His face was bright crimson.

Ashleigh gave him the finger as she ran to Seth's car.

"What's going on?" Seth asked from the driver's seat. "Everything okay?"

She dropped the suitcase into the back seat, then climbed in beside him.

"My dad's just being a total lame-o," Ashleigh said. "I can't leave without him yelling at me."

"Darcy, you come here!" Darcy's dad screamed from the porch.

"He just wants to yell at me for getting pregnant, for the millionth time," Ashleigh said. "Drive, drive, drive. Get me the hell out of here."

"Okay..." Seth backed out of the driveway, and they left Darcy's parents glaring at them from the front porch.

"You sure everything's okay?" Seth asked. "Your parents look pissed."

"We just had an argument," Ashleigh said. "Like we do every day. No big whoop."

Ashleigh lay back in the passenger seat and let the wind blow through her hair. It was a gorgeous Friday evening, with the purple sunset behind them and the night ahead. Orientation began early on Saturday morning, and Seth wasn't a fan of getting out of bed before dawn on Saturday to drive two hours to Charleston, so they were staying in a hotel tonight and tomorrow night.

Ashleigh had been as insistent as she could, without breaking character, that they stay at the Mandrake House, a narrow five-story mansion with a few rooms on each floor. Tommy had already rented a room on the top floor, and Esmeralda would be driving Ashleigh's Jeep to Charleston to join them.

Seth and Ashleigh were staying two floors below Tommy and Esmeralda, which would make things very convenient.

"I wish Jenny was coming with us," Seth said.

"Me, too," Darcy said. In fact, she had advised Jenny not to go. She'd suggested that if Jenny didn't go, Seth would have to imagine life in Charleston without her, and might decide being with Jenny was more important than making his parents happy. "I really like hanging out with her."

"Yeah, Jenny's great." A smile appeared on his lips, and a distant look in his eyes.

Ashleigh wanted to slap him, and then rake her nails back and forth across his face, and then stomp on his dick a thousand times. He had dropped her practically overnight once he started hanging out with Jenny. This infuriated Ashleigh, not just because she'd been tossed out like an old sock, but because she couldn't stand not being in control.

"Do you ever think about Ashleigh?" she asked.

"Sometimes."

"It's weird how she just disappeared like that," Darcy said. "Like presto-change-o, huh?"

Seth looked at her from the corner of his eye, and his forehead wrinkled. He was probably struggling to think of what to say. "Yeah...A lot of people disappeared."

"But you were with Ashleigh forever," Darcy said. "Don't you miss her at all? I mean, if I was a guy, I'd totally want to be with her."

"She wasn't as nice as she acted," Seth said.

"Really?"

"She could be mean," Seth said. "Manipulative."

"Manipulative? Ashleigh?"

"I know you miss her, Darcy, but she was really kind of an evil bitch. She tried to kill me, but she screwed that up, too."

Ashleigh snarled, but she fought it until it was a simple frown. "But everybody loved her."

"Sometimes everybody's wrong," Seth said.

Ashleigh looked into the darkness ahead and tried not to snap. She couldn't stand to hear herself talked about that way.

They turned off Esther Bridge Road onto Highway 63, the road that would take them all the way to Charleston.

Ashleigh had always liked riding in Seth's car, the expensive blue convertible that advertised you were somebody of value and quality. Too bad this would be the last time.

Friday afternoon, Heather got a visit at her office from Chantella Williams, a senior investigator with Homeland Security. The investigator laid a black file folder on her desk.

"This is everything you asked for." Williams opened the folder. The first page showed a birth certificate for Maurice Goodling. "Maurice Goodling. Deceased in 2006, cirrhosis of the liver. Last known address, a Catholic mission in Memphis." She turned the page over. The next one showed a snapshot of a withered homeless man's corpse.

"That can't be right," Heather said.

"Looks like your Maurice Goodling is guilty of identity fraud," Williams said.

"Oh!" Heather reached toward her keyboard. "Then I need to check—"

"Non-residents of Fallen Oak among the infected deceased," Williams said. "You'll find two: Waylon Humphries and Ruby McGussin. Wanted for six kinds of fraud in three states." She turned the page, revealing police mugshots of a thuggish-looking young man with a mullet and moustache, and then a young woman with huge hairsprayed bangs and a death's head moth tattoo on her shoulder.

If Heather squinted, she could just barely see them as the smiling, conservative-looking Dr. and Mrs. Goodling featured on the Fallen Oak Baptist Church website.

"You've had their bodies the whole time," Williams said.

"What about—"

"No sign of the daughter."

"You've done a lot of my work for me," Heather said.

"Are you kidding? After that lab test you sent up earlier this week, this thing got prioritized. A lot of people still want to know what happened at Fallen Oak. Now it's my turn to hear what you know about it. And what you speculate, too."

"What about Jenny Morton?" Heather asked. "Did we look into her background?"

"Far as we can tell, she's never been to a doctor," Williams said. "No medical records. Home birth. Mother disappeared soon after."

"Disappeared?"

"Could be post-partum depression, runs off…"

"Is it possible she died?" Heather asked.

"No death certificate anywhere. Just disappeared."

"What about her father?"

"Local handyman, no steady job. Living on old family land, old little house. There's not much to Jenny, either, judging by her school records. No discipline issues. No extracurricular activities. Good student, but she only got a general diploma. Seems like she was pretty invisible. What do you know about the girl?"

"She might be an immune carrier of the disease," Heather said. "She suffers occasional breakouts of the symptoms, but no long-term damage, as far as anyone knows. Some people think she can infect others at will, or at least chooses to do it maliciously."

"That's horrible," Williams said.

"It may be that something triggered a major flare-up that night," Heather said. "She infected a lot of people at once. But I still can't understand how it works. She catalyzes a fatal reaction, but she doesn't leave any biochemical trace. Nothing viral, nothing bacterial…at this point, it could be little demons with pitchforks."

"Sounds like a perfect weapon," Williams said. "We have to be careful approaching her."

"Are we approaching her?" Heather asked. "How? When?"

"That is under development," Williams said. "But you're going to be part of it."

"I'll have to clear it with Schwartzman—"

"Consider it cleared with Schwartzman, and with anybody you might be tempted to clear it with. We're moving into a high threat level area here."

"Okay," Heather said. "Let's have a closer look at Jenny Morton."

Chapter Thirty-Seven

South Battery, the street in front of the Mandrake House, was blocked off for the festival, so they had to park at a garage a few blocks north of it and walk to the hotel.

"Isn't this so exciting?" Darcy asked. They walked down Meeting Street under a canopy of ancient trees. High stone walls shielded old mansions from the sidewalk, and Seth could only see their upper balconies and the chimneys.

"I hope we can find the place," Seth said.

"Don't worry, I know just what we need to do," Darcy told him.

They walked toward the sound of pulsing music near the harbor. George Clinton was playing. All around Seth and Darcy, clumps of young people walked along the sidewalk or right down the middle of the street, teenagers and college students drawn like moths towards the flickering lights of the weekend-long festival.

They reached Battery and turned left. The crowd was thick here now, and got much thicker across the street at the public park, which looked out onto the harbor. The band was playing somewhere inside the park, past the temporary stalls hawking beer and deep-fried food products, past the cluster of little old ladies protesting the festival with posterboard signs.

The Mandrake House hotel looked like some old Greek temple, with arches and Corinthian columns, and balconies curving out on every floor. The brick steps leading up the front porch were as wide as the house itself. Purple wisteria hung from the gnarled limbs of the old trees surrounding it.

"Oh, it's just like I remember," Darcy said. "I even got us the same room my family stayed in. Two bedrooms, with a little sitting room and a huge balcony."

"That's great," Seth said. He'd let Darcy make their reservations, so he wasn't too sure how much this was costing him. Darcy was at a rough time in her life, though, being pregnant and then giving the baby up for adoption so she could go to college. Seth's dad might yell at him about the credit card bill, but so what?

The clerk was a woman in her forties or fifties who looked at them suspiciously, until Seth touched her arm and healed any little aches or pains she might have had. Then she smiled and flirted with him while she showed them to their suite.

"Each item of furniture you see is a genuine Southern antique," the lady explained. "Most of them antebellum. But your bathroom is one hundred and two percent modern. The shower has a heating-stone floor, and it's big enough for two." She winked at Seth and giggled.

"Okay, thanks," Seth said. He tipped the lady, as well as the big quiet bellman who'd carried up their suitcases, and the hotel employees finally left.

"Whew! I'm pooped." Darcy sat on the couch in the sitting room. She looked out the huge glass doors to the park and the dancing crowd outside.

"You really picked a great place." Seth pushed open the wide glass door to the balcony, letting in a rush of summer moonlight, music and salty ocean air. "We could watch the whole concert from right here. I'm amazed they had a room."

"I guess anything can be arranged," Darcy said.

Seth looked at her, curious. That wasn't a very Darcy thing to say, unless Darcy had copied it from Ashleigh. Then he got distracted by his Blackberry phone playing a sample of Dr. Dre. Wooly was calling.

"Hey, man," Wooly said. "Got your text. Where you at?"

"It's called the Mandrake House. It's on Battery, right across from the park."

"Holy crap, we're like a block from there. We'll be there in a second. Hope you're ready to get *waaaayy*-sted!" Wooly sang the last word.

Wooly arrived with Steven Hunter (whom Wooly called "Skunker") and Adam Branderford ("Aces"), both guys who'd gone to Grayson. Adam had just finished his first year at Charleston, and his first year as a Sigma Alpha brother.

"What's up?" Wooly pounced on Seth, knocking him to the couch and scrubbing his head with his knuckles. "Who's ready to slurp up the mad titty-tang tonight, huh, bro?"

"All right, enough, man," Seth said. He shook Wooly loose and greeted the other, calmer guys.

"Let's get crunk, stunk and locked in the trunk." Wooly unscrewed a thermos, sucked down a shot of vodka, and passed it to Steve. Darcy walked from her bedroom out to the sitting room, and Wooly's eyes widened when he saw the pregnant girl. "Oh, whoa, the record stops," Wooly said. "Hey, Seth? Is this your girlfriend?"

"No, this is Darcy," Seth said. "She's down here for orientation. Just a friend. Darcy, this is Wooly, Steven, and Adam—"

"Okay, good," Wooly said. "Because I was about to say, Seth, dude, you gotta wear a helmet when you play ball. Anyway, we gotta roll, because we got some very non-pregnant bitches waiting out there. Darcy, nice to meet you, Seth…" Wooly made clicking sounds with his tongue while pointing back over his shoulder at the door.

"Darcy's coming with us," Seth said.

"He said what?" Wooly asked the other two guys.

"No, it's okay," Darcy said. "My feet are killing me. I'm just gonna hang out here, you know, find a nice place to read a book."

"That is so interesting," Wooly said. He grabbed Seth's arm. "Come on. Time to get funky now."

"Call me if you need anything," Seth said to Darcy, while the other guys dragged him out of the room.

"I'm good right here." Darcy winked. The heavy old door closed, locking her inside the room.

The night Seth and Darcy left town, Jenny had her last dream of Euanthe.

In the dream, Euanthe walked through the open plaza of the agora, where trade was no longer conducted. Bodies burned on top of a pyramid of wood, and more families were carrying their dead to the fire. The sick filled the temples and the streets, groaning, begging for water and coughing up dark bile. Bloody pustules oozed from their faces and hands, and their fevered and shrunken bodies radiated heat.

So many were sick that no one remained to take care of them, and most Athenians had shut themselves away in their homes, filled with panic at the outbreak of plague, praying to their household gods to protect them.

Only Euanthe did not fear the plague.

She walked past the countless victims and out of the city along the North Wall. This was one of the walls that made the city impenetrable to King Archidamus, stretching all the way to the sea. But she was a weapon that could slip past the wall.

It was a long walk back to the port of Piraeus, forty or fifty stadia. A smuggler waited there to carry her away from Athens and back to her king.

The dream melted forward in time. Now, Spartan hoplites with plumed helmets and bronze shields escorted her again to the tent of King Archidamus, whose army still ravaged Attica, the land on which Athens depended for her agriculture.

It was a cold night, and Euanthe's hair was still damp from the sea. The fires of the army camp were a welcome sight to her.

Euanthe entered the king's tent.

Archidamus sat on a lion-footed chair, reading a scroll. More scrolls were stacked on the table at his elbow.

He smiled at Euanthe when she entered.

"We have reports of plague within Athens," the king said. "The entire city trembles in terror, on the verge of collapse."

"It is my plague that ravages them."

"And what of Pericles?"

"He still lives," Euanthe said. "I released the plague in his household, at a banquet, but he has not fallen ill. I do not know why he survives."

"It cannot be that the goddess favors him," Archidamus said. "Perhaps she is only toying with him."

"Others within Athens plot against Pericles," Euanthe said. "Like the man to whom I was sold. Cleon."

"Then the goddess preserves him so that he may suffer this treachery." Archidamus looked her over and smiled again. "Are you well? How have you endured?"

"I am cold," Euanthe said. "And very hungry."

The king called in one of his guards.

"Timon," King Archidamus said, "Bring the girl bread and meat."

"Should we raise a tent for her, as well?" the hoplite named Timon asked.

"No," the king said. "She will sleep here in my tent, under the direct protection of the king."

Both Euanthe and Timon looked at him with surprise.

"Bring an officer's cot for her," Archidamus ordered. "And several of our least filthy fleeces. Hang a curtain there for her." He gestured at the corner of his tent. "Tell the men to treat her as they would a member of the royal family, and to never touch her, or the curse of the goddess will fall upon them."

Timon departed.

"Thank you for your hospitality," Euanthe said. "And your protection."

"My protection?" Archidamus laughed. "My girl, you are here to protect me. I have enemies among my own people, as Pericles does in Athens. I charge you with the task of striking any who strike at me."

"Yes, my king," Euanthe said.

"I am sorry it came to this." Archidamus poured wine into a wooden cup and passed it to her. Euanthe drank, and it warmed her inside. He drank right from the skin, then wiped his purple lips. "I love the man Pericles, I truly do. He was a great leader in his time. But I have seen him grow addicted to empire, ambitious to rule all of Greece, all of the Aegean, all of Persia. And his people, his democracy, they support this. What we have done—what you have done, Euanthe—is necessary for all of us to live in peace."

Four young hoplites entered, and one presented Euanthe with a plate of bread and mutton. She ate quickly.

The men constructed her bedroom at one side of the king's tent, a cot piled high with sheepskins and a curtain wall.

When they left, the king spoke again.

"I suppose we have raided and pillaged enough for one war season," Archidamus said. "We can leave Athens to rot in its plague. We must return to Sparta for the harvest."

"My king," Euanthe said, "I thought you meant to invade Athens. Was that not my purpose, to prepare it for conquest?"

"Your purpose was to bring it to ruin. Athens no longer births great men. When Pericles falls, Athens will be ruled by rats like Cleon, and the Athenian empire will rot and fall from within."

"But you are pleased with me?"

"By every god, yes, dear girl. In Sparta, you will have a place in my household. I need your capabilities in my hands." He laughed. "I can hardly have you running around the city unwatched. Now go and sleep. I must speak with my men."

Euanthe hurried to lay in the bed. The curtain blocked out the light from the oil lamps, leaving her in a warm and comfortable darkness.

King Archidamus discussed with his officers their plans to break camp, steal anything that was worth stealing in Attica, and return home to Sparta.

Euanthe didn't mind all the men's loud voices as she fell asleep. She felt safe here. The king knew her purpose, and it was an important one. She had found her place in the world, where the goddess Aphrodite Areia intended her to be.

She thought of the king's dark, mirthful eyes and careworn face, and how gently he spoke to her, though he was hard and brusque with his men. A deep peace fell over her, and she slept.

Chapter Thirty-Eight

Jenny spent Saturday afternoon sculpting some new pottery, listening to the *Highwayman* record by Willie Nelson, Kris Kristofferson, Waylon Jennings, and Johnny Cash. The song "Highwayman" made more sense to her now than it ever had.

"I'll be back again, and again…" she sang under her breath, as her fingers worked to create form out of clay.

The phone rang. Jenny grabbed a rag and used that to pick it up, since her fingers were coated and wet.

"Hello?"

"Hey, Jenny, it's Darcy."

"How's Charleston?"

"Good, it's pretty cool. Seth's off touring the business school or some junk. This place has all kinds of historical stuff. Did you know it's the thirteenth-oldest college in the country? I wonder if that's bad luck, being thirteenth?"

"I hope not," Jenny said. "There's enough bad luck in the world."

"Anywho," Darcy said, "We're just, you know, orientating."

"What's Seth been doing?"

"Oh, he hung with some of his old school buddies last night. They seem nice."

"They do?"

"Well, maybe cause I'm pregnant. You know how everybody's nicer to you when you're pregnant?"

"Okay," Jenny said. "But he hasn't…done anything?"

"Like what?"

"Like hang out with girls, or anything like that?"

"Oh, I don't think so. Those guys act like pigs. I don't think any girl would go near them."

Jenny laughed.

"So, here's why I'm calling," Darcy said. "I've been feeding Ashleigh's dog Maybelle, you know? And I forgot to do it last night before we left. So she's probably really hungry by now."

"You want me to take care of Ashleigh's dog?"

"I know you and Ashleigh didn't get along," Darcy said. "But it's not the dog's fault. She's not Ashleigh's dog anymore. She's just a lonely dog with nobody to take care of her."

Jenny sighed. "Okay, I'll feed Maybelle. How do I get in the house?"

"The key's under a fake rock next to the basement door," Darcy said. "I know cause I used to do everything when the Goodlings went out of town. Feed the dog, clean the aquarium, mop, dust—"

"Fine," Jenny said. "Just keep Seth out of trouble, okay?"

"Will do. Cheerios." Darcy hung up.

Jenny opened the back door. Her dad was in the back yard, rebuilding a window-mounted air conditioning unit for somebody.

"Who was on the phone?" he asked.

"Darcy. She wants me to go feed Ashleigh Goodling's dog while they're out of town."

"Seth liking the school?"

"I guess. I haven't talked to him."

Her dad straightened up and rubbed his back. He wiped sweat from his forehead and looked at her. "Jenny, what are you planning to do?"

"Feed that dog, I guess."

"I mean in the big picture of things."

"I don't know. Seth wants me to go to Charleston, but that seems dangerous for me, with all them people. And I know his parents don't want me with him."

"What do you want?"

"I don't know. I want to get out beyond this town, but where I don't have to worry about the pox. Like that Appalachian Trail. You can go slow and hike it for months. That sounds nice, doesn't it? Just walking on and on through the woods, seeing new things every day."

"It does," he said. "You could do that."

"I'd have to do it by myself." Jenny shrugged. "What do you think I should do?"

"Jenny, you done killed half the town," her dad said. "You are way beyond anything I understand. And that's the truth."

His words hurt her feelings, but he was right. Jenny walked back into the house, thinking about the dead bodies she'd left on the town green. Then her dream, the ancient city filled with the sick and dying. She felt ill, and confused, and very alone.

Later, Jenny pulled into the driveway of Ashleigh's house. The evening shadows were already long and dark.

As soon as she got out of the car, she felt like she was being watched. She looked around the cul-de-sac. It didn't look like anybody was home at any house, and one even had a FOR SALE sign in the front yard, which had nearly been swallowed by high weeds.

Jenny walked around to the back yard. It was very secluded, surrounded by old trees with sprawling limbs. A big dry crater yawned open where the duck pond used to be. She hated how isolated and alone she felt, along with that feeling of an invisible eye staring at her from somewhere.

Jenny stopped and looked at the empty pond. She had died down there, and Seth had pulled her out and brought her back. Since then, she'd had occasional jumbled memories about past lives, especially in her dreams. They weren't like normal dreams, where she was participating and affecting what happened. They were more like movies, or reruns.

Seth didn't seem to be having these dreams, as far as he could remember.

Jenny felt like she and Seth were growing more distant from each other, and that worried her.

She walked to the lower patio, built next to the basement door. It was occupied by a park bench and Dr. Goodling's gigantic propane-powered grill. She found the big fake rock next to the door, with the key tucked inside a hollow compartment on the bottom.

Jenny held up the key and looked at the basement door. She didn't really like the idea of going in through the basement, which looked to be mostly underground. She still felt like she was being watched, but there was nobody around, unless someone was watching her from the windows of the house next door. Nobody had ever lived there, though.

The basement door unlocked with a rusty squeak, as if it hadn't been used in a long time. Jenny pushed the door inward.

The inside of the basement was a deep gloom. Jenny found the panel of light switches on the wall and flicked each one, but none of them seemed to do anything. It seemed like all the bulbs were burned out, or maybe the fuse.

"Damn it," Jenny whispered. She would have to find her way in the dark.

Jenny made her way deeper into the basement, her eyes slowly adjusting to the gloom. She tripped over something and sprawled face first, banging her chin on the concrete. She cried out, then looked back to see what had tripped her.

A pink Barbie roller skate, the right size for an eight-year-old girl, trundled across the basement and came to rest against a Christmas tree stand.

Even when dead, Ashleigh was still giving her problems.

Jenny pushed up to her feet and groped forward in the dark, sliding her sneakers along the floor so nothing else could trip her up.

Overhead, she heard footsteps in the house. That must be Maybelle, she thought.

Jenny found her way to the stairs, which were made of unstained boards. She crawled up them on hands and knees, since she could barely see anything more than a few inches ahead of her.

She pushed open the door at the top of the steps.

Immediately, a snarling, furry face filled her range of vision. Maybelle. The Welsh Corgi's mouth opened and closed, but only a hoarse rasping sound came out.

"Hi, Maybelle." Jenny stood up quickly, and the dog backed off a few steps. Maybelle kept up her pathetic attempts at barking as Jenny stepped into the front hall, closed the door, and found her way to the kitchen.

"Look, I'm here to feed you. Stop freaking out," Jenny said. The dog's debarked voice bothered her more than actual barking would have.

Jenny opened the pantry and found the thirty-pound bag of dry dog food, and then located the dog dishes in the laundry room. When Jenny reached for the empty food bowl, Maybelle let out a strangled growl and nipped at Jenny's hand, puncturing her thin summer glove and drawing blood.

"Bitch!" Jenny yelled, but she already felt sorry for the dog. The brief contact, and the slight taste of Jenny's blood, had opened sores along Maybelle's snout. "Aw, crap. I'm sorry, puppy."

Maybelle scampered away, trying to whimper, and hid herself elsewhere in the house.

"Good girl," Jenny said. "Stay away from me."

She dipped the food bowl into the bag and scooped out a heaping mound so she wouldn't need to come back soon. Jenny left the door to the pantry open, too, so Maybelle could get into the big bag if she needed to. Jenny certainly didn't intend to come back—let Darcy check on the dog Monday, and clean up any dog poo on the floor. Ashleigh's house creeped Jenny out.

Jenny glanced into the front parlor, where Maybelle was hiding with her head under a couch, her rump sticking out. The pristine white carpet was already stained with a couple of yellow urine splotches and a pile of dog crap.

Something about the house seemed wrong to Jenny. Everything was put away and cleaned off. There wasn't any dust anywhere, and she could still see vacuum cleaner tracks in the carpet.

Presumably, Dr. and Mrs. Goodling had rushed off to the town square to see about their daughter, who had supposedly been assaulted by Seth. The house looked neatly squared away, though, not one thing left out. Maybe Darcy was keeping up the house, she thought.

Then she remembered one more thing. Last time she'd been here, Ashleigh's Jeep was parked in the driveway, and Ashleigh herself was just a little pile of diseased and broken bones on the front walk.

Today, Ashleigh's Jeep hadn't been there. Jenny's car was the only one in the driveway.

Jenny decided to check the refrigerator, because if the house had really been abandoned for two months, the fridge should be full of mold and rotten food.

She looked inside. Everything seemed new and fresh—the Piggy Wiggly brand milk didn't expire for another week.

"Shit," Jenny whispered as she closed the refrigerator door. Someone was living here.

She immediately thought of the gray-eyed boy who'd given her and Seth an evening of intense waking nightmares. Ashleigh's opposite. What if he'd never left town? What if he was still here, spying on them? She'd certainly felt like someone was watching her, ever since she stepped out of her car.

For all she knew, there was a big black motorcycle in the garage. Maybe the Jeep was in there, too, or maybe he'd sold it for quick cash.

Maybe she wasn't alone in the house.

In another room, something crashed to the floor. Maybe the dog had knocked something over. Or maybe not.

Jenny swore again as she ran for the basement door, instinctively going back the way she'd come. She took them as fast as she dared in the dark, then ran through the basement and out the door. She closed it behind her, but she didn't bother taking time to lock it.

She ran as fast as she could around the house, picking up speed when she saw her car. Jenny looked around. She couldn't see anybody, but someone could be watching from the upper floors of Ashleigh's house, or maybe one of the empty houses nearby.

She sat down in her car, closed and locked the door. Her hand shook as she tried to fit the key into the ignition.

"Calm down," she whispered to herself. She inserted the key, cranked the car, and backed out of Ashleigh's driveway without bothering to look behind her.

As she pulled out, she thought she saw something move in an upper window of the house next door, the one that had never been lived in by anybody. But when she turned her head to look, nobody was there.

Chapter Thirty-Nine

Jenny pulled into her dirt driveway, relieved to see her dad's rusty old Ram still parked there. After her creepy experience at Ashleigh's, the last thing she wanted was to be alone.

She checked over the fence first, but he wasn't working on the air conditioner anymore.

She ran up the front steps to her house and pulled open the screen door.

"Hey, Dad, I think I'll take one of those hoop cheese sandwiches now." She walked into the living room. Her dad didn't reply.

Jenny checked his room to see if he was napping, but his door was open and he wasn't there.

"Dad?" She walked back up the hall. "Dad? Are you here?"

The kitchen table and two chairs were turned over on their sides. Jenny ran into the kitchen. "Dad?"

Broken dishes and cups littered the floor, including fragments of the *Happy Days* collector's glasses. Jenny's dad lay slumped against the kitchen wall, his eyes empty and staring straight ahead.

"Daddy!" Jenny screamed as she ran to him. Something was pinned to the front of his shirt, rumpled brown paper with letters from newspapers and magazines glued to it, like a ransom note. The letters across the top read:

SETH DIES TONIGHT

Beneath that was a crude marker drawing of an eye with a gray iris. The note was signed in smaller cutout letters:

YOU KNOW WHO

Jenny grabbed his shoulder and shook him. "Dad!"

He took a sharp breath of air, looking at her briefly—his eyes confused, seeing her and not seeing her at the same time—and then he rolled onto his hands and knees and crawled away from her, ignoring the broken glass and porcelain that cut his hands.

"Dad, stop! You're hurting yourself!"

He mumbled something and crawled faster.

Jenny wondered if he'd been drinking again, after months of being sober. But this wasn't his usual drunken behavior, either. This was just plain *weird*, and it scared her.

"Dad, where are you going?" She followed him as he crawled down the hall and into his room. He got up on his knees and peeked out the window, then ducked down as if something was about to come hurling through the glass.

"She's coming," he said. "She's watching."

"Who?"

"My daughter," he whispered. "She killed my wife and she's coming back to kill me. Just a matter of time."

"Dad, I'm..." Jenny decided not to finish the thought. If he was afraid of her, maybe it was best not to point out that she was, in fact, his daughter. "What happened? Was somebody here?"

"They're coming for me," he whispered. He peeked out the window again. "They're coming for all of us."

"Nobody's coming for us." Jenny touched his arm.

"Get back!" He howled and pulled away from her. He tripped over a pair of his shoes, and his head knocked into the end table by the bed. The lamp and alarm clock toppled from the table as it crashed to the floor.

"Dad! Are you okay?"

He pulled his knees to his chest and lay on the floor in a fetal position, shivering.

"Dad, answer me!"

"They're coming," he whispered. "They're all coming now."

"Where's your cell phone?"

"It's all gone," he whispered. "All this, it's all gone, they're taking it all away..."

"Is it in the kitchen? Wait right here, okay?" Jenny ran to the kitchen and found his phone on the counter, then ran back to his room. He was shaking, staring through her, terrified.

She didn't know what was wrong with him, but Seth could fix it. Jenny dialed Seth's cell.

"Hey, this is Seth, leave a message." His voicemail answered immediately, which meant his phone was turned off. The voicemail beeped.

"Fuck!" Jenny said. "Seth, it's Jenny. This is my dad's phone. Call back now, okay? It's an emergency. Seriously. Okay? Please?"

She hung up. Her dad got to his feet and stumbled out to the hall, still muttering under his breath.

"Dad? Where are you going now?" She followed him up the hall. His shoulder kept banging against the wall, knocking down framed photographs, as if he were having trouble keeping his balance.

"I got to get the gun," he said. He doubled back and pushed by her, though she tried to stop him. "Before they come back."

"Dad, please, do not do that." She followed him back to his room. He knelt by the bed and rooted underneath it, where he kept his shotgun. "Dad, no!" She dropped down beside him and pulled back on his arms. "We don't need the gun."

"You ain't listening to me!" He looked at her, but he still didn't seem to recognize her. "They're coming for all of us."

"Nobody's coming." The cell phone in her pocket was silent as death. Why wouldn't Seth call back? "Come on, Dad. Maybe you need to go to the hospital." She hooked a hand under his arm to help him up.

"No!" he shouted. He crawled away from her.

"They can help you," Jenny said.

"They're after me." He crawled into the hallway again.

"Nobody's after you." Jenny followed him, trying not to cry now. She didn't know what to do, and there was nobody to help her.

He crawled to a corner of the living and pulled his knees to his chest, head low.

"Dad, please." Jenny took his hands. "Just let me take you to the hospital."

"You ain't taking me nowhere. You get the hell out of my house!"

"Dad..." Jenny couldn't help it, she was really crying now. "Dad, come on. Just get up on your feet."

"What do you want with me?" he asked.

"I'm just trying to get you help," she said. "Come on, stand up."

He looked at her with deep suspicion, but he did let her help him stand.

"This way," Jenny whispered. "It's gonna be okay."

She led him toward the front door, and he leaned heavily on her. She managed to get him out through the screen door and down the steps. Then she guided him toward the car and opened the passenger door.

"Oh, hell no!" He shouted. He pulled away from her and ran into the shed.

"Daddy, stop!" Jenny ran after him.

She found him crouched behind the workbench, looking around. When he saw her, he ducked his head out of sight.

"Dad, come on."

"You're gonna kill me," he said.

"I am not!" Jenny didn't even try to stop her tears from pouring out. This whole situation was confusing and frightening.

"Dad, come on..." Jenny struggled to think of what to do. Her mother's name popped into her head. "Your wife is waiting for you. Miriam."

"Miriam?" He looked up. "Where?"

"We're going to see her." Jenny held out one gloved hand. "Right now. But we have to hurry."

"Miriam," he whispered. He took her hand, and Jenny helped him stand again.

"This way," Jenny said. She walked him out to the car, and this time he was willing to sit inside it. Jenny hurried to close his door and run around to the driver's side.

"I ain't seen Miriam..." he whispered as Jenny started the car. "I ain't seen Miriam since..."

"Just settle down," Jenny said. He was squirming and fidgeting in his seat as they backed out of the driveway.

"Miriam... Miriam..." he whispered. Jenny stepped on the gas. It was twenty-five minutes to the county hospital, if you obeyed the speed limit, which she didn't plan to do.

The longer they drove, the more agitated her dad became. He started slapping at the window by his head. "Where we going?" he demanded.

"I told you. The hospital."

"Aw, no." He pulled at the door handle, and the passenger door opened. The road outside flew past at sixty miles an hour. He lifted one foot from the floor, clearly intending to step out of the moving car.

"Daddy, no!" Jenny grabbed him and pulled him back. The forward motion of the car closed the door. Jenny wished she had automatic locks, or that she'd locked the door or put on his seatbelt before starting the car. Or that her dad hadn't gone completely crazy in the first place.

He stared at the car door, looking puzzled. Fortunately, he didn't make another attempt to open it.

The county hospital was a single-story brick building. Jenny pulled into a parking spot near the front door labeled EMERGENCY ONLY. She ran to open his door.

"Come on, Dad." She held out a hand to him. "We're here."

His eyes narrowed with suspicion at he stared at the hospital. "Where we at?"

"We're just going to the hospital for a minute, and then we'll go back home."

"I don't like this. Where's my daughter?"

"She's coming," Jenny said.

"You better call her."

He pushed himself out of the car and began to stumble across the parking lot, away from the hospital.

"No, this way." Jenny took his arm and turned him around. The brown piece of paper fluttered on his shirt like a child's bib. Jenny tore it away and stuffed it in her jeans pocket.

The clear doors to the emergency room slid apart automatically as Jenny walked him in. The bright fluorescent lights gave the hospital an unreal, washed-out look.

Jenny brought her dad to the front desk, where a bored nurse looked up from a portable TV.

"Yes?" the nurse asked.

"Hi," Jenny said. "This is my dad."

Jenny's dad stood beside her, fidgeting and looking around the waiting room, but not doing anything obvious to indicate his confused state.

"Yes?" the nurse asked.

"He's really off," Jenny said. "Like not making any sense."

"Sir?" the nurse said. "Are you feeling okay?"

"Huh?" He had troubled focusing on her—his head kept moving around. "Just looking for my wife."

"She's been dead eighteen years," Jenny whispered to the nurse. "Almost nineteen."

"Is he on medication?" The nurse looked her dad up and down with a hint of disgust. "Or drugs? Alcohol?"

"Nothing like that," Jenny said. "I don't know what's wrong with him."

The nurse nodded and handed her a stack of forms on a clipboard. "Fill these out. We'll need your insurance information."

"Um..." Jenny said.

"You do have insurance, don't you?"

"Maybe. Dad, let me see your wallet."

Her dad stared at a framed photograph on the wall, which showed a decrepit old general store with a prominent Coca-Cola sign. He seemed lost inside it. Jenny poked his arm.

"Huh?" he asked.

"Your wallet." Jenny held out her hand. "Give me your wallet."

"Oh. Okay." He took his wallet out and held it in her general direction. Jenny took it from his hand.

"You gonna give that back, right?" he asked.

"Yes, Dad." She flipped through the wallet for a minute. "I can't find anything about health insurance."

"Indigent," the nurse sighed. "Go have a seat and fill out those forms. Someone will see you when they're available."

"Okay, thanks." Jenny led her dad to the row of hard plastic seats in the waiting room. She couldn't make him sit, so she let him stand where he was, gawking at everything.

Jenny filled in all the information she could, looking up frequently to make sure he hadn't wandered off. He was trembling and shuffling his feet around, but he seemed a bit calmer now.

After fifteen minutes, she returned the clipboard of forms to the nurse.

"Have a seat," the nurse said. She seemed a lot colder now, having determined that Jenny's dad might be poor and uninsured.

Jenny sat. She reached into the pocket where she'd put her dad's cell phone. The crumpled brown paper was on top of it, so she had to pull that out first. She'd been in such a panic that she hadn't really looked at it.

Now she unfolded it.

SETH DIES TONIGHT.
YOU KNOW WHO.

It was Ashleigh's opposite, Jenny thought. He must have inflicted a massive dose of fear on her dad.

The gray eye was one clue, and so were the words “You Know Who.” That was what everyone called the villain, Lord Voldemort, in the *Harry Potter* books. Ashleigh's first big campaign, when she was a sophomore in high school, was to get *Harry Potter* banned from all the school libraries in the county, on the grounds that it promoted witchcraft to children. The whole thing had just been a big power trip for Ashleigh.

Jenny dialed Seth, but it went straight to voice mail again, so she tried Darcy’s cell phone, though she was a little unsure about the last digit of Darcy’s number.

“*Guten tag!*” Darcy’s voice answered. “You’ve reached Darcy. Leave a message, okay? I will definitely call you back.”

The phone beeped.

“Darcy, it’s Jenny, it’s an emergency. Y’all might be in danger, and I need to talk to Seth right now. Please, please call me back right away.”

She hung up the phone. A nurse was approaching, so Jenny shoved the nightmare boy’s note back in her pocket.

“Mr. Morton?” the nurse said.

Jenny’s dad just looked at the picture of the Coca-Cola sign.

“That’s him,” Jenny said.

The nurse put a hand on his arm and he jumped.

“Mr. Morton, we need to go this way,” the nurse said. She led him toward a pair of double doors that said STAFF AND PATIENTS ONLY.

‘Where are we going?” He was shaking again. He looked back over his shoulder at Jenny. “Where are we going? Where are we going?”

“You’re gonna be okay, Dad.” Jenny’s voice broke when she said “Dad,” and she looked down at the floor to hide the renewed rush of tears behind her long black hair.

Jenny raised the cell phone to her face again.

"You ain't supposed to use those in here!" the front desk nurse shouted. "Take it outside."

"Okay, sorry." Jenny walked to the double doors.

"Can afford a nice, fancy cell phone, can't be bothered to buy insurance," the nurse muttered. The clear Plexiglas doors closed behind Jenny.

Jenny didn't know how her dad's boxy, paint-stained old phone could be considered "nice," but she had much more important things to do than argue with some stupid nurse.

She tried Seth again, and then Darcy. Nobody answered.

Jenny found June's number in her dad's phone and called her instead. June had been dating her dad for a few months now, and she was the only person Jenny knew to call for help.

"Hi, sugar!" June said. In the background, someone shouted an order for two scrambled eggs and raisin toast.

"It's me, Jenny."

"Well, hello, sweet potato."

"Do you know if my dad has any, like, health insurance?"

"Oh, good Lord, what's happened?"

"He's had some kind of…I'm at the hospital, and—"

"Is he okay?"

"He's just had some kind of…nervous breakdown thing."

"Are you at Eldritch County Hospital?"

"Yes."

"My shift's almost over. I'll be there in ten, fifteen, twenty minutes."

"Wow, thanks," Jenny said. "Actually, I have a whole other emergency with Seth, and I have to go find him. So I might not be here."

"What's happening with Seth?"

"That's a long story."

"Well, honey, they ain't gonna let me in to see him. Only kin."

"Shit. Tell them you're engaged. And I'll tell them you're engaged, too. Maybe that will work."

"I guess I do have my ring from my first marriage," June said. "I'll put that on and give it a try. I'll be there in ten, fifteen, twenty—"

"Thanks, June."

Jenny tried calling Seth and Darcy again. She paced in front of the hospital for half a minute, then tried another time. Nobody was answering. She ran back inside to the front desk nurse, who was opening a little jar of fingernail polish.

"Any news on my dad?"

The nurse sighed. "We'll tell you when there's something to tell you."

"Okay, well, I have to go. My dad's fiancé is coming to check on him."

"Whatever."

"I'll try to find if there's any insurance stuff, too."

"Sure you will." The nurse began painting her fingernails.

Jenny ran out to her car and cranked it up, but then she sat for a minute. She didn't like the idea of leaving town when her dad was like this, before she even knew whether the hospital would really be able to help. Maybe they could sedate him, but he would probably still have nightmares.

It was also obvious that Ashleigh's opposite was setting a trap for her. Jenny's dad was just a warning—he was threatening to kill Seth. She felt stupid walking right into it, but the guy did seem like a person capable of murder. And Seth had no idea he was coming—unless the guy had already gotten to Seth.

She took a deep breath and put the car in reverse. She would have to drive all the way to Charleston, and she couldn't even remember the name of the hotel where they were staying. She hoped somebody was answering their phone by the time she got there.

Jenny sped past a Palmetto Bug gas station, towards Highway 63 and the Atlantic Ocean. She felt like the ground had opened beneath her and she was falling fast, and there was nobody left to catch her.

Chapter Forty

"Dude, at the Sig Alph house last weekend, they had sixty pounds of crayfish, six kegs of Heiney, and we ate *all* that shit," Wooly said. "It was off the chain, gang."

"This is pretty good," Ashleigh said. They were sitting on the sidewalk curb—Ashleigh, Seth, Wooly and the other two Grayson boys, Steven Hunter and Adam Branderford ("Skunker" and "Aces," as far as Wooly was concerned). Everyone had a Styrofoam bowl of Frogmore stew, which they'd bought from an old lady at a wooden festival booth.

"This ain't shit," Wooly said. "My uncle makes a mean lowcountry boil. Fat shrimp he catches himself on his boat, hot sausage, corn, potatoes, Old Bay, splash in some Tabasco—bam. That's eating like a motherfucking *king*, S-dog."

"Those are the same ingredients here, too," Seth said. He wasn't liking the *S-dog* nickname Wooly kept trying to apply to him. He poked a shrimp with his spoon. "Those are the basic ingredients of any boil, aren't they?"

"Man, there's ingredients, and then there's fucking *ingredients*, you know what I'm saying?" Wooly said.

Darcy's cell phone rang inside the big canvas purse. Ashleigh pulled it out. It was Tommy, using a prepaid cell phone he'd bought with cash at a convenience store, if he'd followed instructions correctly.

"Oh, criminy," Ashleigh said. She was getting sick of playing Darcy all the time. Being that girl was almost as annoying as hanging out with her. "That's my parents. 'Scuse."

She heaved herself up, and Seth jumped up to help her stand. Ashleigh squeezed his hand, charming him with her love. "Thank you, Seth."

“Anytime.” He beamed at her as she walked away. Sucker.

She found a narrow, relatively uncrowded alley where the buildings tamped down the noise from the band. The phone had gone to voicemail by this point, so Ashleigh called Tommy back.

“She took him to the hospital,” Tommy said. “She just now got him inside. He’s all fucked up.”

“Good,” Ashleigh said. “And she saw the note?”

“Definitely.”

“Perfect. Her next move will be to get in her car and drive to Charleston to save her poor little boyfriend. She’s going to be wary, though. She’s not too stupid. Where are you now?”

“Palmetto Bug gas station. It’s across from the hospital parking lot.”

“Get out of there! You don’t want her to see you, or she’ll come after you instead of down here.”

“She already left the hospital. She didn’t see me.” Tommy said.

“She already left?” Ashleigh snapped. “That means she’s on her way *here*, Tommy. And she’ll drive crazy fast to get to Seth. So get moving, because I need you here first.”

“I’m on my way.”

Ashleigh hung up. Now it was time for the risky part.

She’d planted the seed first thing Monday, sending Neesha’s pictures of Jenny over to that CDC doctor. She’d worried that the government would react too quickly, but they hadn’t. She wanted the information to flow around to prime the pump, but she didn’t want them acting just yet. Now, she just hoped they didn’t move too slowly.

Heather heard the landline ring, but she didn’t move to answer it. That was what husbands and voicemail were for, on a Saturday night when she was watching *Top Chef* on TiVo.

Then it stopped ringing abruptly, and she heard Tricia in the kitchen, screaming, “Hi! Hi! Hi!”

Heather sighed and hurried into the kitchen, where Liam had apparently left the toddler alone with a plate of fish sticks. Fish sticks were scattered on the floor, and Tricia clutched several in one hand. Tricia held the cordless phone next to one ketchup-smeared cheek.

"My mommy's name is Heather!" Tricia shouted to whoever was on the phone. They must have been asking for her, then. "I have fish sticks!"

"Tricia." Heather took the phone from her, and Tricia scowled with indignation. "If you answer the phone, you have to give it to Daddy or me. Preferably Daddy." Then she spoke directly the phone. "Sorry about that. Hello?"

"Are you talking to me now?" a girl's voice asked.

"Yes, sorry, I was—"

"Fish sticks, fish sticks!" Tricia attempted to place fish sticks into Heather's mouth. Heather knelt beside her, wiping away the ketchup smear on her cheek with a Wet One.

"I don't want the fish stick, honey," Heather said. "Especially not up my nose."

"Fish stick!"

"Everything okay?" the girl on the phone asked.

"Yes, sorry, who is this?" Heather asked.

"It's Darcy Metcalf. From Fallen Oak."

"Oh…did I give you this number?" Heather definitely hadn't. Her cell phone, but not her home phone. Which meant Darcy had done at least some light Internet stalking.

"I'm so sorry," Darcy said. "But it's a total super-huge emergency. You know how Jenny killed all those people?"

"Don't worry, we're looking into that," Heather said. In fact, the order had come down that a contingent of Homeland Security officers would go to Fallen Oak on Monday to take Jenny into custody for extensive testing. Heather was supposed to go along. She thought it was a little heavy-handed—it might be best just to reach out to the girl quietly, and only escalate to force if necessary—but that wasn't Heather's call to make.

"There isn't time to just look into it!" Darcy said. "Jenny's in Charleston now. There's a music festival. And she bet her boyfriend, Seth, she bet him that she could kill ten thousand people this time."

"Are you serious?"

"Honest to God! Everyone's even taking bets on how many people will die. It's weird. It's like some people are actually looking forward to it, or at least they don't care. I didn't know who else to call because most people wouldn't know enough to believe me."

"Are you sure about this, Darcy?" Heather felt a cold, sinking feeling in her gut. This was her worst-case nightmare, Jenny going to a densely populated area. And it sounded like the girl actually enjoyed infecting people.

"Yeah, it's horrible!" Darcy said. "You have to do something. The police, or the Army, or something! You can't let her get away with it again."

"I can't just call up the Army," Heather said.

"You'd better find an army somewhere," Darcy said. "Or Jenny is going to destroy that city, and it's gonna be worse than 9/11. I have to go now. Please bring help, okay? Nobody else will." Darcy hung up.

"Jesus Christ," Heather said.

"Cheeses rice." Tricia giggled.

"Don't swear, Tricia." Heather took the girl under one arm, then carried her to the office. She needed to get in touch with Schwartzman, and with somebody at Homeland Security who had the power to mobilize.

Before long, Nelson Artleby would get wind of the situation, and Heather wanted things moving well before that happened. Her first concern was public health, but Nelson's was politics, and that could lead to some very poor decisions.

She called Schwartzman at home.

After Darcy walked away to answer her phone, Wooly turned to Seth.

"Dude," Wooly said, "What the hell?"

"What the hell what?" Seth forked a spicy chunk of sausage into his mouth.

"Why is she with us? Why is she with *you*?"

"I told you, she's my girlfriend's friend, she needed a ride to Orientation—"

"Okay, okay, that's all good," Wooly nodded. "But listen, you can't bring home a sweet slice of titty-tang with the Goodyear blimp parked in your penthouse, know what I'm saying?"

"What do you expect me to do, throw her out?"

"Just park her ass at the Holiday Inn, S-dog. That'll clear your way for a taste of the tang."

"I'm not trying to get laid this weekend, anyway," Seth said. "I just want to get drunk and see Willie Nelson."

"Aw, come on," Wooly said. "It's Saturday night, summertime, Funk Fest—*everybody's* getting laid this weekend. Am I right?" Wooly high-fived the other two guys, who nodded and "Hell yeah"d along with him.

"Whatever." Seth threw the empty Styrofoam bowl into a big steel drum of a trash can. "You guys are gonna pass out under one of these trees and wake up with a dog pissing in your face in the morning."

All of three of them laughed.

"Damn, S-dog, don't hold back," Wooly said.

"Give me that vodka." Seth took the thermos and took a swig, probably two or three shots' worth. It was good vodka, too, very smooth.

They passed it around, while Wooly told a very long and meticulously detailed story about the time he'd almost hooked up with an Asian skater chick, except she barfed and passed out.

"All right, last shot goes to my man S-dog." Wooly passed Seth the thermos, where the vodka was nearly depleted. "I'm gonna make sure you have a good time tonight. Priority one…" He looked past Seth and his eyes widened. "Hit the brakes. *New* priority one. Tap *that* shit."

Darcy was returning, arm in arm with a girl Seth didn't know—for a moment, though, he could have sworn it was Ashleigh. Tall, blond, same build, almost the same tits, even. As if Darcy had specifically sought out someone that looked like her.

"Hey guys," Darcy said. "This is my new friend Allegra. We just totally bonded over some Redheaded Sluts in that bar." She pointed vaguely behind her.

"We totally did!" the blond girl agreed. She was smiling so wide her face was about to split. Closer up, she didn't look too much like Ashleigh at all. She looked kind of East European or Russian, something like that. "I love Redheaded Sluts!"

"Me, too!" Darcy said, and they burst into drunken laughter.

"Did you know she's pregnant?" Allegra rubbed Darcy's belly. "She's so pregnant! And so drunk!"

"Who cares?" Darcy said. "I'm giving it for adoption anyway, right? It's somebody else's problem!"

She and Allegra fell into more drunken laughter, leaning against each other.

Wooly stepped forward to introduce himself.

"I'm Chris," he said. "But everybody calls me Wooly. Cause I'm mammoth."

"Oh, is this the boy you were telling me about?" Allegra asked. Her eyes flicked up and down Wooly's body.

"No, this is Seth." Darcy tugged Allegra past Wooly, closer to Seth. She lay a hand on Seth's arm. "Isn't he way foxy?"

"Oh, yes." Allegra's dark eyes looked into Seth's. "Yes, he is."

Seth felt something like a surge of heat and light in his chest, which spread like molten gold through his body, filling up his head. The incredibly beautiful Allegra seemed to sparkle and glow in front of his eyes. She was everything to him. The past and the future, any other thoughts or concerns, all fell away before her. Every cell in his body cried out with an aching need for her.

"Allegra," Seth whispered, his voice full of awe.

"Yes," she whispered back. Her eyes were locked onto his, and their bodies seemed to drift together, until her hand rested on the back of his neck, and he was embracing her around the hips, drawing her close.

They kissed, and the air around them seemed to ignite. Seth was lost in her smell, her taste, the warm shape of her body against him. He was barely even aware of Darcy's hand still gripping his upper arm.

After a long time, they came back up from the kiss, and their faces parted enough so Seth could admire her eyes, and nose, and cheeks…and those perfect lips…

"Come on, lovebirds," Darcy said. She took one of Seth's hands, and one of Allegra's, and led them away like slow, stubborn horses. They couldn't stop looking at each other.

"Go on, get it on, S-dog!" Wooly shouted behind them, and the two other guys gave drunken cheers. "Daaaaamn, that pregnant chick is a tang *magnet*. Hey, pregnant chick, come back and hang!"

Darcy looked back over her shoulder and winked.

Chapter Forty-One

Heather drove toward the airport, where the CDC's leased plane was waiting. It would ferry her, Schwartzman and a group of first responders. Homeland Security was sending in a flood of people, too, and coordinating with South Carolina state police, Charleston police, and it was rumored that the National Guard had been put on alert. Someone had decided, thankfully, that this was a full-scale emergency in need of strong prevention.

It looked like Darcy Metcalf was going to get her army, after all. Heather just hoped they had biohazard gear.

The situation was volatile and chaotic, which was good, because it meant things were unfolding fast. Heather had been worried that she wouldn't be able to summon a strong enough response, but apparently the picture of Jenny Morton infected with the unknown pathogen, the results of Heather's extremely unorthodox lab tests, and the as-yet-unexplained huge body count in Fallen Oak had made their way to the right decision-makers, despite the rush to cover up the event.

She'd heard that state police had been dispatched to Jenny Morton's house, but they found nobody home, which wasn't exactly reassuring. Heather had called Darcy Metcalf's house, and Darcy's parents said she had gone to the beach.

Heather couldn't help imagining the city of Charleston with thousands of bodies in the street, diseased and contorted like those in Fallen Oak. She shook the image away, but it kept creeping back.

She stepped on the gas.

Tommy looked out at the crowd of people five stories below. From the balcony, he could see the bandstand, which had been temporarily expanded to accommodate the bands and their walls of speakers.

He'd arrived about twenty minutes ago and stashed his motorcycle inside the tall picket-fence dumpster enclosure behind the hotel. He'd rolled the bike behind the dumpster itself, in case any hotel staff took the garbage out. Getting the bike out would be a little trouble if he had to leave in a hurry, but the nearest parking spot was blocks away, and you couldn't make a quick exit when you had to hoof it half a mile and then wind your way out of a parking garage.

He looked back inside the hotel room, where Esmeralda lay on the bed, watching music videos on TV. She had a drugged, detached look to her face that bothered him.

"Esmeralda," he said.

Her gaze drifted in his direction.

"What do you think of all this?" Tommy asked.

"All of what?"

"Ashleigh." Tommy stepped back into the room and sat on the edge of the bed. He looked at the piece of bone hanging on the gold chain around Esmeralda's neck. "I'm not sure about this thing she's asking me to do."

"You've been practicing," Esmeralda said. "You'll do fine."

"No, I mean I'm wondering whether I should do it at all. Ashleigh tells us that this Jenny girl is so evil—"

"She is," Esmeralda said. "She killed all those people."

"But more could die tonight," Tommy said. "All to capture one girl? And bringing in all the cops and feds makes me nervous."

"Ashleigh knows what she's doing," Esmeralda said. "That's what you kept telling me. We had to bring her back because she understands us, and what we are. You said that. You were obsessed with it."

"I still think that, but she's not honest. Watch how she manipulates everyone else. How do we know she's not manipulating us?"

"Because we're her soul family. She told me. We always help each other in all our lifetimes. The three of us belong together."

"I thought you didn't believe in reincarnation. What if she's lying about—"

"She is not lying to us!" Esmeralda sat up and hugged a pillow. "Ashleigh loves us. I know it. And I love her, too."

"Making people feel love is her power. She only has to touch you."

"But it doesn't work on us," Esmeralda said.

"It doesn't work on me," Tommy said. "But I think she cast a spell on you. Has she been touching you a lot, or in any unusual way?"

Esmeralda blushed and turned her head.

"She has, hasn't she?" Tommy asked.

"We have fun together. We both enjoy it."

"You didn't even like her at first," Tommy said.

"I just didn't know her." Esmeralda scowled.

"I know her better now, too," Tommy said. "And maybe I'm wrong, but..."

"You are wrong."

"So…if I wanted to duck out of this whole thing, and hit the road...would you come with me?"

"What are you talking about?"

Tommy took her hand. Fear leaked into her, but he tried to hold it in as much as he could. "I've never been happier than that moment when you first got on my bike. And then riding through the desert with your arms around me. You don't know what that meant to me. Didn't it seem like something good was about to happen?"

"Good things have happened." She squeezed his hand. "We found Ashleigh. She has brought so much into our lives."

"She's using us, I think," Tommy said. "She has her own agenda, and she's using us—"

"*We* are her agenda!" Esmeralda said. "We're only getting rid of this Jenny person so she doesn't kill us. So the world will be safe for the three of us. We can all be together after that, with nothing to fear. Ashleigh is really smart and she knows what needs to happen."

"And what if you had to choose between her and me?"

"I would choose her."

He took her words like a sharp belt lash across the face. Tommy let go of her hand and walked back to the open balcony. "Then the only way I can be with you, is to be with her."

"The three of us, Tommy. Nobody left out."

Tommy looked out at the crowd of smiling, dancing, drinking, kissing people, and he thought about the horror he had to unleash on them.

Jenny sped down the highway towards Charleston as the night grew dark around her. She'd called Seth and Darcy several times as she drove, and left each of them panicked voicemails, but nobody had called back.

A mile marker told her she was thirty miles from Charleston. The further she drove, the slower she seemed to travel, though she kept the needle between eighty and ninety in the countryside. She slowed as she passed through the little towns, where police might be lying in wait for a quick buck.

Doubt gnawed on her guts. She felt horrible for leaving her dad in that condition, when he was acting so confused and lost. Maybe she'd made the wrong choice. Seth had brought himself back from the dead before. Even if Ashleigh's opposite really did kill him, Seth might be able to bring himself back, as long as his body wasn't too destroyed.

And somebody was waiting up ahead for Jenny, using Seth as bait, expecting stupid little Jenny Mittens to take the hook in her mouth. Jenny was doing exactly what Ashleigh's opposite wanted.

She thought about turning back. It was stupid to walk into an ambush, and she needed to go take care of her dad.

Then her phone rang. Darcy, finally calling her back.

Chapter Forty-Two

Ashleigh sat in the antique French arm chair in Seth's room at the Mandrake House. The chair was 19th century, the back and arms carved with images of a woman and gargoyles. It felt like a throne to her. She ate from silver room-service trays: shrimp and grits, sliced heirloom tomatoes, a cheeseburger, a waffle, pecan pie, orange juice and sweet tea. The pregnancy made her crave everything. Besides, she needed to load up on calories to charge up her power, because she'd zapped her latest two victims pretty hard.

Seth and the random girl Ashleigh had picked for him rolled around on the big four-poster bed a few feet away. The girl—what was her name? Alondra?—was already down to her underwear, and she'd stripped off his shirt and started kissing his abdominal muscles.

The girl really was incredibly hot, Ashleigh thought. She was almost as pretty as Ashleigh's last body had been, and nicely tanned, too. Ashleigh was more than sick of thumping around in Darcy's pregnant hippo body. Why couldn't she take this girl's form instead?

Darcy's cell phone, with its stupid cartoon-kitten stickers, sang out a chime. New voice mail from Jenny. Though Ashleigh hadn't answered the calls, she had eagerly listened to each voice mail as they came in. Jenny was even helpful enough to tell how far she was from Charleston in each voice mail, so there had been no reason for Ashleigh to call her back.

"Darcy, Jenny again," the recording said. "I'm about forty miles from there. I really, really need you to call back and tell me where to meet you, or what hotel you're at, or something. Please. Thanks."

Ashleigh decided to let Jenny stew a little longer.

On the bed, the blond girl—Alissa?—was eagerly grappling with Seth's belt. She pulled it off him and ripped open his jeans. Seth unhooked her bra.

"Slow down, guys," Ashleigh said. "You don't want to blow your wad."

The girl paused long enough to fling her bra aside, and it hooked over a lamp. She whipped Seth's jeans off and threw them to the carpet.

"I said slow down, damn it!" Ashleigh shouted.

She heaved herself to her feet, got a head rush, struggled with her balance. The baby woke up and kicked in an annoying way against the wall of her womb, three times, then a fourth, then a fifth. "Stop it!" Ashleigh made a fist and punched the baby as hard as she could, and the little bastard quit kicking.

Ashleigh staggered toward the bed. Seth flung the girl onto her back, and she laughed and wrapped her legs around his hips.

"Wait!" Ashleigh put her hands on both of them, taking control of the situation. "Stop. Cool down."

"But I don't want to stop," the girl whined. She clutched Seth tighter between her thighs.

"This is going too fast," Ashleigh said. "Look. We should play a game. I know the perfect thing."

"That sounds fun," Seth said. "Would that make you happy, Allegra?"

"But I want to fuck," Allegra whined.

"Check this out." Ashleigh reached under the bed and pulled out a length of rope. Ashleigh had tied them herself, upstairs in Tommy and Esmeralda's room on the fifth floor, while Seth was out with his Grayson friends the previous night. Ashleigh Goodling had been a highly decorated Girl Scout in her time, and had brought in a small fortune for her troop pushing those Thin Mints and Tagalongs, even though she overcharged for the cookies and took a cut off the top for herself.

The rope had a noose at each end.

"What are we doing?" Seth asked.

"Just watch," Ashleigh said. She looped one rope around the base of a headboard poster, and then handed both ends of it to Allegra.

"What do I do?" Allegra asked.

Ashleigh put a hand on the back of Allegra's neck. "You want to tie him up. It's always been your fantasy."

"Yeah, I guess it has. Give me your hands, Seth."

"I don't know." Seth looked a little puzzled. Ashleigh quickly took his arm.

"You love this idea," Ashleigh said.

"I love this idea." A giddy smile broke across Seth's face. "I really, really love this idea."

"Anything to make you happy, Seth." Allegra slipped the nooses over Seth's wrists and pulled them tight.

Ashleigh had spent more than an hour on those knots. They were masterpieces, little bunches of knots coiled within knots. Once they pulled tight and small, it would be nearly impossible for Seth to untie them. Seth was no Boy Scout.

Ashleigh grabbed some of the bed's excessive supply of pillows and arranged them over and around Seth's roped hands.

Ashleigh walked to the door of the room and turned back to look, as if she'd just stepped in on them. There was no visible sign that Seth was restrained at all. Perfect.

The girl began to tug Seth's boxer shorts down.

"Honey, no, wait," Ashleigh said. She placed a hand on the back of the girl's neck. "Slow down. Once you get him going, you've only got a couple minutes. Go real slow, like I told you."

The girl sighed. She lay down on top of Seth and kissed him slowly, all over the face.

Ashleigh walked out on the balcony and closed the doors behind her. The last thing she needed was Seth's voice in the background. Out here, there were the sounds of music and lots of people, exactly what she needed.

She called Jenny back.

"Darcy, thank God," Jenny said. "Are you okay?"

"Huh? Yeah, I'm peachy. Why?"

"What about Seth?"

"I guess he's okay. I haven't seen him in a while."

"A while?"

"Coupla hours, I guess. He went off with a bunch of his old friends."

"For a couple of hours?"

"It's okay," Ashleigh said. "I'm having a good time anywho, and I get they don't want some pregnant chick hanging around. And Seth doesn't want to look uncool in front of his friends, and I know what it's like when you don't want to look uncool—"

"Darcy, Seth might be in danger. Are you sure you don't know where he is?"

"Well, I don't see him anywhere, but there's like a bazillion people here," Ashleigh said. "Did you try calling him?"

"His phone's not even on."

Ashleigh smiled. She had pickpocketed Seth's phone, turned it off, and dropped it in Darcy's big canvas purse. Though ugly and horribly big, the purse was turning out to be pretty useful.

"Well…I don't know," Ashleigh said. "I guess I could go back to the hotel and look for him there." Through the glass window, she saw the girl sucking Seth's cock. Ashleigh pounded on the window. When Allegra looked up at her, Ashleigh shook her head and did a cutting motion across her throat. Why wouldn't that slut slow down? Ashleigh must have overdosed her with love. "How far away are you?"

"I'll be in Charleston in ten minutes, but I don't know where to go from there."

"Meet me at The Mandrake House." Ashleigh gave her directions, including which parking garage to use and the best way to walk to the hotel. She figured Jenny would use the same route when she later left the hotel, and that was something Ashleigh was interested in controlling. "I'll just wait in the lobby for you, okay?"

"Yeah. Darcy, everything's crazy right now. I'm so glad to have you as a friend."

"I'm glad to have you as a friend, too, Jenny," Ashleigh said.

"You sure kicked up a big storm," Schwartzman said. He sat beside Heather, looking out the airplane window into a dark, murky night. "You sure this was a good idea?"

Around them, more CDC investigators were clustered around laptops and talking in low voices, as they caught up on the scarce information.

"There could be a serious event tonight," Heather said.

"You better hope there is," Schwartzman said. "The National Guard's on alert. We have state and local police looking for this girl—"

"That could be dangerous."

"—with orders to report if they see her, but leave her alone until we can get a biohazard team out there. Homeland Security's going to be all over that city. This is going to be one hell of a bar tab if you're wrong, Heather."

"But you can imagine what she could do in a city, with a big crowd like that."

"I can imagine things all day," Schwartzman said. "I can imagine Director Voynich asking why we raised the nation's threat level an entire color today, if nothing turns up."

"They still do that color thing?" Heather asked.

"Heather, I'm serious."

"Me, too. I had no idea they still did that."

"Heather—"

"What do you want me to say? If there's a fifty percent—fuck, ten percent, five percent—chance she's going to repeat what happened in that town, shouldn't we try to stop it? Shouldn't we capture her? Quarantine her? Study her?"

Schwartzman tilted his head back and narrowed his eyes, a look that meant he was studying you with possible intent to psychoanalyze.

"That's what you want, isn't it?" he asked. "To study her. You think you'll discover something."

"Possibly," Heather said.

"Something extraordinary."

"We passed extraordinary a while ago, don't you think?"

"What is it you want to know?"

"I want to understand how she does it. There's a lot here that doesn't make any sense."

"And you're going to make sense of it."

"That's what I do," Heather said.

Chapter Forty-Three

When she reached Charleston, Jenny parked at the garage where Darcy had directed her. The garage was nearly full, so Jenny had to park on the top floor. She looked over the city as she waited for the elevator, and her stomach tied itself in knots. So many buildings, so many streets, so many lights shining on people everywhere. She'd never been to any kind of city in real life, and the TV really didn't get across the scale of it, what it was like to have so many people in one place.

She rode the elevator down and stepped out into Meeting Street, where the pedestrians were all streaming in one direction—towards the thundering music festival at the harbor.

Jenny called Darcy.

"Hiya," Darcy said. "Are you here yet?"

"I just parked," Jenny said. "Did you find Seth?"

"Um, kind of."

"Kind of?" Jenny dodged around an artist shilling caricatures on the sidewalk.

"Well, I'm at the hotel, so just come meet me here," Darcy said. "Go down Meeting Street until you hit Battery, then turn left, and you'll see the front doors of the hotel—"

"You already told me that!" Jenny snapped. "What about Seth? Is he hurt?"

"It's hard to explain on the phone. I'll just see you in a minute, okay? I'll wait on the front porch." Darcy hung up.

Annoyed, Jenny jogged the rest of the way. When she hit the intersection with Battery, she stopped and drew a deep breath.

Her worst nightmare lay in front of her. It was a dense crowd as far as she could see in either direction, clumping here and there around vendors offering hot dogs and face painting. She would have to thread her way through a bunch of drunk kids without touching any of them.

Jenny folded her arms in tight and scrunched her shoulders to make herself small. Though she was fully dressed in jeans, a long-sleeve blouse and a pair of gloves, she didn't want to take any risks. A little gap of skin could open between her shirt sleeve and her glove, and if that brushed against someone, they'd get infected.

She turned onto Battery Street. The crowd around her was mostly her age, high school and college students. Jenny watched them hugging, and dancing, and just horsing around with each other.

Darcy sat on one of the half-dozen rocking chairs parked on the front porch of The Mandrake House. She stood and waved when she saw Jenny, leaving the chair rocking precariously far behind her.

"Hey, Jenny! Hey, over here!"

"I can see you, Darcy." Jenny ran up the front walk and onto the porch of the hotel. "What's going on with Seth?"

"Well, um, it's kinda hard to say—"

"Where is he?"

"Up in our room." Darcy held up a plastic keycard marked 303. "But maybe this isn't a good time for you to go up there."

"Why not?" Jenny asked.

Darcy shrugged.

"Just give me the card!" Jenny snatched the keycard from Darcy's hand, then stomped toward the front door of the hotel. She knew distantly that she was being a bitch to Darcy, and she'd probably need to apologize later. But right now, with everything crashing down on her, she just needed to get to Seth. She needed to see that he was all right, and she needed him to make her feel sane again. Not to mention healing her dad and making him sane again, too.

"So I'll just wait for you here, then?" Darcy asked as Jenny stepped inside. Jenny didn't bother answering. Darcy hadn't answered her question, after all.

Jenny passed through the lobby of the hotel, which was stuffed with hand-carved furniture and lots of paintings and rugs, and she jabbed the button for the elevator. She jabbed it repeatedly, then lost patience and took the carpeted stairs two at a time.

She reached the third floor, which was a short hallway with only a few doors. The brass door numbers were sculpted in some frilly font with a lot of curlicues, so it took her a moment to identify 303.

Jenny figured out how to insert the keycard into the slot next to the door handle. She depressed the handle and pushed open the door.

"Seth?" she asked as she stepped into the room. The door opened onto some kind of sitting room, with a balcony outside. Two doors led off from the sitting room, both of them closed.

Behind one door, she heard Seth's voice cry out, as if he were in agony.

"Seth!" Jenny ran to the door and pushed it open. "Seth, what's wrong?"

The scene inside the room hit her hard.

Seth lay on the bed, naked, all the covers shoved down around his feet. His hands were tucked behind his head, under his pillow, just relaxing and having a great old time.

A girl straddled him, moving up and down on him and panting and sweating. For a second, Jenny could have sworn it was Ashleigh—tall, a head of long blond hair, tan all over. Jenny nearly lost her balance.

For one long, paranoid moment, Jenny thought the last several months had been some extremely elaborate game—Jenny's relationship with Seth, and Jenny killing Ashleigh—all of it faked. If anybody could cook up some deception that elaborate, it was Ashleigh.

"Oh!" the blond girl cried out, and she bounced harder on Seth. "Oh! Oh! Oh!"

It wasn't Ashleigh, Jenny realized now, but some girl who looked a hell of a lot like her. Like Seth had been missing Ashleigh and wanted another taste of what he'd lost. Maybe Jenny's pale scarecrow body wasn't doing it for him anymore.

"Seth, what the hell are you doing?" Jenny shouted.

The blond girl opened her eyes and turned to look at Jenny. Definitely not Ashleigh, now that Jenny got a better look at her face.

"Who...are....you?" the blond girl asked, between thrusts of her hips. She smiled dreamily.

"Seth!" Jenny shouted.

Seth's eyes drifted open and his head drooped to the side in Jenny's direction. His grin was drunken and lopsided.

"Hey, beautiful," Seth said. "You came."

"Fuck you, Seth!" Jenny slammed the door. She ran back through the sitting room and out into the hallway, slamming that door, too. She felt like something had just split her in half, ripping her open right down the middle.

She ran to the stairs, angry and numb at the same time. She wanted to cry, but she'd already used up all her tears tonight.

Jenny ran down the stairs. There was a fire exit on the first floor, but it was marked EMERGENCY EXIT ONLY - ALARM WILL SOUND, so she ran out through the lobby of the hotel. The manager, a slim man with a thin mustache and a white suit, gasped as she darted between an elderly couple and out the front door.

She felt broken into pieces. Seth didn't even have the decency to wait until he moved away. She'd already developed some doubts about his commitment, but now it was obvious he didn't intend to stick with her over the long term. Of course not. Why would he want to spend his life with some freak like her?

Jenny raced down the walkway and out to the crowded sidewalk, where she collided with a group of sorority girls in stretchy black pants. She blundered through them and kept walking.

"Oh, ex*cuse* me!" one of them shouted after her.

"What an ugly bitch," another one commented.

Jenny forced herself to slow down and fold in her arms. She couldn't risk infecting people. She had to move slow, even if everything inside her was screaming at her to run.

She wove her way through the clusters of people on the sidewalk. The street was full of people, too, but now a police car was rolling slowly through them, pushing even more people onto the sidewalk around Jenny.

A bright spotlight beam flared inside the police car and swept the crowd. It passed over Jenny, then quickly swung back to her and stayed there. She froze where she was, raised an arm to block the light, and tried to figure out what the cops were doing.

"You," the cop shouted from the car. "You stay right there. Do not move."

The largest morgue in Charleston was at the Medical University of South Carolina, conveniently located a dozen or so blocks from the big music festival. Alexander knew they were all there at the festival—the fear-giver and the love-charmer, the plague-bringer and the healer, and finally Alexander's opposite, the dead-speaker, Esmeralda. That was her name in this lifetime, anyway.

Alexander walked into the morgue at the Department of Pathology wearing blue hospital scrubs and a surgeon's mask. All autopsies in Charleston County, forensic or medical, happened down in these rooms. Just the place he needed to visit.

He passed an autopsy bay where two morgue assistants were preparing for an autopsy. One laid out clamps and blades, while the other wiped down the pale corpse of a gigantically obese man with a thick beard and many badly stretched tattoos. Alexander eyeballed the ceiling-mounted lamps on adjustable metal arms over the autopsy table. Those lengths of metal could be useful.

"This is nasty," said the morgue assistant washing the corpse. He was younger, a white guy with short green hair. "They don't pay me enough."

"That ain't nothing," said the other assistant, an older black man. He was clearly the supervisor, since he was laying out blades instead of rinsing out decaying fat folds. "Just before you started, we had this O.D.'d hooker, every venereal disease you can name growing all over the place. Looked like week-old pot roast down there."

The younger guy made a small heaving sound, and the older one laughed. Then he noticed Alexander approaching the refrigeration unit.

"Hey!" the older morgue assistant yelled at Alexander. "Who the hell are you?"

Alexander didn't stop for questions, but continued on to the wall of little stainless steel doors, each one holding a corpse behind it. It was like one of those Christmas calendars where you were supposed to punch out one cardboard square a day, to find the chocolate treat hidden behind it. He couldn't wait to see what the morgue had for him. He hoped it was full.

He opened one and slid out the conveyor drawer, which held a body covered in a white sheet. Alexander whipped off the sheet, revealing a fiftyish woman in a pantsuit with a shattered arm and a partly crushed skull. It looked like she'd died in a traffic accident.

"Hello, sweetheart," Alexander said. "Want to take a walk?"

He laid a hand on her neck. The dark energy flowed out of him, carrying droplets of Alexander's essence into the dead cells of her corpse.

He opened another drawer, revealing a young man with a bullet wound through the chest, his jersey shirt stiff with dried brown blood. Another drawer held an elderly man who might have died of natural causes. Another held a shrunken boy of eleven or twelve with a shaved head.

"What are you doing?" The older morgue assistant approached him, and his green-haired protégé trailed behind him, looking embarrassed. "Where's your ID badge?"

"Don't you recognize me?" Alexander tugged down the face mask and gave him a big, crazy smile.

"You a student?" the older man asked.

"No," Alexander said. In his mind, he made contact with the bits of energy he'd planted within the bodies around him. "You work with me every day, side by side. You must know who I am."

The green-haired assistant approached, standing beside his supervisor with his arms crossed. He was a short and wiry guy, but he looked ready to fight.

"Stop messing with my bodies," the older man said. "You tell me who the hell you are and what the hell you're doing or you get the hell out of my morgue." He pointed to the door. "In fact, let's just skip to that last part."

"I am simply carrying out my business," Alexander said. "And as for my name, I've had far more than I can remember."

Alexander held up a hand, and the dozen dead bodies slowly sat up behind him.

"I am the vulture circling above from the moment of your birth. I am the eternal force that eats the souls of men and sends the damned to their final suffering." The dead bodies slid off their tables and staggered toward the mortuary assistants. "I am Death, destroyer of worlds."

The dozen reanimated corpses lurched toward the two men, their bare feet shuffling forward one step at a time, their toe tags scraping along the linoleum floor. The corpses raised their arms high above their heads, with their hands hanging limp in the air like they were marionette dolls. All the walking dead dropped their jaws wide open and groaned in unison, shambling closer to the morgue assistants.

Both of the morgue assistants screamed and ran away.

Alexander laughed. He mentally ordered his walking zombies to stop where they were, and they locked up as if playing freeze tag.

He opened more drawers, touched and animated more bodies. Some of them were quite diseased, or a bit gory and mangled, but that didn't matter. He was taking them all. And then he'd be on his way.

Chapter Forty-Four

Seth pulled at the rope with his right hand, which pulled his left hand back against the headboard. Then he pulled with his left hand, and his right snapped back.

"What the hell?" Seth said to the naked blond girl on top of him. "Help me get out of this!"

"But I like it," Allegra frowned.

"I have to go!" Seth said. "That was Jenny! My girlfriend!"

"I don't think she's your girlfriend anymore." Allegra giggled. "You're funny."

"I'm serious here." Seth looked up at his bound hands. He couldn't see them very well when they were close together, so he pulled his right wrist to his face. They were tied with a dense clump of small knots. "Can you cut me loose or something? Look for a knife."

"You want to leave me?" Allegra asked.

"Yeah, look, I don't know what happened here, but this was not a good—"

"I'll tell you what happened." Allegra laid down on top of him and kissed him. "First, we met." She kissed him again. "And then we came here." She kissed him again, and she reached between his legs and took him in her hand. "And then…"

"Stop it." Seth shivered. The girl had some weird hold over him. It almost reminded him of Ashleigh.

In fact, he realized, *she* almost reminded him of Ashleigh.

"You have to help me out." Seth used the fingers of his right hand to pick at the hard little knots binding his left. He couldn't pull anything loose. The girl was some kind of knot-tying genius.

"Please," Seth said.

"Please what?" She kissed him again. "Tell me how to please you."

"Let me go," Seth said. "That would please me."

"No, I'm never going to let *you* go." She kept kissing him. "Never, never, never…"

Ashleigh stood between Tommy and Esmeralda on the balcony of their fifth-floor room at the Mandrake House. Below, the street was thick with festival-goers, but the police presence had swelled from an occasional blue uniform to several squad cars, each of them trundling slowly through different parts of the crowd, occasionally shining a spotlight into the park.

"I don't like this," Tommy said.

"Oh, the cops aren't looking for you, Tommy," Ashleigh said. "Stop being so self-centered." She rubbed the back of his neck. "Now, get ready, because Jenny's going to come busting out in about a minute. You can draw power from me. I'm like a battery for you."

"If you say so." Tommy scrunched up his forehead and squeezed his closed eyes, like he was concentrating hard. Staying focused had never exactly been his strong point, Ashleigh remembered.

Far below, Jenny ran down the front porch steps of the hotel and onto the sidewalk, bumping carelessly into everyone in her path. She was covering her eyes with one gloved hand, and her mouth was trembling hard.

"There she is, Tommy," Ashleigh said. "She's outside, bawling her ass off, poor thing. Are you ready?"

"Just a second…" Tommy raised a finger, his eyes still closed.

"We don't have any time left! She's already out!" Ashleigh glared at the small, pathetic figure of Jenny, trying to get through the crowd.

A police car pulled alongside Jenny, moving very slowly. It blasted Jenny with the spotlight, and she turned toward it, looking confused, blocking the light with her arm.

"Oh, what the hell?" Ashleigh said. "Not yet. We need to have the big show first. Tommy, do it now! The cops are on her!"

Tommy opened his eyes. Ashleigh felt most of her strength drain out of her, and she slumped against the railing and struggled to stay on her feet, practically fainting like some stupid lady in an old black-and-white movie. Esmeralda hurried to support her.

Tommy leaned out over the railing, looking down on the crowd below. He opened his mouth, and out flowed what looked like a stream of very dark blood. It corkscrewed over the heads of the crowd like a ribbon curling in the wind, and then it burst into a cloud of tiny, blood-red spores, drifting out over the festival like gruesome confetti.

The cops had gotten out of the car to chase Jenny on foot, but Jenny didn't yet notice them behind her.

Tommy made a choking sound and stumbled back onto the balcony, and then he fell on his ass, bleached and sweaty and shivering.

Below, the churning of the crowd slowed as Tommy's fear took hold of them.

Jenny's power, when applied to a crowd, created an epidemic.

Ashleigh's power, applied to a crowd, had been known to cause orgies.

When you applied Tommy's fear to a crowd, you got a panic. Maybe even a riot.

Every mob needed a booster, so Ashleigh had brought an electronic megaphone, which featured the jaunty Fallen Oak High mascot Sonny the Porcupine on the side.

"It's the girl wearing the gloves!" Ashleigh shouted through the megaphone. She pointed at Jenny. "See her? She's the one! You have to get her! You have to stop her! You have to kill her!"

Five stories below, Jenny gaped up at the unexpected voice. Ashleigh wondered if Jenny could recognize her pal Darcy at this distance, shouting for a crowd of people to kill her.

A hippie girl with dreadlocks and a nose ring screamed and punched Jenny in the mouth. "Corporatist pig!" the hippie girl screamed.

"That's right, the girl with gloves!" Ashleigh shouted. "Get her! Get her now! She's the one you want. She's the one behind all your problems!"

More people attacked Jenny, punching her in the head and back and stomach, kicking at her legs. The cops arrived as Jenny doubled over, and one of them bashed Jenny in the face with his knee. The panic had hold of everyone, and the crowd crushed in around Jenny, frenzied and eager to attack. Somebody smashed a beer bottle across her head.

"Now we have to get the fuck out of here," Ashleigh said. "You don't want to be here when Jenny does her thing. We could all die." Ashleigh smiled. "But this time they'll catch Jenny. Way too many witnesses, too many cops. They're going to lock her up tight after she mutilates all these people."

"Or they'll kill her," Tommy said.

"That's not so bad for a second-best." Ashleigh turned to Esmeralda. "Are you ready?"

"Oh, yes, I've been waiting." Esmeralda gave Ashleigh a big smile.

Ashleigh cupped Esmeralda's face in her hands. Then she leaned in and kissed Esmeralda hard on the mouth.

"I thought we were in a hurry," Tommy said.

Ashleigh ignored him. She concentrated on disentangling her mind and spirit from Darcy's body. After a minute, she was loose, just a discarnate spirit, and dangerously close to drifting away from these human bodies altogether. Maybe back to the deep and hellish void from which they'd come. She felt a moment of panic.

Then she flowed into Esmeralda. She'd invested a lot of time and energy wrapping Esmeralda tight in the golden threads of her love, like a bug in a spider web. Ashleigh, the great golden spider, moved in to claim her prey.

Ashleigh looked out through Esmeralda's eyes. Darcy was backing away, gaping at her, with a sheen of spit on her chin.

"Oh…" Darcy said. "Oh…GRODY! Why were we doing that?"

"Ashleigh's task on Earth is done," Ashleigh said. "She's back with the angels now, Darcy."

"But…but where are we?" Darcy looked out at Charleston, and down at the rioting mob below, where people were overturning the temporary vendors' booths and punching each other at random. "What's happening? Why, I mean, where—"

Ashleigh put a hand on Darcy's arm, soothing her a little with her loving energy, though Ashleigh didn't have much energy left to spare. She was starving. She needed calories.

Below them, the crowd roared, and they smashed windows up and down the street.

"Come on, Darcy," Ashleigh whispered. "Let's go inside."

"Darcy?" Tommy asked. "Why did you call her Darcy?"

"That's my name, Mr. Angel, sir," Darcy said.

"You relax, too," Ashleigh said to Tommy. She led Darcy inside and shot Tommy a warning glance back over her shoulder. "Darcy, you look so troubled."

"Will someone just tell me where we are?"

"We're in a safe place. Sit down on this nice bed and relax." Ashleigh guided her to the bed. "Good. Now just lie back and close your eyes." She pushed a little more love into the girl.

"But…" Darcy said.

"Sh," Ashleigh said. "You just stay right there. When you feel a little better, we'll explain everything. Remember, we're angels. We'll watch over you. Just close those pretty eyes and relax now."

"Okay." Darcy closed her eyes.

Ashleigh picked up Esmeralda's purse—she would need the girl's driver's license and the rest of her identity. Then she glanced at Darcy's big canvas purse. Her two-hundred-thousand-dollar PayPal card was in there, and assorted other things she might want. She dropped Esmeralda's purse inside it, then slung the big purse over her shoulder.

"Okay," Ashleigh said. "Let's go, Tommy."

"What's happening here?" Tommy leaned in close, looking into her eyes. "Ashleigh?"

"We decided to leave poor Darcy to her own life," Ashleigh said. "Esmeralda agreed I could share her body, for now."

"I don't know if she would agree to that," Tommy said.

"Tommy! Esmeralda loves me."

"Making people feel love is your power."

"That really hurts," Ashleigh said. "You know how hard it is going through life, not sure whether somebody loves you for you, or just because your stupid magic touch makes them feel that way?"

"I never thought of that."

"The three of us belong together, Tommy," Ashleigh said. "I know she loves me because we all love each other. It's not a trick. It's a thousand lifetimes together. You'll understand. I'll tell you all about it. But right now we have to get the fuck out of Dodge before Jenny Mittens turns it all the way up and kills the whole city with us still inside it. Okay?"

Tommy looked at Darcy lolling on the bed, and then he looked carefully at Ashleigh.

"I guess I don't have a choice," he said.

"That's right. Come on. It's time for Jenny to show the whole world what a horrible thing she is."

Ashleigh led the way into the hall, and Tommy closed the door behind them.

As Jenny stared into bright spotlight from the police car, a sudden, profound fear came over her. It was dread and paranoia and confusion all mixed together. The crowd around her suddenly reminded her of the lynch mob in Fallen Oak, the wave of mounting tension just before the explosion, when they'd killed Seth and tried to kill Jenny.

Her heart pounded in her chest, and she panicked and ran away from the police.

"It's the girl wearing the gloves!" a voice boomed high above her. Jenny looked up toward the voice, which actually seemed to come from the roof of the Mandrake House, or maybe one of the darkened balconies. "See her? She's the one! You have to get her! You have to stop her! You have to kill her!"

All around Jenny, the unfriendly faces of the crowd turned toward her, like they were compass needles and Jenny was magnetic north. They pointed at Jenny.

"That's her!" somebody shouted. "The girl with gloves!"

"Oh, shit," Jenny whispered. Her whole body was trembling and she couldn't breathe very well. She needed to do something, but she couldn't think straight. Her mind was blinded by fear.

The crowd closed in around Jenny. A dreadlocked hippie girl threw the first punch, right into Jenny's mouth.

"Corporatist pig!" the hippie girl screamed, and then she spit on Jenny. The girl didn't seem to notice the bloody pustules rising across her knuckles, where she'd made contact with Jenny's lips and teeth.

"That's right, the girl with gloves!" the voice from above shouted. "Get her! Get her now! She's the one you want. She's the one behind all your problems!"

Jenny wondered what the hell that meant.

But those words seemed to open the floodgates—everybody attacked her. Fists pounded her head and her back. Somebody punched her in the stomach and she doubled over. Jenny saw a couple of police jogging toward her and she reached out one hand, hoping maybe they would help her.

Instead, the first cop slammed a knee into her face. Jenny felt her nose crack and a hot gout of blood rush down across her lips. Somebody smashed a bottle over her head.

Jenny fell to the sidewalk and curled into a fetal position, covering the back of her head with her hands. Shoes and sandals and boots kicked and stomped all over her, bruising her ribs, her hips, her legs and arms, the crown of her head. God only knew why everyone had listened to the crazy lady with the megaphone and started attacking her, but Jenny was terrified and didn't know what to do.

There was one thing she wasn't going to do, she decided. She wasn't going to flare up with the Jenny pox and fight her way out of this crowd. Already the pox was rising in her, fueled by her growing fear. With all these people pushing in around her, pulling her hair and pounding on her body, it would be easy to flood them all with infection, even kill them if necessary, and make her escape.

She wouldn't do that again. She couldn't live with one more death on her hands. So she would lie here and let the mob do its worst, even if they killed her. That, Jenny thought, would be justice for what she'd done to all those people in Fallen Oak.

When she'd made that choice, her whole body relaxed. The blows continued raining down on her, but by now she was in so much pain that things couldn't possibly get any worse. She had died before, and it wasn't so bad.

Chapter Forty-Five

Seth gave his right hand another hard pull, and it finally slid free of the noose. All the skin was rubbed off at the base of his hand and his wrist, leaving only raw pink tissue, and the end of the rope was wet with his blood, but he was free. It had taken a horribly long amount of time, and it hadn't helped that Allegra wouldn't get off of him, or stop slathering his face and neck with kisses.

Seth rolled over so that she was underneath him.

"Oh!" Allegra laughed. "Want to go old-fashioned, huh?"

"I have to go." Seth jumped to his feet, dragging the rope behind him, since it was still noosed tight around his left hand. He pulled on his jeans and shoes, grabbed his shirt, and ran for the door.

"Wait!" Allegra screamed after him, sitting up on the bed. "Come back! I need you, Seth!"

Seth dashed through the sitting room and into the hall, and then the hotel's fire alarm began to scream. When he reached the railing, he glimpsed the backs of two people, a young man and a young woman, rushing out the fire door all the way down on the first floor, despite the EMERGENCY ONLY sign warning about the alarm. They slammed it behind them.

Seth started down the stairs, but then something snapped his left arm and hauled him backward, right off his feet, and he sprawled out across the deep-piled rug. He looked up to see Allegra standing over him, stark naked, holding the other end of the rope that was still tied to his left wrist. The rope smeared his blood all over her hands, but she didn't seem to notice.

She wagged a wet, red finger. "Don't you run away from me."

"I have to go!" Seth stood up and tugged at the rope. "Come on, this is crazy."

"Oh, Seth, I love you so much." She tried to kiss him, but Seth turned his head. "Let's get married and have babies. We can go sailing with my parents every summer. Oh, and you can go to the dog shows with my mom! We have a champion Sheltie, Lady Tinkerbelle's Lace."

"Well, all that sounds like it sucks," Seth said. "But I'm in a big hurry here, and you really need to… let go!" He jerked the rope as hard as he could, meaning to wrench it free from her hands, but instead she held tight and stumbled up against him.

"Oh, Seth!" Allegra said. "You could play golf with my dad at the country club. He'd like that. You're a good golfer, right?"

"No," Seth said. "Not even on the Wii."

"You'll learn." She nibbled at his chin. "Sethy-seth. Sethykins."

"Okay," Seth said. "I give up. Let's go back to the room and make out."

"Really?" she chirped. "Yeah, let's go!" And then ran back to the room, dropping the rope in the process.

Seth flung the rope out over the railing, out of her reach, and ran down the stairs.

"I'm waiting!" she cooed behind him. Seth put on speed.

He rushed outside and found himself in the middle of a huge riot. People were punching and kicking each other all over the street, parked cars were overturned, shrubbery was on fire.

He struggled to press through the dense crowd, toward Meeting Street, where Jenny must have parked. It was the only direction he knew to go.

Random strangers punched at his face, and one of the old ladies who'd been protesting the music festival bit Seth's hand.

"What the hell?" Seth backed away from her. The crowd surged like a tidal wave and pushed him back in the opposite direction, past the hotel, and crushed against the side of an empty taxicab. Beside him, a girl of twelve or thirteen got her face slammed against the hood of the taxi's window by an angry fat man. She came up screaming, with a bloody nose.

"Hey, don't do that!" Seth shouted at the guy assaulting the girl. Seth put a hand on the screaming girl's head and quickly healed her face.

The big guy came after Seth, but instead of fighting back, Seth took a chance, seized his arm and pushed his healing power into the guy.

The big guy paused with his fist in midair, looking confused. "Hey, what's going on?"

"Fuck if I know," Seth said, and he pushed past him.

Seth pressed forward through the crowd, but every few feet saw somebody with a broken finger or deep cuts across their face, and he had to reach out and touch them briefly to give them a little healing help—without them noticing, hopefully.

He slowly advanced through the dense, terrified, angry mob. Seth began to fear he might never find Jenny again.

The crowd crushed in around Jenny, and they kept slapping at her head, so she knew she was infecting some people. She lay with her eyes closed and waited to die.

She couldn't understand why everyone had turned on her, but it seemed natural that they would. She was a killer. She didn't belong among good people.

Then the hands jabbing at her turned icy and cold. And these freezing hands weren't punching and slapping, either, but just brushing across her face. Fingers that felt like popsicles jabbed under the wrist of her sleeve and the collar of her shirt, as if specifically seeking out her flesh.

Jenny opened her eyes and found herself looking up at woman in a pantsuit with a partially crushed head. Jenny could actually see fragments of the woman's skull and brain. The young man next to her had a huge red stain on the front of his shirt, and a bullethole.

She was surrounded by cold, gray-skinned people who all looked very dead, and very intent on getting under her clothes and at her flesh.

Jenny screamed.

All of the dead-looking people turned their backs on her, forming a jumbled ring that kept out the attacking mob, though some people could still reach in to give Jenny a poke or a slap.

Each of the walking corpses—Jenny didn't know how else to think of them, without using the word "zombies," which seemed too freaky to contemplate—each one of them dragged what looked like a full-size black body bag in one hand, as if they'd all just unzipped and marched out of a morgue somewhere, but held on to their bags just in case. It was surreal.

A young man who looked a couple years older than Jenny passed through the wall of zombies, who shuffled back and forth to let him pass. He had shaggy brown hair and dark eyes that seemed to glow. A smile twitched his lips.

"Poor girl," he said. "Look what they've done to you." He dropped to a knee beside her, and reached a hand toward her face.

"Don't touch me," Jenny whispered. "I'm poisonous."

"Not to me." He lay his fingers on her bruised, bleeding cheek.

All around them, the slouching zombies straightened up. Each one reached inside its body bag and withdrew a long, slender object. Some of them had wooden mop or broom handles, some had strips of metal, one or two of which had lamps attached at the end, as if they'd been ripped from some operating room ceiling. Some simply had two by four boards.

"What's happening?" Jenny asked.

"Phalanx," he said. "Old Greek formation. Still pretty effective, huh?'

The zombies draped the ends of the body bags over their left arms and grasped the bags' side handles with their left hands. Then they raised the body bags in front of themselves, creating a thick plastic barrier as wide and tall as a person. They weren't exactly bulletproof shields, but they deflected most of the fists and debris thrown by the crowd.

Through the narrow gaps between the body bag shields, the zombies swung their blunt objects, batting back the crowd. They swung in unison, and stepped forward, pushing the crowd back.

All the while, the strange young man was simply looking into Jenny's eyes and lightly brushing her cheek with his fingers. His eyes looked familiar to her.

"Are you doing that?" she whispered.

"Doing what?"

"You're controlling them."

He looked around at the expanding ring of zombies, who were pushing their way into a square formation. "I certainly hope so. I'd hate to see what would happen if they ran wild. They might eat your brain!" He rubbed her forehead and temples with his fingertips. "Kidding. Are you remembering me yet? I know you woke up a few weeks ago. I could feel it like an earthquake, and I was thousands of miles away. Those fuckers in that little town, they tried to kill you, didn't they?"

"Yes," Jenny said. "They did."

He laughed. "Stupid rednecks! Come on, let's get moving." He stood up and held out his hands to her.

Jenny kept looking at his eyes, trying to figure out how she knew him. Every inch of her body was screaming in pain, and she felt like she would collapse any moment.

"Okay," he said. "I get it. Guy shows up with a band of zombies swinging brooms. You don't know what to think. But you should know two things. First, this mob will eventually tear my deceased friends apart, and there goes your security team. Second, there is an army of state police and *federales* on their way to collect you, and I can get you out of here."

Jenny took his hands and stood, but she was wobbly on her feet from her beating. Every part of her ached.

"So, what's your choice?" he asked. "Live or die?"

Jenny looked at him. "Are you Archidamus?" she asked.

"You do remember me." He pulled the glove from her left hand and took it in his own, skin to skin. It was a strange, dangerous feeling to Jenny, touching anybody like that, except for Seth.

"What about Seth?" she asked.

"The healer? He's safe. You're in danger. Come on, we have to hike a few blocks." A wall of flashing blue lights approached from the far end of the street. "Not that way."

He supported her with one arm as they walked, and the phalanx of zombies moved with them, walling them in from the mob.

Those at the front of the square alternating between knocking on people who approached and jabbing their long weapons forward to push people back out of the way.

The zombies on Jenny's left and right simply held up their body-bag shields and only struck people who tried to reach inside. Behind Jenny, zombies walked backwards, holding up the body bags and ready to strike if necessary.

"This is so fucked up," Jenny whispered.

"You get used to it. I'm Alexander in this life, by the way. But you can call me whatever you want. Do you like Euanthe better?"

"Call me Jenny," she whispered.

"We have to move faster, Jenny."

"I can't." Jenny's legs wobbled beneath her.

"That's fine." He picked her up in his arms and began to jog. The zombies sped up with him, and the front line fell into a wedge to pry apart the crowd. The rioting mob seemed to be losing their focus on Jenny, now that the person with the megaphone had shut up, and Jenny had gained a dozen or more scary-looking, somewhat armed protectors. The people who'd been intent on attacking Jenny started attacking each other instead, or bashing in car windows.

"Why's everybody going crazy?" Jenny asked.

"Tommy. The fear-giver. He can make a crowd panic."

"Ashleigh's opposite," Jenny said.

"He wanted you to hit them all with a plague," Alexander said. "It was a trap, but we've wrecked his plans. He didn't have any idea I would show up."

Jenny slid an arm around Alexander's shoulders. It was such a strange feeling to be carried like this, and the strangest part was how comforted and protected she felt. She remembered from her dreams how she had felt in his presence, knowing she'd finally found her place in the world.

She was starting to feel that way again. And it didn't really hurt that he was handsome and strong and had just saved her life.

Jenny laid her head on his shoulder, her face close to his sun-darkened cheek and neck. He wore only a T-shirt and jeans, but the jeans seemed perfectly tailored to fit him, and the black shirt was as soft as cashmere.

He carried her up a side street, into a neighborhood of huge old houses. The crowd didn't follow, and this street was relatively peaceful, with just a band of teenagers throwing rocks at the streetlights. The zombies spread out a little, giving them some breathing room.

Alexander brought them to the driveway of a big Greek Revival-style house, with a black SUV parked in the driveway, nose out as if someone were planning a quick getaway.

"Is this your house?" Jenny asked.

"This house belongs to Wells Fargo bank," he said. "It's for sale. Nobody lives here. So I borrowed the driveway for a couple of hours." He opened the passenger door of the SUV and set her down in the seat. He even buckled her seatbelt before closing her door.

He climbed into the driver's seat and started the engine.

"Where are you taking me?" she asked.

"Somewhere no one will be looking for you." He pulled out of the driveway.

"I have to get back to my dad. He's pretty messed up right now."

"What happened to him?"

"Ashleigh's opposite—Tommy?—hit my dad pretty hard with that fear thing."

"He'll be fine," Alexander said. "The fear wears off after a few hours."

Jenny thought about the time Tommy had attacked her and Seth. They'd had a night of confused terror, but they'd eventually been fine the next day.

"The only person in danger is you," Alexander said. "And I'm taking care of that right now."

He accelerated down the street.

In the rearview, the zombies all fell down at once, like a group of kids playing ring-around-the-rosy. Their pole weapons and body bags littered the street around them.

"Ashes, ashes," Jenny sang under her breath.

"What did you say?"

"Nothing." On top of the deep calm he inspired, Jenny was starting to feel something else—nervous, embarrassed, giddy. She was a little afraid of those feelings...but she liked them, too.

They drove through back streets, through residential neighborhoods, avoiding the swarm of police, Homeland Security and federal agencies that were searching the city for Jenny.

Chapter Forty-Six

Heather rode from the Charleston International Airport in a Homeland Security car. Red flags were already up all over the city. Some kind of riot had broken out at the Southeastern Funk Fest, and local and state police were working to calm things down. The National Guard, already on alert, had been activated and would be rolling into the downtown area momentarily.

Local police had also identified an incident that required CDC attention. A couple dozen bodies had just been found in a big pile in a neighborhood not far from the festival, cause of death unclear. Heather worried that Jenny might have already gotten started on her apparent plan to kill ten thousand people or more. If so, more clusters of bodies would turn up before long, if not a massive-fatality incident.

The Homeland Security vehicle arrived at the incident scene, where police, fire, EMS and a small crowd of onlookers had already gathered. Heather jumped out of the car and joined Schwartzman, who'd been driven by another Homeland Security officer.

"We need to get these people out of here," Heather whispered as they approached the scene.

"Let's see what's happening first," Schwartzman replied.

"It would be a pretty big coincidence if she wasn't involved."

"Shit happens," Schwartzman whispered.

A gray, balding man in a suit approached, looking tired. He glanced at their badges.

"Y'all the CDC folks?" he asked. "I'm Cordell Nolan, county medical examiner. Spoke to you on the phone, I think." He reached a hand towards Schwartzman, who hesitated a moment before shaking it.

“This is Dr. Reynard,’ Schwartzman said. “She’s one of our best epidemiologists.”

“Well, we got us an epidemic of something, but I can't say what.” Nolan shook Heather's hand. “Whole damn city's going up in flames. Anybody with any sense knows you let a few thousand kids run loose in the streets, with music, everything's gonna get wrecked. Mayor was hell-bent this was going to mean money for the city. Now look how much it's gonna cost to fix it back.”

“We're a bit more concerned about these bodies,” Heather said. She looked at the pile of corpses in the street. There seemed to be no rhyme or reason to their age, race, sex, socioeconomics, but they were all barefoot and wore toetags, which was more than a little odd. Body bags were scattered among them, along with random objects like mops and brooms, and what looked like the metal arms of overhead lights from a surgery bay.

None of them had the boils, tumors and pustules indicative of Fallen Oak syndrome.

“Are you bagging them already?” Heather asked.

“The bags were already here,” Nolan said. “Mine are still in the truck. We ain't touched nothing.”

“They came with their own cadaver pouches?” Schwartzman asked. “That's convenient.”

“We ought to take 'em into evidence, though,” Nolan said. “Still gonna use fresh ones to cart ‘em off. Looks like these bodies was already checked in at the MUSC morgue over the past week or so. They still got the toe tags.”

“I'm sorry?” Heather asked. “You're saying these came from the hospital morgue?”

“Yep.”

“How did they get here?” Schwartzman asked.

“Still trying to get somebody from the morgue on the phone,” Nolan said. “Ain't nobody answering down there tonight. Real strange.”

“So...these are stolen bodies,” Heather said. “Some kind of, what? College prank?”

“Take a lot of doing,” Nolan replied. “Need a lot of people to carry this many bodies. Somebody at the morgue had to see something, but like I said, nobody's picking up the horn. Hospital administration's supposed to get back to me any second.”

Heather squatted for a closer look at the bodies. It looked like an assortment of bodily injuries and disease, as well as a few elderly people who might have passed from natural causes. They were all barefoot and hung with toe tags.

"This doesn't make any sense," Heather said. "You'd need a truck to carry all these. There must be witnesses."

"There must be," Nolan agreed. "But the police are spread a little thin tonight, with all the crazy hippies tearing up the city. Thank the Lord we have so many state and federal folks here. Almost like somebody knew a big mess was coming."

Schwartzman looked at Heather with a slight smile at the corner of his mouth.

"Do we have any more incidents like this?" Heather asked.

"If we do, it'll come over the police band and we'll let you know directly," Nolan said. "Now, seeing as how this is mostly a case of theft and vandalism, do y'all mind if we scoop these folks up and get them back in the fridge? There's a City Council member lives in this neighborhood, and it's best to keep things tidy."

Schwartzman glanced at Heather, and she shrugged.

"It doesn't seem like we're needed here," Heather said. "Do what you need to do."

As they walked away, Schwartzman whispered to Heather, "I guess your ass is covered. Not the event you were expecting, but nobody's going to complain about the National Guard being put on alert now."

"Who cares about my ass?" Heather asked. "This thing gets weirder and weirder. I still think we need to find Jenny Morton."

"The cops already have an APB for her," Schwartzman said. "And the Guardsmen are rolling in. This city will be locked up tight. We'll find her."

"I hope you're right," Heather said. "The idea of Jenny running wild out there scares the hell out of me."

Darcy dozed on the nice comfy bed, waiting for the angels to return, until she heard the sudden pounding on the door. Her eyes drifted open, and she turned her head toward the racket.

"I'm sleepin'," she whispered.

A keycard thunked into the lock and the door popped open. A man with a pencil-thin mustache, wearing a seersucker suit with a brass name plate at the lapel, stepped into the room, accompanied by a large black man in gray coveralls and a work belt full of tools.

"Excuse me," the mustached man said. "Are you the only one here?"

"Me?" Darcy asked.

"Yes, you, thank you."

"It's just me. Until the angels come back."

The two men shared a worried look.

"Ma'am," the man said. "I am Pervical Daughtrey, the manager of The Mandrake House."

"Hi," Darcy said. She gave him a warm smile. She was still feeling so good from when the angel touched her.

"Yes," he said. "This is extremely unfortunate news, but it seems this room has been charged to a stolen credit card."

"Oh," Darcy said. "Really?"

"Yes," the manager said. "Really, ma'am. It was recently reported stolen by its owner, whose credit card provider then forwarded the information to us, as you can imagine. Now, if you would be so kind as to surrender Mr. Morris Metcalf's credit card to me, and then I will need you to vacate this room immediately, I'm afraid."

"Morris Metcalf's my dad," Darcy said.

"Oh, I see." His forehead wrinkled briefly. "Would you mind showing me some identification?"

"It's in my purse." Darcy sat up and pointed at the empty chair. "Wait. It was right there."

The hotel manager looked at the empty chair. "Where, ma'am?"

"Oh. Shoot." Darcy looked around the room, but she didn't see it anywhere. "I think that Mexican angel might have taken it."

"A Mexican angel took your purse?" the maintenance guy asked.

"Yeah. But they're coming back. They've only been gone a minute. Or maybe an hour. I forget. They'll be back, though."

"Ma'am, if you cannot provide identification, I'm very sorry to say that you must come down to my office, where you can wait for the police," the hotel manager said.

"Police?" Darcy was getting worried now. This sounded serious. The golden fog over her mind began to lift. "Wait. My purse has to be somewhere." Darcy heaved herself to her feet and looked around the room. She checked under the bed, and in the bathroom. "It has to be."

"There is also the matter of the quite sizable bill you've accumulated," the hotel manager said. "Upwards of nineteen hundred dollars. Given the circumstances, I am afraid my employers would require me to accept only accept cash."

"I don't have money like that!"

"Then perhaps you should not have chosen The Mandrake House for accommodations in Charleston. I must insist you come now and wait for the police."

Darcy moved to gather her things, but she didn't seem to have any. No purse, no suitcase. And how had she ended up in Charleston, anywho? Where were those people who claimed to be angels?

Darcy didn't understand what was going on, but clearly she was in big bunches of trouble.

Ashleigh held tight to Tommy as his bike roared up I-26, the fastest route out of Charleston and away from the whole mess. A convoy of green trucks, the National Guard, flowed into the city on the inbound lanes of the interstate.

She felt exhilarated. Seth had escaped a bit faster than she'd wanted, but besides that, the night had gone extremely well. She knew how Jenny would react once she got cornered. Ashleigh just hoped the scientists got her captured before the soldiers caught up with her. They could keep Jenny locked up and out of Ashleigh's way for years and years, maybe for the rest of this lifetime, if she was lucky.

And poor little Seth would be all alone, too. Ashleigh wished she really had killed him, but it just hadn't been in the cards tonight.

Best of all, any trouble would stick to Darcy Metcalf, not to her. She was just Esmeralda Medina Rios, the lovely girl from California who'd stayed in the background and kept her hands clean of everything.

And Tommy wasn't so bad. He was very acceptably attractive, and she understood how to use him. He was frustrating because he could resist her power. But he wasn't the brightest bulb, and she had fragments of several lifetimes of memories over him. She could press buttons he didn't even know he had.

His power made him extremely useful, and it even amplified her own. They had conquered empires together, here and there across space and time.

She held him tighter. It was good to be alive again, without all the hassle of gestation and birth and infancy. She had a nice new body she actually enjoyed, a new identity, and the whole future ahead of her.

Ashleigh began to think over her options.

Chapter Forty-Seven

Alexander drove only a mile and a half before parking outside a small airport with only one runway. He carried her away from the car, leaving the car doors unlocked and the keys dangling in the ignition.

He opened a spiked wrought-iron gate with a keycard, and then carried her inside, toward the long hangar building.

"I think I'd rather walk now," she said.

"Here you go." Alexander set her down.

"Where are you really taking me?"

"I have a place down in Mexico," he said. "Near the beach. Good spot to lay low for a while, let your trail get cold. Let them run out of steam."

"For how long?"

"Weeks. Months. It's the only safe choice." He opened a small door at the end of the hangar with the keycard.

"I can't do that. My dad…"

"He's going to be fine. I told you."

"But I have to let him know I'm okay. And Seth. Well, maybe not Seth, but at least my dad."

"You can send him a postcard," Alexander said. "Tell him you're in Chicago, or Seattle. I can have somebody mail it for you. But that's it. You've got Homeland Security all over you right now."

"Okay…" Jenny started walking again. He waited to walk alongside her.

"It'll be nice," he said. "You like the beach, right?"

"There's too many people."

"Not at my place. There's nobody we don't invite."

He led her inside the hangar, toward one of several small aircraft. "This is us."

Jenny stared at it. "What is that?"

"A Cessna Corvalis. A little banged up, but it'll get us there."

"I didn't mean…we're taking a plane? To Mexico?" She took her hand back from him. "Who's going to fly it?"

He smirked and opened the plane's right-hand door. "Come on. I'll give you a boost." He held out his hand.

"You're kidding," she said.

"What? These things are easy," he said. "You should have seen my first plane. Didn't even have an enclosed cockpit. Pilot's chair was just a splintery board."

"How old are you?"

"In this lifetime, or adding them all up?"

"Do you remember other lives?" Jenny asked. "Besides Greece?"

"I remember them all." He pointed inside the plane. "We have to go. You're the one in a rush, not me. Nobody's looking for me, not on this side of the border."

"Okay." Jenny looked at him carefully. It made sense that the Tommy guy could give a whole crowd a panic, and clearly Alexander's power lay in another direction. He had come to save her. He didn't seemed concerned about Seth at all—but Jenny wasn't too concerned, either. He seemed to be doing pretty well for himself.

She knew from her dreams that Alexander had been good to her in the past, and that he understood her. It was thrilling to discover another person she could touch, but it also meant she had no real power over him. If he was taking her into a trap, it wouldn't be easy to escape him. Especially when all her major bones felt like broken glass.

"We have a good doctor there," Alexander said. "He'll take care of your injuries."

"I usually heal up pretty good," Jenny said. "Never needed a doctor."

"You took a pretty bad beating."

"When will you bring me back home?" she asked.

"When it's safe."

"Who decides when it's safe?"

"You and me." He smiled. "Jenny, you can trust me. We've known each other a long time, and you know that." He touched her cheek again. She did like how that felt, but it was completely different from Seth. Seth's touch soothed and calmed her. Alexander's made her feel electrified and powerful.

"Okay." She took his hand from her cheek and grasped it tight. "Help me up."

He boosted her up into the cockpit and closed the door.

While the hangar door lifted in front of her, Jenny studied the interior of the plane. It was snug in here, almost like a car. Her palms sweated and her guts knotted up. She had never been in an airplane before, and the idea scared her now.

Alexander climbed into the seat to her left and closed the door.

"I think I saw some OxyContin in here." Alexander opened a console between the seats and handed her a brown pill bottle.

"What are these?" Jenny asked.

"Painkillers."

"Oh, awesome." Jenny unscrewed the cap and tapped one of the red pills into her palm. She swallowed it, hesitated a moment, then took a second one. "Why do you have these?"

"I don't know." He started up the plane and eased it out the hangar door. "I share this plane with a few different friends. Somebody must have left it."

Jenny leaned back in her seat and watched out the window as the plane crawled to the runway. The night was already too unreal, too scary—her dad, then Seth, then the riot…and now flying away with someone from her dreams.

"What's it like?" Jenny asked.

"Mexico?"

"Flying."

"It's great. You'll like it." He took her hand for a moment, and she felt his power flow into her, as if he were intentionally pushing it. She grew much more confident, like she could do anything. And get away with it, too.

"Fuck it," she said. "Let's fly away to Mexico."

"That's my girl." Alexander talked briefly with the control tower over his headset.

He steered it onto the runway, then held the brakes while firing up the engines. The craft rumbled around her, and Jenny clenched the armrests tight.

Then the plane surged forward along the runway, rapidly picking up speed, and Jenny felt pushed back into her seat. She was trembling, and her breaths came short and fast.

The plane jostled her up and down as it shot along the runway, and her teeth chattered together. Then the wheels left the ground and the ride became smooth, though it felt dangerously steep to her. Jenny's heart kicked as she watched the ground drop away below. There was nothing holding them up now. It was like magic.

She watched out the window as the lights of Charleston dropped away on one side. She could see a lot of flickering blue lights there, and a column of National Guard unpacking from their trucks, but they were soon too small and distant to discern.

"Can we really just go to Mexico?" Jenny asked. "Don't we have to show our passports or something?"

"That is the law," Alexander said. "But there are plenty of ways around it, usually involving cash. Or a new black Denali, like the one I just left somebody as a gift."

"Flying isn't so bad." Jenny gazed out over the moonlit ocean. "I think I liked the lift-off part, too."

"It's a perfect night for flying," he said. "The Gulf's calm, the moon's out…"

She looked at him. "What else do you remember about the past?"

"What do you want to know?"

"Do you remember me?"

"I remember you more than anything. Hundreds of lifetimes together. We're always drawn back to each other. Our powers do that." He touched her arm through a huge gash the mob had torn in her sleeve, and she felt the dark sizzle of electricity between them. "We make each other stronger."

"But Seth is my opposite," Jenny said. She was feeling a little confused. Maybe the pain drugs were already kicking in. "Right? That's how we always thought of it."

"He is. And opposites create a powerful charge between them. But our connection is greater. Our powers are complementary."

"What does that mean?"

"You enhance me. And I enhance you. We can only become the greatest, most godlike versions of ourselves when we're together. And I sensed you had been born, somewhere, but I couldn't find you until you flared up bright as the sun a few weeks ago. Then I knew where you were, and I came to find you."

"To increase your power?"

"I have loved you across many lives." He pulled his hand back, and she already missed his electrifying touch. "But we only just met, this time around. And you don't have my curse of remembering."

"You think it's a curse?"

"Every lifetime has its share of suffering." Alexander looked out the windshield at the galaxies of stars. "Forgetting is a gift."

Jenny wasn't sure what to say. She tried not to think of ancient Athens and the diseased bodies heaped everywhere, the smoldering funeral pyres outside the temples. The smell of misery and death. After a while, she asked, "What about me and Seth?"

"You've spent a few lifetimes together, just recently, but your oldest and deepest relationship is with me." He laughed. "Well, that's getting a little weird for the first hour of conversation. You asked, though."

"I did ask." Jenny bit her lip. "You sent me to destroy Athens."

"It was a war. A long time ago."

"And to kill Pericles."

Alexander laughed and brushed his fingers along the back of her head, through her hair, and she felt that dark sizzle of energy again. Again, she felt disappointed when he drew his hand back.

"My strategy was foolish," Alexander said. "Empire is always systemic, Jenny, but we pin it on individual men, all the blame and revulsion and glory. I made that mistake, too. His death only brought us Cleon and many more years of war."

"But if that was Seth, then the Jenny pox wouldn't have hurt him."

"The Jenny pox?" He grinned, lighting up his dark, magnetic eyes. "You are so cute this lifetime."

"But I'm right. And history says he died of the plague."

"Or, just possibly, somebody poisoned him and made it look like plague. Pretty believable, when everyone else is dying of it, especially if you get the body to the pyre fast enough. Somebody who wanted to clear the road for another politician. Someone ruthless and clever."

"Ashleigh?" Jenny asked. "Ashleigh killed Seth to make way for Cleon?"

"That's where I'm putting my bet. Sounds like her, doesn't it?"

"It does."

"Of course, it's all ancient history now," Alexander said. "But the more you use your gift, the more you'll remember."

"It's not a gift," Jenny whispered. "And I don't want to use it."

It was colder inside the aircraft, now that they were thousands of feet in the air. Jenny folded her arms around herself. It was strange and scary how he'd stepped out from her dreams and into the world like this. Part of her felt safe and comfortable with him, even crazily attracted to him, but she didn't know if she could trust that part. He seemed dangerous, with all his knowledge of the past.

And even if he'd been good to her twenty-five centuries ago, she didn't know anything about what kind of person he'd become since then.

"How did you know to come protect me tonight?" she asked.

"I came to Fallen Oak to find you, but I then saw the fear-giver in town, and spied on him." Alexander paused a moment, as if thinking something over. "He's in league with my opposite, Esmeralda."

"What's the opposite of making zombies?"

He laughed. "She can only listen to the dead. I command them."

"Why aren't you interested in her? If she's your opposite?"

"For one thing, she always hates me," Alexander said. "She's a part of their faction."

"What faction?"

"The love-charmer, the fear-giver," Alexander said. "Your enemies and mine. I came here for you only, Jenny. I have no interest in her."

"Is anybody else on our side?" Jenny asked. "And what are the sides, anyway? Why do we have to fight?"

"We've always fought," Alexander said. "That's why we need to be together now, while you're in danger. Your power and mine will be at their peak, if we need them."

"I don't ever want to use mine again," Jenny said. "I can't do any good for anyone. I'm just a monster."

"You're my beautiful monster." Alexander gave her a smile. His eyes reflected the stars and the black night sky. "And I love you for what you are."

Jenny looked deep into the night, into the vast darkness of the unknown.

THE END

ABOUT THE AUTHOR

J.L. Bryan studied English literature at the University of Georgia and at Oxford, with a focus on the English Renaissance and the Romantic period. He also studied screenwriting at UCLA.

Find more of his books at jlbryanbooks.com.

9595623R0017

Made in the USA
Charleston, SC
25 September 2011